The Belen Hitch

NEW
MEXICO

Santa Fe

Albuquerque

40

285

Belen   Vaughn   Fort
                                        Sumner   Clovis
(La Jefa)
              60

                                                  Portales
Socorro   285
                                                Elida

              380
                    Carrizozo   206
                    Lincoln

         54
25   Ruidoso   Roswell

                                   82
              Alamogordo

    10
         Las Cruces

Carol Cooperrider

The Belen Hitch

a Sasha Solomon mystery

Pari Noskin Taichert

UNIVERSITY OF NEW MEXICO PRESS | ALBUQUERQUE

11   10   09   08   07   06   05   1   2   3   4   5   6   7

Library of Congress Cataloging-in-Publication Data

Taichert, Pari Noskin, 1958–
The Belen hitch a sasha solomon mystery / Pari Noskin Taichert.
p. cm.
ISBN 0-8263-3915-8 (alk. paper)
1. Women public relations personnel—Fiction.   2. Railroad museums—Fiction.
3. Tourist trade—Fiction.   4. Art museums—Fiction.
5. New Mexico—Fiction.   I. Title.
PS3620.A35B45 2005
813'.6—dc22
2005007132

DESIGN AND COMPOSITION: Melissa Tandysh

To Peter, Hope, & Lily with love.

"Art that doesn't shock—isn't art. It's window dressing."

—*Phillipa Petty*
at the opening of her forty-year retrospective
at the Metropolitan Museum of Art, October 23, 2004

one

"AIIIIIEEEE, HA, HA, HA!!" wailed KANW—my favorite radio station—as I drove, one hand holding a cup of java and the other tapping rhythm on the steering wheel. 7:30 A.M. Zoom, zoom on the freeway, my Toyota pulling to the right at the high speed. In less than half an hour I'd be interviewing Phillipa Petty, the internationally known artist—*and* royal witch, according to Mom, who'd been her friend for a couple of centuries.

I drove through sleepy Belen feeling optimistic for no good reason. Just being on the road, pushing my business plan forward, was enough on this frisky fall morning.

Over the railroad track onto a little blue highway, I wound my way toward the secluded house owned by the cantankerous painter, who'd made the tiny community of Las Jefas her home for more than fifty years.

Another turn, then down a long, dirt drive, ka-bumping my coffee all over the place. Who cared? Nothing could faze me. Sure, I had other clients—but this was my second gig as a roving PR pro marketing the little New Mexican towns I loved.

"*Vida triste, vida dolorosa*," I sang along with my mourning *compadre*, windows open to wake me at this ungodly hour. Trumpets brassy with woe sighed as they lost volume and the last measures of the song faded away. One final swig of caffeine before I silenced the music and parked the car.

A wooden bridge girdled a sludgy irrigation ditch; beyond that stretched a cobbled walkway. Then steps. Why did anyone need so many steps? I climbed them, huffing by the twenty-seventh, cussing by the thirty-first.

I rang the doorbell.

"Ms. Petty?" I called, nudging a yellowed cottonwood leaf with my foot. "Anyone home?" I pushed the button again. "Hello? It's Sasha Solomon . . . Hannah's daughter." I pushed the bell again.

"We have an appointment." I kicked the screen door. Just a bit.

Inside the house, a phone jangled. It was an old sound. I imagined the machine, a black rotary job, heavy and inconvenient, with iffy reception. The perfect instrument for an aged and contradictory artist like Petty. Just when I had the image secure in my mind, I heard a recorded voice, a beep, then another voice much like my mom's. A moment later, a dial tone droned an empty, sad sound. Obviously, Petty liked to make everyone wait.

"All right. I get the picture," I muttered, rapping on her window this time. The glass refracted light like tin foil and my once tidy brown braid unraveled in its reflection.

I pulled a brush from my purse and proceeded to straighten up, puckering my lips with new color, and trying to assess the pantsuit I'd chosen. A bit tight, damn it. I still needed to lose those ten pounds. If I were vain, I'd pluck my unruly eyebrows too. Bob, my semi-boyfriend, always picked at me about how little I did to "present myself to the world"—his words, not mine. I always told him, "Hey, this is New Mexico. We go for natural here. If you want a fashion model, go to Paris."

My nose itched. I pinched it, forestalling a sneeze, and tapped the window again. "Anybody home?"

Did the lady have a hearing problem? It hadn't sounded like it on the phone yesterday when we'd spoken.

A little look-see wouldn't hurt anyone, would it? So, I, uh . . . Petty's front doorknob turned with just-greased ease.

"Hello?" I let myself in. Morning sunbeams filtered though thick curtains and barely illuminated an overstuffed pink couch that resembled anemic lox. Vases filled with dead roses the color of dried blood covered bookcases that had never known magazines, let alone books. Fine but copious dust served as a major element in her interior design.

A hissing noise, a burning smell.

I found the kitchen, its windows fogged from steam spewing out of a large pot of boiling water. The liquid, now down to its last quarter inch, had left a high white mineral rim. Two plump loaves of burned-black bread dried in the oven.

"Ms. Petty?" I turned off the appliances.

A dark corridor beyond the kitchen led to brightness. I took out my new digital camera—a toy I hoped to convert into a work tool as soon as I figured out how to use it. Maybe I'd catch the artist at work in her studio. Almost to the door, I saw the puffy top of a foot in a rubber-soled tan shoe. A knee-high, flesh-colored stocking had inched its way down the age-speckled leg that lay motionless in the perversely cheerful sunlight of a greenhouse-like structure. I snapped a photo, then another, before I realized what I was doing. My trembling fingers clicked a third picture as I lowered the camera back into my purse.

"Ma'am? Ms. Petty?" I said, tiptoeing farther in.

The artist sprawled face up on the floor, a jumble of death. She clutched a paintbrush in one hand, the handle of a large ceramic coffee mug in the other. Dried blood crusted around the opening of her right nostril. A horrid, corrosive smell—like rotten eggs—slammed into my nose. I tried to hold my breath, but was too late.

I ran down the hall and found the toilet in time to throw up. In my life, I'd only seen two dead people. The first had been horrifying, the man brutally murdered. Today, it was an old lady who'd expired, a heart or brain that had given out. But the proximity of death, the smell and look of it, rendered me limp.

I staggered back to the studio, picked up my dropped purse, and pulled out the cell phone. My throat hurt, my nostrils burned. I dialed 911.

There was nothing to do but wait.

An unfinished life-size painting rested on two easels, its human figures faceless. One held a broken crucifix. Another stomped on a silver chalice.

No surprise there. Petty earned her fame though blasphemy, debasing beloved religious icons with vigor—Moses kissing a pig, Buddha driving a BMW. Her most famous painting, *The Cross-Dressing Christ*, had thrust her into artsy-fartsy spotlights in Paris, New York, and later,

Berlin. Hey, controversy sells. Gallery owners and museum curators loved her.

Petty earned other responses as well. Millions of religious devotees—Christian, Moslem, Jewish, and Jain—hated her guts.

I'd followed her career for years, as had many a New Mexican interested in her art. From a technical standpoint, she merited her reputation as a master painter. In this artist's deft hands, oil paints became the pulse of a beating heart, anger on a parsimonious mouth, the tear in a blood-shot eye.

Technique can go only so far, however. There's the small question of subject matter. Petty excelled at shocking and alienating. I've gotta say, the Moses thing upset me, and I even eat pork. If her life's goal centered on offending, she'd succeeded in spades. No wonder she and Mom got along so well.

Mom. How am I going to tell Mom?

The thought yanked me back to the here-and-now horror of the artist's death.

Striving to holster my increasing panic and revulsion, I surveyed the room further. A clutter of images dampened my adrenaline: an orchid wilting, bunches of herbs drying upside-down on a laundry line. An overturned tuberous begonia, its thick branches broken and oozing.

Windows stood open. Others had round cracks, resembling shot-out windshields. Belen's mayor warned me Petty had earned enemies in his town. Good thing they'd only broken glass.

The phone rang again, two times. Then Ms. Petty's recording sounded its terse command, "Leave me a message."

"Philly?" Mom's voice, panicked, with a frightening feebleness, filled the house. "Philly? What's happened? Philly! Answer me! Philly!"

Where was the phone? Not in the hall. Not on this table or that dresser.

Beeeeeep. Too late.

I realized I was panting, not from the search but from anxiety. Mom's fear squeezed the air out of me and tightened my throat. My lungs worked double time, my heart quadrupled its arrhythmic beats.

Why did Mom sound so scared? It couldn't be a coincidence that she'd called while I was supposed to be interviewing Ms. Petty. I'd heard

4

of people having premonitions about their friends being in danger. Maybe Mom sensed the artist had died. That could make my job easier when I went to tell her. No. Telling her would be awful no matter what.

I went back to Petty's studio. Papers lay willy-nilly on a wooden table and some had cascaded onto the floor. My stomach revolted again, my throat seared. I swallowed hard and stepped closer. Next to her body lay a black-and-white photograph of three people leaning against a 1957 Ford T-Bird, a hardtop convertible, with its wonderful portholes and ostentatious tail fins. It had to be Mom's car—white exterior with red leather interior—the car I'd learned to drive in. The paintbrush in Petty's hand obscured the faces but I recognized one woman's stance. To get a better look, I stooped so near I could detect the artist's musty odor sneaking through pungent baby powder.

Mom looked straight at the camera. The edges of her lips tipped up with a smile I'd never seen before. She wore cloppy shoes and bobby socks. Her pleated skirt triangulated out from her young hips to below her knees. Had she really had such a small waist? Her hair! A black poof-up top with a weird indentation as if someone had smashed his hand right in the middle of it and hairspray had shellacked the assault in place. Her ponytail was only hinted at, but I knew it was there tickling her mid back. I'd seen it in other cherished pictures from the same era.

The woman beside Mom had to be the one now at my feet. Lithe and blonde with an impish expression, Phillipa Petty stood arm-in-arm with the man. With her other hand, she shielded her eyes, perhaps to get a better view of the photographer. The man she held had short dark hair and eyebrows that slashed across his forehead as if they'd been drawn in black permanent marker. He, too, smiled as his tie blew to one side, and his other hand held a highball glass midway to his mouth.

Outside Petty's studio, sirens now shrilled, making the room even colder. With a cough, I stood up, then bent again, succumbing to the temptation. I wanted the photo. I wanted to own that frozen image of my mother—young, beautiful, and alive to the world's possibilities. Petty wouldn't need it now. From what I knew, she'd never been married, never had kids. This picture was *mine*. Finders keepers. I put it in my purse.

Ah, Mom. How would she deal with this blow? The loss of a woman she'd known longer than I'd been alive. A dear friend whose artistic career she'd helped to launch more than forty-five years ago. Maybe I'd give her the photo—her friend ambered in that long-ago happy moment.

Footsteps pounded up the stairs and across the wooden porch. A hard knock sounded. I walked through the kitchen and into the living room of a house that had become too familiar. Another knock, closer to a thud this time.

"I'll be right there," I called.

two

"YOU FOUND HER JUST like this?" said Detective M. Garcia, a few minutes after introducing himself and following me into the studio. Now, he stepped around Petty's body, concentrating on his footing.

"Yes, sir." I cleared my throat, wondering why my hay fever was acting up.

"Did you touch anything? Anything at all?"

"No, sir."

If I told the policeman about the photo, he'd take it away—file it in a folder, throw it in a drawer. What harm could there be in me taking something that I valued so much more than he possibly could? That little picture could jog Mom's memory. It could lead to a story I'd never heard. Or, perhaps more important, it would comfort her when I spoke about her friend's death.

"You're sure?" he said.

"Yes, sir."

He smiled.

I smiled back.

"I didn't realize people were so polite in Albuquerque. 'Yes, sir, no, sir.'" He glanced at Petty and paused as if ready to ask me another question, a quick narrowing of his espresso-brown eyes, but nothing more. "Come on. Let's talk in the living room."

We passed through the kitchen with its cloying smell of burned baking.

"Oh." I stopped. "I did touch something. I turned off the oven and the stove in here," I said. "I think she'd made some interview for our bread. I mean, bread for our interview."

He squared his shoulders to face me.

"I sound like an idiot," I said.

"Most people do in this situation." He beamed me a lopsided grin, sniffled and continued out of the room.

Like a confused puppy, I followed.

Garcia sat down on the plush girlie couch, his fit body out of place—a Slim Jim surrounded by strawberry ice cream. Five, ten years older than I, Garcia's skin glistened caramel-colored in the odd light. He had short blue-black hair that would have curled if given the chance, age spots on his forehead, and strong cheekbones in a face never smoothed by botox.

The detective rubbed his temples. "Tell me more about the interview with Miss Petty."

"It was supposed to be at eight." I sank into the bloated chair opposite him. "I'm working on a project for Mayor Flores."

Garcia had perfected the raising-eyebrow technique, asking questions without words.

"I've been hired to assess the best use of the Harvey House." I flipped into PR mode, my confidence rising.

"Really?"

"Yes. The train people want a train museum. The artists want an art museum."

"And?"

"Would you mind if I get a glass of water?" My throat bugged me, the rawness more noticeable with each swallow.

"Are you all right?"

"Yeah." I coughed, then stood. "It must be allergies."

"You were talking about the project," he said, tailing me into the kitchen. He moved past my outstretched arm. "Here, let me get your water."

I sat at the pineapple-yellow-topped table, part of a cheesy dinette set, replete with mod Peter Max–style flowers. It would have been all the rage in the sixties.

The solid bell of Petty's phone rang through the house. Detective Garcia looked up. "Do you know where the phone is?"

"I couldn't find it."

"It rang earlier?"

I nodded. He handed me a glass of lukewarm liquid and left the room. I drank and listened.

The machine beeped and I heard Mom's voice again. "Philly? Philly! Answer the phone this minute!"

I thought I heard Garcia say something, but couldn't be sure. His footsteps traveled down the hall and he came back into the room.

"Who was that?" I said, trying to be nonchalant.

The detective wrinkled his face until he looked like a Shar-pei. "I didn't pick up in time. Do you think you recognize the voice?"

I cleared my throat once more, made a face, rubbed the front of my neck. "It sounded a little bit like my mom. She and Ms. Petty are . . . were . . . old friends."

"Really?" The slight contraction of his eyelids, the single twitch of his lower lip bespoke his interest. "Did your mother know you were coming here this morning?"

"I doubt it." A white lie that could be true. Garcia's curiosity made me feel protective—as if Ms. Petty's death were more than it seemed and my mother had helped. Ludicrous. Mom couldn't tie a shoe without an occupational therapist to coach her. I made a big show of looking at my watch. "Gee, I'd better get back to Albuquerque."

Garcia held my gaze a moment more than was comfortable—for me—and then noticed my empty glass and refilled it. "So, your mother and Miss Petty were friends," he said as if he hadn't heard me and seated himself at the table.

"Yessir."

"'Old friends,' you said. How long have they known each other?"

So much for deflecting his interest. "Since before I was born."

If he leaned any farther forward, he'd be lying flat. "You've known her all your life?"

"No, I haven't. I mean, Mom's talked about her and I've seen her every once in a while. But they sort of had a falling out when Ms. Petty became famous." Could I have been digging myself a bigger hole if I tried? And Garcia just sat there letting me do it. "They reconciled years ago," I quickly added. "But you know how it is. Just because someone is your parent's friend, doesn't mean she's yours."

"Miss Petty didn't visit? Come over for Christmas?"

"Not really." He had to know from our last name that we were Jewish. He was messing with me and I didn't like it. "Don't forget that she had residences in other countries. I think she only moved back here full-time a few years ago." I emptied the water glass again. Anything I said sounded suspicious and that was just plain stupid. Petty was old. Old people die. What was the big deal? I returned Garcia's assessing stare with tempered defiance.

"So, tell me about the project," he said.

"I've got to make a recommendation."

"Train people or artists?" Amusement lit his eyes. He canted back in the chair and balanced it on two legs.

"As I understand it, the artists want to use Ms. Petty's work as a touristy centerpiece." I swallowed with an unpleasant thought. "Actually, her death isn't going to help their cause at all. I don't know if she made any legal provisions for them." I might be out of a job even before I started. Damn, my throat hurt.

"And the train people? What do they want?" said the detective.

"Oh, right." I looked out the window to see if something was blooming, something pregnant with enough pollen to cause my throat to burn. I swallowed with more pain. "The train guys want to revive the whole Harvey House concept with a restaurant, girls in white uniforms, the works."

Garcia shook his head, then laughed.

"What?" I said.

"No wonder Tony hired you. A local would never touch it."

"Why?"

"They hate each other—the trains and the artists. It's like that old saying about oil and water, only worse," he said. "You're a courageous woman, Ms. Solomon."

"Come on. It can't be that bad."

"For your sake, I hope it's not." He chuckled.

"Well, I like challenges," I said, getting up for another glass of water.

"Good thing." He waited for me to sit again. "Okay. Let's get back to this morning."

I drummed my fingers on the table, then stopped, aware of Garcia's gaze. When I counsel clients for television appearances, I focus part of my advice on nonverbal cues. Right now, between the bad throat and my fidgeting, I looked guilty—like I was hiding something big.

"What time did you get here?" he said.

"I arrived at eight on the dot." I tried to look him right in the eyes, to project confidence. After all, I didn't kill Ms. Petty. She was stone dead when I got there.

"What did you do?"

"I rang the doorbell." I moved the glass an inch forward, then moved it back. Oops. Indecision was another indicator of nervousness. I wasn't nervous; I felt sick.

"Did you notice anything odd? Out of the ordinary?"

"Not really." I shifted position on the chair, massaged my throat.

"Then what?" he said.

"I rang the bell again."

"What did you think when she didn't answer?"

"Actually, I thought she'd blown me off. It happens a lot in my business," I said, scratching my forehead a millimeter below my widow's peak.

"How did you get in?"

"The door was unlocked."

Hand to his chin, his eyes cued me to continue.

"Ms. Petty was old," I said. "I thought maybe she couldn't hear me."

"You said you thought she'd blown you off."

"I did." Why did this feel like an interrogation? "But I wasn't going to go without . . . I don't know," I said. "I don't give up easily."

"So you let yourself in."

"Yes, sir." I scooched forward, picked up the empty water glass. Put it down.

"And?"

"I called out her name a couple of times and then started looking for her."

He got up, refilled my glass and placed it in front of me. "Did you notice anything odd?"

"I heard a noise and followed it here, to the kitchen, and saw the water boiled down to nearly nothing. And the bread. Then I went into her studio and found her."

"Tell me exactly what you saw," he said.

"She was just lying there."

"On her back?"

"Yes, sir."

"Did you notice or do anything else? Open some of the windows, maybe?"

"As a matter of fact, when I came into the room, there was this awful smell. Toxic almost. It made me sick to my stomach. I threw up in the bathroom."

"You threw up because of the smell?" he said.

"I don't know. I think I threw up because I found a dead lady."

"Hold on a minute, will you?" Garcia left the room.

I reached in my purse for a chunk of candy bar. My fingers brushed the photograph. Was it wrong to keep it? Why would it be? This wasn't a crime scene. An old lady had kicked the bucket. That's all. The police didn't need to know about one little photo.

But I did. I wanted to talk to Mom about it. To find out who the guy was—to see if she remembered who'd taken the photo in the first place.

"Okay. Where were we?" Garcia said, returning. He sat down, elbows on the table, his back flagpole straight. "You noticed the smell and got sick. What happened after that?"

"Nothing much. I dialed 911 and waited."

"Where?"

"I don't know exactly. Here and there," I said. "I paced. I'm not sure."

"Ms. Solomon, try to remember."

I nodded, closed my eyes. "I walked around the studio, mainly." My voice caught. I turned my head, sensing someone behind me.

"What?" said the detective. "Is something wrong?"

"No. It's okay. I'm just tired," I said, feeling spooked. I could have sworn someone was standing right in back of me, breathing decay onto my neck. A few months ago, I would have seen whatever it was—would have done another shing-a-ling with reality—in a hallucination. I took a breath and thanked the universe I'd found a good, cheap Doctor of Oriental Medicine—a.k.a. D.O.M. Hair-thin acupuncture needles, stinky *moxa*, and little black tarry pills had stopped the visions for now.

I opened my eyes wide, stretching the muscles and releasing the tension behind them.

Garcia watched me. Waited. His next question came in a whisper. "Did you touch her?"

"God, no!" I shook my head, backed my torso away from him, repelled by the thought.

"Did you notice anything else? Anything at all?"

I turned again, convinced someone was about to touch my shoulder. The air felt cooler on the side of my face. What was wrong with me?

"Ms. Solomon?" Garcia's voice pulled me back, rescued me.

"What?" Suddenly hot, I looked at my sweating palms.

"Did you notice anything else?" he said, yet again.

"Not really."

"Are you sure you're all right?"

"I think I'm just shaken up."

"It's not surprising, given what you've just been through." He waited two beats before handing me his card. "If you remember anything else, give me a call."

"I will." I reciprocated with my card. "I work from home. You can reach me anytime."

"Thanks." He pocketed the contact info and stood. "I hope the project goes well for you."

"Project?" Oh, yeah. "Me, too."

"Let me know if I can help."

"Thank you," I said, wanting out of there before I got any weirder.

"And, Ms. Solomon?"

"Yes?"

"You might want to see a doctor about that sore throat of yours."

three

SUNLIGHT BOUNCED OFF THE fall-garbed trees, flaming them against a sky so blue it stung. Thirty minutes after I started the drive home I hit Albuquerque's city limits. Thanks to more good New Mexican music, I'd shed my freaky feelings—which I attributed to the creepiness of being in a house with a dead person—and focused on the day ahead. As to whether the mayor still needed me for the Belen job, well, I'd continue billing hours until he told me to stop.

Idling at an intersection with cell phone in hand, I prepared to call my friend Darnda Jones. She'd recently become a client and I wanted to set up a meeting for later that day. Before I could push the first number, it rang.

"Hi, Sasha. I was wondering if you could stop by this morning. I've got an idea for that press release you wrote," said Darnda.

"I wish you'd stop doing that," I said.

"What?"

"Anticipating my calls."

You see, Darnda is a psychic. The real McCoy. She's got a special talent, too. Darnda can talk with anything alive *and* anything that ever was. Yep. Ghosts, squirrels, cherries. She can talk with mold, ants, and Africanized bees. Get this, she's made scads of money hiring herself out as a sort of paranormal pest controller to wealthy, wafer-thin clients in gold-kissed Santa Barbara, the Hamptons, Monaco. Her last job was at a mansion in Indian Hill, a community in Cincinnati, for a children's birthday party. The kids were going horseback riding and mommy didn't want any bugs to bother them. I kid you not. Now Darnda has self-published a book and wants to go on the national lecture circuit to train other people to talk to cockroaches, ticks, . . . whatever.

"Something's wrong with you, Sasha," Darnda said. "I can feel it."

"Don't I know it," I said, merging onto I-25. "Look, I've got to go. I'm stopping by Mom's." Now, in addition to having to tell her about Ms. Petty, I had to warn her just in case Detective Garcia's unnatural interest transformed into an impromptu interview. "How about we meet at the Flying Star on Menaul in a couple of hours?"

"Okay, but—"

"I'm driving," I said. Darnda hates it when people drive and talk on their cell phones.

"All right," she said. "I'll see you there."

After turning into the parking lot at St. Kate's, Mom's rehab hospital, I decided to call Bob, a.k.a. Mr. Humdrum. We'd been suffering from mediocrity for months now, but hey, a boyfriend in the hand is worth two in the . . . no, that wasn't right. And the sex? Well, I'd have to give it a .05 on the Richter scale.

"Robert Kalco, PC," said his thirty-fifth secretary.

"Hi, this is Sasha—"

"Ms. Solomon, Mr. Kalco is unavailable."

The snippiness in her voice brought out a perverse urge to squelch it. "How are you today, Allison?" I said, all sugar and candied violets.

"He's at lunch."

"This early?" I got out of the car. "Well, how are *you*?"

"I'll connect you to his voice mail."

"No thanks," I said before she could get rid of me. "Just tell him I called."

Miffed, I bumped my knee on the steering column getting out of the car and headed toward the facility where Mom grappled with the detritus from her latest stroke. On the building's glass-door entrance, a neon-pink piece of paper proclaimed in black magic marker, "Under New Management!" I'd liked the old management just fine. In the days since Hatch Healthcare had taken over the hospital, the only change I'd noticed was a distinct slip in employee morale—and more mildew in Mom's shower. Maybe I should have Darnda ask it to relocate.

With a swish of air, the doors opened and I walked into the antiseptic and somehow sleazy world of rehab. The receptionist's jaw worked with chewing gum—or tobacco—as she acknowledged me with a dip of her chin before returning to her tabloid.

St. Kate's depressed me. Getting old depressed me. Some days I'd arrive and couldn't make it past the lobby. Mom's decline shocked me anew with each visit. Worst of all was her mental unpredictability. Her short-term memory shimmied in and out of places I could only guess at.

One constant remained. Mom's long-term memory, overburdened with its grudges and disappointments, held as vivid as a nuclear flash. As long as I could remember, my mother had worn her irritation like her once-daily red lipstick, loud and abundant. Our relationship, feisty at best, converted to hostile in a single breath.

I continued through a more solid set of double doors into the Brain Injury Unit. Tacked on the outside was another bright pink piece of paper with a handwritten note: "Please check in at the nurse's station."

Tacky, tacky. They could've at least paid for someone to desktop publish their signs. Instead they'd opted for cheap, and it looked it. Talk about bad first impressions. If I'd been their PR consultant, they wouldn't have dared to post this crappola.

Okay. The vexation helped distract me, but not enough. Mom's room was just a few doors down the hallway. The trick was to storm ahead with confidence, to push aside the dismal thoughts about aging, uselessness, and death. Reckless and forward-moving I slammed into Rita, a nurse's aide.

"Well, as long as we're this close, give me a hug," she said, embracing me with lung-deflating enthusiasm. She let go, straightened her pastel peach uniform, and assessed my expression. "You summoning up courage?"

"Always."

"Well, don't bother. Your mom was asleep when I checked on her a little while ago," she said. "Peaceful as a baby."

"Yeah, right." Bad health, limited mobility, and the proximity of death had intensified Mom's negative disposition. When she wasn't busy torturing herself, she picked on me.

"Honey, imagine what it's like to be in your mother's head," Rita said. "She knows something's wrong but can't fix it no matter how hard she tries."

"It still hurts."

"Of course it does. And it hurts *her* even more." Rita's lips settled into a frown. She gave me a little shove. "Go on. Be a good girl."

I nodded and continued to Room 104. The gods smiled down upon me; Mom wasn't there. Sunlight fought the dinginess of the gray bedspread but couldn't vanquish it. I sat down and waited, assuming Mom's nap had been preempted by one of her many therapies—physical, occupational, speech. I should have known her schedule. Another failing on my part. Bad daughter. I rubbed my neck; my throat bothered me worse than it had in Belen. I felt a heaviness, born of the institutional room and my own insufficiencies.

Helping Mom had become an unsolvable puzzle to me. I'd given up urging her to eat, cajoling her to want to live. My words of encouragement grated, more than soothed, her aggravated soul. Our story was too complicated. My entire childhood, I'd wanted a mom who stayed home and baked for me—not someone who felt so abandoned and exhausted herself that she didn't have extra energy to love.

I pulled out the photo of Mom with her friends and tried to imagine her happy. I strained to remember a time when her laughter flowed unfettered by worries about money or babysitters or having to make the macaroni and cheese I insisted on eating every night. But I couldn't do it. My imagination just wasn't that strong.

All my years of yearning for the mother she couldn't be had turned into an emotional black hole. I knew I was being unfair, self-indulgent, and still I couldn't get past it. So, people like Rita and Paul—her boyfriend—provided loving sustenance. I occupied myself with Mother's business affairs, her bills and charitable donations. Each month, I fielded the maze of insurance claims she accumulated. My work was the stuff of little emotion and lots of paper.

"Where's your mom?" Rita appeared at the door's threshold.

"Probably at therapy," I said, putting the photo back in my purse.

"She doesn't have therapy now."

"Maybe she went for a walk," I said, knowing the idea sounded flimsy.

"I swear she was asleep a minute ago." Rita came in, knocked at the bathroom door. "Hannah? You in there?" She peeked in.

"She's not there," I said. "I would have heard her."

"You stay here." Rita's rich skin lost so much color I could see the acne scars on her face. "I'll be right back."

Her alarm infected me. I looked under the bed, in the closet, as if Mom might be playing hide-and-go-seek. A minute later, Rita returned with another woman.

"Where's your mother?" The stranger's accusatory tone notched my anxiety tighter.

"And you are . . . ?" I said.

"Mrs. Hartman. The charge nurse." Think Nurse Ratched, only more officious. "Now, where is your mother?"

"Shouldn't I be asking you?" I shot back at her.

"When did you last see her, Rita?" said Mrs. Hartman.

"Fifteen minutes . . . a half an hour ago at the most. She was asleep."

"Don't you people watch your patients?" I said, sounding shrewish.

"Ms. Solomon, I'd appreciate if you'd stay out of this," said Mrs. H. "Your mother is an adult. She really isn't our responsibility."

"Like hell," I said. "How could you lose my mother?"

"There's probably a good explanation," she said.

"There'd better be."

Both women left the room. I followed. They looked in the water therapy area, the supply closet, up one hall and down the next.

"Don't you have some kind of intercom system here?" I said, irritated with the inefficiency of our search.

"Hannah!" said Rita.

And there she was, placid in a royal purple robe, propelled in a wheelchair by her friend Gilda. Her eyes held no spark, her lips no trace of a smile meant for me.

"Mom! We were worried," I said. "Where were you?"

"We took a little walk, but Hannah got tired," said Gilda. "I didn't know you were coming, Sasha."

"It's all right." I hugged myself to quell the trembling. "I'll be back in a minute." How dare she worry me like that? I went into the nurse's lounge to get a soda pop and a renewed perspective. The carbonation burned with each quaff, my eyes watering in response. I might have uttered a few inappropriate words. I turned to see Rita studying me.

"What's wrong?" she said. "You sick?"

"No. It's my throat," I whispered. "It must be hay fever."

"Not this time of year." Rita motioned me over. "Let me take a look."

"Don't be silly. It's nothing." I winced. "Mom scared me."

Rita tsk-tsked and guided me out of the lounge to the nurses' station. "Open up."

"You're not a nurse."

"Open up."

I opened my mouth.

With a tongue depressor in one hand and an examining light in the other, Rita stared into my troublesome gullet. "It's swollen and bright red back there," she said. "You better go home and get in bed."

"It's just my throat. I don't feel bad."

"Well, it looks bad."

"Rita, it's just allergies."

"That's not what allergies look like. That's what a virus looks like," she said. "That's what *strep* looks like. You want me to call over a real nurse? Mrs. Hartman? Get *her* opinion?"

"Sorry," I said, realizing the insult I'd dealt her.

"Forget it," she said. "Go home."

"What about Mom?"

"I'll tell her you had to go. She's got Gilda there. She'll be fine."

Still unsettled from the adrenaline rush of Mom's brief disappearance, I realized it'd be better to visit her when I'd calmed down. Any excuse to escape St. Kate's oppressiveness.

I scurried to the parking lot and had my hand on the car door before I remembered my original mission—to tell Mom about Phillipa Petty. On some level, she already knew. Why else would she have called Petty's house like that? I didn't really think the police detective would interview her. Paranoia. That's what had made my synapses tingle during our conversation. Why would Garcia bother to contact Mom? This wasn't a murder case. He wouldn't disturb her; he had no reason to.

Relief and gratitude, cowardice and guilt—I felt them all at that moment. I'd need to find a good way to tell Mom about Ms. Petty. A gentle way. This would hit her hard, snap another bone in her fragile emotional balance. A few hours, even a day, wouldn't matter; Mom would have the rest of her life to miss her friend.

four

"READ MY LIPS, DARNDA. I have *not* been poisoned." I mooshed the chocolate and espresso ice cream together. A fourth bite of the cold glop didn't help. My throat still burned. "You're way off," I said.

"I don't think I am." Darnda nibbled frosting off her éclair. She sat opposite me, her corkscrew gray hair pulled back in an ineffective ponytail. She wore a too-tight black T-shirt, her bust stretching the picture of the rock band Kiss to even more garish proportions. The leather vest didn't help either. Or the biker-chick mini skirt. We'd talked about this a dozen times already. If she wanted national credibility, to do the talk show and lecture circuit, she'd have to look the part—at least a little. Instead, Darnda looked like the founder of a senior citizens chapter of Hells Angels.

She caught me staring at her get-up and winked. "You like?"

"Yes, I like it. And reporters will like it, too—for all the wrong reasons. You don't want to look cheap, Darnda. You want to look wise."

"Like a mortician, maybe?"

"You know what I mean."

"Tell me more about the dead lady," she said.

"Look. I love you, Darnda. You're my closest friend. But maybe we shouldn't work together," I said. "You're rebelling against my simplest ideas. About how you dress. Right now it works with the people who hire you because you've built a good reputation. But in order to appeal to a broader audience, you'll need to—"

"Give me a break, *Mom*." Darnda bit into her pastry with such force its filling leaked out of the sides.

"Speaking of Mom, did I tell you she called Ms. Petty's house three times while I was there? It was like she knew something was wrong."

"Just because your mom's memory is shot to hell doesn't mean she can't pick up on stuff," said my friend. "What'd she say when you told her?"

"I couldn't." That led to a recitation about what had happened at St. Kate's. I massaged my neck while I spoke and wondered if I'd created a little groove—or a swollen red ridge—in my flesh from doing it so much. "This has sure turned into a crappy day."

"No kidding." Darnda closed her eyes, then opened them halfway, concentrating on something just above the crown of my head.

"Don't," I said.

"What?"

"You know. Don't read me."

"I want to be sure you didn't carry some of that lady's essence with you when you left."

"Yuck!" I leaned back, away from Darnda.

If she noticed the action, she didn't show it. After a few seconds, she said, "I hate to say it, but there's something there." She shook her head and her ponytail came undone. Loose, her geriatric mop sproinged around her face like thousands of miniature slinkies.

My cell phone chirped. People at surrounding tables reached for their briefcases and backpacks, checking theirs.

"Sasha Solomon," I said, squinting back at Darnda while she tried to read me again.

"This is Detective Garcia." Pause. "How's your throat?"

"It's been better." I stuck my finger in the ice cream, licked it.

"Your throat's still bothering you?"

"Yes," I said. "Why?"

"How about your eyes?"

"My eyes are great," I said, rubbing them. "What's going on?"

"I'd like you to go to the hospital and get checked out. You may have been exposed to something at Miss Petty's house."

"What do you mean 'exposed'?" I felt dizzy.

"Some of our men are exhibiting a respiratory reaction after being in her studio."

"Respiratory reaction? What's that mean? Are you saying I've been poisoned?"

"It's possible," he said. "We won't know for sure for a few days."

"I've been poisoned," I said. *I'm going to die.*

"We're not sure."

I felt the room shift, as if its foundation had suddenly lost a supporting corner. Something pounded in my ears.

"Sasha?" said Darnda.

"Ms. Solomon?" Garcia said.

"You can't be serious," I said.

"We're not certain. But just in case, you should get checked anyway," he said.

Light-headed, I felt my breathing speed up—along with a definite decrease of oxygen.

"Come on, Sasha." Darnda stood up.

"I understand you're upset," said Garcia—his voice slow and even—*patronizing*.

"Don't you handle me," I said too loudly.

"You need to calm down," he said. "The fact you're walking around bodes well."

"Oh, right. Just marvy." With the spoon, I pulverized my ice cream.

Darnda moved the bowl out of my reach. I scowled at her and pulled it back.

"You said the windows were open when you entered Miss Petty's studio?" said Garcia.

"Yes." I picked an ice cube out of my water and held it to my forehead. As it melted, little rivulets rolled off my eyebrows, paused on my lashes, and plopped onto the table. "They were all open like that."

"All right."

"Was Ms. Petty murdered?" I said.

Garcia didn't respond.

"Detective Garcia? Do you think she was killed?"

"No comment."

"I'm not a reporter," I said. "I'm a victim."

"Ms. Solomon, we're wasting time here. Get to the hospital. I'll be in touch."

"I can't go to the hospital," I said.

"Why not?"

"I don't have health insurance."

Garcia's sigh could've powered a wind generator. "Go to a clinic, go to a doctor. Just see someone about this." I heard voices in the background, a couple of coughs. "I'll call you later," he said before hanging up.

Darnda sat down again, her pale blue eyes shrouded in concern. "You need me to take you to the hospital?"

"I don't want to go to the damn hospital."

"If it's about money, Sasha, I can lend it to you. No biggie."

"Oh, yeah, like you're rolling in dough. I know how much it cost to publish your book. You don't have thousands of dollars to spare." I drew a circle in the puddle with my pinkie. "I certainly don't."

"Don't be an idiot, Sasha. You've been poisoned," she said.

"Why don't you use your voodoo on me. Talk to the poison, find out what it is."

"You really want me to?"

"Yes." I braced my hands on the side of the table, awaiting the invasion. I had no idea how it would feel, or if I'd feel anything at all.

Darnda, on the other hand, bent her head forward. Her hair covered her face. I could see the pink of her scalp in the part in the middle and a white spot where the pigmentation was going. She put one hand on top of mine and remained in that position long enough that I wondered if she'd fallen asleep.

People at the tables near ours stared at us openly. The guy clearing trays and dishes stopped to ask if she was all right.

At last, Darnda looked up and said, "Nothing. I can't get anything. It's not organic—or retains so little organic material that I can't connect."

"So, what does *that* mean?"

"Well, it was probably made synthetically—in a lab. I don't know. I don't usually try to talk to poisons, Sasha. I'm good, but not that good."

"Great." I pulled out another ice cube. "Even if I went to the ER, what would I say? 'Gee, I think I've been poisoned but I can't tell you what it is or when it happened or anything at all. And oh, by the way, thanks for charging me two million dollars and making me wait three days for the privilege of telling you.' That sounds like scads of fun." I could feel the heat in my face, the thump-thumping of the veins near my temples.

"You're being stupid and stubborn, Sasha, and neither becomes you." When Darnda is angry, her cheeks turn as red as sour cherries. Right now, she was working on a color I'd never seen before. "I know I'm going out on a limb here—but maybe a doctor could *help* you."

"This is useless. I'm going home," I said.

Darnda's lips disappeared in an inward bite. She took a long, long breath and released it. "Let's start over. I've got this friend who—"

"I don't want to see one of your friends. I saw enough groovy healers when I worked at TrueHealth."

"Let me finish!" Rarely does Darnda raise her voice.

I shut up. Nodded.

"He used to be an ER doc—now he's a pharmacist and works over at Poison Control. If you won't go to the ER, maybe he'll talk to you. As a favor to me. Okay?" Her stare dared me to open my mouth. "Poison Control. You've been poisoned. You think that might work? Or is that too *groovy* for you?"

I didn't move, didn't know whether to nod again or shake my head. The restaurant was strangely quiet. Without turning, I looked sideways. Pretty much everyone near us had stopped eating and drinking.

"Well?" said Darnda.

"Okay," I said in a whisper. My forehead hurt from eyebrows raised too far in strain. "But you know what? I'm going to find the sonuvabitch who did this to me. And I'm going to nail him to the wall."

"He didn't do it to you, Sasha. He did it to that poor old lady."

"All right then. I'll find him for the both of us."

five

POISON CONTROL DOESN'T GET a lot of drop-in business. The wheezing, blue-faced, choking crowd goes to hospital emergency rooms. Still, I was expecting something a little more—I don't know—*medical*. Housed at the University of New Mexico in Albuquerque, the state's cutting-edge repository of poison knowledge is such a humble place you'd walk right by if you weren't hunting for it. Sure, it's identified with a sign—about the size of a mosquito.

When you walk through the dark glass door, you're greeted by an unimpressive receptionist's desk made of cheap white plastic. To the right is a cramped room with a bank of seven computers—large-screen monitors—and phones. These are the call-in stations manned by pharmacists who stare at data on those screens, have toxicology info at a keystroke, and pal around with each other when the phones don't ring. Alas, the phones ring too much.

Peter O'Neill, MD, PharmD, MPH, and a slew of other abbreviations, met us at the desk. He wore a green button-down shirt and a serious expression. "You should really go to the ER if you're worried," he said, ushering us outside to a weathered wooden bench. "I haven't worked as a doctor for a couple of years now." His intent gaze magnified blue eyes topped with kohl-black brows. Pretty much a fatal combination for me, the whole Celtic *gestalt*.

"Thanks for making an exception," I said. Even in pain, I appreciated his broad swimmer's shoulders, the narrower hips, his many defined muscles hinted at through his cotton clothing. I bet we'd have good-looking kids.

"I haven't yet." He and Darnda exchanged glances. She scratched a mole on her cheek. With her mouth closed, she pushed her tongue against that same cheek. The action had a practiced air to it—as if it was a long-time signal they'd shared. His boyish grin made me rethink his age, taking it downward to thirty-something—definite stud-muffin territory.

"Tell me why you think you've been poisoned." His soft, professional voice jolted me back. He was too young for me anyway.

"I don't know if I've been poisoned," I said. "The police seem to think I have . . . by something in the air in Belen in an artist's studio. They think it killed her. But all it's done to me is give me a nasty sore throat and a whole lot of anger." I averted my eyes, embarrassed by the situation and by taking this man's time away from people who really needed it.

O'Neill frowned and acquired a serious doctor air—the one where he tells you you've got six months to live. "You have no idea what it was?"

"No," I said. For some reason, I didn't know what to do with my hands. They didn't feel comfortable in my lap, or on the bench, or in my hair.

"Any trouble breathing? Tight chest, wheezing, that sort of thing?"

"Just this sore throat. That's all." I felt foolish and incredibly attracted to him. I scanned his hands for a wedding ring.

O'Neill stayed *my* hands with his. He waited until I met his stare. I felt a zing of energy that flushed my face before I could take a breath.

"You're going to be okay," he said.

"How do you know?" My voice did one of those loop-de-loops associated with boys just this side of puberty.

"I've got some experience with this," he said. "Remember?"

Again, the damn cell phone chirped. I didn't want Peter O'Neill to let go of my hands.

Darnda noticed. She opened my purse, answered the phone, and said, "Sasha, it's the police."

"Hello?" I didn't bother to keep the irritation out of my voice. I put one hand to my cheek, realized what I was doing and let it drop to my lap.

"Did I catch you at a bad time?" said Garcia.

"Sort of."

"This won't take long. I need you to keep quiet about all of this," he said.

"That I've been poisoned?" I didn't like the squeaky thing happening to my vocal chords.

"Calm down. Have you been to the hospital yet?"

"I'm at the doctor's right now," I said.

Darnda and O'Neill shook their heads like parents catching their kid in a fib.

"I'm glad to hear that," said Garcia. "Does he have any questions?"

I wanted to ask why he thought my doctor was automatically a man. Of course, O'Neill wasn't *really* my doctor. I proffered my phone in his direction. "Do you have any questions for the detective?"

O'Neill took it and identified himself. "That's right . . . Poison Control . . . sure, if you need to . . . not too serious . . ."

"He's not married," Darnda whispered into my ear. "He's always been too busy for much of a social life."

"Why are you telling me that?" I whispered back, still trying to listen in on his side of the conversation.

"I don't have to be psychic to see you're attracted to him."

"Am I being that obvious?"

Darnda's smirk dimpled her generous face.

"Ms. Solomon?" O'Neill held out my phone for me.

"Nice guy," said Garcia. "Now, back to the other thing. Please hold off on telling people about Miss Petty."

"Can I tell my mom?"

"Must you?"

"Yes."

"It'll be in the news, anyway. Just don't give any details. I—hunh?" Voices mumbled in the background, something thudded. Garcia got back on the line. "We're saying she died under suspicious circumstances. You can use the same language."

"So, she *was* murdered."

"When will you be back in Belen?"

"Was she murdered?" I said.

"Morning or afternoon?"

"You're not going to answer my question?"

"It's not your business," Garcia said. "When will you be back in this area?"

"Tomorrow morning."

"Stop by on the way down."

Darnda and the doctor had gotten up, affording me some privacy. They stood by the entrance to Poison Control, talking. Their laugher carried through the air like birdsong.

"You're across from the chamber, right?" I said, wishing I could hear what they were saying.

"No. I'm in Los Lunas."

"What?" I shook my head in surprise.

"I'm with the state police, Ms. Solomon. I've gotta go." He disconnected.

I looked at my cell phone for a second then put it back in my purse. When I walked over to them, O'Neill cast a smile my way that would've hooked a prize trout. He reminded me of some kind of romantic Druid. I would've liked to see him in animal skins, hair a bit longer, flowing around his face. . . .

"Ms. Solomon, I'm sure with just a bit of bed rest, you'll be fine," he said. With a slender and well-manicured finger, he moved a curl of hair from Darnda's face. His hand evoked images of tickling and touching bare skin. I blushed. "But, I'd feel better if I knew someone was staying with you tonight. Just in case you have a more serious reaction."

"Damn it to hell," said Darnda. "I can't do it, Sasha. I've got my grandkids every night this week." My friend was between husbands right now. She went through them with amazing regularity. You'd think a psychic would have better foresight.

"Bob'll do it," I said.

"Sasha," said Darnda.

"He'll do it," I said.

"Good," said O'Neill. "Tell him to watch for changes in your breathing. If you start having a hard time, you need to get to a hospital immediately."

"This is too weird," I said.

I liked watching O'Neill's lips. They had a texture I wanted to explore, firm and yummy. Whatever I'd been exposed to must have affected my brain. He reached into his pocket and pulled out a wallet. The card he handed me bore the gray and turquoise logo of the University of New Mexico. Reaching in again, he unfolded a small pen and wrote on the back of the card.

"This is my home number," he said. "If something happens, tell your friend to call me. He doesn't need to worry about the time. I don't sleep much."

"Okay," I said. "I'm sure he wouldn't mind if you called, too." I handed him my card. "Anytime. Really."

"I'll keep that in mind," said O'Neill. Then, before he went back into the building, he tossed me a wink full of promises I wanted him to keep.

"What was that?" I said to Darnda.

She just smiled and walked me back to the car. This was the story of my life: I had to be poisoned to meet an attractive man.

six

WHEN YOU'RE IN A sour mood, don't add lemon juice. Darnda and I had parted ways after the Poison Control visit. I didn't really feel like having her razz me more about O'Neill anyway. Don't ask me why I decided to stop by Bob's office. Maybe I wanted sympathy. Maybe I thought a personal visit would clear up my ambivalence about the guy. Turns out, I was right.

Though just past three o'clock, the lobby felt beyond empty, abandoned. No light shone to greet clients—or a poisoned girlfriend.

And then I heard them.

His broad laugh, her giggles, on the other side of his thick door. I thought about leaving, letting it go. Then she squealed and giggled again.

"Hi there," I said, bursting into the room.

She straddled his lap. Both of them having a bit o' afternoon delight behind his desk. Bob's head was buried underneath the front of her shirt.

"Gosh, I don't think we've met," I said, holding out a hand to shake hers.

She jumped up, leaving my boyfriend's thinning hair stiff, pointing in twenty different directions as if he'd just been electrocuted. His mouth shone with saliva.

"Sasha," he said.

"I know, I know. Law requires so much research nowadays. It's hard to keep up," I said, then put on my best sneer. "Or maybe I should say, 'it's hard to keep it up.'"

"Sasha, this isn't what you think," he said.

"Sure it is," I said.

The woman's pantyhose had sagged at the knees. She tried to sneak past me. Her makeup at first glance had seemed flawless. Now I could see the cracks, the smudged lipstick.

"My name's Sasha Solomon," I said, blocking the door.

"Ann," she said.

"Nice to meet you, Ann." I glanced at my nubby fingernails. "So, how long have you been a slut?" I thought my tone showed tremendous civility, all considered.

"Sasha!" Bob—fastening his pants—came to Ann's side, put his arm around her waist. "Don't go," he said to her. "I'll straighten this out."

"I'd like to see you try," I said.

"Give us a few minutes," he said to his new squeeze. She nodded once and pushed past me, assured of her position in this little power struggle.

When she'd gone, Bob said, "I was going to tell you."

"That you're a sleazebag?"

"Yes. No. Not that."

"What were you going to tell me, *Bob*?" I played with his name, popping the consonants so that it exploded. Each time I did, he jumped. Just a little.

"That we needed some space."

"That you wanted fresh nookie, *Bob*."

"There's no need to be crude."

"Don't tempt me, *Bob*." I leaned against his rosewood conference table. We'd made love on that table. I checked it for smudges. "Fresh prints. Gee, I wonder how these got here?"

He quickly wiped them with his shirtsleeve. "Sasha, let's talk about this later."

"I'd rather talk now. Annie-baby can cool her jets a few minutes more."

"There's no need to take it out on her."

"Bob, you've been the one taking it out on her. In and out." I grinned; it *was* sort of funny. Sick funny.

"Sasha."

"Oh, screw it, Bob. I'm not even that offended. She looks like a whore and you've been acting like an idiot lately. Now I know why."

"She's a very well-respected attorney."

"You forget, I'm a very well-respected PR pro."

"Is that a threat?"

"Statement of fact," I said with a wicked smile.

"I don't want you to leave until you swear not to breathe a word of this to anyone."

"Who would I want to tell?" Let's see . . . I bet someone in the media might be interested.

"I don't like the tone of your voice," he said, tucking his shirt in and straightening his tie.

"And I don't like *you* right now. Not one little bit."

He crossed to the door and stood before it, big and bulky and—for the first time since I'd known him—outright ugly. "Sasha, I don't need to remind you what libel is, do I?"

"Tell me how it's libel when I catch my boyfriend *in flagrante.*"

"We weren't screwing."

"Oh, excuse me. You must have been playing find the boob. Well, here I am," I said. "Now let me leave or I'll do something really stupid. And you know I'm capable of some really stupid stuff."

He stood aside. "I don't want it to end like this."

"I do," I said, slamming the door in his face.

But that wasn't enough.

Who knew how long Bob had been screwing long-legged, lusty-lawyer Ann? Had there been other women before her? I stood on the other side of his door for, maybe, six seconds, letting the doubts bubble until they erupted.

Hot faced, heart pumping, I burst into the room. I wanted to do something bad. Really bad.

"Sasha!" said Bob, his hand extended as if he'd been about to open the door.

Eyes searching for the right target, I didn't speak. What would satisfy my anger and sense of betrayal? Ripping his Persian rug? Nah, too time consuming. Throwing his chair out the window? Too much work.

Ah. That'll do it.

"Sasha?"

I opened my purse, pulled out my key chain, and walked to the far side of Bob's flawless conference table. When I reached the end farthest from him, I stopped and selected my longest key. The one to the Toyota.

"You wouldn't dare," he said.

"Oh, really?" With a beautiful—I thought—flourish, I dug the key into the pricey wood and held it down as I scratched the length of the table. Though a big man, Bob couldn't quite reach me.

My ex spluttered, "You . . . you . . ."

I zeroed my sites on the door.

Then ran like hell.

seven

CATS HAVE NINE LIVES. A dog's first few years weigh seven times heavier than human ones. And for any forty-year-old woman who still toys with the idea of having a child, one month equals a year. Seen that way, I'd wasted a decade on Bob.

Clichéd tears of laughter and anger dribbled down my cheeks on the drive home. Another round of repairs on Fourth Street made a mess of the already antiquated road and paralleled the feelings of upheaval carousing in my heart. Poor poisoned me, traded in for a younger model.

Leo da Cat, a mercenary orange-and-tan tom who'd adopted me a couple of years before, ran in front of the car when I pulled into my unpaved driveway. With the nonchalance only a cat can assume, he sauntered to the front door and regarded me with feigned disinterest. I missed stepping on his tail by a quarter inch.

Ears back, he hissed.

"Don't start with me," I said.

Leo ran into the cool adobe house and headed for the kitchen before I'd even gotten my purse unhitched from the door handle. My shoe caught on a piece of metal in the doorframe and I fell onto the brick floor. Cross-legged, I cried again, trying to put the heel back on the Ferragamo.

Leo licked his thin black lips and arched his back, hinting he wanted me to pet him. But when I held out my hand, he shrank away from it.

"That's not fair," I said. "Come here." He jumped into my lap, his tuna breath comforting with its familiarity. He purred and kneaded my thigh, using his claws just enough to make a point. "Oh, Leo, what am I going to do?"

He jerked away when I tried to nuzzle my teary face against his side. Darnda tells me that if I want real love, I should get a dog. She says they're not emotionally conflicted, not selfish, like cats. I say, just because she can talk to animals doesn't make her an expert. Well, technically it does, but some things in life should remain a mystery—and cats are one of them.

Feeling utterly rejected, I went into the kitchen and searched for food. The scotch scorched, the instant vichyssoise seared. I paced my little house, frustrated by every attempt at solace. I wanted drugs. I wanted to go to sleep. I wanted this to be over.

Instead, I paid my bills. I paid Mom's bills. Prepared invoices, stared at the computer, and killed time. At one point, I took out the photo of Mom I'd found at Ms. Petty's and used several magnets—the ones with words on them—to create a frame around it on my fridge. The frame became a kind of nonsensical poem as sad and disjointed as I felt.

Then I went back to the computer and played Bounce Out and FreeCell. Eventually, I found myself surfing the web, *Google*-ing the names of former boyfriends. Leo twitched, ensconced in his kitty dreams on the couch. Around eight, the phone rang. I put on the headset.

"Go to hell," I said, expecting Bob, and searching my *casita* for something to throw.

"I must have the wrong number."

"Who is this?"

"Peter O'Neill . . . from Poison Control," he said.

"Ohmigod. I'm sorry, Dr. O'Neill."

"Let's start over," he said. "Hi. How're you doing?"

"Not great." My throat still felt like someone had scoured it with a cactus.

"May I talk to your boyfriend?"

I blubbered something.

"Ms. Solomon?" Mariachi music blasted behind his voice. "Are you all right?"

"Everything's wonderful," I said. *Pitiful, just pitiful.*

"Your boyfriend isn't there, is he?"

"Not exactly."

"I knew it," said my own private Druid. "When you left, I had a feeling you'd try to do this alone."

"Believe me, it wasn't my choice." I went into the kitchen and got the can of whipped cream from the fridge.

"Have you had anything to eat?"

"Not really. Well, sort of." I squirted the sweet stuff into my hand—it tasted metallic. I gave up, went to the sink and rinsed it off.

"I'm at Monroe's. How about I bring you some flan?"

"Would you?" I sounded more pathetic with each answer. Were Druids into human sacrifice? If I kept this up, he might get the wrong idea.

"Tell me where you live."

Ten minutes later, O'Neill knocked at the front door, a brown paper bag in his hand. "You've been crying. Are you in pain?"

"You could say that," I said, wiping an errant tear from my cheek. "I'm fine." With a hostile kick, I knocked my pair of ruined high heels to one side of the room. I could feel O'Neill observing me—and judging me by my messy home, my angry movements. "It's a long story."

"You can tell me later. First, I want to see that throat of yours." He pulled out a flashlight. "Say, 'Ah,'"

"Why does everyone want to look in my mouth?"

"Indulge me." He sat down on my futon couch without being asked and patted the cushion next to him. "Come on. Then you can tell me your woes and I'll tell you mine."

"Why are you doing this, Dr. O'Neill?" I walked over to him.

"Peter." He patted the couch again. "Well, you're Darnda's friend. And, I'd feel responsible if I saw your name in an obit." He turned on the little light. "Now, open wide."

"Well?" I said.

"I think you'll live, Ms. Solomon." His kind smile broke me.

I started crying again. "My name's Sasha," I burbled.

And unlike Leo, O'Neill . . . Peter . . . let me nuzzle against his shoulder. *Why couldn't Bob have done this? Just been there for me?*

Peter held me closer and cooed, "It'll be all right. Don't worry. It's okay."

I liked the feel of his arm, muscular beneath the long-sleeved turquoise T-shirt. I closed my eyes and let the tears dribble out. He dabbed them with something soft. My breathing steadied. He hummed a tune I didn't recognize, didn't need to recognize. My hunched shoulders relaxed. Warmth suffused me. . . . I fell asleep.

Ch-ch-cheep! Ch-ch-cheep!

I moved my leg and tumbled off the couch. Above me, still snoring, was Peter. His shirt had crept up to reveal the kind of abs people hire private trainers for. In the early morning light, his long eyelashes echoed the angelic curls gracing his forehead and beyond.

The phone continued to ring. I yawned, out-of-it to the point I hadn't moved to answer the insistent sound.

Peter sat up, saw me on the floor, blinked, and glanced around the room.

"What time is it?" he said.

"I dunno." I stood and yanked down the sheet I used as my front curtain to get a better look. The phone stopped ringing and the answering machine clicked on, the volume low.

"In that case, good morning," he said. "How's your throat?"

"Good as new," I said. "What happened anyway? I don't remember a thing."

"We made mad passionate love."

"Don't I wish." I turned fuchsia when I realized I'd said it out loud. "Oh, God. I didn't mean that."

Peter grinned, eyes twinkling. "Don't look so mortified. I'm the one who was inappropriate."

"I don't remember a thing." I yawned again.

"I have that effect on women."

"I—"

"I'm teasing you," he said. "Actually, I'm pleased you went to sleep so easily. Being poisoned isn't exactly trivial. It's exhausting."

Poisoned. I thought of Phillipa Petty—her old-ladyness, her deadness, that puffy and pale leg—then shook my head to banish more images. Outside, birds chattered and chittered in the new day. I bumbled into the kitchen on autopilot and ground the coffee.

Peter watched from the doorway.

"Do you have time for something to eat?" I said, turning my back to look in the fridge.

"Where's a clock in this house?"

"Above the front door."

I had my back to Peter, my attention focused on scrounging breakfast, when I heard his laugh. He'd found the timepiece—a kitschy pink cat from the 1950s with rhinestone-encrusted eyes that moved side to side and a sparkling pendulum tail.

"I've got to be at work in ten minutes," he said.

"Too bad."

"Yeah." He tilted his head as if to see into my soul. "You sure you're okay?"

"I'm just fine, *doctor*. Couldn't be better," I said. "My throat is happy as a clam."

"A clam, hunh? I've never met a happy one." He walked to where I stood and touched my shoulder, looked into my eyes.

I tensed. This could be one of those romantic moments when the violin music swells and a harp takes the solo.

"Nice sleeping with you, Ms. Solomon," he said, his breath warm with a kiss to my forehead, his hand resting on the doorknob to leave.

eight

"GARCIA," THE DETECTIVE SAID, picking up on the second ring.

"Hello," I said. "This is Sasha Solomon."

"How are you feeling?"

"Throat's as good as new." I sprayed a shot of whipped cream— it tasted fine now—straight from the can into my mouth. Okay, it wasn't the best breakfast. But milk is protein, right? And protein is good for you, right?

"What was that?"

"Nothing," I said, swallowing and shaking the can for another hit. I spritzed the next course onto my hand and added mini–chocolate chips. Did you know that chocolate has been proven to be an effective anti-depressant? At this rate, I'd be happy all day.

"Ms. Solomon? What can I do for you?" He said it quickly, as if he were harried.

"Do you still want me to stop by this morning?"

"Yes. Please do." Click.

"Okie dokie," I said to the dial tone. "I'll be there in a few minutes." I added more chocolate to my next mouthful.

Before leaving, I listened to my messages. Darnda had called. Yesterday, I'd meant to give her a second draft of the press release I'd written and talk about my ideas for the pitch we'd use with reporters. We had to be sure she seemed credible or she'd get the wrong kind of attention and no one would take her seriously. Maybe we could use a couple of her more famous clients for testimonials. Heaven knew, she'd worked for enough movie stars. We'd use them—and anything else I could think of—to launch her national campaign with a nuclear bang.

The trick was to reach her. Darnda didn't answer her phone much, and she didn't use email or faxes. All of this was done to protect herself from unwanted energies. I'd learned not to take her silences personally. They rarely had anything to do with me, anyway. I left her a message.

On the way out the door, I squirted a dab of whipped cream into Leo's bowl and bid him adieu. I took another snort myself and then ran into the kitchen to put the can back where it belonged. Another handful of chocolate wouldn't hurt either.

Twenty-five minutes later, I pulled off the freeway in Los Lunas. The tan blandness of the state police substation blended in with the dirt surrounding it. Whoever had landscaped the front had a real fondness for tumbleweeds and gravel. In New Mexico, we talk about xeriscaping—using plants that conserve water and look nice. Well, this was *zero*-scaping.

Dressed for my midmorning interview with the first of the train guys, I knew I looked good. Though my nutrition had suffered this morning, my efforts to present a professional demeanor hadn't. I'd pulled back my brown hair into in a sexy bun and applied an almond-warm lipstick to an otherwise make-up-less face. Sure, the skirt came up a little too high, but it exposed decent legs. My last pair of heels pushed me to a solid 5'6".

Garcia didn't notice a spot of it. Neither did anyone else. Grim-faced, the detective guided me through a maze of cubicles to his own. He pulled out a grimy metal chair for me. It screeched across the concrete floor.

"Why didn't you tell me about your mother's relationship with Miss Petty?" Garcia said.

"I did."

"Not quite."

"I said they were very close."

"I suppose you did. But you somehow neglected to tell me they were best friends for decades, that they were in touch daily."

I looked at him. "I'm sorry, I didn't think it was important."

He cleaned his nails with a pocketknife.

"When we talked, I didn't know Ms. Petty had been murdered," I said. "What does Mom have to do with this, anyway?"

"She left seventeen messages on Miss Petty's answering machine yesterday." Garcia snapped his knife closed.

I scrunched forward in the uncomfortable chair.

He sat back.

"How much do you know about my mom?" I said.

"Enough."

"Do you know she's in a rehab hospital?"

He nodded.

"Do you know she's got problems with her short-term memory?"

"I got that impression." He leaned his head back an inch, chin forward. "Why don't you explain it to me anyway."

I did. As I spoke, I caught myself fingering the outline of my digital camera through the scuffed leather of my purse. If I told the detective about the pictures I'd taken, he'd confiscate my new toy. They were probably out of focus anyway.

"Have you heard of withholding evidence?" he said, frowning.

"Yes, sir," I said, also thinking about that photo of Mom I'd snagged.

"Why do I get the feeling there's something you're not telling me?"

"I have no idea." I made eye contact though it would have been easier to look away. Someone laughed in another part of the room. I thought I smelled cigar.

Garcia got up. "You wait here. I'll be back in a minute."

Phones rang. Men paused to talk with each other. The smell of coffee, deodorant, and mouthwash hovered thick in the air. Someone coughed, and another person sneezed three times in a row. Garcia returned holding a Styrofoam cup, its contents steaming. He sat down, took a sip. He frowned some more.

"Your mother was very worried about Miss Petty—every time I spoke with her and in the messages she left." He rubbed the bridge of his nose.

"Did you tell her?"

He shook his head. "I thought you were going to."

"I haven't had the heart to yet."

I thought I saw compassion touch his eyes, but he said, "What are you waiting for?"

"The right time, I guess. Yesterday wasn't," I said.

"Wouldn't it be better coming from you than from me?"

"Of course it would. But you know, she probably won't remember it five minutes after you or I tell her." I stared at his coffee, hoping the hint would spur him to offer me a cup. I really wanted to drink something stronger and to drink a lot of it.

"When did your mother last see Miss Petty?" He noticed my gaze, picked up his cup, and drank.

"I have no idea." I looked at my watch.

"Am I keeping you?" His face hardened.

"No. Yes. I don't know," I said like an idiot.

"What *do* you know, Ms. Solomon?" Almost playful.

"I know telling Mom is going to be one of the hardest things I've done lately. I know she's going to be devastated—over and over again—by this."

Garcia sighed. "I need to speak with her again soon, Ms. Solomon. If you want to be the one to tell her, you'd better do it quickly."

I felt my whole body tense at the thought of him alone with Mom, of him trying to interview her. "You can't see her alone. She'll get too upset."

"What do you suggest?" Garcia finished his coffee and threw his cup into the military-green metal garbage can next to his desk.

"Maybe we could go together. Or I could meet you there. I'd sit in the back and wouldn't say a word," I said.

"You think she'll be calmer, that she'll talk with you there?"

"More than she'd talk without me."

He shrugged, glanced at his own watch, and pushed back his chair. "I need to be somewhere right now. What's your schedule for the rest of the day?"

"It's pretty loose. I've got an interview in an hour or so, then I was going to spend some time getting to know Belen."

Garcia chuckled. "You won't need much time for that."

"You'd be surprised."

"I probably would be," he said, rising. "I'll call you around noon and we can set up a time to go see your mother."

"I can't guarantee she'll make any sense. Her short-term memory's shot."

"So's yours. We've already talked about that," he said. "Just be available when I call."

nine

ERNIE MERKIN'S HOUSE DIDN'T pretend to have a lawn, or a yard. The square of land in front consisted of sun-baked dirt dotted by undistinguished rocks and surrounded by a chain-link fence. No stairs graced the non-existent porch—first dirt, then door—nothing to ease the transition. The doorbell was a buzzer.

Through the black screen, Ernie resembled an animal kept too long in a cave. Pasty-faced with Shar-pei wrinkles, he said, "You, Solomon?"

I nodded, "Yessir."

"Well, you might as well come in." He unlocked the screen door. Inside, the only natural light struggled through bent venetian blinds.

I followed him via the living room into a dingy kitchen, dirty dishes on the counter, in the sink, the smell of old food verging on decay. He saw me assessing and said without humor, "The maid comes tomorrow."

I sat across from him at a rust-colored table, the legs wobbly. His eyes were the color of juniper, his hair brown as dried mud and whitened at the edges with age. He gave the impression of leanness, though he had a paunch, like he'd given up exercise or given in to beer.

"Thank you for meeting with me," I said to start what seemed like an already stalled interview.

"Sure." He reeked of resentment. He drank from an oversized mug, the liquid amber—maybe scotch. Perhaps his silence was alcohol induced.

"I'd like to start with some basic questions about the Harvey House project."

"Anything you say, lady."

"Okay. I understand you'd like to see the building restored to its original splendor—the Harvey Girls, a B and B, and train museum. Is that right?"

"Sure."

"Can you tell me why this is important to you?"

"It's not."

"Excuse me?"

"It's not important to me."

"But your name is on the list of people to interview for the project."

"You want the canned answer? I'll give you the canned answer," he said. "Trains have been my life. Whether I like 'em or not, they're there every minute of my day and night." He drank the mug's contents down, looked at it, and went to a cabinet to pull out a gallon jug of whiskey. With his right hand, he hefted it out and swished it side to side, his eyebrows raised in invitation.

Ten in the morning.

"Want some?" he said.

"Sure." I didn't, but this guy wasn't going to talk without a drinking buddy.

Back at the table, he placed a jelly jar, one-quarter full, in front of me.

"Down the hatch." He held up his mug and winked.

We chugged the harsh booze. He refreshed our glasses and we repeated the ritual.

"You're okay," he said.

"Thanks."

Through the loosening power of shared drinks, I sensed a different him. A younger man. It was one of those twinklings, here then gone. His dimples must have broken hearts, his hands caused shudders of desire. And those eyes, long ago clear, must have nailed women to whatever bed he wanted.

"So, what do you really want to know?" he said.

"Why don't you start with what it was like to work on the railroad?"

"You got all day?"

"Sure," I said.

"No, really. How far back you want me to go?"

"Tell me how you got into railroading in the first place. Did you love trains?"

"Nah. I never loved trains." He snorted, looked at the glass in his hand. "They're big dumb beasts that can kill you faster than you can blink an eye." He drank, wiped his mouth with the back of his hand. "After I finished high school, I got married and had to support the wife somehow. I didn't want to go to college, didn't want to borrow money from my parents or hers, so I started as a brakeman for the Atchison-Topeka line here. Simple as that."

Why had he married so young? Why trains, if he didn't like them? What was the deal with borrowing money? So many questions I wanted to ask. So few were my business. "What's a brakeman?"

"Just like it sounds, we set the brakes. Used to be, a hundred years ago, guys would ride on the top of every third car, in all kinds of weather, to set brakes. When I started, the crew would be a head brakeman, a couple of other brakemen up and down the train, the engineer, and the conductor. Nowadays, it's just a hoghead and conductor," he said. "And I figure they're not long for the world either."

A child screamed for its mother outside. Ernie got up and closed a window I hadn't realized was open.

"What's a hoghead?" I said.

"Lady, do you know anything about trains?"

"They're big and have little red cabooses." As I said it, I wondered if the humor would offend.

His smile raised up a fraction of his expressionless face; it could have been a frown. "Think about it for a minute. Those forty-, sixty-, eighty-ton cars don't do anything by themselves, not unless they're on a hill or the track's bad. You use the engine to move and kick the cars where you want 'em. It's like a giant puzzle putting together trains, getting them where you want 'em, figuring out what's gone wrong." He yawned. "Trains are a half-mile, maybe a mile long. You have to check the knuckles, walk the train and make sure the air's bled."

I stared at him, unable to swim my brain past his unfamiliar terminology.

"You really want to learn about trains, what I should do is take you down to the tracks," he said.

"I'd like that." I drank the last drops of whiskey. "Do you mind answering a few more questions?"

Merkin waited.

"Do you think the Harvey House and train museum are a good idea?"

"Listen, lady. The reason my name's on that proposal paper is that they needed some rank and file to sign it. To make it look like we're all one big happy family. What the hell? I'm getting my retirement. I'm set up good. They want me to sign some stupid piece of paper, give me a bonus for doing it, who'm I to say no?"

This was news.

"So, you don't think it's a good idea?" I said.

"I don't really care. There're so many foamers out there, it'll work. And if it saves that building from turning into a blasphemous place, well, it's got my vote."

"Foamers?"

"Yeah, people who love trains." He got more booze and his voice got all fake smarmy. "Oh, trains are *sooooo* romantic. Don't you just love them? They're like riding *mysteries*." His voice resumed its gruff tone. "Tell you what. One time I was working the yard and caught some idiot trying to steal the plaque, the train's number, right off the engine up front. He coulda been killed up there. We were switching with a hump and a car coulda smashed his ass like a bug. And *oh*, he just *loved* trains. That's what foamers are. Crazy idiots who think trains are the be-all and end-all." He shook his head.

"Don't people who work on trains love them?"

He gave me an ah-come-on look. "Grime, noise, being treated like shit. Oh, yeah, I just loved that."

"But why did you spend so many years on trains if you didn't like them? Why'd you become a conductor?"

"Work's work. Pay's pay." He made sure I was looking him in the eye. "From the time I started on the extra board, became a boomer, the life was in my blood. And when there was work, the money was good. What's a kid with no education and all alone going to do?"

"I thought you said you were married."

"Wife's dead," he said. "Dead to me, anyway. She left years ago. Trains and family don't mix."

"But—"

"Look, it was what I knew and the money was good." He straightened up. "You need anything else?"

"Not right now." Actually, I wanted to take a couple of pictures of him and his home, a reminder that my life could be oh, so much worse. But I didn't bother to ask.

He got up, headed into the front room, and opened the door.

"Can I stop by again if I've got more questions?" I paused on the other side of the screen.

"Sure," he said. "If you bring the booze."

ten

TIPSY AND DISPIRITED, I decided to find a cup of coffee and try for an interview with someone on my artsy-fartsy list. In the almost empty Denny's, I got out my cell phone and dialed.

Three rings, then an elderly voice snarled, "I don't want any."

"Excuse me. Is this Mrs. Lydia Herndon?"

"Who wants to know?"

"My name is Sasha Solomon. I got your name from Mayor Flores."

"Humph."

"Mrs. Herndon, I'm looking into the Belen Artists Guild proposal for the Harvey House. Would you have some time to talk with me today?"

"I don't see why anybody gave you my name," she said. The contrariness in her voice sounded permanent.

"You're president of the guild, aren't you?"

"For the moment."

"Mrs. Herndon?"

"What time is it, anyway?" Her mumble told me she was asking herself. "Oh, I suppose you may as well come now."

"Thank you."

"I don't see how I can help you."

"I'll be there in just a few minutes."

While I finished my coffee, I wrote down questions to ask about the Harvey House project, the Artists Guild, and Phillipa Petty.

From what the mayor had told me, the painter had planned to give several of her most famous works to the project if the artists could secure a commitment from the city to promote it. Enough Petty paintings in one location in the Southwest might turn this unknown town into a modern-art mecca. The controversy groupies from California and Texas would come for sure if *The Cross-Dressing Christ* were part of the package.

I popped a breath mint into my mouth and drove through Belen's downtown area with its new Burger King and Taco Bell alongside boarded-up storefronts. Was the town big enough to support a real tourist industry? I made a mental note to visit the chamber of commerce to talk with the executive director. The exec would have a feel for the local merchants' perspectives on both projects. Restaurants, hotels, souvenir stores—all of these would be necessary to sustain development of the Harvey House. Without the business community's goodwill, neither proposal would be viable.

Becker Street was off the main drag and in the direction of the Harvey House. I stopped at a prim little home. Someone stood in the front yard. Clothed in one of those standard-requisition old-lady flowered dresses, a white-haired elderly woman held a water hose with a pesticide container attached to it. Her concentration focused, she aimed the stream of poison at her rose bushes and muttered as she moved it up and down. The water spewed with such force that the woman had trouble controlling the spray.

It was the intensity of her mission that struck me. Leaves from the bushes jounced and flapped, some breaking off. I didn't want to surprise her. I didn't want pesticide to end up all over me.

A car drove by and honked. Sure enough, the hose lifted and turned toward the noise. I jumped out of the way just in time. Liquid flew in front of me in a malicious arc before splashing the sidewalk.

"What are you looking at?" said my next interviewee.

"Mrs. Herndon? I'm Sasha Solomon. I just called," I said, finishing the strong mint and yearning for another to cover my boozy breath.

"Why didn't you say so?"

"You looked busy," I said.

"Well, don't dawdle. Come in." She continued attacking the bushes. "What are you waiting for?"

I lifted the latch on the amber picket gate to let myself through. She had her back to me as she strode through puddles, her flip-flops drenched. Drops flecked her rainbow-veined legs. I jumped from dry spot to dry spot in the small river she'd created.

"Aphids." Mrs. Herndon turned to look at me. "Every year I buy those damn lady bugs and every year they fly away. Just like that." She snapped the fingers on her free hand. "And so every year I end up spraying poison, from here to Kingdom Come, just to get a few lousy roses." She turned off the hose. "Well, that ought to do 'em," she said. She walked up the cement stairs to her fuchsia-trimmed porch and opened the screen door.

Mrs. Herndon wasn't much of a housekeeper. Magazines straddled the arms on her couch. Plastic grocery bags covered the rest of it. A pile of clothes huddled in a corner of the living room. I followed her voice into the kitchen, a big, bright room at the back of the house. Painted flowers, vines, and birds adorned the walls. While they were colorful, they had an elementary-school feel to them—the kind of decoration you'd find in a kindergarten classroom.

"Sit down," she commanded.

I pulled out a chrome chair with a plastic Kelly-green cushion from a table topped with the same color. My hostess puttered—water in a teakettle, spoons on the table, milk into a creamer, cookies onto a plate—all the time talking to herself.

This felt like a show, somehow. A deliberate effort to put me in my place. After five minutes of the performance, I said, "Excuse me. I don't want to take up too much of your time."

"All I've got is time."

"Okay. I'd—"

"Oh, I just hate aphids, don't you?" she said, coming to the table with the steaming kettle and several tea bags. With a loud exhalation, more appropriate for someone weighing twice her hundred pounds, she parked herself across from me. "Every day I get up and hope they'll all be dead. But nothing doing. Someone brings them in by the truckload every night, right up to my house. No one else I know has these problems." She poured the water into both cups. Mine was chipped. "What did you say your last name was?"

"Solomon."

"Any relation to that phony Hannah Solomon up in Albuquerque?"

"Excuse me?"

"Hannah Solomon."

"She's my mom."

"Huh." She narrowed her eyes, studying me. "Yes, I can see the resemblance now that you mention it."

"How do you know my mother?"

"She used to slum it down here in Belen, before she got all high-and-mighty."

"My mom?"

"She owned that gallery just off the plaza in Old Town, right?"

"Yes, but it's been at least thirty years since she closed it." I'd loved that gallery. Happy, happy memories. The art alive with so much energy I wanted to eat it. The crazy, creative people with untamed beards, cigar breath, rosy noses, and pieces of candy and hugs for me.

"She carried nothing but junk," said Mrs. Herndon, stirring her tea. The spoon clanked loud enough to crack enamel.

I bit back my first response. "Did you exhibit with her?"

"She wouldn't know good art if it bit her in the ass."

"I don't know why you'd say—"

"So, how's your mother nowadays?" She spoke through ungenerous lips, her tone peckish. "Philly mentioned they'd spoken the other day."

"Really?"

"Isn't that why you're here? To talk about what's happened?" She dumped four teaspoons of sugar into her drink, saw me watching, and said, "Diabetes. I've had it for years and I'm sick and tired of doctors telling me what I can and cannot eat."

To protect us both from a bad scene, I decided to take the conversation far from Mom. "Would you mind telling me a bit about the Belen Artists Guild?"

"What do you want to know?"

"Who are the major players? What's your mission? That kind of thing."

"Oh, that's priceless. Major players? Mission?" She cackled. "You don't have any idea what you're talking about."

"How about you setting me straight?" If she'd known me, she would have marveled at the control I exerted to keep my voice calm, my scowl molded into a tense smile.

"Well, let's see." She took a drink of her tea, added another teaspoon of sugar. "I guess you'd like the history and all that rot, first?"

"Wherever you'd like to start."

"Back before Philly was God's gift, she was an artist just like anyone else. She grew up here, you know?"

I nodded, sipped the generic tea.

"Well, we were talking one day about how being an artist is such a solitary kind of life. No one but another artist understands how creativity works, how it needs to be nourished." Mrs. Herndon smacked her lips. "Plus, no one in the world knew there were artists working down south in New Mexico—well, your mom did, but she didn't count. Anyway, it was 'Taos this, Santa Fe that.' Belen wasn't even on the map as far as real dealers were concerned."

"You could make the same argument today," I said, wanting to slug her for continuing to insult Mom.

"Exactly!" She slapped the table. "Well, Philly and I decided we should try to get the artists down here together to help each other, to support each other, that kind of thing." Her crustiness receded as she continued. "We got a group of people together, Maggie Soames, Dick Ortega, Fran Junquist, your mom—though I don't know why she gave a hoot—and others. Our first meeting was right here in this kitchen."

She stopped, remembering something. Birds gossiped outside, their shadows speckling the brightness of the room with movement.

"I had no idea it started right here," I said to get her going again.

"Even then, no one could agree on a damn thing," she said. "Maggie wanted to have a minimum skill level to qualify for admittance into the guild. Dick—that brown-noser—thought that anyone who wanted to join should get to pay their two bucks and hobnob with us—even amateurs." She picked up a chocolate-frosted butter cookie. "I just wanted to get a big enough group that we'd be taken seriously by the bigger gallery owners, by the folks with real clout and contacts, unlike your—"

"I know, *my mom.*"

Herndon's pale green eyes clouded, hostile.

"Weren't there galleries here?" I said.

"Just look around you. Who'd think of having anything in Belen? It's a wasteland. Has been. Always will be."

"That's not fair," I said. "Why do you think Ms. Petty was so willing to donate her paintings to your project? Because she believed in this town—and you all—to make it happen."

"First of all, her name was *Miss* Petty. She couldn't abide by that 'Miz' business," said Mrs. Herndon. "And you're just too naïve about everything."

"I'd love to understand." I'd stopped taking notes because I'd pressed too hard with my pen and had ruined the paper. Still, that was better than decking the snarky old woman.

"Philly didn't believe in a thing except Philly. She moved here to be left alone. If she'd had her druthers, she'd've lost touch with the rest of us years ago."

"So, why didn't she?" I said. "Why'd she volunteer to give your project millions of dollars worth of paintings if she was so selfish?"

Lydia Herndon stood up and in a trembling voice said, "Young lady, no one has the right to use that tone with me."

"Oh, so it's perfectly fine for you to dis my mother and to bad-mouth *Miss* Petty, but I can't call you on your contradictions? Is that it?" *Yep, that's the way to conduct an interview. Very professional.*

Her face had turned radish red. "This interview is over."

"Thank God," I said, gathering my things and rushing out of her house. Once through her gate, I felt tremendous relief, as if I'd escaped a rabid animal. With each distancing step, the sun shone cleaner, the day warmed toastier.

I opened the car and let the hot air escape before sitting down. Hand on the hood, I looked at Mrs. Herndon's now dry walkway, the white residue from the pesticide visible on the ground.

Poison. Phillipa Petty had inhaled poison. I had, too.

Believe me, I was going to make the S.O.B who'd done it to us . . . pay.

eleven

MY STOMACH BUBBLED WITH irritation after the lousy interview. When upset, eat.

I drove down Belen's main drag and noticed The White Way Restaurant, its parking lot full with an early lunch crowd. Although the name of the place made me think of New York—and Belen was the size of a thimble in comparison—Mayor Flores had said it had the best burgers and fries in town. Who was I to question a bureaucrat?

Inside, the diner hopped. I found a seat at the counter and listened to snippets of conversation.

"She's burning in Hell, blaspheming the way she did," said a shrill voice behind me.

"Never was a part of this community anyway," said another.

Phillipa Petty's death had hit the local gossip train.

"Come on, Nick, no one deserves to be murdered," said a woman, her murmur soft.

No *suspicious circumstances*; she'd used the M-word. I turned to find the speaker. She sat at a table with an older man. Her tawny hair bracketed a face that reminded me of a new penny, shiny and round.

"I guess you caught me." She noticed my gaze alight on a napkin she'd begun to fold. I caught a glimpse of eyes, messy hair. It looked like a quick portrait. Of me?

"Mind if I take a closer look?" I said, leaning to get a better view.

"It's not very good."

"I'd love to see it." I slid off my stool.

Her face reddened but she opened it anyway. Only the flowers on the napkin impeded my likeness in the cheap blue ink.

"What do you mean it's not good? It's wonderful," I said.

"I'm still learning. See?" She pointed to the drawing. "I didn't get your nose right. It's too sharp. And here . . . your chin has that nice tiny dimple and I completely missed it. I always have trouble with chins."

"It really is *very* good," I said.

"Why don't you join us?" The words somersaulted out of her mouth. Their speed gave the impression that she sought to deflect further praise.

"Thanks," I said.

The man rose to hold out a chair. Old. Probably her dad, his skin damaged from too much sun for too many years.

"Thank you again," I said.

"I'm Cherry. Cherry Hutchins," she said. "And this is my husband, Nick."

"Nice to meet you. I'm Sasha." Everybody shook hands, then stared at one another in that uncomfortable silence born of unfamiliarity. The waitress, an older Hispanic woman who moved with the authority of an owner, brought my green chile cheeseburger, fries, and Dr. Pepper.

"Sasha what?" said Cherry.

"Solomon."

"Sounds familiar. Are you from around here?"

"No, I'm from Albuquerque."

"Really? Usually people go the other way," she said.

"Actually, I like it here. I'm working on a project for Mayor Flores."

"That's where I heard your name! You're that consultant Tony hired," said Cherry. "Well, welcome to Belen." She seemed pleased. "I was hoping to run into you."

"Let me guess, you're an artist."

"Aspiring."

"Aspiring, my foot. This lady has more talent in her little finger than most anybody I know," said her husband. He waved a ketchup-bedipped french fry at me. "And I dare you to find a nicer person south of Canada."

"How come Canadians are nicer than me?" Cherry pecked him on the cheek before he could answer. "You're the one who found Philly, aren't you?" she said to me.

"Yes."

"You poor thing."

"Yeah, it was pretty awful."

The conversation halted again. We ate our food, lobbed half-smiles back and forth.

"Did you know her?" I said once my plate held only a piece of chile nestled in a blob of mustard.

"Everyone knew Philly," said Nick.

"What was she like?" I said

"She was a nasty, mean—"

"That's best left alone," said Cherry. "Tell me, who've you talked to so far?"

"About Miss Petty?" I said.

"No, the Harvey House."

"Just the mayor when he hired me, and Ernie Merkin. And I had a brief interview with Lydia Herndon."

"Oh, you poor, poor thing." Cherry pressed her lips together until they'd lost all color. Her laughter detonated a second later. When she'd brought her mirth under control, she said, "I don't know what's worse, finding Philly or speaking to Lydia unarmed."

A giddy twittering replaced conversations at several of the tables around us. Cherry turned and gestured with one hand for everyone to be quiet.

"Shusshhh!" she said again, then winked at me. "And I suppose Lydia was a fount of joy and happiness."

"Actually, our interview ended abruptly."

More laughs from the peanut gallery.

"Oh, don't pay any attention to her," Cherry said, smiling. "Rudeness is just part of who she is." Her tone held affection in spite of the slight. "If you want, I'll call her. She usually listens to me."

"She'd better. You do all the work," said Nick.

"Well, I've got the time," said Cherry.

"Ree's vice president of the Artists Guild," he said. "She does all Lydia's work on top of her own." He pushed his chair out from the table, mumbled something, then kissed his wife on the top of her head. "I'll pick up the boys. You take your time." He shook my hand. "Nice meeting you."

Cherry watched her husband leave.

"He's my knight, defending my cause even when I don't need it," she said in a voice only I could hear. The love warming her eyes would have melted an iceberg.

"You're lucky." Bob had crushed my hopes of ever having such a knight.

"Don't I know it," she said, nodding the waitress over. "Can I buy you a piece of the best chocolate cake in town?"

"Nick's already taken care of it," said the waitress. "I was just waiting for you girls to finish up." She went behind the counter and cut the cake.

Cherry took another napkin from the dispenser and began to doodle. Her ability to catch life in a couple of lines amazed me. I wished I could translate the world so easily onto paper.

"Do you mind talking a little bit about Miss Petty?" I said, watching her blue pen capture the essence of a mother waiting with her young child at the register.

"Not at all."

The waitress returned with two slabs of cake, each the size of a college textbook. "Want coffee or milk with this?"

"Water and coffee for me," I said, irritated at the interruption.

54

"I'll have a Diet Coke," said Cherry. The waitress left again. "Are you staying in Belen or heading back to Albuquerque?"

"I'll be here as much as I can. It's better to talk with people in person."

"I know what you mean. They're not as honest when they're talking on the phone."

I nodded, ready to get the conversation back to Miss Petty.

Again the waitress—depositing drinks and lingering to wipe invisible food from the tabletop.

"I tell you what," said Cherry. "I'll call Lydia and tell her to be nice. If you want, I can tag along. She won't dare misbehave in front of me."

"Why not?" I said.

"My shining personality." Cherry batted her eyelashes. "No, really. Lyddie's got an ornery exterior but she's a pussycat."

The waitress snorted and left to the sound of a bell from the kitchen.

Cherry sipped her soda. "Did you know Lydia Herndon raised six boys on her own? And she still managed to paint."

"No, I didn't know." My opinion of her shifted a millimeter toward compassion.

We paused for a bite of cake. Cherry ate from the bottom up, saving the best for last. Not me. I started with the frosting.

"What are you going to do while you're here?" said Cherry.

"Maybe you can help me," I said. "I want to spend at least one night in town to get a better feel for the place. Any suggestions?"

"The Hub Motel." She took two mouthfuls without bothering to chew.

"You're pretty emphatic. Why?"

"I don't want to spoil the surprise. Trust me. You'll love it." Cherry finished her cake with the speed of someone who knows she shouldn't be eating so much.

My cell phone rang as I mimicked her technique.

"That your phone?" she said.

Mouth still stuffed, I nodded and pulled it from my purse.

"Let me get it for you." She pressed the button to answer it. "Sasha Solomon's office . . . I'm sorry, she's not available right now. May I take a message?" Cherry grinned. "Yes, this is her secretary." She abandoned her professionalism. "Moises! Was that you I saw out on I-25 this morning? Don't you have anything better to do with taxpayers' money?" She laughed at the response.

I drank coffee, feeling impatient, not wanting to miss the fun.

"She's right across from me eating chocolate cake," said Cherry. "Where are you? I'll buy you a piece. Oh, okay. Well, don't forget dinner this Saturday. You promised."

"Hello?" I said, wondering who was on the line.

"So, you've found Belen's treasures," said Garcia.

"Excuse me?"

"Cherry Hutchins and the White Way's chocolate cake."

Garcia and Cherry were friends? Well, why not?

"Ms. Solomon?" he said.

"Yes?"

"Let's go talk with your mom."

twelve

WE CONVENED IN THE White Way's parking lot. People passed us, waving to Garcia, everyone his old chum.

"Don't you trust me?" I said.

"Do I have any reason not to?"

"No," I said, feeling guilty about the various pictures I'd neglected to mention to him. If he kept trusting me, I'd break down and have to tell him.

"Good. Let's get going. You lead," he said, opening my car door for me.

Have you ever traveled thirty-plus miles knowing a state cop was following you? I couldn't speed. I couldn't take my hands off the steering wheel. I couldn't turn up my music too loud. I couldn't do a damn thing except drive.

By the time we arrived at St. Kate's, my hands sweated and my hair—forget the nice bun—collapsed upon itself in lifeless clumps.

"Will you let me go in first? Sort of prepare her?" I said, hurrying though the doors into Mom's unit.

"Let's not make this a bigger deal than it is." He kept up with my pace.

"Can I at least introduce you?"

"I don't think that's necessary," he said.

"You're not going to give me an inch, are you?"

"I don't have you on a leash, Ms. Solomon. Should I?"

Rather than answer, I walked into Mom's room. She lay in bed, eyes fixed on the television suspended from the ceiling opposite her. On the table next to her, a plastic water jug held drooping zinnias. The room smelled of old meatloaf and strawberry gelatin. I spotted the uneaten food, now cast to her left on the mobile tray. Another water jug perspired with melting ice, its excess liquid about to drop to the floor.

I grabbed a couple of tissues and wiped up the puddle before reaching for the television's volume control to mute the talk-show drivel.

"Hi, Mom," I said.

"What took you so long?" she said.

"What?"

"You were supposed to be here this morning. Where've you been?" She saw Garcia. "Jack? What are you doing here?"

I looked at the detective and shrugged my shoulders an inch.

"Hello, Mrs. Solomon. I'm Detective Garcia," he said, showing her his badge.

My cell phone chirped. "Not now," I muttered.

"Sasha?" said Bob.

"Go to hell."

"Who are you talking to?" said Mom.

Garcia glared at me. With an abrupt point of his index finger, he signaled me to take the conversation into the hallway.

"We need to talk," said Bob.

"I don't think so." I hung up. It felt good to do it—even though slamming a receiver down would have been more satisfying than punching a little button. Before I could get in the room, my phone rang again.

"I'm too busy for this," I said.

Rita passed me on her way to a patient's room next door to Mom's. She went in with a loud, "It's time for your medicine, Mrs. Jones."

"I was going to tell you," Bob said.

"Who gives a flying f— oh, why am I even talking to you?"

"Because we need to talk."

I stared at my cell phone.

"Sasha?"

I'd had, like, no time to process the fact that my boyfriend was screwing someone else, and here he was pressuring me *to talk about it.*

Rita returned, gave me a bright smile and a pat on the shoulder on her busy way to another room.

"Sasha, are you there?" said Bob.

Oh, I had boxcars full of responses—so many, in fact, that I couldn't speak. Instead, I shook my head, disconnected again, and turned off the phone. A nurse clipped me on the way to another room. The bump reminded me that Garcia and Mom were alone.

I should have known.

Mom's eyes inflated with tears. The detective held her hand, his words inaudible across the room. I pushed past him to hold her. Our embrace—weak on her part, encompassing on mine—lasted until her heaves gentled into hiccups.

"Mom?" I said, helping her settle back onto the pillow. "Mom."

"How could this happen?" she said.

I glanced at Garcia, wondering how he'd told her—if he'd mentioned murder.

"I just talked with Philly today," she said. "How could this happen?"

"What?" said the detective.

"Mom, you're confused. She died yesterday," I said.

"Ms. Solomon," said Garcia.

Mom snorted. "She called me this morning and told me about her new painting."

"That's impossible," I said.

"Ms. Solomon, I'm warning you," said Garcia.

"It is not," said Mom. "Philly told me it's called *St. Francis Dances*. It's got a strip-joint motif. She's already got a buyer."

"Oh, God," I said. I liked St. Francis—the birds, the *Canticle of Brother Sun*. Why did Phillipa Petty have to mess with the good guys?

"Did she mention the buyer's name?" Garcia positioned himself in front of me, so that he was first in her line of vision.

"Bruce Rains," she said.

"Who's he?" said Garcia.

"A collector in Chicago."

"Wait a minute," I said. "She couldn't have told you this, this morning."

"She did," said Mom, moving to the side to include me in her view. "You're jealous."

"Of what?" I stood up.

"Of the fact she's put me in her will. She said so today."

"Really?" said the detective.

"Why would I care about that? She wasn't *my* friend," I said.

"She's going to send me a copy this week," she said.

"Oh, Mother. You're confused."

"I am not."

"Ms. Solomon, would you mind coming with me for a minute?" Garcia said to me. "Excuse us, Mrs. Solomon."

"Jack, I'd love some water with that bourbon." It was a coy request, coquettish.

Disbelieving, I looked at her; her smile was smug.

"I'll get you that water, Hannah," said Rita on her way into the room. "Do you need that pillow fluffed while I'm at it?"

Garcia and I moved into the corridor and I put my hands over my eyes in frustration. A nurse's light blinked on over a patient's doorway. I thought about telling Rita, but I liked the extra attention she gave Mom. It made me feel better about St. Kate's.

"Ms. Solomon," said Garcia.

"Do you see what I mean? Her mind's gone," I said. "She's crazy."

"She is and she isn't," he said. "You've got to stop interrupting her."

"How can you say that?" I said. "She's nuts."

Unmerciful eyes locked on mine. "Stop feeling sorry for yourself."

Rita stepped into the hallway just in time to hear him say it. She shook her head at me in silent recrimination.

"I am *not* feeling sorry for myself," I said to them both. Rita continued tsk-tsking as she headed to the room with the nurse's light. I looked at Garcia. "You heard Mom. She's lost it."

"Look, I know it's difficult having a brain-injured parent," he said. "But if Miss Petty talked with her this morning, then that's what I'm going with."

"I don't think I'm the best person for this," I said, watching a family roll a middle-aged man in a wheelchair past us. He slumped, his face unnaturally relaxed. Their smiles at us held desperation rather than friendliness.

"For what?"

"For being here," I said. "Paul would be better."

"Paul?"

"Katz. Her boyfriend," I said.

"I'll talk with him as soon as I can. But you insisted on being here right now, so you're going to stay until I say you can go." Lest I forget, Garcia *was* a cop. Everything about his manner—from the tense jaw to the determined stare—screamed authority.

"But you said it yourself, I'm not helping."

"That's beside the point," he said.

There was a hum. The detective checked his pager, took out a cell phone. "Garcia," he said, eyes focused on the ceiling, the tiny phone at his ear. "She did?"

I watched him.

He noticed and turned away from me. "I'll be there as soon as I can," he said, hanging up. "I've got to go."

"Does it have to do with this case?"

When he'd finished writing a note in his PDA, he turned to face me. "I'll talk to you later."

thirteen

AFTER TRUCKLOADS OF ADMONITIONS from Garcia not to talk about Miss Petty with Mom, the detective and I bid each other *adios* in the parking lot. I got in my car. He waved goodbye. I waited until he was out of sight, then went back to Mom.

Thinner by ill-spared ounces each time I saw her, Mom now sat in an olive-green chair. The cardiologists kept her one step away from starvation. The less she weighed, the less work her heart had to do. I'd had awful dreams of her losing the rest of her poundage before my eyes, her skin hanging on fragile bones that broke and disintegrated into ivory piles of dust.

"I'm sorry about your friend, Mom," I said.

She didn't speak.

I went to her, crouched at her feet to peer into her face. Deep hurt had furrowed her brows, dug wrinkles around her mouth, and gouged canyons on her once smooth forehead. But a change had happened in the mere minutes since I'd last seen her. It was as if someone had used her soul for target practice.

"Mama?"

"She can't be dead," she said.

"I saw her," I said gently. "It's true."

"You knew and didn't tell me?"

"I tried yesterday, but you weren't in your room. Then I got sick," I said. "Remember?" As soon as I uttered the word, I cringed. Somehow, using that verb near her smacked of cruelty.

"I don't remember anything about anything," she said, her face splotching a reddish blue. Her frustration morphed into confusion. "How could I have talked with her today?"

"I wish I knew."

Mom asked me to help her back into bed. When she settled, she pointed to a newspaper on the other bed in her room.

"Read it to me," she said.

The article about Petty contained nothing new. Detective Garcia masterfully spouted the kind of bland quotes that encouraged reporters to commit *hara-kiri* from boredom. An obligatory sidebar chronicled the artist's career. I knew a different, more interesting, version.

Long ago, Mom's gallery served as the booze trough for a generation of New Mexican artists. Raymond Jonson and some of the original members of the Taos School would stop by when they were in town. Mom knew all the biggies and, in the early sixties, she introduced Phillipa Petty to every one.

Through connections and talent, the young artist got a full scholarship to study at the Chicago Institute of Art, then flew off to Europe for more training. She painted her life-size *The Cross-Dressing Christ* while in Rome—of all places—and achieved international notoriety that quickly translated into beaucoup bucks.

In her catty moments, Mom said Miss Petty had left her in the dust once she'd hit the big time. At some point, they'd renewed contact. And now, supposedly, Mother was in her will.

Mom's closed eyes tricked me into thinking she'd fallen asleep. I folded the newspaper as quietly as I could.

"You know, Philly didn't have a nice bone in her body," she said.

"So why were you such good friends?"

She continued as if she hadn't heard me. "It's the truth. She was mean to the core. Mean, opportunistic, and arrogant."

I'd always been curious about their relationship. The accumulation of time Mom had spent complaining about Petty would surpass decades. "Why did you stick around?"

"Loyalty, I guess. And she could be fun . . . crazy fun, in spite of the acid." Mom smiled. "You know, she slept with your father. Did I ever tell you that?"

"Not that I recall," I said, almost holding my breath, afraid any motion might silence her. She'd been mighty secretive about Dad's infidelities. I'd had to learn too much on my own.

"I caught them on the kitchen table. Can you imagine? Right next to the pimento olives and celery I'd put out on the relish tray." Mom laughed.

"What did you do?" Scandalized and pleased with the image, I strove to keep her talking.

"I watched for a while—they were too busy to notice me—and then I went to the garage, picked up the trashcan, and dumped a week's worth of garbage on them."

"Oh, Mother. You didn't!" I grinned. They deserved it.

"Sure I did."

"Then what?"

"I made dinner for the both of them—as if not a thing had happened—and made them eat it. Just to watch them squirm."

That spunk, that feisty flame whispered memories of Mom when she'd been a vital, dynamic woman. In a way, her actions paralleled mine today with Bob. The realization kindled a feeling of connection with her. A compassion. I couldn't conceive of what it was like to live with her iffy memory, though I understood her unsteady take on reality too well.

"Hey, Mom? Why'd you call Detective Garcia, 'Jack'?"

"Did I say that?"

"Yeah. You called him 'Jack'."

"I can't imagine what I was thinking," she said. "I hate this."

This could have been anything. I watched her straighten her bedclothes. A lab technician came in and took blood. A nurse stopped by to chide her for not eating her meal. When they both left, Mom turned on the television, her most dependable companion.

I stood to leave.

"Sasha, I need you to do me a favor," she said.

"What's that?" I moved the tray with her water to one side of the bed and sat down.

"Find out who killed Philly."

"Mom, I'm not a detective."

"She was killed, you know." A conspiratorial glimmer lightened her eyes. The promise of a secret revealed colored her voice.

"How do you know that?"

"Policemen don't stop by just to say hello. He had an agenda." She dipped her head once, sure of her assertion.

"You're right, he did."

"And Philly told me she had a bad feeling, like someone was after her."

Ah. Maybe that was why Mom had called her friend so many times yesterday. "Miss Petty said that?"

"She did indeed."

"Why didn't you tell Detective Garcia?"

"Who?"

"Mom, don't go off on me here," I said, sensing her attention slip away. "Why didn't you tell Detective Garcia? The policeman."

"He was a nice boy, wasn't he?"

"Mom, hold on. When did she tell you she had a bad feeling?"

"This morning, sweetie," Mom said. "Right after I opened the gallery."

"Look at me." I held her face level with mine. Her dry, cool skin was too thin. Her chin poked sharp against my hand. "What did Phillipa Petty tell you?"

"Phillipa?"

"Your friend Phillipa Petty . . . the one who died yesterday."

"Philly's dead?" she said.

"Yes, Mom." *Poor woman.* In sympathy, I let my hands flop to my lap. "I found her on the floor. There was nothing anyone could do."

"Why didn't you tell me?" Fresh tears formed, puffing her eyelids.

I wondered how many times she was going to relive this moment of pain.

"Oh, my God," she said.

"Mom, I need you to focus. Do you remember what you were just saying? You said something about her having a bad feeling about something."

"I did?" Her gaze searched the room as if it held the answer. Her eyebrows tightened into lines that her lips duplicated.

I nodded. "Try, Mom. Try to remember."

"It's so hard," she said, her breath faster with the effort and frustration.

"I know, but try. Please."

"She was killed," she said slowly.

"That's right," I said.

"You've got to find him."

"Who?"

"Whoever did this to her."

"Mom, who killed Phillipa Petty?"

"How should I know?" Indignant. Her tone had changed from working with me to anger against me for being so dense. Of course she didn't know, she seemed to say—why would I expect such a thing?

I quivered with the need to scream, then hugged myself to stop the shaking, willing patience into my fraying nerves. "Mom, you almost had it. You almost gave me something to work with."

"You've got to find out who killed Philly," she said.

"That's what the police are trying to do. That's why they came to see you," I said, knowing my words wouldn't mean much to her now that she'd made her decision. Oh, how I wanted to run from her room and never come back!

"No. You're the one who can do it. You found that one in Clovis, didn't you?"

"Mom." How could she remember something from months ago and not a few minutes before? The atrocity of her mental lapses suffused me with additional fury. Once, her mind had been like a fine painting, but stroke after stroke—the paint thinners of brain injury—had created a horrid mess. I tried not to be angry at *her*.

"Why do you come here if you won't do anything for me?" Her voice deteriorated into a whine, the beginnings of manipulation through guilt.

"I'll see what I can do," I said evenly.

"You never do anything I ask," she intoned. "Miss Know It All. You're so much smarter than me."

"Mom. That's enough."

"Have I told you what happened to me when you were born? Your father left me alone in the hospital." Always the same chorus in the ballad of my birth. "And you, you were so big I had to have a c-section. They cut me open. Twenty-four stitches. Did I tell you that?"

I got up and headed for the door.

"Don't you walk out on me. I never walked out on you," she said. "Never. Not through the divorce. Not—"

"I'll look into it," I said. "Okay?"

Satisfaction cloaked her with its unearned success. "That's all I'm asking you to do, sweetheart."

fourteen

SASHA SOLOMON, *Super Sleuth.* In addition to the stupid alliteration, the whole idea felt as false as the calm with which I tried to stifle my exasperation. Mom couldn't help her zigzag lucidity, not a stitch. But knowing that didn't make anything better.

In the car, I coaxed my blood pressure to return to this galaxy. After a couple of minutes or ten, I still saw spots. Since it wasn't yet safe to drive, I pulled the digital camera out of my purse and looked at the photos I'd snapped at Petty's the day before. Amateurish at best. Blurred images with dots and outside glints of reflecting light. Two pictures of her lying on the floor. A third—probably taken when I was going into shock—had an off-center quality, like something a kid would shoot, fumbling to hold the camera and press the button at the same time. From what I could tell, the photo included the stack of papers that had fallen onto the floor and part of the easels beyond. Utterly useless. I thought about deleting them, but decided against it. Maybe I'd show them to Detective Garcia after all. Maybe I'd show them to Mom to help her grasp her friend's death, to make it real.

What to do?

Go home. Feed the cat.

Leo stretched on the doormat, his coat warm when I rubbed his tum. He purred. Without warning, he extended his claws and locked onto my arm. I ripped it away and nursed the scratches while unbolting the door.

Open windows allowed an afternoon breeze to swirl through the house. I'd left them closed but my landlady, Josie, must've thought the place needed airing. I didn't mind. She'd often stop by to feed Leo, wash dishes, or sweep when she thought I was on the road. Since I hated housecleaning, her occasional efforts seemed more beneficent than intrusive.

I skirted the unused Nordic Track, now bedecked with underwear, and headed into the kitchen—not hungry, but determined to eat anyway. In the fridge, I found the last quarter of a garlic bagel and an Almond Joy. Voila! Instant *croissant au chocolat.* I topped it with whipped cream, grateful my throat felt fine now. My midafternoon snack merited fresh coffee. While it brewed, I thought about how to integrate my work in Belen with finding the creep who'd brought new pain to Mom's life, messed up mine, and abbreviated Petty's.

Mug in hand, I walked back into the front room toward the bedroom. In the hallway, my answering machine's light blinked its hysteria. Instead of playing back a message, the tape rewound to the beginning. Josie must have accidentally tapped the record button when she'd come through.

I flopped onto the futon couch, placed the coffee on its wide arm, and remembered Peter's face in slumber. Well, I didn't have to worry about being faithful to Bob anymore. Maybe I should pursue it with the new guy. Or not. The last thing I needed was another relationship.

You're getting a little ahead of yourself, here.

Something sharp and hard poked me. I reached underneath my tush and rescued a red rock. Faceted to catch even the most hesitant light, its diameter must have measured at least two inches. It looked like a garnet—or a ruby—but was bigger than any I'd ever seen. I put the stone close to my eye, the color so rich it reminded me of solidified Chianti.

The gemstone must belong to Peter. I searched for my purse, found his card, and dialed. He wasn't there. I left a message, surprising even myself when I said I'd stay in Belen for the night and would call him tomorrow. Twirling the stone in my hand, my smile grew. I had an excuse to be in Peter's life for one more day.

I sipped the coffee and made plans. The decision to overnight in Belen gave my immediate life a purpose. My actions fell into a neat sequence: pack, feed the cat, clean the litter box. Call Bob to tell him about the trip. *Scratch that.*

The thought of Bob brought bleak feelings of being unlovable. Seemed like I was always looking for love—from Mom, from my philandering father, from boyfriends, from the damn cat.

On cue, the phone rang.

"Where've you been?" said Darnda. "I've been trying to reach you for hours."

"It's a long story. You sound out of breath. Are you okay?"

"Can I come over? I'm in your neighborhood." I heard a car honk through her phone, then a passing motorcycle.

"Darnda, are you on your cell?" *This must be serious.* "What's going on?"

"I'll tell you when I get there."

Before I had the litter box cleaned, Darnda knocked on the door. She was dressed in tight purple jeans that emphasized the bulges of her hips. The T-shirt she wore had holes around the shoulders from too much wash-'n'-wearing. She hadn't bothered to try to contain her hair; it bounced as she entered my house.

"You remember that lady in Rancho Mirage? The one connected to absolutely everyone in Hollywood? Remember she said she knew someone at *The Other Side?*"

"Yes . . . I do." Since its launch two years ago, *The Other Side* had become one of those hit television shows that regularly attracted millions of viewers. It exposed quacks and lauded paranormal workers who appeared to be the real thing. The expensive set and Barbie-&-Ken talent lent a sort of *Entertainment Tonight* feel to the show—with movie stars and corporate muckity-mucks regularly featured—as if fame equaled intelligence or scientific accuracy.

"Well, the Rancho Mirage lady—her name's Carol, by the way—called me today and said a correspondent from the show wants to talk with me. Her name is Karen Kilgore and she's thinking of doing a story on me. On me! Isn't that great?"

"Slow down, Darnda." I guided her to the couch, where she stood vibrating excitement. I gently shoved her so that she sat. "Have you talked with this Karen Kilgore yet?"

"No, my client gave me Karen's phone number and told me to call her." Darnda got up. "What's wrong? I thought you'd be delighted. This is the big-time, Sasha. I can get the word out to millions of people. Why are you looking at me like that?"

"Like what?"

"Like the proverbial deer caught in the headlights, my dear."

I sat next to her. Getting Darnda this kind of exposure was good—great, in fact. But I hadn't had a chance to coach her on media interviewing yet. We hadn't discussed her key talking points or refined the stories I knew she'd want to tell. Getting onto *The Other Side* was a tremendous opportunity; I just didn't want to see her portrayed like some kind of idiot. Face it, I didn't want my friend to be mocked. *Okay, okay.* The first thing to do was to find out what kind of angle the reporter was thinking of for the story.

"Hello? Earth to Sasha." Darnda tapped the back of my hand. "Why are you upset? Am I missing something?"

"No, it's not that," I said, getting up to close a window. "We've just got so much to do before you can talk to reporters. Any reporter." Leo tried to get in, but got stuck. I didn't help and he gave up. "You want to be taken seriously, don't you?"

"Of course I do."

"Can you trust me on this? Will you let me call her?" Where to start? What would help Darnda the most and get her ready the fastest?

"But Carol told me to call her."

"Trust me. She won't mind if you have a publicist. It'll make you appear more professional." And it'll buy me some time.

Darnda squinted at me. I knew what she was doing.

"Stop it. I promise I'll call her today," I said, going over to the Nordic Track and dumping the clothes on the floor. The skis stuck a little from lack of use, but the movement helped me think. "Meanwhile, you can contact some of your more famous clients and see if any of them would be willing to be interviewed about your work. Compile a list with contact info and call me when you've got three confirmed names. I'll start concepting your media kit and bio." I began to sweat. "Do you have a decent photo?"

"I have a couple with movie stars, mainly locals like Julia Roberts, Val Kilmer, Shirley MacLaine. Would those be okay?"

"And maybe some heavy hitters from industry, too. Didn't you do something for Bill Gates?" I nodded, breathing more heavily than I should have been. I needed to exercise more. Yeah, but when?

"I'll see what I've got at home," Darnda said, ready to be helpful rather than pushy. At least I'd accomplished that much.

"If you can get written permission from any of them to use those photos in the kit, that'd be excellent." I got off the Nordic Track and went into the kitchen for the whipped cream. Holding the can at an angle, I offered some to Darnda.

"No way. I know where that can has been." She wrinkled her spider-veined nose.

"Chicken." I looked at my watch. "Darnda, we've got tons to do. And right now, I have to go back to Belen. But I'll get started on what we need to do today."

"You still don't seem happy about this, Sasha."

"I'm tickled pink. I just didn't expect to go into warp speed without checking the spaceship first." I paused for a slug of whipped cream.

Darnda watched me, her eyebrows high, waiting.

When my mouth was mostly empty, I said, "We haven't even really talked about your goals, your real goals . . . like money, or teaching, or some karmic thing that only you know about."

"It's the money," said Darnda. "I want lots and lots of it."

"Don't give me that. You're not that mercenary." I returned my food to the fridge and poured a few mini–chocolate chips into my hand.

"I'm just surprised at how quickly things are moving. Of course, with you, I shouldn't be."

"You're up to it, Sasha. It'll work out great. I have total faith in you." Darnda flashed a smile full of love and confidence. She hugged me, smelling of lavender and lemon. "Call Karen today. I just know she's going to be wonderful." With a lighter squeeze, she bade me goodbye.

Darnda's enthusiasm, compounded with an excuse to be in touch with Peter O'Neill, should have propelled me into Happyland. Neither did. As soon as I was out of her lava-hot joy, I cooled back into a basalt-gray mood.

In the car, I distracted my dour thoughts by concentrating on the drive. I looked for touristy milestones and special points of interest but found depression. The southern stretch of Albuquerque's outskirts morphed into junkyards, unkempt factories, and businesses resembling delinquent strip malls. Beyond the grimy buildings and wrecked cars lay denuded desert, its fragile ecosystem so disturbed from development only dirt remained.

I cranked on the radio—hitting a good *cumbia*—and things began to look better. The change coincided with the entrance into Isleta Pueblo. Radio pulsing, windows open and wind blowing my hair, I banged my hands on the steering wheel as if it were a conga drum. My life could be fun, if I just let it be.

Darnda on The Other Side. *What a kick!* I imagined her—from the kooky hair to her refusal to polish her image for anyone—with those plasticine Hollywood types. It was bound to be electric. I just wanted to make sure she wasn't the butt of any nastiness from people who measured beauty by how many millimeters they'd sliced off their noses and inches they'd added to their breasts.

Right at the place where I crossed the river—Isleta Lakes to my left—the trip took on a rural feel. Cottonwoods, weeping willows, fields of alfalfa, and other crops now golden and dry. Black boulders of the mesas, the Manzano Mountains to the east, the bluffs to the west of the highway. Then past ticky-tacky Los Lunas, and on to Belen with three—count 'em—three freeway exits.

The first one revealed the entire small town in a single straight shot, and the sight wouldn't inspire a fig. I had my work cut out for me here, too.

That's what PR was about, though—image, reputation, and relationships—whether they were for a single client such as Darnda or an entire town. And it's what I liked to do.

Moments later I entered the Dayspring Deli—the place to see and be seen in Belen. It also served a decent café latte—strong coffee and upstanding foam. I sat at the only available table, one of its legs stabilized with a pack of matches, and let ideas bubble and mix in my brain.

After a few more slugs of coffee, I opened my interview notebook and reviewed notes from the conversations so far. Opposed to the art museum idea and unenthusiastic about the train museum, Ernie Merkin was probably a dead-end. However, his comment about blasphemous art intrigued me—had he known Miss Petty personally? Maybe he was good for something else. After all, I was Sasha Solomon, *Super Sleuth*.

I finished my drink, decided to get a room at the Hub Motel, and, maybe, to visit a liquor store later that afternoon.

Merkin would appreciate the present. Asking him about Petty could be a place to start. Well, it was as good as any.

fifteen

BELEN, A.K.A. THE "Hub City," lures the occasional tourist off the interstate with promises of *Hotels!* and *Restaurants!* Much of what the tourist sees, alas, are the same chain businesses that can be found in other cities along other freeways in this great country.

Not so, the Hub Motel. I should have known from the way it abutted Belen's main street. Where parking should have been, there was, well, a big wall. Then a don't-blink-or-you'll-miss-it turnoff into a driveway leading to a pebbled lot.

On skittering ankles and in scratched shoes, I entered the courtyard and stopped midstep. Pink everywhere—a gloppy color like cream cheese and strawberry jam mixed together—kind of like the couch at Miss Petty's place. Alhambra arches, a gazebo with icicle lights. An alabaster sculpture of a Greek goddess supervised a waterfall's trickle while life-size ceramic deer grazed on colored gravel in small herds.

This was high kitsch. I had to catch my breath before continuing to the office. I sat on the nearest wrought-iron bench. A stone's throw away, water spat, jumped, and spilled into pools around a dozen fountains, causing plastic goldfish and rubber ducks to bob. I counted seventeen birdhouses in one tree.

The owner of the motel came outside to greet me. White hair cropped so close I could see the freckles underneath, willow thin but strong in a defiant way, she held out her hand to shake mine, her grip sure. She wore a metal pin with her name, Lucy Hardraker, above her heart.

As we walked the short distance to the office, she bent several times to pull weeds.

"Damn interlopers," she said.

"Pardon me?"

"Drinking my water and forcing themselves through my beautiful rocks." Lucy Hardraker spoke in a blur of words, her accent thick and difficult to identify.

The registration area seemed doubly dark due to the sudden contrast from the outdoor brightness. I blinked. Walls covered with paintings, family pictures, and brass ornaments began to distinguish themselves from the shadows.

"You staying for a week or a month?" Ms. Hardraker said.

"Excuse me?"

"A week or a month?"

I liked the question, the assumption of staying a spell, of cooling my jets. "Just tonight."

She frowned and took two keys from a rack. "I'll give you a choice of rooms today. But I can't guarantee I'll be able to do that every time."

Number twelve: Textured light fixtures hung on either side of a queen-size bed enshrouded in a red bedspread. Robin's-egg-blue walls studded with *schlocky*, fake western masterpieces—cowboys around the campfire, Native Americans looking wise, herds of buffalo. Sprigs of paper blossoms in an urn vied for attention with fake tulips and philodendrons in pots.

I wanted to package the hotel as a destination in itself. Look for tours specializing in gaudy Americana. My mind swam with marketing possibilities. Forget the Harvey House, the Hub Motel could launch its own campaign and make a bundle.

"Number eleven's one of my favorites," she said, opening the door to white walls, a four-poster bed, scads of paintings and brass wall ornaments, five framed mirrors. Fake daffodils and hyacinths, a large plastic rubber plant. An easy chair overlaid with a brown-and-green-checkered blanket rocked when I sat in it. I couldn't resist its welcome.

As soon as Ms. Hardraker left, I let go of the overnight bag, kicked off my shoes, and thumped onto the bed. Outside light goldened the walls, giving the cluttered place a pleasant, cozy feel. If I'd had a favorite great-aunt, this would have been her bedroom. I checked my cell phone to make sure I'd turned it back on and then rolled onto a spot on the bed where the sun had warmed the covers. I let myself relax and fall asleep.

In my dream a sick sparrow perched on a gaudy birdhouse, its song too perky for its dull feathers. The damn thing wouldn't shut up.

That's because it was my phone.

"Hello?" Sleep scratched my voice.

"Sasha?"

"Peter?" *Omigod, omigod, omigod!* I sat up.

"Yes. How are you?" he said.

"Just fine. I'm great. How are *you*?" Then I remembered, disappointed. "You're calling about your garnet."

"Ruby," he said.

"It's a ruby?"

"Yeah."

"Wow," I said, sounding like a dope. "I guess you want it back."

"I do. How about now?"

"I'm in Belen." I pictured him in a sexy Druid garment. Were Druids sexy? Well, he had on this animal-skin drapey-thing that only covered one side of his chest—like a toga. Maybe I was thinking of a caveman.

"Where?"

"Belen," I said. "It's about twenty-five minutes south of Albuquerque."

"What are you doing there?"

"Work. I'm a consultant. I work all over the place." *Brilliant repartee, Sasha.*

"Huh," he said, then cleared his throat. "Well. How about I come down there? I'm new to New Mexico. It'd be an adventure."

"You must really want your rock back. Problem is, I left it at home."

"Actually, I'd like to see *you*, too."

"Really?" My voice actually squeaked. I winced with embarrassment.

"Don't sound so surprised." He laughed. "Maybe we could grab some dinner."

We'd already spent a night together and he hadn't tried anything. And the poor guy probably didn't know many people. Loneliness had spurred me to impetuosity before. Why not have dinner with a new friend? A new, handsome friend.

"I'm staying at the Hub Motel," I said. "Why don't we plan on six or so?"

"The Hub Motel. Great. I'll be there."

I pressed the "off" button and thought that if I'd been a decade younger, and a dozen pounds lighter, I would have jumped his bones. Maturity had replaced passion. It was a sad, sad truth that at forty, my dallying days had shriveled into minute-long fantasies. My body image had gone down the tubes as well; thighs pitted with cellulite can be pretty humbling. Propelling myself off the springy bed, I unpacked, dumping clothes into a drawer.

Then, because I'd have to do it eventually, I dialed the number for Karen Kilgore at *The Other Side*. After being vetted by a perky receptionist, I was sent to Kilgore's voice mail. You can't deduce much from a recording, but she sounded polished and professional enough. My worry meter went down a couple of notches. The next hurdle would be to see how strong the tie was between Darnda's client and the correspondent. If Kilgore didn't respond in a day or two, I'd make one follow-up call. If she still didn't respond, I'd ask Darnda to talk with her buddy in Rancho Mirage.

Water gurgled outside when I opened the door to late-afternoon sunlight. I felt restless—had an urge to wander. The practical thing, the thing I *should* do was to schedule more interviews. I should get that bottle of whiskey and visit Ernie Merkin. Nah, too depressing.

Or, I could scare me up some other clues about Miss Petty's murder.

sixteen

I DON'T KNOW WHAT I expected at the turnoff to the artist's house. Maybe a few dozen cop cars, a mobile crime lab. Something. Instead, a bird chirped, a dog barked. Crime scene tape laced the front of the building. Other than that the place was, well, dead.

The irrigation ditch smelled today of mud and decaying leaves. I leaned against the car, my legs outstretched to catch the sun's warmth. My gams used to be one of my main attributes, sleek, muscled, and tan. Too many skin-cancer scares later, they almost glowed in their puniness, each vein a blue map with hints at varicose detours. Freckles popped out as I watched. Tough to break a lifelong habit of sun worship. I shook my head but didn't move for cover.

As I perched there thinking about nothing, I saw, then heard, a car coming up the drive. The tip of a battered old Lincoln Continental, grayed with an uneven paint job and too much solar glare, came into view. Its dingy roof had spawned plastic curls as the material separated from the metal frame. The vehicle lumbered and bumped on the dirt as if shocks had never been installed.

The newcomer parked with sloppy nonchalance in the middle of the drive. Slender-bodied and petite, she slammed her car door. "No one's supposed to be here," she said, her shrill voice halting the twittering of birds. "Who're you?"

"Nice car you've got there," I said.

She stared at me, dipped her head to spit on the ground, and raised it again. A late-season hummingbird whizzed past us. The woman grunted, held her thumb up, index finger horizontal—and pretended to shoot it. "Pow," she said. "Now, who are you and what are you doing here?"

"I could ask you the same." This felt like one of those really bad Westerns, the kind made in Italy in the sixties. Or maybe a cop show. I could almost hear the twanging of an electric guitar in the background.

The woman sighed, lifted her arms, and began braiding her long black hair. Just one strand of the braid was thicker than all my hair put together.

"Okay," she said. "My name's Celia Ortega." She looped the braid into a bun and fastened it upon itself somehow. Eyebrows imperious, she signaled she was waiting.

"Sasha Solomon. Pleased to meet you." I held out a hand, which she neglected to shake.

"So, what are you doing here?"

It was an interesting question. Of course, she could be one of those clues I'd thought about scaring up.

"I heard Phillipa Petty lives here," I said.

"You a reporter?"

I did a little self-deprecating shrug, hoping she'd take that as a *yes*. Her dark eyes scrutinized me. I didn't like Celia Ortega.

"Phillipa Petty was murdered. If you were a reporter, you'da known that." A mean expression crossed her olive-skinned face and settled into a grimace, as if it were her default expression. I noticed a mole, its hair untrimmed, on her left cheek.

"I've been out of the country," I said, not owing this nasty woman the truth.

Lips scrunched in a disbelieving scowl, she said, "Where?"

"Iraq." My voice dared her to ask another question.

Instead, she snorted and pretended to shoot another bird. The woman had definite *machismo* issues.

"So, what are you doing out here?" I tried a casual tone, as if our entire conversation up to that point hadn't happened.

"I came to clean up. Miss Petty needed help since she was so old." Ortega nudged a rock near her foot, then kicked it. "Woman had no business being out here."

"Would you be willing to be interviewed?"

"Who do you write for? One of those papers in Al-bu-querque?" I guess she didn't like the local rags.

"No. I work for *Arts in America*. It's a magazine." This lie was about to bite me, I could feel it.

"Then what were you doing in Iraq?"

"Writing about the looted treasures at the national museum."

"I don't want to be interviewed," she said.

"Come on. I bet you have some interesting stories. Stuff that no one else knows."

Her face hardened. "Did you know pride is one of the seven deadly sins?"

Was it me, or had she just skipped a groove?

"I've heard that. Yes," I said.

"You ever seen her stuff?" She kicked another rock.

"Some of it."

"You see the one where she blasphemes Jesus Christ? That one?"

"Yes," I said.

"What do you think of it?" She studied me, eyes hungry for my answer.

"Technically, she's a master oil-painter," I said. "There're only a few other people who can match her skill. But I don't care much for her subject matter."

"You see this?" With one hand, she reached down the front of her T-shirt and pulled out a big silver cross on a chain. "You *care much* for this? Do you?"

"I'm not a Catholic, if that's what you mean."

"It's not about being Catholic. It's about accepting Jesus as your savior," she said. "Have you welcomed him into your heart?"

Answer "yes," and it'd be a serious lie. Answer "no," and I'd become an ignorant soul ripe for proselytizing. I opted for a sort of affirmative grunt.

People hear what they want to hear.

Ortega's manner changed in a nanosecond. An ardent smile replaced the frown. She took my hand and walked up the stairs with me to the porch. We ducked under the crime scene tape. She led me to a stuffed and yellowed plastic chair. It wheezed when I sat in it.

"Then you know what I mean about Miss Petty's pride. She thought she didn't need God, that she was better than Him. That's called *hubris*. And now she's dead," Ortega said.

"Yes," I said.

She patted my hand, her face eager. "Tell me about it. Tell me about when you accepted Jesus into your life."

Call it a moment of conscience, I don't know, but I didn't want to play this game anymore—to mess with this woman's obvious faith. How to save face for both of us? Words floundered, none good enough to speak.

Celia Ortega patted my hand again.

I took a deep breath, not knowing what I'd say but vowing it'd be true. "You know, my relationship with God is such a private thing . . ."

"Of course it is. I understand." Her sincerity embarrassed me.

"I think I'd better go," I said, uncomfortable now.

"You don't have to leave. I can show you her house, maybe tell you a story or two, now that I know you're not on her side."

For all I knew, Celia Ortega could have killed the artist or she could know who'd done it. If my faith burned as strong as hers did, I'd hate an artist whose mission centered on mocking everything I cherished.

But I just couldn't take advantage of the situation, not after the wrong I'd done here. It wasn't a question of God smiting me or going to Hell. That's not in my Jewish lexicon. But being a good person is. Continuing my deception—pretending to be a reporter, to be saved— stank of an internal dishonor I didn't want to own.

"I don't write obituaries," I said, working to disengage from the myth I'd created. "I'm not the best person to talk with you." Well, that part was true. Maybe I should introduce her to Detective Garcia.

"You sure?" she said.

I nodded, afraid of emitting any more fibs.

Ortega accompanied me to my car, then gave me an unexpected hug.

"God be with you," she said.

"Thanks. You, too."

When she headed back to the house, the air around me chilled, a private mini–storm front. I sensed a malevolence just out of view, the kind of feeling you get when you're in a dark, unfamiliar hallway. If you turn around quickly, you'll see something you don't want to see—and so you move forward with an uncomfortable stiffness, not allowing your neck to move.

Ortega ascended the stairs to the porch. I moved my head slowly around, hoping not to see anything out of the ordinary. No horror awaited me, but the cold remained—a cloying sensation accompanied by a wet underground smell. Decay. I reached in my purse and popped a black herbal pill and unlocked the car door, still sensing something off-kilter. At the driveway's edge, the cold ceased. I looked in the rearview mirror.

The housekeeper waved goodbye, her hair haloed by an unseen light source, and her cross shining close to her heart.

seventeen

HANDS WHITE ON THE steering wheel, I made it back to Belen. My trembling dissipated as I passed now familiar landmarks—the White Way, a car dealership, the used bookstore. With more than an hour to kill before dinner I decided to check out the Harvey House. I also wanted to give my herbs time to work before going near Peter.

Located on North First Street, then up a small hill, the Harvey House stood dwarfed by acres of train yard beyond the chain-link fence bordering its now empty parking lot. Built in the late 1800s, the structure had gone through many incarnations, the most recent being a small museum dedicated to Fred Harvey, the pioneer food magnate, and his famous restaurants. I went to the door and peeked in its lifeless, darkened glass front. I knocked anyway.

"I'm coming, I'm coming," called a man's voice before he came into view. "Hold on a minute. I'll be right with you." I stuck my nose against the glass and saw him, maybe sixty years old, graying hair. With a jangling of keys, he yanked at the door twice before it opened. "May I help you?"

"I'm sorry to bother you." I looked at my watch. "I thought you'd still be open."

"Abbreviated hours after Memorial Day," he said.

"Does the museum have private tours?"

"We do." He hadn't opened the door all the way yet. "Are you interested?"

"I sure am." I got my calendar out. "Can I sign up for the next one available? I'm helping Mayor Flores decide what to do with this building."

"You are?"

"Yes, sir."

"You're the lady Tony hired?" He stepped a bit closer.

"I am."

"Mike Gracey," he said, extending his hand. His wore dark glasses on a face that had once been fleshy, his jowls rippling when he smiled.

"Sasha Solomon."

"I can give you a quick tour right now, if you've got the time."

"I don't want to impose."

"You don't know me well enough yet, but you'll find out I don't make an offer if I don't mean it. I'm too old for that." He bowed and let me in. "Well? Are you going to make an old man wait?"

"You're not that old."

"Eighty-five last May. That's old by anyone's clock."

The beveled and leaded windows couldn't hint at the potential of this building. Polished wood floors glistened and offered large open spaces adaptable for any number of uses—exhibits, a grand lobby, a restaurant. Outside, a train horn blew and, two breaths later, the locomotive rumbled past, shaking the ground beneath us with its tons of power.

Gracey held his ground, waiting for the noise to subside. Then he motioned me to follow.

"This here is a model of where a Harvey Girl might sleep at night," he said, leading me into a space smaller than most bathrooms. "And here's her uniform. Do you know that if a Harvey Girl got a single drop of food on that white apron of hers, she had to put on a new one?"

I tried to imagine being a young, innocent, upstanding girl from the Heartland—a Harvey Girl. It was too much of a stretch.

"Here's the museum office. Not much to look at," Gracey said, continuing the tour. "Do you know some people say Fred Harvey was the father of fast food?"

"But I thought his whole goal was to provide really good food."

"Fast food used to be good food," he said. "Whenever a train came in, late morning or middle of the night, Fred Harvey had his people ready to serve a wholesome, tasty meal. Now the train companies contract with places that serve pre-made pizzas and cardboard burgers."

"I heard something about Mr. Harvey not liking profits."

Gracey stopped to look at me. "He liked profits all right, just not when they got too big. As a matter of fact, if one of his restaurants made too much money, he'd get angry."

"Why?"

"Because that meant the restaurant was cutting corners, not serving generous enough portions or not using the finest ingredients. Fred Harvey was a stickler for excellence."

"Can you imagine?" I laughed from incredulity.

"You want to go upstairs?"

"You sure you don't mind?"

"If I do, I'll tell you."

We ascended the prim but elegant staircase, a solid and polished piece of carpentry. No cheap veneer here. Gracey's hands touched lightly on the banister, like he'd lived in this building all his life.

The second floor formed a C with small rooms along most of the edges and a few in the middle. These had been used to board the sweet, apple-cheeked Harvey Girls stationed in Belen. Each outer room contained at least two big windows with good natural light.

We stepped into one of the rooms. I looked at the Manzano Mountains to the east, blue with distance, beyond the train yard. A wide veranda encircled the entire second floor. If restored and rezoned, it might be used for cocktails and train watching. Or maybe exclusive parties for arts patrons.

Two public bathrooms with several toilet stalls had once served dozens of girls and their chaperones. We'd need to work on the plumbing to get it up to code for visitors or overnighters. And no elevator to the second floor—we'd have to take care of that too, for the ADA regulations.

Another locomotive thundered past, the vibration rattling the windows.

Easier to see this as a train museum and B & B—heavy on the Harvey House motif—than an art museum. Train buffs would love the rumble and tumble, the smell of diesel, the clanking and screeching of boxcars being hitched together and uncoupled. For train enthusiasts—*foamers*— the booming of that much steel and power brought excitement and pleasure. And that's who would be the only audience for actually sleeping here. The trains clanked through town all day and night.

Art connoisseurs would be less likely to appreciate the grittiness of train life, the grime, the noise, the almost squalid feel even at midday.

I wasn't being fair. The people who wanted an art museum must have thought this through. The problem was, I didn't have much of a proposal to go on. The artists had written up a couple of pages about why their idea was so good, how it would generate scads of cash, hike up those gross receipts. But they hadn't answered the questions I had now, such as: "What about the noise?" and "What are you going to do with the upstairs rooms?" and "Won't every train knock your precious art right off the walls?"

Nailing that down was my job. That's why I'd been hired.

Of course, the train contingent—with their twenty-page, professionally prepared proposal—made glowing claims as well. They'd attract an international audience; old and young alike would "flock" to this railroad mecca.

"Miss Solomon?"

"I'm sorry. I'm thinking about this whole Harvey House idea," I said.

"I bet you are."

"What do you think? Which idea do you like better?"

"What are my choices?"

"You don't know?"

"Just testing," he said and winked.

"Which one do you think would be better? Art or train museum?"

Gracey scratched his head, looked at his feet, looked up at me then down again. We stood there for a few minutes—him presumably considering the idea, me waiting.

"Mr. Gracey?"

"I want you to come with me," he said, leading me out of the room and toward another at the far end of the hall. In the corner, the space had four windows and a marvelous view. Damn! It felt like the home I'd searched for my entire life. Four walls and four windows.

"I like this room," I said.

"You do?"

"Very much."

"So does our ghost," he said.

eighteen

"A GHOST?" I SAID.

"Yep. She lives here, knocks around upstairs and down," said Gracey. He sounded like he'd told the story a thousand times.

"Have you seen her?"

"Not me. But a couple of other docents have," he said. "She mainly comes out at night."

"What does she look like?"

"Oh, she's a Harvey Girl through and through. Puffed-up bun, spotless uniform, heels that click when they come down the stairs."

"Wow. Was a Harvey Girl murdered here?" I said, goosebumping at the thought.

"No. Why?"

"As I understand it, ghosts hang around places where they've got unresolved business," I said with authority.

"You know a lot about ghosts?" Gracey's smile had an amused edge to it.

"Not exactly. But that's what people who know say."

"Sounds too serious for me," he said. "And they haven't met our girl. She's as friendly as can be."

"Really?"

"Yep. Her only *unresolved issue* is that she misses waiting on people, serving them a good cup of coffee and a wholesome meal."

I squinted, trying to see her. Nothing. I'd be happy to see a nice ghost. Maybe there were little tarry green or blue Chinese pills that could do that for me. What would my acupuncturist say to that?

Gracey watched me. I realized I'd been silent. For how long? "You still haven't told me which proposal you prefer," I said, walking toward the stairs.

"Which do you think?" He said it like an instructor hoping for the right answer.

"Okay. You don't want to tell me," I said. "That's okay."

"I thought I just did."

"You don't care for either one?"

"Bingo." He stopped to catch his breath and with that action I knew I'd overstayed, though I could tell he'd never say so.

"Actually, if I was leaning toward anything, it'd be the train museum and Harvey House idea," he said. "But the amount of work they'd have to do on this old building might hurt it more than it could stand."

"If it were up to you, what would you do with the place?"

"Leave it the way it is," he said.

We shook hands at the door. Gracey locked up and headed to his car. I hung back, taking in the place, the spectacle of the train yard, its oil and other burning smells, the grime of it. To a train lover, this would be heaven.

And a ghost? That opened up even more markets.

The low hum of an incoming locomotive—yet again—amplified to earthquake proportions as I sat on a wrought-iron bench under the building's veranda. How could anyone sleep with this kind of noise and jostling? Train buffs might love a sleepless night, but the art crowd's glitterati would be basket cases by morning.

Sitting there, I realized my many hours at Mom's gallery as a child had set my biases like super glue. While I loved artists, I hated collectors. Alas, they'd be a big chunk of the target audience for the art museum. I'd have to get past my own prejudices to figure out how Lydia Herndon and others planned to deal with the intrusion of the trains at this location.

I leaned back on the bench, letting the cooling air whoosh across my face, and closed my eyes. Beyond the yells of men working in the yard, I heard the crunch of a car on gravel but ignored it in favor of a few more moments of calm before I got all hot-and-bothered about dinner with Peter.

"An odd place for a nap," said Detective Garcia.

I opened my eyes. "Detective. How'd you know I was here?"

"I saw Mike Gracey at the gas station." He held out a hand to help me up. "Come on, let's walk."

We passed through the nearly empty parking lot and down the hill. "That's the train headquarters for the area," the detective said, pointing to a low, dull building surrounded by cars. We wandered onto a tree-lined street, the houses small with pitched roofs, painted fences, and fall leaves piling in front of their doors.

"Tell me more about your mother," said Garcia.

"What about her?"

"She knew Miss Petty a long time."

"So did a lot of other people," I said.

Garcia's pager hummed. He unclipped it from his belt, looked, then put it back.

"You need to make a call?" I said.

"Your mom."

Why was he obsessing on Mom? "You think she knows something?"

He looked up at the blue sky through a cottonwood tree, its remaining leaves bright yellow. Didn't say a word.

"Even if she did, we can't just give her a pill and make her coherent," I said, waiting.

"How much time are you planning to spend down here?" he said.

"Enough to get the job done."

"What?" He stared at me now. "Hours? Days?"

"Why?" I had a nasty hunch about his question.

"Do you remember your mother talking about Miss Petty's will?"

I kneeled to pick up a penny—heads up—on the sidewalk. "Yeah."

"We're still looking for it," he said.

"And you think Mom knows where it is? You must be kidding." Then it hit me. "You want me to baby-sit her in case she says something important?" I shook my head. "No way."

"She said Miss Petty promised her an inheritance. That you're jealous about it." A vociferous crow flew overhead. The detective stopped to watch its flight.

"You could ask her boyfriend to do it," I said.

"Mr. Katz."

"Yes," I said, catching the scent of something organic burning. A good smell in the air—in spite of the idiocy of any manmade fire in a state facing another year of drought.

"Was Miss Petty *his* friend as well?" Garcia was walking too slowly for my liking.

"How should I know?"

"Take an educated guess," he said.

"I don't remember hearing anything about it."

"Is Mr. Katz a religious man?"

"You can't be thinking he'd have anything to do with her murder."

Again, he didn't answer. Instead, he veered for a pile of leaves and crunched his way through them—a gratifying noise. He smiled.

"Have you seen him?" I said.

"Not yet."

"He's small. Think a short Napoleon," I said, throwing the penny so someone else could benefit from finding it. "He'll help. I can't."

We retraced our route.

"You know more about what I'm looking for," said Garcia.

"Yes, but I've got a lot of work on my plate right now. This job here in Belen. And one of my clients is going to be on national television." Okay, I was stretching the truth but I couldn't be holed up with Mom for days on end. "I can't just drop my work. Plus, you're wrong about Mom, anyway. She's mostly *off* her rocker," I said. "Get this— Mom said Phillipa thought she was in danger—like she was that character, you know, the one in the melodramas. The Perils of Pauline? I mean, how cliché can you get?"

Garcia faced me. "Let me get this straight. Your mother said that and you didn't bother to share it with me until now?"

"What's the big deal? It's another one of her fantasies."

"So you're a psychiatrist, too, Ms. Solomon?" Garcia kicked a can off the sidewalk. It landed with a ka-chink and rolled to a stop in the middle of the street. He resumed walking. "What were her exact words?"

"Phillipa called Mom and told her some man had come back or something like that." I shook my head, suddenly aware that I'd started thinking of the artist by her first name. As if in her death—and my search for answers—she'd become a friend.

I refocused on the conversation. "I tried to get more out of Mom but she flipped into Lala-land again." My lack of sympathy for Mom's mental problems sounded harsh, even to *my* ears. I felt guilty for it—

and defensive. "Am I supposed to call you every time she says something like that? Even if I think it's absolute bull?"

"Colorful, Ms. Solomon." He rubbed the bridge of his nose. "Why don't you let me decide what's *bull* and what's not? It's my job. But I can't do it if I don't know about it." He stopped again, his face yielding no clue as to what he was thinking. "I'd appreciate if you'd tell me these things when they happen."

"I can't be there twenty-four-seven," I said. So, it was back to the "will she or won't she baby-sit her mama" routine. I wasn't going to do it. No way. Nope. No siree, Bob.

"You can be there more than you are," he said.

Another train. Its force rattled more than my legs. Garcia's pressure did too.

"I'll try." I took a quiet, slow, and deep breath.

"I guess I'll have to settle for that." Garcia moved back from me and rolled his shoulders in such a way that his polished holster flashed in the waning light.

nineteen

DRESSED IN JEANS AND a royal-blue T-shirt, Peter stood emanating health, youth, and sensuality. His smooth arms caught the sunset's uneasy pink and gold rays in the patio at the Hub motel. Shadows fondled his muscled chest.

Moth to flame, moth to flame. I felt myself melting. *He's too young.*

"Hi. How long have you been sitting here?" I said, my voice laced with self-control.

"A few minutes. The owner told me to make myself comfortable." He reached for my hand, the warmth of his touch a balm.

"What do you want to do?" I squeaked.

"I brought some Guinness. We can sit here and watch the sunset, then look at the stars."

How dare he be so handsome?

"You've got a long drive home." I cleared my throat. "You sure you want to drink?"

"That's very responsible. But I'm one step ahead of you," he said. "I got a room. So drinking shouldn't be a problem."

A room? He'd gotten a room? *Talk about temptation.* No, no, no. The last thing I needed was another man. A virile young pup to distract me from everything and everyone. I moved a step away from Peter, afraid that another touch would dissolve my spectacular restraint.

He stepped forward.

"Then Guinness it is," I said, knowing I should say something else.

Peter tilted his chin just so—a dimple I'd not noticed before beckoned.

My skin tingled. My heart watusied. "Do you mind waiting while I freshen up?" I said, worried that my black pills weren't working, that I'd see some stupid hallucination and turn the moment with this hunk into a scene from *Psycho.*

"I'd wait a long time for you." His words sprinkled my skin, awakening receptors and making me squirm.

After I'd worked the lock, I lunged into the room and plopped onto the bed, my eyes squeezed closed. A breath. Heart beats skipping, a full-body hot-flash. Menopause? I cracked my eyes open a millimeter. No, this wasn't the result of a mind gone haywire; the reaction was simpler than that. I wanted hot sex with Peter. Right then. Right there.

Sighing, I went into the bathroom. The cold water felt lukewarm against my boiling libido. But I kind of liked the feeling of having that gorgeous guy out there attracted to me. And me to him. The zing of it sent prickles skittering under my skin. I splashed more water on my face and continued the internal monologue about responsibility, men and their superficiality—about what he would do when he saw my frumpy body. A million reasons not to open the door and go outside.

Lust triumphed.

Peter had been busy in my absence. Two flowered paper cups book-ended him on the bench. The sun didn't have far to go now; it was probably morning in China. I sat down next to him and watched as the various lights and lamps in the courtyard sizzled to brilliance.

"I had a feeling the owner wouldn't want us drinking beer out of the can," he said, handing me a cup.

"Guinness tastes good in anything." I scooched away from him, then let my back relax. "I've had it out of soup cans before. This is positively civilized." I chewed the inside of my lip, listened to cars out of view.

Peter moved a tad closer, enough that his fresh scent mingled with the humidity caused by the fountains and the fragrance of still-blooming roses. It would be easy to lean on him, to put my head on his shoulder, to smile, and maybe kiss that first and most precious kiss. I bet it would be sensational, a real head-to-toe kiss.

"This is nice," he said.

My sigh was the quick kind, one of frustration rather than content-ment. "You know, Peter, I'm wondering what we're doing here."

"Drinking fine beer. Sitting companionably."

Was I misinterpreting the whole scene?

Straight-backed now, I said, "Why did you really come down here? To Belen?"

He shrugged, gave an innocent smile. "I wanted to see you."

I wanted to snuggle in those dimples, or maybe just curl up and take a long restful sleep. Who was I kidding? Sleep wasn't what I wanted. "I've got to be at least ten years older than you are."

"We're not exactly Harold and Maude," he said.

"I'm not ready for another relationship." Whoa. If that didn't scare him, nothing would.

"One step at a time, Sasha," he said. "How about a friend?"

I shook my head a fraction but said, "Oh, I'd like that."

twenty

I AWOKE IN A foul mood, angry to be alone in the lumpy bed. Predawn. 5:30 A.M., to be exact. What an idiot! I could have slept with Peter last night. But no, I'd parried his advances in the name of rationality, of "taking things slow." I'd told him about what had happened with Bob—minus my impromptu tabletop sculpting—and then his advances had dulled to sludge.

The hot shower cooled before I ran out of regret. Shivering in the early morning chill, I dressed. *Should I knock on Peter's door? Have a little cuddle before sunrise?*

Sleeping with Peter would be a stupid move right now. *What was so great about being smart? Sex. I wanted sex.* I kicked a shoe out of my way. Maybe I could consider sex after I was done with the Belen job. Yeah, that was it. I'd finish the job and use Peter as my reward.

I sat down with the laptop and tried to concentrate. My fingers slowed as I keyed in the dismal highlights of my research so far. A murdered artist. Lydia Herndon—the living definition of the word "antagonism." Ernie Merkin, that charming, gung-ho supporter of the train museum/Harvey House concept. At least I'd gotten some insights into railroad culture from him. Oh, and a friendly ghost—that was something. In all, I didn't have squat to make an informed recommendation to the mayor.

If I wanted to sleep with Peter before menopause, I'd have to do better than this.

Straight shooters on both sides—that's what would launch me into his arms. Cherry might be a good interview. I scanned my list. Wallace Crawson, retired railroad exec. The mayor said the guy was a major force behind the B & B concept. I probably should have interviewed him in the first place. Also, there had to be some artists—with decent manners—to flesh out their side of the picture.

With sex as my motivator, I made several notes, fingers rapping the keys with satisfying smacks as the ideas burst into existence. When I finally looked up, the sun was high enough to provide good natural light. I pulled the curtains back.

The day had more purpose now. I'd see about interviewing the director of the chamber of commerce and, maybe, that railroad guy. Then I'd go back to Merkin—when I'd had a couple of successes to fortify me—for his take on local reaction to Phillipa Petty, the blaspheming queen. This round of interviews would give me more names of people to interview, to get an even clearer picture. It always worked like this. I'd start with the outer layer, the obvious sources. Little by little, I'd find the important ones, the key players, not obvious to outsiders.

Though I wanted to spend the whole day in Belen, I also needed to check in on Mom. With what had happened—her momentary disappearance and Garcia's interest—fresh in my mind, I wasn't about to trust the *new, improved* management at St. Kate's. I'd aim for late afternoon to spend time with her. By then I'd be ready for a break.

Peter tapped on my window, his hair still wet from a shower. I opened the door and the electricity between us crackled. He angled his head to one side and moved closer to me. I held my breath, scared to move. His lips on my cheek, the lightest of touches, and *damn it*! I wanted to jump him.

An hour later, even the waitress asked if we were newlyweds.

Breakfast sat iffy in my stomach, the byproduct of too much caffeine, grease, and innuendo. At a little before nine, I knew I'd have to send my handsome hunk back to Albuquerque if I wanted the reward I now promised myself in return. Maybe I could lose twenty pounds before I saw him again. Cut down on the whipped cream. Go on a fast. Start an exercise program.

"I'm getting mixed signals from you, Sasha," he said to me, stirring nonexistent sugar in his coffee.

"I guess I'm a little confused."

"About what?"

"Me. You. Men in general," I said. "I'm probably going to be screwed up for a while about the whole Bob thing."

"I'm not Bob."

"I know that," I said, playing with a drop of coffee on the table. "It's just, well, I'm not willing to go down that road again. Not yet."

"Who's asking you to?" Peter said.

"I know you're not pressuring me. Not at all, Peter. But, I think it'd be best if we wait until I'm done with my work down here before we get to know each other better." My chair had grown too hard. I watched a waitress deliver a plate of eggs dripping with orange-ish grease to the table next to ours. "If I push, I can probably be done by the end of this week," I said. "Then, if you're game, we can celebrate—Japanese Kitchen has great sushi, or we can go to India Palace, or Saigon Restaurant for Vietnamese—we can do anything you like."

"I'd like to spend more time with you today."

I shook my head.

He put his spoon down. "I sound pretty desperate, don't I?"

"Not to me."

"No, really. I haven't been honest with you."

Here it comes. I knew it.

"I just got out of a long-term relationship, too. You and I, we're both rebounders," he said. "I'm sorry."

"For what?"

"Forcing myself on you."

"Oh, please. Force yourself on me anytime." Had I really just said that? My face sequenced through several shades of red—each more intense than the last.

Peter laughed. "Okay. When?"

"When I'm done here in Belen."

He stroked my hand, toyed with my fingers—their nails uneven but clean.

"Peter, listen to me. I want to see where this might go—with both eyes open and without reference to Bob," I said, enjoying the physical contact. "Give me some time. Please."

"I'll try," he said, putting my hand down with care and then standing to leave.

"I *will* call you," I said.

His kiss—on my forehead—sent a shock of green hurtling down my spine and out the bottom of my feet. I looked under the table to see if the energy had left a puddle.

It had.

twenty-one

HAVING BANISHED MY SEXUALITY back to Albuquerque, I had no option but to work.

First stop: the chamber of commerce. Belen's propaganda machine occupied a tiny storefront on Dalies Street. A display in its window honored businesses that'd been in the town for twenty-five, fifty, and one hundred years. Continuity as a theme brought civic pride, but to outsiders it was as exciting as a saltine.

Next door, a run-down movie theater, adorned with one of those great old marquis that evoke a grander time, perched like a dare. The city of Clovis had turned a similar building into an active performing arts center. Did Belen have the same *moxie*?

I pushed open the chamber's small glass door and put myself in the shoes of a tourist. Above the door hung a miniscule wind chime, its soft tinkle welcoming. I scanned the lobby—no chairs. Freestanding racks touted Belen's vitality with scads of brochures extolling Valencia County's points of interest, organizations, tourist attractions. Another rack held so many business cards, I had trouble removing them. Two handfuls later, I'd collected enough for future reference.

Beyond the onslaught of printed materials, a counter where—presumably—a receptionist should have been. And past that, a long unlit hallway.

I leaned over the countertop, searching for a sign of life or a buzzer to let someone know I'd come in. Alas, the wind chime hadn't done its job.

"Hello?" I said. "Hello? Is anyone here?"

"I'll be right there," said an unseen woman.

I shuffled through the cards while waiting: a cactus and bicycle shop, four insurance agents, the P & M Farm Museum, realtors galore, a massage therapist, the local Masonic Temple.

High heels clicked on the linoleum floor.

"I'm sorry. Have you been here long?" said a wisp of a lady in a navy-blue suit, her hand poised to shake mine.

"I just got here."

"Well, my receptionist—we use volunteers—called in sick a few minutes ago and I've been on the phone trying to find a replacement." Her wire-rimmed glasses caught sunlight from the storefront window. I couldn't tell what color her eyes were. "Not a very friendly greeting, I'm afraid."

"Couldn't be helped."

"You know what? Let me put up a little sign, here at the desk, so people know to come on back," she said. "It'll just take a minute."

In profile, she appeared older than I'd first assumed, perhaps early sixties. Her short salt-and-pepper hair sparkled under the fluorescent overhead fixtures. I thought I detected a bit of a pull where jaw met ear, possibly the remnant from a facelift. Her makeup frayed at the edges, a missed spot toward the bottom of her chin, the tiniest clump at temple and hairline, as if she only planned to speak to people face-on.

Her manicured nails topped smooth but wrinkled hands, a single gold band on the left one. She straightened.

"There. That's done," she said. "Would you like a cup of coffee?"

PR tip: It's always a good idea to accept beverages proffered by potential interviewees; it puts them at ease—even if you're waterlogged. "That'd be great."

We stopped at a dollhouse-size kitchen with cartons of bottled drinks stacked against a wall, boxes of candy bars, and a four-burner coffee machine.

"You hungry? Help yourself," she said, pushing a wad of thick red licorice toward me. "Cream?"

"Thank you."

She stepped over containers of bagged potato chips to get at the fridge. Inside, prepackaged sandwiches, a fruit plate, and half a pineapple glittered in their cellophane wrappings.

"Nice pickings," I said, pouring milk into the coffee.

"We're Party Central," she said, noticing me staring at the food. "Grab yourself a plate."

"Maybe in a few minutes." I followed her out of the room.

Her womb-like office had no windows, its fake wood paneling making it darker yet. At one end sat a desk bedecked with several stacks of manila folders with a hodgepodge of papers sticking out of them. A clunky computer hummed beyond the disarray, its hard drive dominating more than half of the surface.

"Let's sit here," she said, moving toward a shiny fake-marble–topped table. Eight thick leather chairs encircled it. "Well, that's better. Now, what can I do for you?"

"Mayor Flores hired me to look at the proposals for the Harvey House."

"So, you're Sasha Solomon," she said.

"The one and only." I wondered which of my reputations had preceded me.

"Sue Evans, executive director of the chamber."

We shook hands again. Drank our coffee.

"I heard you worked wonders in Clovis with their UFO initiative," she said.

"It was a fun project."

"Jan Cisneros says you're a creative dynamo."

"She's the dynamo in Clovis, not me," I said, smiling. When I'd created the plan for my traveling PR business, I'd hoped the grapevine would buzz in my favor. Already my first job on the road—the one in Clovis—had given me a head start in Belen.

"I hope your work here isn't too boring after space aliens," Evans said, eyebrows raised in a tease.

"Hey, I hear you've got a ghost."

"Whatever works." She laughed and finished her drink in one gulp. "Now, what do you need from me?"

"Opinions mainly," I said. "What does your business community think of the two proposals? Does one look better than the other to your constituents?"

She frowned in concentration but said nothing.

"Also, is there any money anywhere earmarked for tourism? For sprucing up downtown?" I said.

"Let me take those one at a time." Her eyes unfocused for a moment, as if she were accessing information deep in a mental filing cabinet. "I'm going to answer you in a roundabout way here, so bear with me. All right?"

"Sure."

"There are a few fundamental things about Belen that you need to understand. First of all, this is an old community. It was here long before the trains came through. So there's a kind of local tradition you might not find in other communities." Evans rested her head in her hand, her fingers bent. Her gaze passed beyond me again. Then she lightly slapped her free hand on the wooden surface and renewed eye contact. "There's also a strong religious tradition. Even though many families are moving away from Catholicism, everyone still goes to church on Sunday."

"I bet Phillipa Petty didn't make many friends with her art." I felt like a real P.I.

"What made you say that?"

"I was supposed to interview her the day she died."

"Oh, well, yes. You're right. Her art offended many people here," Evans said.

"So, everyone prefers the train museum and B-and-B concept?"

"Not exactly."

"Really?"

"It's a question of practicality. Would we really be able to attract enough people to sustain the B and B, to pay chefs and servers, maids, and so forth? An art museum would be infinitely cheaper to run. With Phillipa Petty's name, we could position ourselves as an art destination. There's a kind of appeal in that."

"The advertising alone—in those high-end publications—would be astronomical," I said. "And I bet the insurance on Miss Petty's paintings—"

"We'd have to factor that in, of course."

I swiveled in the chair. "How much money do you anticipate making off the Harvey House?"

"The site itself would have to break even. We're also banking on the added value of increased tourism—more customers for our gas stations, restaurants, hotels—attracting more business to the area."

"Wouldn't the B and B be in competition with local businesses?"

"Not if we played it right."

"Do you have a dollar amount in mind?"

"When it's established?" She frowned. "Two, three hundred thousand throughout the year? Somewhere in there. If we can up the ante, it'd be great."

"You really think you can pull that in?"

"It's a good goal, no matter which proposal. Don't you think?"

"I think it's ambitious."

"Did you know that Miss Petty provided money for the art museum in her will?" Evans fiddled with a pen, began doodling on a scrap of paper. Another artist?

"I had no idea. How much?"

"She didn't say. I expect we'll find out soon enough."

"So, you prefer the art museum?"

"Personally? No." Evans got up. "Do you want more coffee?"

"Sure."

"I'm a Latter Day Saint, Ms. Solomon. Have you seen her painting of Joseph Smith?" she said, her back to me.

"No."

"She has him surrounded by children dressed as strippers." Framed in the doorway, Evans turned to face me. "Can you imagine?"

I sighed. "Nothing was sacred, was it?"

"The woman didn't know the meaning of the word." Evans left the room. A minute later, I heard her pour our drinks.

While I waited, I studied the photos on her walls. An abundance of talking heads—dignitaries, mainly male—shaking hands with other people I couldn't identify. Pictures of groundbreakings, of men and women smiling with their shovels poised and feet ready to press into parched earth.

"Just because I can't abide by her art doesn't mean it wouldn't be the best alternative," said Evans after her silent return.

"Did you know Miss Petty well?"

"Not really," she said, sitting down again. With an upraised hand, she invited me to do the same. "But whenever I spoke with her, she was good for a donation of some sort—be it money or a cute little custom-made card she'd paint for a specific occasion."

"Really? That sounds out of character, somehow."

"Personally, one-on-one, she wasn't bad. For example, when the Artists Guild approached her with their proposal, from what I heard, she embraced it."

"But people here don't like her art," I said.

Evans cocked her head a tad to the left. "Granted, it'd be a problem. But I think we could pull it off if it meant more money for Belen."

"You're not worried about vandalism?"

"The whole time she lived here, no one ever defaced her work. Nothing, not her studio or anything else, was ever harmed."

"She *was* murdered."

"Not by a local," said the executive.

"How can you be so sure?"

"Why would someone here kill her? People who might be angry about her art had already tolerated it for decades. As far as I know, nothing's changed. And, like I said before, she wasn't bad as a person. A bit crusty . . . she liked her privacy. But she cared about the people here and about Belen."

"She sure had a funny way of showing it. Mocking the very religious symbols people in Belen care so deeply about."

"That's true." Evans nodded. "But I bet you didn't know that she put the chamber in her will too."

"Really?"

"Yes." She finished her coffee. "A couple of weeks ago she called to tell me she'd done it. She wanted to make sure we'd have the money for the Harvey House project—no matter what."

"Amazing," I said, trying to adjust my image of the husband-stealing, icon-smashing artist. The air grew cooler. A sudden sadness passed through me. Beyond Evans, I sensed a presence but saw nothing more compelling than fake paneling. "And now she's dead."

twenty-two

YOU KNOW HOW YOU begin to notice small things and they acquire a special significance? Or you feel the embryo of a hunch, its first flutter? Well, while I'd been talking with Sue Evans, I started seeing three words with a too-coincidental frequency. Little words all with the same sound: *to*, *too*, and *two*.

"Okay, this is too weird," I said aloud. *Too*. I sat in my car outside the chamber and wondered if I was cracking up. "What's the deal with *too*? Or *to*? Or *two*?" On the opposite side of the street, the Belen police station parking lot held four squad cars. *Two times two equals four.* One of them pulled out, the policeman cruising past me with the stare smeared on his face.

I must look like a lunatic talking to myself. I smoothed down my hairdo and tried to make sense of this sudden, odd obsession with the three words. A train's horn sounded down the street. *Toot.* Maybe that's what I was looking for—not a homonym for *two* after all. That felt right; if I could grab the thought and force it a little farther. *Toot.* Trains and poison? Murder . . .

My cell phone chirped and the almost-formed connection sharded into nothingness.

"Hello?" I said, the annoyance in my voice too audible.

"Hello. Is this Sasha Solomon? Karen Kilgore here, from *The Other Side?* Returning your call, I've got some business in Santa Fe this weekend and thought I could do a pre-interview with Darnda Jones midafternoon on Friday in Albuquerque. I'm afraid that's the only time I've got on this trip. We could do it in my hotel room. I'll be staying at the Hyatt. Would that work for you?" She finally took a breath.

It caught me off-guard.

"Hello? Do have the right number for Sasha Solomon?" she said.

"Yes. Hi."

"Well, will that work?"

"I—"

"Good. Darnda sounds like the real deal. I just love people who're the real deal. Don't you? Well, I'd better get going. How about two-thirty? That's all I can spare. I'll be traveling under my married name, Murphy, Karen Murphy. Can't wait to meet you."

The dial tone cued me that the conversation—if you could call it that—was over. Oh, this didn't bode well. I'd have to work with Darnda between now and Friday. Sounded to me like Karen Kilgore wasn't in the habit of listening. Darnda would have to be assertive in a subtle way—not off-putting—to make sure the story we wanted to tell penetrated Kilgore's pattering mind and mouth. I sighed and the damn phone rang again.

"Yes?" I braced for another verbal barrage.

"Ms. Solomon?"

"Detective Garcia." I wondered if he could hear the relief in my voice.

"Where are you?" he said.

"Belen."

The Belen policeman cruised by in the other direction and made sure I saw him watching me. He spoke into a hand-held microphone; I could see its curly chord attached to his dash.

"I'll buy you lunch," said the detective.

"Did something happen?"

"How about the White Way at noon?"

Why was everyone so free with my time? Didn't they know I had to work? "I—"

"Great. See you then." He disconnected. Two hang-ups in less than two minutes. Two. To. Too.

"Arrrrrrrr!" I yelled, hitting the power button on the phone and jamming it into my purse. The knock on my window felt like a natural consequence.

"Yessir?" I said.

"Are you all right, ma'am?" the policeman said. He stood tall as a basketball player. Brown hair short, shaved face clean. Emotive as concrete.

"I'm fine," I said. "Why?"

"You've been parked here for more than an hour. It's a half-hour zone." He pointed to a sign. "See? Thirty minutes."

"I'm sorry. I had no idea I'd been here that long."

"You sure you're all right?" He'd bent to my level, eyes not visible behind reflective sunglasses, presumably gauging whether he had probable cause to search my car.

"Yes, officer."

"I'm going to have to write you up." He straightened, flipped open a pad, and clicked a pen.

"Oh, please don't," I said with great despair. Believe it or not, I'd never gotten a ticket, not for anything. One of my few perfect records. That . . . and disgusting boyfriends.

He hadn't begun to write yet. Again came the bend, the stare, a shake of his head. "All right. You can go," he said. "But pay more attention next time."

"Thank you so much," I gushed, starting the car and beginning to shiver. Guilt catching up with me, I suppose. But why did I feel guilty? I'd done nothing wrong.

Well, technically, I had. The question was: When would I tell the detective about the photo I'd snagged, and the ones I'd snapped? Two different instances of wrongdoing on my part. *Two.*

twenty-three

NOTHING SETTLES RATTLED NERVES better than a boring interview; it was time to check in with my employer. I clicked on my phone—just in case someone else wanted to hang up on me—and drove to his factory. Unless you've lived in a small town, you probably wouldn't know that most mayors tend to have other jobs—ones that pay real money—in addition to their titular duties. Belen's chief, Antonio Flores, owned Tierra Avonite, Inc., a manufacturing interest at the north entrance to town.

I sat in the lobby of his pre-fab building, drinking the cup of mud-colored water his young secretary had offered as coffee. What Flores saved on designer java—and a whole lot more—went into glossy, four-color sales brochures like those arrayed on a table next to me. I picked one up and learned about the wonders of Avonite—a decorative polymer used to cover countertops, tabletops, and, according to the brochure, a great many things in between.

"Ms. Solomon?"

"Mayor," I said, rising to shake hands.

With cheekbones high and a nose hinting at royalty, Flores's only deficit was his height. Even with his thick-soled shoes, he still fell into the pipsqueak category—even shorter than my 5'4". In spite of his humble altitude, he commanded attention. Maybe it was those iris-leaf-green eyes shining in a desert-brown face. He looked good to me, handsome. I guess I was in one of *those* moods—horny.

Flores led me to a plain office, appointed with furniture befitting Ernie Merkin. The only item that stood out was a table, dead center in the room, its inlaid top a mosaic of golds, purples, pinks, and tans. Avonite, I presumed.

The mayor pulled out a chair for me. I could smell his sweet, spicy cologne. If I'd known him better, I'd've asked for the name of it.

"So, how's the project going?" he said, sitting down.

"Not as well as I'd like. There've been a few unexpected developments."

"Like Phillipa Petty's death."

"No kidding," I said. "Speaking of which, I can't believe people here would really support the art museum idea. Not with Miss Petty's subject matter."

"You wouldn't think so," he said. "But there's more to it than that. I want to show you something." He opened a filing cabinet almost as tall as he was, removed a folder, and handed me two pieces of paper. "Here, look at these"

Deer Tonio,
Petty is the Devil's Spawn. Someone should do something about her. You run this town, Tonio. Keep her out. Or some-buddy else will have to.

Raul

Dear Mayor Flores,
I know Jesus says we should turn the other cheek but I am finding it difficult to be a good Christian with Miss Petty living so near by. Did you know she came to our church last Sunday? What horrible thing is she going to paint next? Isn't there any way you could ask her to move or something?

Maybe up to Santa Fe or someplace that doesn't love Jesus the way we do?

Sincerely,
Bitsy Ford

I looked at Flores. "And this is supposed to make me feel better?"

"Now look at this," he said, proffering a card. An impressionist watercolor of Petty's bridge, the irrigation ditch lined in a flurry of greens, reds, and browns, graced its cover. The artist had created a pointillist sky of multiple blues. A gold-leaf signature lounged in a corner.

"P-two?" I said.

"P-squared," said the mayor. "Phillipa Petty."

"She made this? It's lovely."

"Open it."

Inside there was a handwritten note, the penmanship shaky, the ink a flamboyant purple.

Tonio,

Happy Birthday. May you be blessed with the joy of each coming year—even as we are all blessed each day—by knowing you.

Philly

"She wrote this?" Talk about cognitive dissonance.

He nodded and took the papers from my hand. "So much of life is a contradiction, Ms. Solomon. Philly was no exception. She incited anger with her religious art but her motivations were good."

I frowned.

"You don't believe me," he said. "I asked her once about her paintings."

"What did she say?"

"That people have gotten too complacent." The mayor fondled the front of the card as he spoke. "That they've let religious symbols replace the hard work of spirituality. And that it was her job to make them stop and take a long look at what's important about God and what's man-made pomp."

"For some reason, I didn't think she cared much for God."

"Philly was a deeply spiritual person."

"She had a funny way of showing it," I said.

He turned the card over in his hand, opened it, read the note, and closed it. Shook his head. "Nothing funny about being murdered."

"I didn't think that was common knowledge."

"I *am* mayor," he said.

"I didn't mean any offense."

"None taken. Even if I wasn't mayor, something like this can't be kept secret in a small town. Everyone knows. Philly was too high-profile."

"Do you think she was killed because of her art?" I wanted someone to 'fess up to it, to admit her nasty images could have inspired murder.

"It's the only reason I can think of," he said.

Ah. "Do you think you might know who did it?"

"No," he said, "because it wasn't anyone local."

"That's what Sue Evans said. She also told me Miss Petty had taken care of Belen in her will."

"That's what I hear, but I don't have any details."

"None?"

"I suspect it's a trust for specific projects. Philly talked about that kind of thing before," Flores said, tracing a design on the table with his thumbs. "The interest off of some kind of endowment for arts education in the schools or a performing arts center. That kind of thing. But she never told me if she actually did it."

"But why couldn't it be someone from Belen?" I said. "Like that Raul? That was a mean-spirited letter."

"He's all bluster. That letter was written to *me*, not Phillipa." Flores opened his hands as he spoke, palms outwards. I noticed thin white scars around both his wrists. "I know my people. They didn't like her but they respected her. They respected what she'd accomplished," he said. "It had to be somebody from somewhere else."

"Okay," I said.

"You look skeptical."

"I want to believe you."

"Then do." He leaned forward. "Belief is a very important thing."

To break the tension I said, "Do you know why she felt compelled to leave money to Belen in the first place? She must have known how people felt about her."

"Personally? I think it was a perverse impulse. A rub-your-nose-in-it kind of thing," he said. "If we spend her money, it'll be a constant reminder that she was part of this town."

"That brings me back to the art museum," I said. "How can it fly with all that religious hostility?"

"Money has a way of dampening umbrage. If it brings in substantial revenues and increases tourism, the chamber members would support it." He caught my second glance at his wrists and pulled down his shirt cuffs. "They'd be the ones to sell it to their extended families. It could work. With some effort."

I straightened my back in the chair, thinking.

The mayor returned the Petty folder to its place in the cabinet.

"You know, in order for either plan to work, Belen is going to have to invest real money in cosmetic renovation," I said. "Right now, tourists aren't going to consider this a destination. And once they're here, boarded-up storefronts on your main streets don't say, 'Hey, this is a great place to stay a while.'"

"Our economy is worse this year than last," he said, turning to face me. "I'm mayor because I'm willing to do the job for free and because I've kept far more people on the payroll than my business merits. That's just me. Several of our other civil servants took pay cuts to make budget."

"So, renovation is out of the question," I said.

"Unless Philly left us a fortune."

twenty-four

I STILL HAD TWENTY-FIVE minutes before my rendezvous with New Mexico's finest. On a whim, I drove south past the White Way and onto the same highway that would lead to Phillipa Petty's house. Instead of turning left at the train tracks, I stopped at the post office.

Housed in a yellowed building that looked more like a large mobile home, the post office sported a steady line of people opening boxes to retrieve letters and magazines, buying stamps, and shipping packages. A portly woman with black frizzy hair served each customer with a smile of recognition, a personal comment—*That knee feel any better, Jorge?* and *Your mom back from the hospital yet?*—and pat of solidarity on the hand of those who looked like they needed a human touch.

I stood at the back of the room, watching and wondering how the woman knew every person so well. Of course, she must have known Phillipa, too.

When the area cleared, she said, "Can I help you with something?"

"I'm not sure," I said.

"I feel that way sometimes." She worked on something behind the counter, out of sight. Not rebuffing me, not pressuring either.

Emboldened by her averted gaze, I said, "Did you know Miss Petty?"

"Philly?"

"Yes."

"I did." Her voice gave no clue to her feelings about the artist.

"Did she collect her mail here?"

The woman stopped her work. "Now, why would you be interested in that?"

"Because I'm the one who found her the other day. Because I'd like to understand her better, to understand—"

"Why someone would murder her?"

"Yes," I said, no longer surprised at the common knowledge.

She held up a coin. "Phillipa Petty was like this quarter. One side bright and worthwhile, the other—well, I don't know. Pure evil. How she could live with both sides warring in her is beyond me."

"Did she come in often?"

"No."

"So she didn't have a box here."

"No."

Outside, the sound of more than one car door slammed. Another wave of customers.

"Do you think someone could have killed her because of her art?" I said.

The woman gave me an assessing look. Her attention moved past me to the opening door. "Phillipa's paintings made a lot of people mad."

"You talking about Philly?" said a gray-topped man, his corrugated face evidencing years of outdoor work. He had the kind of bushy eyebrows—white and plentiful—that begged for clipping.

"I was asking about her," I said.

"Who are you?" he said.

"I'm the lady the mayor hired to figure out what to do with the Harvey House."

"She's the one who found Philly," said the woman.

A couple of other people came into the room and stopped to listen.

"Philly knew how to use those oils. No one can take that away from her," the man said.

"So what?" The challenge came from a small woman wearing an off-white crocheted sweater. "What good is talent if it's used for blasphemy?"

"Talent's talent," he said.

"You know that isn't true. Anything used for evil is evil itself," the small woman said.

"Maria, you're too black and white. Philly's work was all about symbolism, about separating outward representations from the crux of spirituality," he said.

"You with your big words. 'Outward representations' my foot," she said. "You're as bad as she was, Jerome." She gave his name the Spanish pronunciation—"Herom."

"Who's next?" said the woman behind the counter.

I looked at my watch and realized I only had two minutes to get to my lunch date. Still, I tapped Phillipa's defender on the shoulder. "Sir?"

"Yes?"

"Did you know Miss Petty well?"

"Sure did," he said. "But I don't know you."

"Sasha Solomon," I said, extending my hand.

"You related to Hannah Solomon up in Albuquerque?"

Seemed like everyone in Belen knew Mom. "I'm her daughter."

He stepped back from me, as if trying to get a better view. "Yes. I can see the resemblance now. Same eyes. You've grown quite a bit since I last saw you."

"I'm sorry. I don't remember—"

"No reason you should. Must have been thirty-eight, thirty-nine years ago. Your mom had that gallery in Old Town." His hazel eyes had a milky quality to them. I noticed because they seemed to clear for a moment.

"That's right. May I ask your name?"

"Must you?" Resignation weighed down his simple words.

"Excuse me?" I said.

He smiled. "Hold on a minute, I'll talk to you when I'm done here."

This was important; I could feel it. My back against the wall, I observed the quaint scene and hoped Garcia wouldn't be too put out about having to wait for me. It didn't matter. I was going to stick around to talk to this Jerome guy.

When he finished his business, the man came toward me. "Ah, there you are. My name's Jerome Whitaker," he said, escorting me out to the parking lot.

"*The* Jerome Whitaker?"

He bowed. "You can touch my jacket, get a feel for fame. And no, I won't read your latest manuscript and I won't give you a blurb. If you want me to give a speech, you'll have to go through my publicist."

"I don't want anything from you," I said, amazed to be talking with the Nobel prize–winning novelist. "You live here?"

"Where else?"

"I guess that sounded pretty stupid." I'm not often in awe of celebrity—but Jerome Whitaker ranked up there with the best: Vladimir Nabokov, Jane Austen, and Mark Twain. I'd read every one of his fifteen books at least three times.

"You look pale," he said. "Are you all right?"

"I'm just pleased to meet you. That's all."

"I see," he said. I sensed him waiting for me to calm down and start acting like a grown-up again. "How's your mom doing these days?"

"Not so great."

"I'm sorry to hear it. She was a pistol when I knew her."

My phone rang. *Yippee.*

"Solomon," I said, holding up a finger and widening my eyes to request Whitaker's patience for a minute or two.

"Where are you?" Garcia's irritation crackled.

"I'm on my way."

"I hope so," he said.

"It'll take me about ten minutes to get there."

"I'll order for you. Now."

Whitaker handed me a torn scrap of paper with a phone number on it.

"Hold on, Detective," I said.

"Detective? You must be important," said Whitaker, his eyes sparkling with mischief. "Call me. If I don't pick up, leave a message. *Sasha*, right?"

I nodded.

The author did the same before yanking open the door of a dirt-swathed Ford pick-up—one of the old ones with rounded fenders and those headlights that look like freestanding frog's eyes—a real collector's item. The truck fit the man. He tipped an imaginary hat my way.

"Remember me?" The voice barked in my phone. "I'm counting the seconds, Ms. Solomon, and I suggest you don't be late. One . . . two . . . three . . ."

twenty-five

"... **SEVEN THOUSAND AND EIGHT**, seven thousand nine," said the detective, standing up to greet me.

"You didn't really count that whole time," I said.

"Do you know that for a fact?" He sat down. "You psychic or something?"

I stopped, my rear end six inches above the chair, unhappy with his reference. "What does being psychic have to do with anything?"

"You tell me."

"Nothing. It doesn't have anything to do with anything."

"There you go again. Holding out on me," said Garcia, shaking his head in obvious mock disappointment.

"I'm not psychic." I managed to get parked in my chair and held my hand over the burger in front of me. Still warm. "Who've you been talking to?"

"People." Garcia unfolded his paper napkin. "Want to tell me your side of the story?"

"There's nothing to tell."

"As I understand it, you're on a first-name basis with all kinds of ghosts."

"I've got it under control now," I said. "Who'd you talk to, anyway?"

"Some of the folks up in Clovis."

"I figured. But why?"

"I was curious. One cop to another, that kind of thing."

"I can't believe Henry would've said anything."

"LaSalle? No, not him. I spoke to your buddy, Agent Frenth, the FBI guy."

"He's not my buddy," I said too quickly.

"Yeah, that's what I figured." Garcia chuckled. "Turns out he holds grudges. Your buddy had a lot to say about the case up there." He dumped a mound of catsup onto his plate. "He mentioned something about a ghost and you drinking too much."

"It didn't happen like that," I said. "And I don't drink too much."

"Depends on who you're talking to."

"Ernie Merkin drinks too much."

"Who?"

"It doesn't matter."

"Why were you late?" said Garcia.

"I met Jerome Whitaker."

"Who?"

"Jerome Whitaker. You know—*A Storm of Crows* and *Nantucket Rodeo*—the author."

The detective blinked—a deliberate and unimpressed action.

"He won the Nobel Prize for Literature a few years ago," I said, mixing catsup with red Tabasco sauce and pepper. I tasted it with a spoon and added more hot sauce.

"For that, you were late."

"You don't get it, do you? Nobel Prize. Great writer."

"Ms. Solomon, I've got six new homicides this week—spread across hundreds of square miles—and a pile this high of other active cases." He held his right hand over his head for a minute. "I'm not interested in literature. I'm interested in solving crimes before someone else gets murdered."

"Okay," I said. "I'm sorry I'm late."

"Accepted." He opened his burger and picked out a piece of green chile to eat before speaking again. "We tracked down Miss Petty's will."

Though he spoke in low tones, a hush vaulted through the restaurant. Forks stopped clinking on plates, conversations stilled.

"You couldn't find her will?" With all the attention now on our chit-chat, I felt I needed to be clever. "That sounds like a cheap plot device in an amateur novel."

"Back to the literature again? Well, I'm sorry to sound *amateurish*, but Miss Petty wasn't what you'd call organized. She also didn't have a local lawyer." He lifted his burger and then put it back down. "Why am I justifying myself to you?"

There's a time to keep quiet and a time to talk. I stuffed several fries in my mouth before I said anything else to tick him off.

"Anyway, we found it," he said.

"Is that what you wanted to talk about? The will?"

"You're brilliant." He winced, rubbed his eyes. "I'm sorry. That was uncalled for."

"No problem." I dipped one of the fries in my catsup concoction, tasted it, and smiled.

"Your mother was right," said Garcia.

"Right?" I said. "No way."

"Half right."

"No way." I took a big bite of the burger and hoped he'd elaborate.

Instead, he ate, too. People at the tables around us began talking again, the hum reassuring. In the kitchen, someone dropped some dishes. The crash and clatter traveled into the dining area and people applauded in the perverse way they do—to relieve tension or commiserate.

After a few minutes, I said, "How was Mom right?"

"Miss Petty changed her will recently." Garcia's words worked like a pause button on the diners. He took a breath and their actions resumed.

"Yesterday morning? After Miss Petty had been dead for two days?" I said.

"Almost," he said. "She changed it over the weekend and we think she died trying to send a copy to your mom."

I drank my water, not wanting to look at him. I wanted my mom far away from anything having to do with Phillipa Petty—on the other side of the universe. Because if she wasn't, she might be in danger, too, and that was too much to think about.

"There was an envelope near Miss Petty's body." He paused. "It was addressed to your mother."

I knew he wanted a reaction from me. The one I gave him probably wasn't what he was shooting for. More french fries into my mouth. A swirl and then a counter-swirl of the straw in my milkshake. If I evaded his eyes long enough, he might go away.

"It looked like it was empty, but whoever killed Miss Petty was in a hurry. We found a little paper fragment in it with both type and handwriting on it," he said. "Through the miracles of modern science we found it matched Miss Petty's will. She was mailing your mom a legal copy the morning she died."

"You think the killer took the will?" Why was Phillipa sending it to Mom? What was *in* the damn thing?

"Unless you did," Garcia said.

"What?"

"Did you touch that envelope?"

"No."

"Or anything else?"

"No," I said, peeking at him and hoping he wouldn't notice. "Not really."

"Not really?" He stared hard at me. "You are familiar with the idea of tampering with evidence? Of messing with the integrity of a crime scene?"

I took another large bite of the burger and began picking at a piece of nail on my little finger.

"What aren't you telling me?" he said.

"I took a picture," I said, expecting him to yell at me.

He leaned back. "What kind of picture?"

"Black and white . . . from the fifties, maybe. It had Mom and Phillipa and a man I didn't recognize." I sneaked another look at him, not long enough to read his face. "I didn't think it was important."

"Then why did you take it?"

"For sentimental reasons. Mom looked happy, carefree. . . . I haven't seen her look like that in years . . . ever." I smashed a fry with my finger. "And I thought it might help her deal with Phillipa's death." I picked up my fork and smashed another fry; it was kind of therapeutic—plus, it gave me a reason not to look up. "I didn't think there was anything wrong with taking it. I didn't know she'd been murdered. Remember?"

He sighed and pushed his plate of food to the middle of the table. "Where was it when you found it?"

"On the floor, near one of her hands."

Detective Garcia closed his eyes and shook his head slowly. His lips resembled wire. "Let me see it."

"I don't have it here. It's at home."

When he opened his eyes again, they held no anger—just disappointment. "You make sure I get it before tomorrow."

"I'm sorry," I said.

"It doesn't matter what you are," he said. "You lied to me and that makes me wonder what else you've lied about."

I wanted to say "nothing," but that wasn't true. I still had those pictures I'd taken with my digital camera. Ah, crap. Should I tell him?

He pulled his plate back and began to eat again. Mouth full, he said, "Your mother's right—she's going to inherit a lot of money from Miss Petty."

While not conciliatory, his tone eased my stomach pains. I digested the info along with the rest of my burger, then started working on the fries and milkshake again. A child's high-pitched giggle sounded behind me.

"Tain, tain," the kid said.

"Chugga, chugga, chugga," said an adult.

The child responded, "Toot, toot."

I shuddered and with a jerk turned to look at the youngster. She returned my gaze with a shy smile.

"What?" said Garcia. "What is it?"

"Nothing." *Toot.* Trains.

"You okay? You just lost all your color."

"I'm fine," I said, troubled by the coincidence.

A man, his light-blond hair fashioned in a buzz cut, stopped at our table. He wore work clothes and a leer for both of us. With an age-spotted hand on Garcia's shoulder, he said, "Moises, aren't you supposed to be working?"

"I am," said the policeman. "More than you, anyway."

The man winked at me. "Lunch with a pretty young woman? That's work?"

"You're just jealous," Garcia said.

"I'm too old to be jealous." They both laughed, gave each other a hearty *abrazo*. The man went to the register to pay. By the time the detective's attention returned to me, I'd decided that my obsession with words that sounded like "to" was just that—another stupid obsession.

"Where were we?" he said.

"Mom and her magnificent memory," I said.

"It's better than you think," he said.

"Maybe. But it's ninety percent mush."

"Have you seen her today?"

"I haven't been home yet. I spent the night here."

"With Peter O'Neill," said Garcia.

"Adjacent to Peter. Not with him. Separate rooms," I said. "How'd you know that?"

"This is a small town. People talk."

"It's against the law to have dinner with a man?" Now I was irritated.

"Of course not." The detective waved his white napkin in fake surrender. "But I figure if you have time for pleasure, you can make time for more important things."

"Like what?"

"We're back to your mother."

"We've gone over this already."

"My request still stands."

"So does my response," I said. "Look. I'll talk to Paul. He's there most of the time, anyway."

"Ah, but I know *you*."

"I'll call Paul and introduce you," I said.

Garcia flicked his wrist to expose a watch, the old wind-up kind, and blew out a lungful of air. "Gotta go. Call me later." He picked up the check and the ten-dollar bill I held out for him. After paying, the detective turned to nod a curt goodbye.

"You going to be available when I call?" I said.

"I'll drop everything the minute you ring," he said on his way out the door. "Don't forget that picture."

twenty-six

IF YOU WAIT A couple of breaths in a small town, you're bound to run into someone you know. Or, in this case, someone ran into me—literally.

I hadn't noticed Nick Hutchins enter the noisy restaurant until he bumped into my table. My back was to the door and I'd been too busy concentrating on what to do next. Funny how circumstances sometimes oblige.

"Hello," I said. "Would you like to join me?"

"Looks like you're done," he said.

"I need a little dessert."

"Well then, I don't mind if I do." Dressed in a flannel shirt and worn jeans with a prehistoric belt cinched around his thin waist, Cherry Hutchins's husband made eye contact with the waitress. She nodded and started to pour coffee into a mug.

"Can I have a piece of the chocolate cake?" I asked when she came to our table. Mr. Hutchins watched me. "How're Cherry and the Artists Guild?"

"Fine. Just fine," he said with a finality that threatened to bury our conversation under a layer of discomfort.

"Mr. Hutchins—"

"Nick."

"Nick." I paused. "So, how long have you lived in Belen?"

"Forever."

"You grew up here? What was it like when you were a kid?"

"Smaller. Friendlier. Everybody knew everybody then." He poured cream into his coffee and added a packet of fake sugar. "I don't know."

"Did you know Miss Petty when she was a kid?"

"We're . . . we were . . . the same age. We went to school together from kindergarten on up. I knew her brother, too. And all of her parents."

"*All* of her parents?"

"Her dad divorced her mom. Married a couple more times after that."

I let that soak in for a minute. "Where does her brother live?"

"He died a few years ago. Funny thing, too. He was a priest."

Nick was full of useful tidbits. What if Phillipa had some other relative—someone no one had thought about for years—who wanted her money? Maybe the brother had had kids before he became a priest. Maybe he became a priest because of his blasphemous sister. I bet his kids would have hated their wealthy aunt. What would Garcia think of that?

". . . I even knew *your* mom way back when," Nick was saying when I tuned back in.

"My mom? But she came from Chicago."

"She used to pal around with Philly and her crowd." He smiled at the waitress when she brought our food. "Thanks, Sarah."

"Did you spend time with them, too?" I assessed my cake—it was a much smaller piece than I'd been served before. Fewer calories. Maybe I *could* lose some weight before seeing Peter again.

"Me? No." He took a bite of his grilled cheese sandwich. "But years ago, before you were born, your mother used to come down at least a few times a week. Boy, she was sure a looker back then." He opened his sandwich and put in a couple of potato chips, took another bite that crunched, and then added some more.

"What was she like?"

"Philly or your mom?"

"Both, I guess." I started in on the frosting—with a spoon.

"Well, your mother was young, pretty, and full of ideas. She was a real regular here, for many years."

"When did she stop coming?" A wonderful, rich smell distracted me—homemade red-chile sauce—it's almost as good as the smell of roasting green chiles. Sarah served platefuls of enchiladas to the people at the table next to us. Even though I'd already had lunch, I felt hungry again. Hungry for more than a measly piece of cake.

"It was the summer after that writer moved here for good. The famous one. The drinker."

"Jerome Whitaker?"

The air pressure in the restaurant changed. Nick looked toward the door. I twisted around. Ernie Merkin had walked in. A wake of silence followed the man, and something else, something malignant. If I'd been with Darnda, she would have commented on his aura—probably the color of week-old roadkill.

"Do you know Mr. Merkin?" I jutted my chin in his direction.

"Sure I do. I worked with him for years."

"On the railroad?"

Nick nodded, his mouth full. "At one time, it was the best job for men who wanted to make decent money."

"Did you like it?" Without it's gushy topping, the cake didn't appeal. Too dry. It needed whipped cream or warm fudge sauce. I cut it into pieces with my fork, playing with it like a kid.

Nick shrugged. "It was okay. Hard on my family, though."

"Would you mind if I asked you a few questions?"

"That's what you've been doing, isn't it?" Though he said it gently enough, I could tell this interview was almost over.

"I'd like to ask about the Harvey House. Would that be all right?"

"Cherry has her heart set on the art museum."

"What do *you* think?"

"What Cherry wants, I want." He added the slices of dill pickle to his sandwich.

"If Cherry wasn't in the Artists Guild, would you still support the art museum?"

"Nope."

"Because . . ."

"Miss Solomon, I'm not a religious man, but I don't make fun of other people's religions, either. It's as simple as that. Phillipa's art is disrespectful." He finished his food and coffee. "Doesn't the world have enough disrespect as it is?"

Merkin left a minute later with a takeout bag. Nick watched him go.

"Mr. Merkin isn't particularly enthusiastic about the train museum idea," I said, following his gaze.

Nick grunted. "Ernie doesn't like much of anything."

"Do you think the train museum could fly?"

His lips twitched. "Funny choice of words."

I rolled my eyes. "You know what I mean. Do you think it has a chance of succeeding if the art museum is a no-go?"

"Sure. There're a lot of people out there that love trains. They're part of our American heritage, you know." He drank his water. "You spiffy up that building, put a few good-looking gals in there, have 'em serve wholesome food, and make people feel welcome. I think it has a good chance." He shook his head. "Don't you go telling Cherry I said that."

"I wouldn't dream of it."

"That's right," he said. "Because I won't let anything or anyone hurt my Cherry."

twenty-seven

BY THE TIME MY car rolled into St. Kate's parking lot, my mood had darkened to a sewer brown. It stank, too. I felt like everyone wanted something from me—Garcia, Mom, Darnda, even Peter—and I couldn't satisfy any of them. And then there was the no-start job in Belen. I'd made negligible progress, considering the time I'd dedicated to it.

Bad attitude. Lousy disposition. A rotten way to start a visit with Mom.

Through the automatic doors, down the hallway, I paid special attention to the old people today. Sure, Nick Hutchins was still vigorous. But the warehoused men and women here lay in dingy beds and half-sat in dull scuffed wheelchairs. Frail, life-drained, and expressionless, their minds and bodies betrayed them. Growing old was the pits.

"Consider the alternative," was one of Darnda's favorite sayings. Stepping past a woman strapped into her chair, the large veins on her arms the most colorful thing about her, I wondered if the alternative was so bad after all.

"Sasha?" a Russian-accented voice said at my side.

"Paul, just the person I was looking for," I said. "How are you?"

"Have you seen your mama?" Mom's boyfriend wore a blazer and pressed slacks, his tie a solid navy blue. He looked unusually weary, as if he'd left half his spunk at home.

"I just got here," I said, walking with him toward her room.

"Ms. Solomon?" The voice was female, unfamiliar, and nervous.

"Yes?"

A taupe-suited woman approached us, wearing her officiousness like perfume. Hospital administrator, for sure. Eyes looking this way and that, her manner overwrought, a trapped bird bumping against an invisible cage.

"You're Sasha Solomon?"

"None other."

"Susan McGuire."

I shook her moist, extended hand. The woman waited a beat before coughing.

"And this is my mother's friend, Paul Katz," I said.

She nodded but didn't shake his hand, then looked at me. "May we speak alone?"

"Sure." I turned to Paul. "Excuse us for a minute?"

"I'll wait in Hannah's room," he said.

I knew his expression from past experience—worry masqueraded as docility. He unfolded an afternoon newspaper and cocked his head to urge me to follow the bureaucrat.

Her thick heels thumped on the linoleum. Good solid shoes. The kind I imagined prison matrons might wear. She unlocked a door marked "Authorized Personnel Only." Inside, semi-stocked shelves of hospital supplies stood floor-to-ceiling tall.

"Sorry for the impromptu office," she said.

"No problem," I said.

She picked up a cellophane-wrapped bed pad off the floor and stuffed it into a shelf. "Now, don't be alarmed. Your mother seems to have gone AWOL again." She said it almost like a joke. Ha, ha, isn't your mom just a silly old goose?

"What? This is the second time in two days!" Zing! There went my blood pressure. "What the hell is going on? Can't you keep track of your own patients."

"They're *residents*, Ms. Solomon, not patients."

"You're arguing semantics with me?" I took a breath. "How long has she been missing this time?"

"Since this morning. We've been trying to reach you." She pulled a piece of paper from one of her skirt pockets. "This is your number, isn't it?"

"That's my home phone. Didn't you have my cell number?"

Pause. It was like we were on a ten-second delay.

"We left messages," she said.

I retrieved the little phone from my purse. "Look at this. See? This is supposed to flash if there's a message. Plus, I've had it on all morning. No one tried to call me. Don't lie to me." I jammed the cell back into its hiding place.

"Calm down," she said. "She's probably gone out with one of her friends again."

Possible, but improbable. "Why didn't you call Paul?"

"He's not family."

"Of course he is. What is this? Some kind of new policy? Mrs. Sanchez—the old administrator—didn't object to calling him."

"Didn't you read our new policy statement?"

"Is it your policy to lose your residents?"

She winced.

I began to pace. Pause. I understood her hesitation now. She balanced everything she said against a possible lawsuit.

"That was uncalled for," she said. "Your mother has a history of wandering off by herself."

"Two times does not a history make. Plus, she can barely walk." I know my face was red. My underarms felt wet and uncomfortable.

"Her walker's missing." Another cough. McGuire sounded like I had when I'd been poisoned. Well, she should be coughing; she should be choking. I considered helping her with option number two.

"How can you keep letting this happen?" I looked around the room as if it could give me an answer.

"Your mother is an adult, Ms. Solomon. She has the right to leave if she chooses. Blaming us won't solve the problem." McGuire should have sounded sorrier, more upset. Worried, at least. Her false banality was laced with the kind of pseudo-patience she must have used to manage her charges. We looked at each other for a solid two minutes.

"Exactly *when* did someone realize Mom wasn't here?" I said.

McGuire removed a white hair from the sleeve of her jacket. "A nurse noticed she was gone when she came on shift this morning."

"Who?"

"Rita—"

"Where's Rita?"

"She's on the floor taking care of patients."

"Who's looking for Mom?"

"We have people on it."

"So, what should I do? Call the police?" I said. "I'll call the police."

"There's no need for that yet," she said.

"None of your staff noticed a frail old lady leaving the place?"

"This is not a restricted facility." Oh, she was definitely handling me.

"No, but it's supposed to be a *safe* facility. A secure one."

Her pregnant pause could have birthed sextuplets. "Ms. Solomon, we tried to call you several times." Snitty.

"You didn't try very hard," I said. "You're acting like none of this is your responsibility."

"Your mother *is* of sound mind, isn't she?"

"You know she's not."

"We're not a restricted facility." McGuire needed a better PR person if that's what she'd been instructed to repeat. Her object here should have been to make me happy—at least show some sincere emotion—not defend her little fiefdom.

"We're not doing any good here," I said, tugging my shirt down and preparing for action.

"We're doing everything we can."

"Oh, please. You didn't even try my cell phone. No one bothered to call Paul. Don't give me that crap." I headed back to Mom's room.

If I wanted to see real emotion, I got it there. Paul balanced on the edge of Mom's bed. Rita, pallid and flustered, sat next to him. Both rose when I entered. The room smelled fresh, like someone had wiped away my mother's very existence with disinfectant.

"Any news?" said Rita.

"Nothing," I said, pushing the phone toward Paul. "They're acting like this is our fault. Paul, can you call everyone you know who might have decided to give Mom a ride? Start with Gilda."

He nodded and began to dial, then said, "Why didn't they call me, Sasha? I told your mama I wouldn't be in until this afternoon. I had a funeral this morning, then lunch with Irv. I could have been here right away. Why didn't they call?"

"Some stupid new policy, Paul. We'll straighten it out later," I said. "All that matters now is finding Mom."

"She's all right," said Rita, patting my hand to comfort herself. "I can feel it."

Paul's face had lost what little color it normally possessed. I could see each broken capillary, pale childhood scars, the purple line of a recent skin cancer biopsy.

He noticed me watching him, shook his head, and hung up the phone. "Where could she be, Sasha?"

The hours dribbled by. Rita had been called back to work by an irritated Mrs. McGuire.

Evening came.

So did Mom, dressed in one of her Chinese scholar's robes. A young man in a peach-colored uniform pushed her in a wheelchair.

"Where have you been?" I said, my anxiety ember-hot.

The attendant removed Mother's slippers and helped her into bed. "I'll see about getting you some food, Mrs. Solomon. Okay?"

"That'd be nice, Oliver," she said.

He shook his head and pointed to his nametag: Frank.

Paul put his arm around Mom. "Hannah, we were so worried."
"Why?"

"We didn't know where you were," he said.

"I told everyone I was going to the gallery," she said. "I couldn't miss Philly's opening."

"Oh, Mother," I said.

twenty-eight

"SASHA." RITA NABBED ME in the lobby. She wore a thin raincoat and one of those net scarves that older women use to keep their hairdos fresh. In her hand curled an old *People* magazine, its cover torn.

"Have you been here this whole time?" I noticed the chair she'd been sitting in. The indentation looked permanent.

"I went out to dinner but couldn't get your mama out of my mind. I kept calling from the restaurant to see if she'd shown up." Rita lowered her voice. "I didn't want to go back on the floor—politics, you know—and I knew you'd come out eventually." Rita sat back down and I joined her. "I'm so glad she's all right. Could she tell you where she went?"

I shook my head, the tears less than a breath away. "I don't know how much longer I can take this."

"As long as it takes," said Rita. She put the magazine in a large bag. I caught a glimpse of multicolored yarn, thick needles.

"You knit?" I said.

"Have for years." She snapped the bag shut. "As a matter of fact, your mama has helped me with a couple of projects while she's been here." Rita smiled. "I just love that woman. She's so much fun."

"You're talking about my mom, right? Hannah Solomon?"

"Oh, stop it." Rita chuckled. "Just the other day, she was telling me about her friend down in Belen, that artist, and all the adventures they used to get into. I sure wish I could have known her then."

"Yeah, me too," I said. The lobby had grown darker since we'd started talking. A teenage girl—nose pierced, earlobes plugged—sulked past us, followed by an older woman.

"Didn't your mama tell me you're working down there in Belen right now?" said Rita.

"I'm surprised she remembered."

Before Rita could respond, a scratchy recording announced the end of visitors' hours. We both stood up.

At the door, I said, "Rita, I don't know if I've told you this before . . . but I really appreciate all you do for Mom."

"I know that, honey."

We stepped out into the cool evening. The mountains stood a deep and silent blue. One pale pink contrail was visible to the west.

"Did you know that artist, Mom's friend, is dead now?" I said walking her to her car. "I keep having to tell her, over and over again."

The nurse's aide sighed. "This world just isn't fair, is it?"

We hugged goodbye. The lonely parking lot echoed our mutual melancholia. I tooted my horn at her before turning left onto the street.

At home, Leo's absence seemed like a benediction—a respite from unpredictability. I kicked off my shoes, hissed at my answering machine with its frantic blinking, and went straight to the bar for a scotch. This wasn't the day for abstinence. I poured a generous splash. Then another. Found an old ice cube in a bowl in the back of the freezer. The photo of Mom accused me from the refrigerator's door. I went back to the front room with it, feeling incredibly sad, lonely, for the woman Mom had been before my birth.

Paul and I hadn't been able to get any valid information from Mom. She'd gibbered about going to Belen, seeing Phillipa and other old friends, having a burger at the White Way. All a mishmash of fantasies and memories. I wasn't convinced she'd even left St. Kate's. It was just as possible she'd wandered into a room and had been sitting there—in her own little world—for hours. I didn't think Mrs. McGuire would ever tell me the truth—even if she discovered it.

Unsettled, I plopped onto the couch—and saw Peter's ruby glistening like an angry zit right where I'd left it the day before. Cute, smart guy. The only problem was, well, he was a man and men were pretty low on my list at the moment. I picked up the ruby and weighed it in my hand. My bank account had about fifty cents in it. My IRA . . . what IRA? Think again. How much would a nice-size ruby bring at a jewelry store? A pawn shop? Though the futon felt good, I got up to find the yellow pages and turned to the section listing local appraisers. There was one on Lomas, fairly close to my house.

What am I doing? It's not mine.

On the couch once more, I moaned with the frustration of the past few days. I'd lied—more then once. I'd impersonated a reporter to get information. I'd taken evidence from the scene of a crime. This behavior, all of it, reeked.

Maybe my New Age doctor could prescribe a pill for honesty or, better yet, a pill that could give me some insights. Hell, I didn't want insights! I wanted to delete the last few days. To take back everything from the moment before I'd discovered Phillipa Petty's prone body.

One scotch down, a fresh one in hand.

Two hours later, I sat in a tepid bubble bath, the water murky with dirt, soap, and sorrow. I'd descended into the kind of funk reserved for true self-loathers. The phone rang twice during the plummet. I thought I heard Detective Garcia; he wasn't worth getting out of the tub for. Spasmodic beeps from the answering machine indicated that the message tape had hit its end once again. Those couldn't all be calls from St. Kate's.

A more likely scenario: Leo had stepped on the machine out of vengeance for my lack of attention. It'd be just like him to act out. Another man. Well, another male, at least. Men. My pale blue hands and feet were ridged and creased in white from sitting too long in the tub, an alien topography. I ran, nude, to the front room. More scotch. Back to the tub.

Leo sauntered into the bathroom, took one look at my face, and left.

I sank underneath the water, moved my head back and forth, and felt the wonder of longish hair pulling against the liquid. Eyes open again, I studied the cracks in the ceiling and a line of mildew arching its way along one edge.

Waitaminute. How'd Leo get in?

In one motion, I leaped out of the bath and grabbed a towel, wrapping it like a dress around my body.

"Leo?" I said. "Where are you, kitty?"

Leaving wet puddles on the cool brick floor, I ventured from room to room, searching for the cat. Not on my bed. Not on the couch. Not under the couch. The towel came undone. I tightened it.

"Tuuuuuuunaaaaaa," I sang, trying to entice him. "Fresh tuuunaaa."

In the kitchen, the door to my patio stood wide open. Dizzy from the scotch, I stared at it. In the interim, Leo slinked into the room and circled close to me. With his sandpaper tongue, he licked my wet leg, rubbed against it, purring, waiting.

He walked to his bowl, sat down, and looked at me. When I didn't move, he came back, repeated the rub-purr routine, and returned to his bowl.

"What? You think I'm going to give you fresh tuna?" I said. "When have I ever given you fresh tuna?"

On his next pass at my leg, he bent as if to lick my foot. Instead, he bit my big toe.

"Hey!" I said.

He moseyed back to the bowl. I could almost hear him thinking, "Stupid human. What's it gonna take for you to perform?"

I opened a can of smoked oysters for him. Pushed the door closed and tried to remember if I'd opened it when I'd gotten home. Had I really been distracted enough to have done it without realizing? No, the lock needed lubing; working it required intent. Plus, the evenings were cool enough I wouldn't want to hike up my first few heating bills of the season.

Leo growled when I removed some of the oysters from his bowl. I rinsed them in the sink and made appetizers with a pack of crackers I found in a drawer—must've pocketed them from a salad bar. In the living room, sitting on the couch, I thought about eating something else. The can of salmon might still be okay. The crackers weren't too stale. There was always whipped cream.

The wet towel fell off when I changed my position. With critical eyes, I surveyed my body—pouching stomach, too many freckles on my arms. Middle age. I frowned. More red mole things had spouted on my thighs since yesterday's shower. My toenails needed cutting.

Stop being paranoid. I must have opened the door.

I pulled the towel back on, happy to look at its cheetah design rather than my unloved body.

Nothing to worry about, I told myself. *Everything's fine.*

Great. Things were great. Really. Couldn't be better. Mom was safe. Oh my God!

The ruby was gone.

twenty-nine

MY CALL TO THE Albuquerque Police Department's non-emergency number elicited apathetic questions from a female clerk.

"Look, someone broke into my house, while I was in the bathtub," I said, trying to convince her to at least pretend to be interested.

"And they stole a ruby," she said. "And it wasn't yours."

"I know it sounds ridiculous, but the real crime was the breaking-in part. Not what was stolen."

"I'll send an officer," she said. "It might be a while."

Gee. "Thanks."

I dressed in a respectable black sweat suit, one with no holes. Ate the can of salmon straight—no dishes, no crackers. Took a few drags on the can of whipped cream. And waited. And fell asleep.

Leo's claws dug into my chest with the policeman's first knock. The cat scrambled toward the back door, no doubt thinking it might still be open. Thud. I heard him grunt when he hit it. Any other time it would have been funny. Oh, what the hell? I laughed. Then I filled my lungs with as much air as I could, released it in a satisfying huff, and opened the door.

The uniformed policeman entered, eyes already narrowed.

"You alone?" he said.

"Yessir."

"Anyone else here?"

"No, sir. I'm alone."

He put a hand on the television. "I thought I heard laughter."

I remained silent. The last thing I wanted was for him to think I was nuts.

He stopped to look at me. "Show me the door."

We walked through the living room. I pointed to the couch's wide arm. "That's where the ruby was."

"What kind of ruby?"

"A really big one," I said, thumb and index finger shaped in an O. "Like this big. It wasn't mine. I was taking care of it for a friend." We'd come into the kitchen. I unlocked the back door and showed him how much it had stood open.

"Why were—" He stopped himself. "You're sure you didn't leave it open?"

"I'm sure."

He surveyed my messy space—the empty can on the counter, the unwashed dishes in the sink, the single oyster in Leo's bowl. "Well, it doesn't look like forced entry."

"I didn't *let* anyone in."

"Who else has a key?"

"My landlady."

"You talk to her about this?"

"No. But she didn't do it."

He lowered his pad and pen. Shook his head. "How do you know that?"

"She would have said something or called my name," I said. "She wouldn't have just come in and taken the ruby."

"Is it possible the *friend* you were keeping the ruby for stopped by and your landlady let the person in?"

"No, it's not possible."

His gaze landed on the bottle of Glenlivet. I could feel him judge me against it. My credibility plunged as he focused on papers strewed on floor and tabletop, the two pairs of panties and a bra hanging from the Nordic Track.

"Aren't you going to dust for fingerprints?" I said.

"I don't think it'd be much help." He peeked into the darkness outside the door, saw the fake rock in the pot next to it. "You keep a key in that rock?"

"Yes."

"Check and see if it's still there."

I did. "Oh, no."

"You'd better change your locks first thing tomorrow morning," he said, frowning.

"I'll do that."

It was ten when the officer left. Three policemen in a day, enough to make anyone stop for reflection.

Who could have taken the key? Peter? *God, I hope not.* Only one way to find out. I dialed his number and let it ring five, six times. I thought about calling Poison Control, but stopped. People with real problems needed those lines open; plus I wasn't sure I wanted to tell Peter his gemstone was gone—or find out he'd taken it without asking.

Should I go to a motel tonight? I pouted in the living room. Then moved the Nordic Track to block the front door. I pouted in the kitchen. Then moved the table and chairs to block the back door. At least I'd hear it if someone tried to break in—this time.

Bone tired and brain weary, I grabbed Leo—incurring a scratch in protestation—and went to bed.

thirty

MORNING CAME IN WITH a snicker.

My head hurt. My body had a teeter-totter queasiness that worked its way into every nerve ending. For some reason, my eyes squinted reflexively with each quick glance out the window. I couldn't keep them open.

My lousy mood had intensified through the night. The only thing to do, before I became totally inert from self-flagellation and self-pity, was to cram my day so full of work I wouldn't have time for anything else.

Interviews. It'd be a magnificent day for interviews. I could ask open-ended questions and let other people think for me. Taking notes wouldn't be too difficult once I'd had seven or eight cups of coffee.

Professional autopilot has its advantages. In less than an hour, I'd called Josie to ask her to change the locks and had set up three interviews. I also planned to stop by Ernie Merkin's for a little chat about Phillipa. There, my day would be exhausting, but at least I'd feel like I was doing something positive, forward moving—money generating.

Then, if time allowed, I'd go hang out at Mom's and see what ditties might emerge from her fantasy world. That'd put me in good with Garcia.

As to the missing ruby, I hadn't worked out an explanation yet. But I kept thinking about Peter and wondering if he'd let himself in and had taken it. I could imagine him not wanting to disturb me—wanting to respect my request about waiting. Still, if that were the answer, it gave me the creeps.

I used a black magic marker to color in the scuffs on my high heels and clear nail polish to stop the run in my knee-highs. My mother's discarded pantsuit fit well enough, though I had to use a safety pin because one of the hooks had come off the slacks. No problem. The top was a sort of tunic thing with a loud enough design that no one would pay attention to the outfit's other flaws.

Four cups of coffee bullied my woozy brain cells into coherence. Crackers topped with whipped cream would have to hold me until I found something in Belen. The carbo and caffeine buzz ratcheted up my energy level more than I'd thought possible.

I tried Darnda again, to tell her about the appointment with Karen Kilgore and to see if we could squeeze in an hour for media coaching before the interview. Of course, she didn't pick up her phone. I left a message and told her to call me as soon as she got it. I didn't know how we'd accomplish what we needed to do, but I wasn't going to let her crash and burn.

The file I'd created for my friend bulged with ideas and when I pulled it out of the cabinet, I felt guilty about how little time I'd devoted to her project since the Belen thing had come up. Well, I'd be done in a few days and could focus more on her and my other miscellaneous clients. Speaking of other clients, I was scheduled to go back to Clovis in a couple of weeks to train their newbie PR hire and to help with the groundbreaking of a museum I'd proposed.

"What are you looking at?" I said to Leo. He'd perched on the couch and followed me with only his eyes. I tested it. Only when he absolutely couldn't see me did he turn his head. "I'll be back before you know it."

He twitched his tail and left the room. I put out a bowl of fresh water for him, replaced the oyster with some dry food, then did a double check on all the doors. The house secure, most of my work in the car, I headed back to the Hub City.

The drive got faster with each trip. I had to remember to keep my PR hat on, to see the various marketing points along the way. Maybe today would be a good time to take a short trip south of Belen to check out what a visitor from Houston or Phoenix might see coming north on I-25. If the interviews turned out to be duds, that could be plan B.

On an impulse, I swerved off at the Los Lunas exit and stopped by the state police station. Garcia wasn't there. Relieved, I left the envelope with Mom's picture with the receptionist. Then *vroom vroom*, back onto the freeway.

My first appointment was with Wallace Crawson, a retired railroad engineer whose name had been on Mayor Flores's short list. Crawson had been pleasant on the phone, happy to talk with me. He lived in Rio Communities, like Ernie Merkin, but *west* of Highway 47—near the country club.

Location, location, location, *baby*. While Merkin's yard mimicked landfill, Crawson's donned mosaic stepping stones cutting across a browning lawn of groomed Kentucky bluegrass. The path led to over-size bronze doors. While Merkin's house scowled in disrepair, Crawson's two-story confection sported nary a crack in its blonde brick façade. I'd call the building early McMansion, complete with Doric columns and a front entrance designed for Zeus's dad.

My outfit felt leisure-suit tacky in these surroundings. Perhaps I should enter through the back door. Instead, I pressed the front bell and released a carillon version of "I've Been Working on the Railroad." Of course.

A middle-aged Hispanic woman, dressed in a black maid's uniform with white apron, opened the door. I handed her my card. She nodded and led me to a sunroom that smelled so good my mouth watered and I had to swallow hard.

"Mr. Crawson will be with you in a moment," she said. "Would you like a croissant?"

"That would be lovely. Thank you," I said, hoping I hadn't drooled.

"Would you like some coffee?"

"Thank you. I would."

The strong drink had an almond kick. The thick cream hinted of chocolate. Even before Crawson came into the room, I was in love. A minute later, he clicked down the hallway, his shoes bearing cleats. "No, no. Please don't get up. I'm sorry to be late," he said. "I thought I could get a few holes in before you came." Solid gray hair and a sun-bronzed face to match his doors, Crawson had eyes as green as fresh peas. He wore a subdued golf outfit, beige and tan and, alas, plaid.

"I see Maria has taken care of you. I'll just change my shoes and be right with you," he said.

Maria must've been listening through the intercom. She came in carrying a silver tray and placed a plate laden with a dozen golden pastries before me. The china set had a stylized gold "C" in each ceramic center. A four-inch square of butter covered the letter on the smaller plate. Two cut-crystal bowls of jam with sterling spoons—yes, they had the "C," too—completed the spread.

It's not that my early-morning queasiness had settled, it's that the food looked so good. I ate the first croissant recklessly, crumbs dotting my outfit and flaking to the floor. Crawson returned halfway through my second one. Thank goodness I was consuming it with more decorum.

"Thank you for agreeing to meet me on such short notice."

"The pleasure's all mine, I assure you," he said, circumventing my next bite of pastry with a power handshake—two-handed and solid. "Anyone who's going to help put the Harvey House to good use is a friend of mine."

136

I didn't want to take notes; I wanted to finish this croissant and have another. The butter was unsalted and the orange marmalade just bitter enough.

"Pardon my asking, but how have your interviews gone so far?" he said.

"They've been interesting." I wiped my hands on the cloth napkin and picked up my pen.

"That's a safe word, isn't it? *Interesting*. Doesn't give me any information at all." He was affable enough, but I wouldn't want to have to negotiate with him. I bet he sharpened his claws on anyone who crossed him.

"Well, I've met someone who's supposed to care who couldn't care less," I said. "Another person who makes the artists look like a bunch of biddies. And a dead woman. I stand by *interesting*. Wouldn't you?"

"Given those, I would, too," he said. "Too bad about Miss Petty."

"Did you know her?"

"Only to say hello, to nod at, at a Rotary meeting."

"She went to Rotary?" Phillipa and Rotary didn't fit in the same sentence.

"As a guest. She wasn't a member herself, of course."

"What was she like?"

"Quiet at the meetings, not much to interest her there, really. Just a bunch of geezers talking business. I never understood why she came in the first place." He cut his croissant in three equal pieces, buttered them in sequence, and arranged them in a line.

"What do you think of her art?" I said.

"I don't care for it," he said. "It's not my definition of art."

He measured exactly one silver teaspoon of strawberry jam onto each piece, making sure it stayed in its order, part of a regiment of slathered pastries. Crawson, the jelly tactician.

"What is?" I said.

"Allow me to show you."

I followed him into a gentleman's study complete with country fireplace, wood paneling. An Anglophile's dream. Above the mantelpiece hung a large oil painting of an English hunting scene—horses trotting, dogs scampering, men dressed in goofy jodhpurs and tweed jackets with their crops raised ready to whack some poor animal. A hint of mist rose over the valley where the hunting party rode.

"That's art," he said. "Or, this."

Off we went into another room, its walls hung with portraits of people better left unpainted. They all had the stodgy air of old money and too much inbreeding. Fish-eyed, cheeks red-stained rather than rosy, the women's scowls made no attempt at smiles. Men frowning with superiority, their faces pasty pale and strained. All looked as if being caught in a portrait was beneath them.

"That's art," Crawson said again, now leading me back to the sunroom.

All that aristocracy made me hungry. I attacked another croissant.

"Solomon. That's Jewish, isn't it?" he said.

"It's Russian."

"Jewish, though. Right?"

"Yes."

"We had a brakeman named Solomon. Jim Solomon. First Jew I ever met on a train who wasn't a hobo. You any relation?"

"I don't think so," I said, writing to avoid his eyes.

"It was back in nineteen-seventy, seventy-one. We had a shortage of young men willing to work. The war, you know." Crawson trisected another croissant. "As I recall he was a good worker, that Jew."

"It's part of our ethic. Doing a good job." From the décor and the "art," the last thing I'd expected was this level of provincialism.

"Good workers. Yes. I'd heard that somewhere about your people," he said.

My stomach flip-flopped. I turned the page in my notebook and prepared for another stellar interview.

thirty-one

"WE'D FINANCE THE TRAIN museum from private donations to start," Crawson said, many minutes later. "We've already secured several hundred thousand here in Belen. When we start to really kick in on the fundraising, I'm sure we'll be able to get more."

"Who'd manage the museum?" I asked mainly to keep myself awake. Bombastic rhetoric coupled with a good breakfast can be lethal to concentration. I half expected him to pull out a cigar and develop catarrh.

"To start, it'd be a consortium." He sipped his coffee, right pinky extended. "Those of us who front the initial investment."

"Would you be able to use the Fred Harvey name for the restaurant?"

"We've been in contact with the family. I'm sure some kind of arrangement could be made." He rubbed his thumb and first two fingers together. "Most people understand this."

Subtle, very subtle. I had to be civil to this guy, but he'd begun to bug me. Okay, I'll admit it. I stopped liking him a while back. "What's the average age of a train enthusiast?"

"Are you thinking about the elevator problem at the building? That American Disabilities idiocy? We think we can get around it," he said.

"Actually, I'm wondering if it'll draw younger people, too. If you'll be able to grow an audience from newer generations instead of depending on people who have fond memories of the old Fred Harvey restaurants."

"You're young and you sound like you do."

"I loved the old Alvarado Hotel in Albuquerque. My mom used to take me there for lunch." I thought about the waitress who'd always given me extra cherries in my Shirley Temple—and those little paper umbrellas. "I had my first lobster at the Fred Harvey restaurant at the airport ages ago."

"And I bet the food and service were superb," he said. "Maria!"

She came in and cleared our plates and remnants from breakfast. Out of her apron came a silver-handled crumb brush to clean the tablecloth.

"I remember the magic of the Alvarado," I said. "And the lobster. He was the only living one Mom could find in the whole city. He looked tired—with his single claw—and he limped. But he tasted good to me."

Maria returned with new plates, mother-of-pearl-handled fruit knives, and a bowl of apples and oranges. Crawson took an orange, cut circles in the skin at top and bottom, then vertical lines at exact half-inch intervals.

I didn't dare crunch into an apple. Maybe if he left the room I could stick one in my purse for later.

"What else do you want to know?" he said, peeling the perfect strips off the citrus.

"Is it accurate to assume trains attract an older crowd?"

"Why does this matter?"

"For your audience. I'm looking at Belen and trying to see it through the eyes of your primary customers." I took a deep breath to enjoy the orange's fragrance, fresh and sweet.

"Good idea."

"So, are they older?"

"I'd say so. Most above fifty."

"Do you think there's enough of a younger crowd to keep it going when this generation is gone?"

He made little cuts in the membrane of each piece and removed the seeds that had dared to grow there.

"I think we can cultivate an audience," he said. "That's one of the reasons for the overnight concept. We'll lure the older folks in with the trains. The younger ones will come for the novelty of it. And there's always Ernestine."

"Who's she?"

"Our ghost."

"I've heard about her. But not by name." I picked up an orange and contemplated the knife trick. "Have you seen her?"

He spread his orange pieces into a flower pattern and leaned back in his chair. Eyes intense, lips pressed, he appeared to be assessing me, deciding if I was worthy of his next comment. I just hoped it wasn't about Jews again.

"My wife sees her," he said.

"Really? That's great." I put down the orange. "May I speak with her sometime?"

"Why not now?" Did I detect relief in his voice? "She's at the club."

I looked at my notes. The ghost angle tickled me; it'd be fun to work. Also, I had a hunch it'd yield a bigger audience than the train contingent realized. "Great. There's only one thing that bothers me about people actually staying at the Harvey House."

"The noise," he said.

I nodded.

"We've thought about that. Older folks don't sleep much anyway. No, no." He held a finger up to stop my interruption. "I know we can't depend on that. We've spoken with an architect and a window expert to see how to soundproof or minimize the noise."

"And what did she say?" *Feminine singular. Let's see what he does with that.*

It was the only time I saw the man look discombobulated, neck slightly back, eyes confused—but he regained control quickly. "There are many things we can do. Will do. *If* the proposal's approved."

"What about all the shaking? When those trains pass, the whole building moves," I said.

"Not a problem. For an enthusiast, that's part of the excitement. Sheer locomotive power. It's an awesome thing." He picked up another orange and rebooted the surgery program.

"Sounds like you've thought of everything." I know it was an inane comment. But so were most of his answers. Apparent, flippant, and too easy.

"We're ready to go as soon as the mayor gives us the green light. We've started a foundation already—K-T-A, Keep Trains Alive."

"Catchy," I said, but he paid me no attention. *Ktahhhhh.* It sounded like something Klingons would say.

"One of our board members is a building inspector, so we shouldn't have a problem with getting it up to code. I'm sure we can work around some of its obvious deficits." He was on a roll now. "Another of our supporters has connections to a collector who'll sell us authentic furniture from the era—at cost." Unguarded in his enthusiasm about the project, Crawson became boyish; I could picture him running in a field—somewhere in the Midwest where it was green—to wave at the passengers on a train. I wondered if he'd been the kind of boy who put a piece of long prairie grass in his mouth.

". . . and of course, I'm still active in several train organizations," he said. "I don't know if you've done your homework on me—stop me if you know this—but I'm a bit of a celebrity on the national train circuit."

"Indeed?"

"Yes. My family has been in trains almost since their beginning in this country."

Locomotive blue blood. That explained a lot. "That should be a big help."

"Believe me, it'll be more than that." He stood. "Let's see what Sugar is doing."

Unsure I'd heard correctly, I kept my mouth shut and followed him to the garage. It held a silver—of course—Cadillac, a good American gas-guzzler.

"Let's go to the club and see if my wife is available to speak with you," he said.

Four minutes from point A to point B. We didn't talk in the car and I didn't have time to admire the grounds at the Belen Country Club. Crawson ushered me into the place with the sureness of long membership. Through the lobby, down a hallway to a windowless room where women dressed in cashmere cardigans and knit slacks played bridge with all the concentration and annoyance of regulars.

"Sugar," said Crawson to a thin woman with poofed-up, straw-blonde hair. Her pants were Pepto-Bismol pink. Her sweater matched them over a cotton-embroidered blouse. Semi-circle reading glasses dangled from a gold chain around her neck.

"Not now, Wally, I'm busy." Her accent was Texan maybe, or deeper south.

"I've got someone who'd like to speak with you."

"Well, you'll just have to wait," she said, shooting me a glance of sheer vexation.

In that instant, I knew we wouldn't like each other. It wasn't her nasty tone or unwillingness to meet a stranger that made our enmity so immediate and apparent. The response was much more visceral than that, like cats that catch a whiff of each other on the breeze and hiss, claws extended, teeth bared.

"We'll be in the hall," said Crawson, guiding me out with a hand at the small of my back.

True to his word, we stood in the drab passageway watching uniformed workers scurry through. We still didn't speak. Waitstaff and gardeners walked by us without a single hello. I looked at my hands, suddenly conscious of how my chewed fingernails might appear to women with manicures.

A few minutes later, Sugar retrieved us.

"Sorry to be rude, dear," she said to me, her smooth face unfamiliar with remorse. "We were about to have a grand slam."

"That's all right," I said. "Is there somewhere we can sit?"

"Oh, my goodness. How uncivil of me," she said, her hostess smile superglued in place. "Wally, would you do the introductions, please?"

He obliged with a "Sugar, this is Miss Solomon. Miss Solomon, this is Sugar."

"Solomon, that's Jewish, isn't it?" she said.

"Yes," I said, wishing I had horns on the top of my head—for the shock value.

She actually sniffed—a haughty action not lost on her husband or me.

"Sugar, Mayor Flores has hired Miss Solomon to pass judgment on our proposal for the Harvey House." His tone held a warning for her to behave.

"Imagine that," she said.

"Yes, indeed," I said.

thirty-two

"DO LET'S FIND SOMEPLACE to sit," Sugar said, as if it hurt. With that, she turned heel and led us away from her bridge mates' inquiring ears.

We alighted on flowered couches in the front foyer. I wondered who would breach our collective silence first. I knew I couldn't just ask her about the ghost. I bet she disliked me enough to deny having seen the Harvey Girl.

"Sugar, I told Miss Solomon about your experience with Ernestine."

"Why! You didn't!" she said with breathy indignation.

I focused on taking notes, not observing her because I knew one misinterpreted glance would shut her down. Arms across her chest, lipsticked fissures around her mouth, this woman didn't want to talk to me.

Just a little peek—in time to see her glance at her husband. His eyes, unrelenting, focused on her face. His glower not quite masked.

"Oh, all right," she said. "What would you like to know?" The accent remained, but not the Scarlet O'Hara routine.

I waited two beats before saying, "Please tell me a little bit about her. What does she look like? When was the first time you saw her?"

"Well, let me see," Sugar said, her index finger to her cheek. "I'd just begun serving as a docent."

"The Harvey House museum has been one of Sugar's pet projects," said Crawson.

"More than that," she said. "I helped put it on the map, if you don't mind me saying so." Her practiced modesty gave all Southern women a bad name.

"That's impressive," I said. Maybe flattery would work on her.

"Why, thank you."

Did I mention her fingernails? Manicured to pearl-pink points.

"Did you see her right away?" I said.

144

"Not for a few months. It was in late spring, I believe . . . yes . . . our fruit trees were in full bloom. Did you notice the orchard in our back yard? Peaches and cherries. Italian plums, the sweet ones."

"Sug," said Crawson, "I'm sure Miss Solomon is in a hurry."

Her face pinched slightly in response, but her voice remained syrupy. "I had stayed quite late one night filing, or some such thing in the office, when I heard a noise upstairs. Of course I went to investigate and that's when I saw her the first time."

A couple dressed in golf clothes, the gaudy kind only wealthy people dare to wear, walked in. They exchanged greetings with the Crawsons. Pretended to ignore me. Left.

"Now where were we?" said Sugar.

"You were telling me about your first sighting of Ernestine."

"Oh, heavens, yes," she said. "Well, I hadn't expected to see anything, but there she was, hovering in a corner of the room."

"What did you do?"

"Frankly, I thought I'd had a bit too much vodka at lunch." She tittered. "No, seriously. I closed my eyes, counted to ten, and she was still there, an angelic little smile on her face and her white apron practically glowing in the dark room."

"The lights were off?"

"Only the light in the hallway was on. The room itself didn't have one."

"And you're sure she was there?"

Sugar gave me an irritated look, as if I'd asked an imbecilic question. "Miss Solomon, I've seen Ernestine at least . . . what?" She opened both hands—her palms were pink, too—and looked at Crawson for confirmation. "Maybe thirty times?"

He nodded without returning her glance. He waved to someone beyond my view.

"I've lost count," Sugar said, turning to see who had caught her husband's attention.

"What does she do?" I said.

Sugar sighed and refocused on me. "Oh, Ernestine's really rather cute. She seems to enjoy serving coffee, and plates of food—at least we think that's what she's doing." Sugar turned around again, preoccupied with something.

"Anything else?" I wanted to finish this interview. To get on with the day and to connect with Darnda.

Back again, Sugar pursed her lips and said, "Well, she doesn't stay in her room. She goes all over the building. Ned says he sees her most often in what used to be the kitchen."

"Does she speak?"

"Not to me. Ned claims she's a regular chatterbox when he sees her."

"Ned?" She'd used the name twice. Could her hint have been any more obvious?

"Nelson Trafferty. He's the night custodian."

"Wonderful." I made a note of his name. "Are her appearances predictable? Are they linked to a time of night or date . . . anything like that?"

"I haven't thought much about it." Sugar scrunched her eyebrows. Thinking probably hurt the poor dear. "I'd say we see her more often in the winter. The windows are always closed. I know that."

"Would you be willing to go on record saying you've seen her?" I was imagining media interviews, possibly a video short either for an exhibit or as a press release to television stations. Maybe I could mention it to Karen Kilgore and get *The Other Side* interested. That'd give the train museum great exposure.

"People will think I'm daffy," Sugar said. "What kind of record?"

"Maybe on television or in print?"

"Oh, I couldn't do that," she said. "Television?"

"It might be a way to attract more people to the museum," I said.

"Honey, has Linda Bivins ever been on TV?" said Crawson.

"Why, I don't believe she has." A naked, snarky smile streaked across her face.

"Would you consider it?" I said.

"Only if Wally's train museum is part of the bargain," she said, taking his hand in hers. The proprietary motion wasn't for me.

"Of course," I said.

"Hello, Francine," Crawson said, eyes alight with pleasure, to an approaching woman dressed in lime-green slacks and sweater. She gave a microscopic smile before tapping her watch. "Sug, are you coming back? Violet has to leave in an hour," she said.

"I'm ready, Frankie," said Sugar. Then to me, "I really *must* get back to my game."

"May I call at a more convenient time?"

"Arrange it with Wally," she said, already halfway out of the room. "I'd love to help."

Yeah, right. I looked at Crawson.

"Are we done here?" he said.

"I think so."

"Good. I've got an eleven o'clock tee-time."

"I can walk back," I said, making his day.

"You're sure?"

I wondered what he'd do if I changed my mind. "I could use the fresh air."

"Well, that's that," he said, standing up. "Good to meet you. Glad to help. Call if you need anything else." And then zippo, he turned his back on me, as if escaping.

I sat on the couch, shoulders hunched, and completed my notes while the interview remained fresh. A pair of sturdy stockinged legs in white shoes, with thick white rubber soles, stopped before me.

"I'll just be a minute," I said, thinking management had decided to throw me out.

No movement from my bouncer.

"Almost ready." I finished the last sentence and then looked up.

"I heard you talking about the ghost at the Harvey House," she said. Her black hair shone; it was pulled back tight behind her sienna-skinned face. Age indeterminate. High cheekbones, teardrop eyes under meticulously shaped brows. Her exoticism rebelled against her clean subservient uniform.

"We were," I said, putting down my pen.

She glanced left, then right. "Her name isn't Ernestine. It's Eulalia." The woman shifted the weight on her feet. I thought about asking her to sit with me—but didn't. She'd probably get in trouble. "Eulalia isn't a ditzy waitress, either."

"No one said she was."

"If you talk with *them*, you'll hear it. They think she's cute, like a toy or something." The intensity of her protestation was more real than anything else I'd heard that morning. "And she *doesn't* talk to them. They're all making it up."

"You've seen her, too?"

She nodded. "She was my great-grandmother . . . part Pottawatomie, but no one could tell. She had really light skin, a small nose."

"Really? I thought Fred Harvey mainly recruited from the East Coast."

"Mainly the Midwest. She was born in Oklahoma but her dad moved the family to St. Louis when she was little. The whole Indian thing was a secret." She lowered her voice to a whisper. "It wasn't a good time to be Indian. They were ashamed."

"So, your great-grandmother grew up and became a Harvey Girl?"

"That's right."

"Thank you for putting me straight." I held out my hand.

She shook her head slightly—even shaking hands with the *help* could be offensive to the country club crowd, I guess. Still, she stood before me, her message far more important than the mere words she uttered.

"It's not what you think," she said. "I mean, I've seen my ancestor and she does talk. But most of what I know comes from her diary."

My mouth opened in amazement. "She kept a diary?"

"She wrote a paragraph every night." If we'd been somewhere else, her smile would have been much bigger. "Great-grandmother adored working at the Harvey House. It was like her one moment of independence before she settled down and got married."

"Do you know I'm helping Mayor Flores figure out what to do with the Harvey House?"

"Yes, I do."

"May I call you for more information?"

"I suppose," she said. "But I can tell you right now which one *she* prefers." Eyes still watching for something, the woman frowned. "I'm late for work."

"What does she prefer?"

"The bed and breakfast."

"Why?" I said.

"She gets lonely."

thirty-three

THE COSMIC SYMMETRY IN pushing the B & B idea appealed on so many levels. Eulalia, the resident ghost, could serve her customers endlessly if she wanted, and they'd love her. Adore her. It'd be perfect for part of a successful marketing plan. It'd give it sustainability. Everybody was interested in ghosts.

Eulalia's great-granddaughter, Lucy Whitaker, had given me such a wonderful present—far more than Sug had. I put the young woman's phone number into my wallet and left, grinning at my luck. *Lucy Whitaker*. In Belen? *She's got to be related to the writer*.

A crisp late morning's air cooled my cheeks when I walked back to Crawson's house. A good pre-winter kind of feeling. Yards still held traces of green but I could almost taste the moments of surrender as grass and trees succumbed to fall.

What I really wanted to do now, or as soon as I could, was to spend the night in Eulalia's room. Curiosity and pragmatism spurred the impulse. Sure, it'd be cool to see a *nice* ghost. Just as important, though, I needed to get a feel for how often trains came booming through town during the wee hours, how it felt to sleep upstairs when the building shook from all that serious locomotion.

If the train contingent got its way, I'd propose restoring Eulalia's room to its authentic look, complete with furniture from the period. I'd suggest creating a special place solely for ghost hunters, psychics, and paranormal enthusiasts. *Big market there.*

I began to feel the same frustration I'd experienced after finishing my job in Clovis. My specialty—the reason people paid me the big PR bucks—was to come to a town, scope it out, meet and interview scads of people, come up with a plan, write it up, submit it, and leave. Sure, the folks in Clovis might call me for a little training, crisis management, an additional idea or two, but I didn't *implement.* It'd be fun to see one of these jobs through—start to finish. I guess the upside was I didn't have to deal with budgets, zoning meetings, and politics. I sighed anyway. I was always the wedding planner, but never the bride.

"Enough of the melancholia," I told myself while I unlocked the car door. My luck was changing here in Belen. I'd had a couple of really good interviews today already. Next on my list: Nila Markowitz, another member of the Belen Artists Guild. I backed out of the Crawsons' driveway and headed toward the other end of the universe— an undeveloped plot due east of town.

Ritzyville begone! Markowitz's house was an aluminum trailer atop a high foundation of cinderblocks. Its cluttered front yard had dozens of trashcans full of broken glass, glistening jewels in the sunlight. Two large pieces of plywood stood on sawhorses on either side of the front door like insect wings. An opaque substance covered all the windows from the inside.

In a weird way, this reminded me of Phillipa's place. It had that artsy feel to it; a cockeyed manifestation of a private world constructed exactly to fit an internal vision. Art with a capital A—done in quest rather than market planning.

Pit bulls in a neighbor's lot strained at their ropes to bark at me. A small breeze picked up miniature whirlwinds of dust, making me feel gritty. If Markowitz had a car, I didn't see it. The clanking of too many wind chimes came from behind the trailer. I paused at the door, looking for steps into her place. There weren't any.

"Hello?" I thumped on the trailer's warm exterior.

"Just a minute," a muted voice returned.

Honking overhead presaged winter, the Canadian geese making their migration to the Bosque del Apache bird refuge farther south. I heard a loud bang, then "Shit!"

The door opened and a roly-poly woman in tight-fitting shorts and a low-cut T-shirt, her cleavage bulging, bent over to lower a stepladder. The veins in her legs—spiders and super-novas in dimpled flesh. She could have been anywhere from forty to sixty years old.

"Come on in," she said. "Sorry for the mess."

Hot. The place sweltered. I took off my jacket and wished I could remove my tunic as well. Sweat pooled at the elastic in my bra.

Constellations of mobiles hung from scores of thick dowels in a grid across the ceiling. Surfaces screamed with piles of colored glass shards. All of the windows had wooden-framed stained-glass mandalas made from beer-bottle browns and greens, rare blues and reds.

"Find a seat," she said. "You want something to drink? I've just heated some Atholl Brose. It's great this time of year. Takes the chill off, you know."

The chill?

She disappeared behind a bead curtain, its clicking reminiscent of my dope-smoking adolescence. But no psychedelic black-light posters littered her walls. Rather than the tarry smell of marijuana, scents of posole—that magnificent stew of hominy and pork topped with red chile—and oatmeal wafted through the trailer.

Dumbstruck by the visual and olfactory overload, I cleared a pile of newspapers from a metal chair—checking to make sure there were no errant pieces of glass—sat, then looked up. Each suspended piece of each mobile contained a mini-mandala evoking Tibetan and Navajo religious art. The one above my head was made entirely of small individual letters—no words, just the art of the letters.

"So, what do you think?" Markowitz said, reappearing with two mugs filled with steaming liquid.

"These are incredible. They must take you forever."

"Just about," she said. "Here."

I took the cup and stared at its milky contents.

"It's Atholl Brose." She lifted a small swatch of carpet, tossed it to the floor, and harrumphed into a cross-legged sit. "You've never had it before?"

I shook my head, watching lumps float in the drink.

"I make it just the way my granddad did," the artist said. "Try it."

The first sip surprised, the second elated, a mouthful of oatmealy, honeyed, whiskyed warmth. "This is . . . well, it's wonderful."

"People think I'm crazy but I just love a mug or two, late morning. It keeps the inspiration flowing. And I only use steel-cut oats, so it's actually nutritious."

"That's why I drink Guinness," I said, half-joking.

"Atholl Brose is better for you." Markowitz wiggled herself into a more comfortable position. "Now, what would you like to know about our plan?"

"Tell me how you're going to keep the artwork up on the walls with all those trains thundering through," I said, taking another sip.

"They're something, aren't they?" She stretched out her legs, touched her toes, then straightened her back. "First of all, if you've been to the Harvey House, you know there are already things on the walls. So, it's not as impossible as you might think." She reached for her toes again before continuing. "One of our members' sons works as an exhibit designer. He graduated from Philly's alma mater, the Chicago Institute for the Arts. He's agreed to help us with the mechanics."

"He's not worried?"

"Not particularly."

"What about the constant noise from the trains? Won't that disturb your collectors and connoisseurs?"

"The trains aren't as frequent as you might think," she said. "And we've begun pricing soundproofing. At least on the first floor."

"You don't think they'll offend finer sensibilities?" I'd begun to feel light-headed and put the drink on a TV tray to my side.

"How much do you know about art collectors?" she said.

"A fair amount. My mom owned a gallery for years."

"Well, please don't be offended, but your question seems a bit naïve." She bent her knees out and touched her heels together to stretch the insides of her legs. "In my experience, collectors will come to the art. The more rustic or weird the place, the more appealing it is to those 'finer sensibilities.' For example, I've got buyers from all over the world who come to this crazy place. They sit right where you're sitting, drink what you're drinking—or mint juleps in the summer—and shell out obscene amounts of money for the privilege of being near mystical, creative me."

"Yes, but the museum you're proposing will feature Phillipa Petty's work. It'll draw gawkers and protestors—you might get one of those situations like they have at abortion clinics." I don't think she meant to be patronizing, but she was. "Won't that scare away the collectors?"

"Bring the protestors on!" Markowitz held out her hands and wiggled her fingers to invite them. "I'd put my money on the publicity working in our favor—that's part of the reason Philly's paintings command such high prices in the first place. People who buy art want more than the mere painting or pot. They're looking for a particular experience of the world," she said. "There are the thrill-seekers and those who simply love the creative spirit and in some way hope it'll rub off on them. An old, elegant building with rumbling trains evoking mystery and adventure—and even protesters—will be a plus. Trust me."

"You've obviously thought it through." I drank the last of the Atholl Brose, wanting more. "But I still don't see a large enough audience to sustain the art museum project over time. What are the long-term marketing plans?"

"First of all, Philly's paintings use timeless images, so they'll never be dated. And with her murder, well, it's awful to say, but that'll benefit the museum." She rose with a grunt. "Would you like some more?"

"I don't think I'd better," I said.

"Your call," she said with a shrug.

My phone rang. Nila laughed and took my mug with her while I answered it.

"Sasha, that's great about Karen," said Darnda. "I can't wait to meet her."

"What are you doing at two or three today?"

"I was going to—"

"Actually, I don't care what you had planned, Darnda. Come to my house at two-thirty for some heavy-duty media training. This is it." I nodded a thank you to Nila for the second drink. "I love you dearly. However, if you want to be my client, no excuses. You come."

"I'll be there," said Darnda. "Bye."

I put the cell phone back in my purse. Nila had positioned herself for more extensive stretching on the floor. "Sounds like you need to leave."

"Not yet," I said, enjoying a gulp of the warm brew. "What can you tell me about Miss Petty?"

thirty-four

"PHILLY WAS AN ABSOLUTE witch," said Nila, now on her third drink. "There was a time when she'd shoot at people who rolled up her driveway if she didn't know them."

"No." I giggled; it was my third drink, too.

"I kid you not." With her thumb, she smashed a small black ant scaling one of the veins on her mid-thigh. "And, she used to drive around town in this big salmon-colored Buick Electra—you know, one of those cars as big as a boat. Only she stuck reproductions of her paintings on it and would switch out the images every couple of months." Nila giggled. "God, I thought she was going to get killed."

Her head went down as if someone had slapped the back of it. The only sound in the trailer, the plinking of glass in the mobiles above, dancing in an unfelt current. When she looked up, her eyes watery, the good-natured smile on her lips now quivered. She opened her mouth to say something, then closed it. "I guess someone finally got fed up enough to do it, " she said, dabbing her eyes with the knuckle of her index finger. "Such a damn shame."

"You knew her well?"

Nila nodded, the tears insisting on release. "I'm sorry."

"For what?"

"For this." She waved a hand, then wiped her eyes with it. "I still can't believe she's dead." She sniffled and straightened her back from its sorrowful slouch. "You asked me something?"

"How long did you know Phillipa?"

"Pretty much my whole life. She was kind of a mentor to me." Nila pointed to her work overhead. "When I first started making these, I sold them at local arts-and-crafts fairs, you know, those kinds of places. But when Philly saw them, she went crazy. She got what I was doing and how much work these babies took." She rubbed her temples, sniffled again. A grin scampered across her face. "Philly is the reason I'm selling internationally now."

I looked around her trailer, trying to reconcile "international artist" with the humble sloppiness of what I saw.

"I know. This place is a dive," Nila said. "But you've got to understand, I love living like this right now. I figure I've got another ten, twenty years of being a bohemian before I have to do the old-age thing. In the meantime, I'm socking all the money I earn into secure bonds and blue chips, so I'll be able to live my dotage in style. That, plus in the winter I rent a nice little place in the Cap St. Jean Ferrat in southern France. I'm not doing too badly."

"You go to the Côte D'Azur?" Talk about cognitive dissonance. I couldn't imagine her hobnobbing with elitist French film stars and old European moneyed families.

"I've been doing it every winter for sixteen years. Thanks to Philly. She taught me how to market my work. Got me into big galleries. Talked me up to collectors. Bought some of my first pieces for more money than I'd ever seen in my life." Nila stood up and leaned against a table. "I used to work as a waitress at Pete's. Philly gave me fifty thousand dollars, this trailer, and land—just like that—showed up at my parents' house and handed me a check and told me to quit my job so I could do my art. I was eighteen years old."

"So why do you say she was a witch? It sounds like she was a fairy godmother to you, " I said.

"She was both. Nastier than mold most of the time. But when she believed in someone, she did everything, and I mean everything, to help that person succeed." The tears came anew.

"Who else did she help?"

"Oh, some lady in California who was wheelchair-bound and did these incredibly intricate pen and ink drawings. Poor thing died a couple of years ago." Nila cleaned her nails with a yellow-handled screwdriver. "And a guy named Sym Calhoon who makes sculptures out of found materials—trash, really—he's pretty well known now. People like that. I'm the only one around here that I know of."

"Do you know anyone in particular who might want to kill her?"

"Whoa. You skipped a groove," she said, putting the screwdriver down and picking up a pair of fingernail clippers. "You practicing to be a policeman?"

"No." I smiled. "My mom and Phillipa were good friends."

"Figures. I was wondering why we'd left the art museum idea."

"Was it that obvious?" I'd had too much to drink; my conversation wasn't tracking.

"Yeah, but it ties together," she said. "Philly really believed an art museum in the Harvey House would work. And she knew a helluvalot about art marketing." Nila bit her lip. Let it snap back out. "Personally, I wouldn't give a damn about the project if it weren't for her work. Her paintings are hung all over the world, but only a couple of them are exhibited anywhere in New Mexico. I'd really like to see the ones she had on loan to all those museums everywhere else come home." She looked me in the eye. "You know?"

"Yes, I do," I said. "Mom has all this artwork in her house— Schleeters, Baughmans, a few really good Raymond Jonsons. I'd hate to see them leave the state."

"You from here, too?"

"Born and raised in Albuquerque," I said.

"Other people just don't understand what this place is about, do they?"

"Depends."

"No, it doesn't. Most people who move here try to change it in one way or another. They plant grass—of all things—in a desert. They try to politicize us. They bring their activism, their racism, their yearning for fancy restaurants and upgraded stores in the mall."

"And yet you support a museum to bring more tourists in," I said.

"You don't have to like people to make money off of them," Nila said. She picked up a smooth-edged square of deep-blue glass. "Belen could use the money. We need all kinds of infrastructure repairs, sewer lines and streets. We need more cops. So, if we exploit people's wallets without convincing them to live here, it'd be fine." She clipped the nails on her right hand as she talked. "You've been looking at the trains as a deficit in this whole equation. But think of it this way—people who don't like the noise they hear on the way to the Harvey House, or inside it, won't be tempted to move here. That's an advantage."

"I doubt the chamber would agree."

She turned her head, looking over her shoulder through the bead curtain, then back to me. "You know what? I'd really better get back to work. I've got a show in L.A. next month."

What did I say? "Would you mind if I take a couple of pictures of you before I go?" I don't know why I asked, maybe just because I liked her.

"Sure. Let's do it outside. I don't like people seeing my home."

"I don't plan to publish these."

"We can do it outside." She huffed when she got up to open the door. Pushing out the little ladder, she motioned for me to go out first.

The sunlight stung and I blinked, wondering if I'd be able to see well enough to shoot the photos.

When she saw my camera, Nila came over to me. "Do you like your camera? I've been thinking of getting a better one of these."

"It's okay. I don't really know how to use it well yet."

"Do you mind if I try?"

"Not at all." I handed her the instrument and struck a goofy pose.

She pushed the button, then said, "How do I see the picture?" She pushed another button and gasped. "Where did you take this?"

I rushed to her, remembering the photos of Phillipa's studio. "I thought everybody knew I found her that day."

Nila's tears dribbled down her cheeks as she cycled through the three photos. "What's that?"

"What?"

"That." She pointed to light reflecting out of the studio window.

"Probably sunlight."

"I . . . don't . . . think so." She stared at it, turned the camera vertically. "Do you mind if I download it and take a closer look?"

"I'm sure it's some kind of mistake."

Nila shook her head. "I don't think so. It looks too round, like it's a reflection off of a lens."

We scaled back into her trailer. Nila turned on a computer I hadn't noticed, transferred the photos onto her large monitor, and said, "Oh, shit."

"What?"

She pointed to the monitor. "See? There's someone there. You can just make out the head. See? That round part there . . . above the reflection."

"I don't see it."

"Right here. God! Someone must've been watching Philly through a telescope. Sick bastard. He was watching her die."

"You're jumping to conclusions. It could have been something else."

"I don't think so."

"Can I have my camera back?" It struck me that I wasn't the only one who occasionally *saw* things. Nila was so desperate in her grief she imagined a person where a simple reflection existed.

"Have the police seen these photos?" she said.

I took too long to respond.

"You didn't show them? This is important, Sasha. Even if you can't see it, I can," she said. "It's there."

I made a noncommittal noise, a kind of assent without actually lying.

"Who's the detective working on the case?" She detached the camera from her computer and handed it back to me.

"His name's Moises Garcia. He's a state cop."

"You know—a few minutes ago you asked who'd want to kill Philly."

I nodded.

"I wasn't ignoring you," Nila said. "Don't get me wrong—I loved her. But I think a better question would be, who *wouldn't* want to kill her?"

thirty-five

I COULDN'T SHOW UP at a Nobel Prize winner's home perspiring whiskey, so I opted for cheese enchiladas soaked in thick red chile, salsa that kicked with each dunking of tortilla chip, and *sopaipillas* that could have floated out of my hands if I hadn't burdened them with honey. Yes, Pete's definitely went on the "assets" side of Belen's tourist column.

Sated and much less tipsy, I headed for Jerome Whitaker's hacienda. Turned out the writer lived off the same highway as Phillipa, a few miles past her house.

Far down an unpaved drive, the small adobe blended into its surroundings as if it were trying to hide.

The place wasn't exactly shoddy, but it wasn't tip-top either.

A couple of chickens pecked at scattered feed in the front yard. A freestanding fountain—powered by a bright orange extension cord coming off the porch through the screened front door—trickled and served as a birdbath for the wrens and finches that flew up into trees when I slammed my car door.

"Sasha," Whitaker said, coming into the yard to greet me. "Let me give you a tour of 'Rancho Raton.'"

"Funny name for a homestead," I said.

"But appropriate. You'll notice I've got a pride of cats." As if to illustrate his remark, he nudged a tortoise-shell kitty now purring at his leg. "Pests," he said, smiling and bending to pet it. "They hang around because of the mice—I don't do anything to encourage them."

"I can see that you're a regular ogre."

Whitaker nodded. Large cottonwood trees, their leaves Midas-touched, shaded the yard. "That's where I get my best work done. Thinking. Plotting." He pointed to an oversized hammock. "Winters—stuck inside—are hell for me. It takes all I can do to stick my butt in the chair and force myself to write a single, decent sentence."

This folderol didn't follow the articles I'd read about him—the ones describing his tremendous discipline—and lauding his work. I remembered two in particular—one from a critic who described the author as the only contemporary poet who clothed his masterpieces in prose, and another in which a reviewer for the *New York Times* noted, "Whitaker's writing is akin to heaven, and much more plausible."

Oh, I wanted to ask how he came up with his ideas, how he coaxed words into such spectacular and new combinations. Though he might have answered me civilly, I could feel he wasn't one of those authors who wanted to pontificate. Self-satisfied in the truest sense, Jerome Whitaker didn't need to prove himself to idolaters. I'd never met a person who exuded more self-confidence.

"You're awfully quiet," he said.

"I'm worshiping you," I said.

Whitaker chuckled. "A kid with Hannah Solomon as her mom has no reason to worship anyone. You've got superior genes. Don't belittle them; it's unbecoming." He untwisted a piece of wire from an eye-hook attached to his house and a high piece of chicken wire. "I've never had time to make a proper fence." He opened a small gap and said, "Hurry up. Don't let the chickens back here."

I squeezed next to him, close enough to smell the good smell of his real sun sweat, and looked him in the face. Older by thirty years—my dad's age, if he'd lived—Whitaker was sexy as hell. He winked at me.

I shot past him, into a patio of *bancos* and bricks—an insane tessellation of hues—blood orange, ochre, and mahogany. Rough, inexact geometric pieces of flowerpots, mirrors, glass, and rocks. Everything, from floor to color-encrusted pillars supporting the tin roof, consisted of inlaid adobe.

"You ever heard of Antonio Gaudi?" said Whitaker.

I gawked. "It's incredible."

"I've been working on it for years." He walked to one of the earthy seats and sat down.

"Do you know Nila Markowitz?"

"Her work inspired me to give this a go. Although I don't have the eye she does, or the patience. I just do this to get away from my writing." He pointed to a stand of hollyhocks, pale pink and white. "Determined flowers."

"They're gorgeous."

"Just tenacious," he said. A whispered breeze tickled wind chimes into a chorus of Asian tones. Whitaker closed his eyes and listened for a moment. "This is where I come when I need to turn off my overactive imagination."

"I don't want to sound trite, but it's really amazing here."

"Well, that's as good a word as any."

I rested my back against a banco's solid support.

"So, why are you interested in Philly?" he said, his hazel eyes now focused on mine.

"Two reasons. I'm trying to figure out if her paintings would be enough of a draw to breathe life back into Belen's economy."

"You talking about the art museum idea?"

"Yes."

"It'll never work," he said.

"Why?" I said.

"I'm speaking from experience here. Controversy is a powerful short-term marketing tool but I don't see it as the cornerstone of enduring success. Today's shock is tomorrow's boredom."

"Miss Petty managed to make good money at it her whole life," I said.

"But she's dead now. I suspect her paintings will lose some of their emotional value with each generation."

"What do you mean?"

"Without a live target for hate, Philly's art will be judged on its own merits entirely. And I don't think it'll draw the crowds the Artists Guild hopes and needs." He tented his hands, interlocked fingers, and rested his scruffy chin upon them. "Belen's too small, too unknown in arts circles to become a modern-art destination. And Philly's works—though master-pieces—are simply too unpleasant for most people to make the trip for."

"Roswell's in the middle of nowhere and it's managed to make modern art fly."

"You're right. But space aliens fire the imagination, too. And the town had the support of the Anderson and the Hurd families. Both known and respected. There's no one in Belen who can come close with a name or money."

"What about you?"

He laughed. "First of all, while I might have the name, I don't have the money."

I didn't believe him. His books were required reading in high schools and colleges across the country. He'd won enough prizes to fill an Olympic-size swimming pool. Scores of his novels had been turned into movies. The man had money.

"Don't give me that look," he said. "I'm paying for a reckless youth. And I'll be paying for it until I die. I've got alimony from five different divorces and college tuition for at least eight kids."

"It's your own fault," I muttered.

"I'm not saying it isn't," he said. "Besides writing, sex is the one thing I've always been good at."

I cleared my throat—I guess that explained Lucy Whitaker—and looked at my notes. "So, the art museum idea won't fly."

"You're an uptight little thing, aren't you?"

"No, I'm not," I said.

"You are, too. When was the last time you slept with anyone?"

"That's none of your business."

"You're just like your mother. All this sensuality bubbling under the surface and a complete refusal to enjoy it."

"You're not going to get my goat, Mr. Whitaker."

"Jerome," he said.

"This isn't why I came, *Jerome*."

"No, you came to find out about Philly and your mom."

"What about them?"

"Come on."

"What?"

"You didn't know?" He sighed. "Far be it from me to tell secrets."

"Mr. Whitaker, what are you talking about?"

"You want some coffee?" he said, standing up.

"No. I want to know what you're talking about. What do you know about Mom and Phillipa Petty?" I'd gotten to my feet, too.

Back turned to me, he headed into the house. "We were lovers."

"You and Phillipa?"

"The three of us. Together."

thirty-six

"YOU NEED SOME MORE?" Whitaker said, handing me a second glass of water.

"You had a ménage à trois," I said.

"Fancy name."

"But you did. When?"

"Late fifties . . . early sixties." He shrugged. "Everybody was doing it. Free love and all that rot, you know." He measured coffee beans into an electric grinder.

I sat at his kitchen table. Whereas his backyard delighted the eye with its whimsy, his interior design was early monastic. Bare adobe walls, rustic wooden furniture. All meant to soothe and quiet. I, however, felt anything but calm.

"You're telling me Mom did this while she was married to my dad," I said. "I don't believe it. Mom would never have an affair."

Whitaker slouched, but said nothing. He poured water into the coffee maker.

"I don't know why, but you're just making this up," I said.

That got him. He came over to me, pulled a chair to face me, and brought it so close I pushed mine back. He inched toward me again.

"Why are you such a prude?" he said, taking my reluctant hand in an insistent grasp. "This happened close to forty years ago."

"I am not a prude." I pulled my hand away. "It's just a surprise. That's all."

He bent forward, elbows on knees. "Show me."

I leaned away from him, the chair's back slats digging into my skin. "What are you talking about?"

"Sex. Here and now. Show me you're not a prude."

"That's just perverse. You want to make it with Mom's daughter? Is that why you granted this interview?" I started to rise, but he held my thighs down with unexpected force.

"You're not going anywhere until we're done with this."

"Let go of me," I said, scared that this septuagenarian might try to rape me.

"For all I know, you could be *my* daughter," he said.

My entire body deflated in shock. I shook my head. Beyond him, I thought I saw a wisp of color. It lasted only a second or two. The room grew cold.

"Hannah stopped coming here so suddenly." Whitaker released my legs and said, "Then I heard she was pregnant. I've wondered for years. Don't get me wrong, it could have been your father. But I've always wondered. After that summer, your mom never spoke to me again."

I continued shaking my head.

"Look, you came here to ask me about Philly," he said. "Why don't you focus on that now? There's nothing we can do about the other, anyway."

I hugged myself against the chill.

"Are you all right?" said Whitaker. He turned around to see what I'd been looking at. "Oh, Jesus Christ, Philly, leave her alone." He put a now gentle hand on my leg. "Don't pay attention to her. She'll go away."

"Who?"

"Philly. Phillipa. She's standing right over there. I thought you saw her."

"I don't know what I saw," I said, reaching for my Chinese pills.

"Well, I do. You saw Philly—or some hint of her." He scratched his cheek. "You been seeing her for long?"

"Not seeing her so much as sensing something. Ever since I found her," I said.

Chin resting between thumb and first finger, lips obscured, he mumbled.

"Excuse me?" I said.

"She's been a regular pain in the ass," he said, dropping his hand to his lap. "Just like when she was alive. Always causing trouble."

"You don't sound too sad that she's gone," I said.

"Well, she isn't *gone*, is she?"

"That's not what I meant."

"I know exactly what you meant," he said, one side of his mouth sucked in. "Am I sad she was murdered? Yes. Did I expect it? Yes. Do I give a rat's ass who did it? No." Whitaker went to the cabinet and got two chipped mugs. "Dead's dead."

"But waitaminute. Don't distract me," I said. "You hallucinate like I've done before?"

"I'm not sure it's the same, Sasha. But I see things that other people don't." He filled a teakettle with water, used a match to light the old stove. "Why do you think I live in the middle of nowhere?"

"To get your writing done?"

"That's part of it."

"And to keep distractions down," I said.

"That's right." He walked to a freestanding cupboard, then brought a tin of fake creamer to the table. "Suffice it to say, you ail from your daddy's affliction."

"You don't know you're my father," I said.

"You don't know that I'm not."

thirty-seven

DAD. POP. DADDY-O. Father. Five-foot-seven Armand Solomon could be summed up in four other words, too: louse, womanizer, and superb businessman. Dead now for more than ten years, he rarely made it past the mental fortresses of self-protection I'd nursed during a childhood and adolescence of neglect. In some ways, he had been more of a phantom than any ghost or vision I'd ever seen. Home no more often than a bad cold, he expected filial devotion when his own parental ambivalence erupted at the slightest provocation.

But he'd left his fortune to Mom; the attorney contacted her just days after Dad's death. Mrs. Solomon the fourth or fifth—I'd lost count—tried to contest the will. She only gave up when she realized Dad had reaffirmed it as soon as he found out the cancer had metastasized to his marrow. Two weeks later, he shot himself in the head, his wife asleep in another man's arms during a junket to Palm Springs.

Someday his fortune might come to my sister and me, if it wasn't all used up in Mom's health care costs.

I kept the radio off on the drive back to Albuquerque, preferring instead to think about Dad and Whitaker's outlandish claims.

In the grand scheme of things, my daddy double helixes didn't matter a speck. A night's fun or passion had yielded me. I kind of liked the idea that a world-famous novelist had imprinted his DNA in me. It was certainly more thrilling than an import-export whiz.

The question remained: Should I ask Mom?

I still didn't have a good answer when I got home at two. Leo tore out the door as soon as I cracked it open. Fine by me. I had a lot of work to do in a half-hour. Going to the hall closet, I unpacked my video camera, a big tape recorder, and a couple of trouble lights. I positioned all of them for Darnda's interview—I'd seat her on the couch, with bright lights in her face, and unforgiving instruments to record every screw-up and "um" she said. Normally, I'd rent a studio for the session but this was a rush job—we had to do it today.

With fifteen minutes to spare, I powered up the home computer and typed questions—the kind of stuff I thought a reporter might ask. The kind of stuff that might force my friend way off track, make her sound like an idiot. Better to discover her weaknesses with me than in a real interview. I'd give her a second, a third chance. An audience might not.

"Here," Darnda said, arriving with two grapefruit-size crème brûlées from Satellite bakery.

"We can use them as a reward after the session," I said, and put them in the fridge. "This is what you'd wear to an interview?"

Her bra-less breasts tugged at her teal Rattlesnake Museum T-shirt and the short leather skirt did nothing for her legs but expose their paleness and dimples. Her boots looked like they were alligator skin. "You didn't say it was a dress rehearsal," she said.

"If you want national attention, everyday—every hour—is more than a dress rehearsal—it's always performance time. You've got to get yourself in the right mindset for this, Darnda. If you're going to be big-time, you've got to think big-time."

"This is how I like to dress. It's comfortable."

"That's fine with me, my friend, just be sure it's what you want to project to your audiences." I sat her down on the couch. "I know what your outfit says to me. Let's get through this session and you can decide what it says for yourself. You can watch the tape and do a self-critique." I turned on the lights.

"Damn, Sasha, that's bright."

"If you're in a television studio, it will be, too. The lighting will definitely be different than what you're used to." I moved behind the video camera so she couldn't see my face. "There will be people all over the place, some wearing headsets. There will be equipment in front and around you, maybe a microphone or two suspended overhead. You can't be distracted by any of it."

She pulled her shirt down to cover her stomach, messed with her skirt. "This is weird, Sasha. I can't believe Karen Kilgore will put me through this."

"She probably won't, but I want you to be prepared for the most unpleasant kind of interview. That way everything else will seem easy." I looked at my questions. They weren't at all nice. "You ready?"

"Shoot."

"Ms. Jones, I understand you spent two years in a mental institution."

"What's that got to do with anything?" Darnda said. She'd already begun to sweat. Her hands were fisted and her eyes belligerent. "Nobody's going to know about that."

"If you go national they will. Someone from your past will try to cash in. Now . . . three, two, one . . . answer the question."

Her eyes were going every which way, making her look shifty, dishonest. She cleared her throat, scooted forward, then back.

"I'm waiting," I said. "You're before a live audience. Do you want the question again?"

"Fuck you, Sasha."

"Maybe later," I said.

She laughed and took a breath. "Okay. I think I've got it." She took another breath. "I was institutionalized when I was a teenager. The diagnosis was adolescent schizophrenia, but that was in the dark ages. Things have changed a lot since then."

"Good save, Darnda. That kind of humor will put the audience in your hands."

She smiled.

"You ready for another one?"

"I guess."

"You claim you can talk to anything living or that once lived. So, can you talk to my shoes because they're leather and were once cows? Or can you talk to the cantaloupe in the green room? How about this coffee?"

"Honey, if you give me enough time and a good enough reason, I could communicate with the plaque on your teeth—"

"Darnda."

"Well, it's true. You know it."

"But it's not good to alienate the interviewer or to seem combative."

"Okay, let me try again." She straightened up, squinted, and tried to smile right at the camera. "Well, Karen, those are interesting questions. In a nutshell, yes, I could talk to—or, as I like to say, 'communicate with'—all of those things. But for me, the really important question is, why would I want to communicate with them? There has to be a good reason because it takes a lot of effort."

I clapped my hands. "Darnda, that was great. You did three marvelous things just then. Number one, you complimented the interviewer without being smarmy. Number two, you clarified your terms. And number three, you brought up one of the questions you want to address. Good job."

"Can we take a break?"

"Not yet. Three, two , one. . . . Can you show us how you talk to something right now?"

"Sure."

"Darnda, don't leave it up to the interviewer. Know some things you'd be willing to do before you go into the interview. Let's try it again. . . . Can you show us how you do it right now?"

"I'd love to. Is there a parent with a baby in the audience? Or an animal?"

"Tell me what you're going to do in each case, Darnda. Let me see what I think."

"Well, if there's a baby, I'll ask it questions about its family—you know, about siblings or other relatives, or if it's been sick lately. And if it's an animal at home, I'd ask if the person had someone at home. If so,

I'd communicate with the animal and have the person in the audience call home to see if the animal did what I asked him or her to do. That kind of thing." She was so matter-of-fact about it. Confident, too.

"Those might work. Can you think of anything else that might work with the audience?"

"Well, you know I could communicate with her coffee or whatever, but I don't think the audience would believe I was actually doing it. The same goes for cancer in someone's body or something like that." Darnda tugged at her microscopic skirt again, wiped her forehead with the back of her hand. Not good.

"Okay, that's a situation I want you to think about a little more. See if you could come up with something splashy, something visual for television."

"I'll try."

"Now, you know you'll be asked about your clients and some of the jobs you've had to do. Are you prepared to talk about them?"

"Some of them—but I do keep most of my clients confidential." She squinted into the light. "You know, Sasha, you haven't asked me anything about my book or about how I can train other people to do this, too."

"I haven't asked because I think you'd be able to answer those kinds of questions without too much difficulty. I want to address the stuff that you might not have considered."

"Oh, come on. Ask me an easy question."

"Tell me about your name."

"Well, you might not know this, but I come from a large family." She relaxed into one of her favorites stories. I'd heard it many times before. "I have seven sisters."

"Any brothers?"

"Not a one. That's actually how I got my name. I was raised on a hardscrabble farm in Oklahoma. My mom had all of us at home. When I was born—I'm the youngest—my dad was still hoping for a boy. The story goes that when I popped out and the midwife held me up, Dad said, "Darn ta hell, woman, why'd you have another girl? And 'darn ta' became Darnda because Mom had run out of girls' names by then." She grinned. "How was that?"

"Cute, but too long. Cut it down."

"Sasha, this is a pain in the ass. Why do we need to do it?"

"Because I want you to have a feel for talking with people who aren't necessarily on your side about this psychic thing."

"You do know I've met those kind of people before."

"Of course I do. I used to be one of them myself, but it's been quite a while since you've been challenged." I turned off the bright lights. "You make all this money and have a good reputation that keeps building on itself. But reporters and media people are a different breed and if you're going to open yourself up to them . . . if you're going to actively try to get their attention, you'd better learn how to handle them, and yourself with them, before we go much further." I turned off the video camera and took out the cassette so that she could have it. "I want you to take this home and study it. See what looks good and what looks lousy. We can talk about it before you meet the famous Karen Kilgore. And we'll do more of this kind of training before you actually go on camera. I just really wanted you to have a feel for it."

"Gee, thanks."

"How about some crème brûlée?"

Darnda got up and followed me into the kitchen. "I think I need a hug first." She held out her arms. "That was rough. I didn't like it at all."

I hugged her back. "Doing it to a friend is horrible. But better me than Jay Leno."

thirty-eight

LESS THAN AN HOUR later, I pulled into the lot at St. Kate's. For some reason, the lobby smelled like ammonia today, toxic rather than antiseptic. A new receptionist nodded a greeting and asked me to sign in—a procedure I had hitherto ignored. The place seemed unnaturally calm, like they'd drugged all the patients so the staff could take a cigarette break. Maybe it was my mood. Though Darnda and I had made nice-nice, I still felt bad about putting her through such a quick and unpleasant session—even though I knew she'd benefit from it. Would I benefit by knowing the truth about Whitaker's assertions?

Sunlight glinted on the windows, exposing streaks. They reminded me of the reflection Nila had noticed in the photo. I was sure she was crazy. There was no head in the photo. It was a trick of shadow or foliage.

Mom wasn't in her room. At the nurse's station, an older woman whom I didn't recognize said Mother was outside on the terrace enjoying the beautiful day. The "terrace" loosely described a square cement "garden" bordered by rocks and pyracantha bushes—their berries bright orange. Several people in wheelchairs sat motionless, some staring at their hands, others sleeping.

On a bench at the farthest end from the door sat Mom, back straight, both legs directly in front of her. And in front of them, a walker.

"Hi, there," I said, with more cheer than I felt.

"Help me get back in," said Mom. "I need to go to the bathroom."

I waited for her to show signs of effort, a strain of arms as she tried to lift herself up, a tensing of calves. Instead, she looked at me, expectant.

"Can't you get up?" I said.

"I need your help."

"Lift your elbow. Grab the walker."

Her arms were now so thin they reminded me of bare twigs. When she held the walker firmly, her knuckles white, I positioned myself behind the bench to help her stand. What would have taken a healthy person three minutes took her ten. But she made it to the bathroom without an accident and then, exhausted, shuffled to her bed.

"Sasha, this is no way to live," she said.

"Consider the alternative."

"I have."

Thank God, a nurse came in.

He wrapped a blood pressure cuff on Mom's arm and mumbled something when it slipped. His ugliness continued through two attempts to find her wrist pulse. Without warming his stethoscope, he placed it on her chest, causing her to inhale sharply.

"He certainly was a delight," I said when he'd left.

"They all are."

"Even Rita?"

"I haven't seen her for days." Mom pressed the television on, turned the volume up.

I must have dozed to the drone of a program because I woke with a start, disoriented and uncomfortable. Mom was asleep, her hands tensed in raptor like talons. Paul sat next to me in the other free chair, his eyes lackluster, his white hair flat.

"Paul, I didn't hear you come in," I said.

The pitiful smile that lifted his lips shuddered into a frown. In a whisper, he said, "Sashala, I spoke with Detective Garcia."

"What happened?"

Paul took a handkerchief from a hidden pocket and pressed it against his nose, then dropped his hand to his lap. "He asked me again and again about your mama and that Miss Petty."

"Were you able to tell him anything?"

"Only what your mama has said."

"Did you ever meet Phillipa?"

He shook his head. "This is not a happy subject. Your mama often tried to persuade me to see this woman, to have lunch with the two of them. Or dinner. But I always refused."

"Why?"

"Why would I want to meet a blasphemer?"

"But she just did that in her art," I said. "She was trying to make a point."

"That the symbols people hold close to their hearts should be ridiculed?" Paul's raised voice awoke Mom.

"Children?" she said.

Paul and I looked at each other, the same question in both of our eyes.

"Hannah," he said. "Did you have a good rest?"

"I had such a terrible dream," she said, reaching for his hand.

"It's over now," he said.

"No, no. It isn't. Not with Philly dead," she said. "I almost saw him, Paul."

"Who?" I said.

"Philly," said Mom. "You're here?"

"No, Mom. It's me. Sasha."

"Philly? What's happened to you?"

Mom's gaze moved from my face, past my shoulder. I spun around, afraid of what I might see. Nothing was there. Nothing but the curtained window leaking its tepid afternoon light.

"She was painting," Mom said. "She'd let him in, to talk, to explain. But he didn't want that. He wanted sex. After all these years, he wanted her again."

"It's all right," said Paul. "Everything's fine."

"No, listen to me. This wasn't the first time. He nearly killed her before. She told me. They'd never made love—he raped her every time. Beat her, ripped her clothes, whipped her, tied her up."

"It's okay, Mom," I murmured, worried by her agitation. I'd moved to the other side of her bed, to be out of Paul's way and to see her more clearly. My back to the door, I could hear the banging of dinner trays as they were pulled from their carts. Cheery voices of dietary workers cajoled people, pretending that the meals they served weren't tasteless and gray. A smell of institutional food, with its heavy sweetness, intruded.

"Mrs. Solomon, it's time for dinner," a woman said from behind me.

I turned to see the speaker.

"Celia?" I said.

"You?"

thirty-nine

"YOU'RE THE REPORTER, RIGHT?" Celia Ortega said, holding a tray.

"Yes," I said. "I didn't know you worked here."

"I just started." She came into the room and served Mom. "Here you go, Mrs. Solomon. A nice hamburger and salad. Doesn't that look good?" Her loud voice had that condescending tone some people use with older adults, as if their mental capacities have diminished along with their hearing.

"Isn't it a long commute?" I said.

"Nobody'd hire me in Belen after they found out who I worked for." She cleared the sliding patient's table, removed the silverware from its place in the folded paper napkin. "I'll be back in a minute with some coffee. It says here, you want coffee."

Mom didn't answer.

"This is Celia Ortiz," I said. "She used to work for Phillipa."

"Ortega," she said.

"Sorry," I said.

Mother stared at her food and didn't look up for the introduction.

"Mother?" I said, curious at her rudeness.

"Hannah?" Paul had picked up on her deliberate snubbing, too.

"Oh, that's all right," said Ortega. "These old folks don't know what they're doing half the time. I remember my grandma. She lost her marbles early and never found them again." She laughed at her joke. "I'll pray for you, Mrs. Solomon."

"I don't want your filthy prayers," said Mom.

"Hannah!"

"Mom!"

Ortega batted the incivility away with a flick of her hand. "It's okay. She probably doesn't know what she's saying." She pushed the food a little closer. "Now, you eat up, Mrs. Solomon. You need your strength. I'll come back in a while to pick this up."

"Thank you," I said.

Seconds later, we heard Ortega's same loud voice in the next room, as if she were reading from a script.

Mom said, "Bitch."

"You know her?" I said.

"I can't eat this food, Paul. Get me something from the cafeteria. Anything." Mom pushed her dinner away.

Paul went out the door, following her command.

"You don't like hamburgers now?" I said, convinced she was yanking Paul's chain to feel her own importance. Being stuck in a rehab facility left little room for self-esteem—Mom had to create her own sense of self-worth where she could.

"That woman poisoned Philly's food," Mom said. "She told me all about it."

I sat down.

"You don't believe me, do you?" she said.

"Why did Phillipa keep her on if she was doing that?"

"She didn't. She fired her sorry ass."

"When?"

"A month ago, maybe two. But that woman kept coming back." Mom spit the words out.

"Why did she think she was being poisoned?"

Mother turned her head away from me with a grunt.

"Mom? Why?"

"I know you think I'm just making this up."

"No, I don't. I'm asking because I want details. And after you tell me, I'm going to call Detective Garcia and tell him," I said. "But I want as much information as you can give me first."

She folded her arms across her chest in disbelief.

"This is important, Mom."

She nodded again, but didn't relax her pose. "Philly felt absolutely fine before that woman started working for her. And then, each day, she started feeling worse and worse." Mother shifted her position and looked at me. "She said it was like a stomach flu that wouldn't go away. Cramps, diarrhea. She lost ten pounds in the first month. Another six the next."

"Did she say why she thought Ortega was doing it?"

"Religious fanatic."

I heard quiet footsteps and got off the bed to make room for Paul. Instead, Ortega came in the room. "Why, Mrs. Solomon, you haven't eaten a bite. And here I've brought your coffee."

"Thank you," I said. "I'm sure she'd like a cup."

Mom's eyes widened.

Ortega poured the drink and waited.

Paul came in with a dinner tray.

"Thanks, Paul," I said, grabbing it from him. "I'm starving."

I moved to one of the bedside chairs and made a big show of eating a french fry. "These are great."

"Aren't you going to eat, Mrs. Solomon?" said Ortega.

"She likes to take her time," I said.

"What's the matter with her? Can't she talk?"

"It comes and goes," I said, knowing Ortega had heard Mom's recent nastiness.

Paul's deliberate stare belied his confusion, but he had the good sense to stay quiet.

"These sure hit the spot," I said. "Why don't you try one?"

He took my cue and sat next to me. He picked up a fry.

"Well, I can't wait all evening," Ortega said. She turned to face me. "You can stick the tray in one of the racks in the hall when you're done."

"Thank you," I said, imbuing my voice with as much sincerity as I was able to muster.

"Don't you give her anything off your own plate," she said. "Your mother's on a restricted diet."

"Yes, I know."

"Well, okay," said Ortega.

"Good to see you again," I said.

Mom had brought the hamburger to her mouth. I thought she was faking it, playing along with the game to get Ortega out of the room. Instead, she took a bite. Chewed and took another.

"See?" I said. "She just needed to get hungry."

"Okay." Ortega nodded.

As soon as she left, Paul switched the trays.

"Give me back my hamburger," Mom said.

"I brought you a nice turkey sandwich, Hannah. Look, it's just the way you like it."

"I want my hamburger."

Paul switched the trays back.

"Mom, don't eat that," I said, pulling away the food Ortega had served. The plastic cup of coffee spilled onto the plate.

"Why not?"

"Not again," I said.

"Why won't you let me eat my hamburger?"

Paul repositioned the sandwich in front of her.

"I don't want a turkey sandwich. I hate turkey sandwiches. I want my hamburger." Mom's sulk nearly convinced me to let her eat the damn food.

"Mom says that woman poisoned Phillipa Petty while she worked for her," I said to Paul.

"Which woman?" he said. "The one just now?"

"Yeah."

"She knew Miss Petty?"

"She worked for her. When I met her she said she was her housekeeper. But she must have cooked for her, too."

"Sashala, you need to call that policeman," said Paul.

"I want my hamburger." Mom pouted.

"You don't have to eat the sandwich," he said. "How about some fries?"

"Well, I like the fries." Mom began to eat.

"This is too much of a coincidence," he said to me.

"I don't believe in coincidences, Paul."

forty

"I'VE GOT ONE OF those gems you were waiting for," I said a few minutes later. With Ortega hovering near Mom's room, I'd opted to use my mobile office—the car—for the telephone call.

"Tell me about it *after* you tell me about the photos you didn't tell me about," said Garcia.

"Nice sentence," I said.

"What? Oh," he said. "I can do without the grammar commentary."

"Did Nila Markowitz call you?"

"That's beside the point. You had pertinent evidence—more evidence—and you deliberately withheld it. Just what do you think you're doing, Ms. Solomon?"

The steering wheel was cool. I ran a finger over the part that had dented when I'd hit it with a stainless-steel travel mug. What could I say to placate the detective?

"Did you hear me? Do you realize how stupid it is to withhold information?" said Garcia.

"I'm getting a bad idea about it," I said. "Look, here's the truth. At first, I thought you'd confiscate my camera."

"I could have downloaded the photos. I didn't have to take your whole camera."

"I know. I realize that now. It just shows how totally moronic I am." I took a big breath. "But with everything that's happened, I forgot them for a while. And then when I remembered them again and looked at them, well, they looked like crap. I wasn't intentionally trying to deceive you. Oh, hell, you can have my whole camera if you want. I never want to see those stupid pictures again. But I've got to say, Nila Markowitz is crazy. The only thing those pictures show is that I don't know how to use my damn camera."

"Are you done?"

"Yes."

"Good." He let me stew for a minute. "Now you listen to me and you listen real closely. Nila Markowitz has more sense than you do, Ms. Solomon. She's smart enough to know we're better equipped to make judgments about the relevance of information than she is," he said.

"Yes sir," I said.

He cleared his throat. "What I need to know now is—do you have any more surprises for me? And what you need to know is—I hate surprises and I will not tolerate any more of this piecemeal information flow. Be straight with me now or be ready for punitive action."

"I'm not holding anything else back. Really," I said with total sincerity. "The whole reason I called was to tell you something . . . in case you can use it."

"What is it?"

"According to my mother, Phillipa Petty's housekeeper—Celia Ortega—was poisoning her."

"She just mentioned it out of the blue?"

"Not quite. Ortega just got a job at St. Kate's. I turned around and there she was, serving Mom dinner. I introduced them to each other and Mom went ballistic." I rolled down one of my windows. The whooshing sound of rush-hour traffic sounded like a river—probably as close as Albuquerque would get to water this year. I tried to remember what rain smelled like but got a nostril-full of exhaust and hospital food.

"Did your mother accuse Ms. Ortega to her face?"

"No. She just refused to eat the food and acted like a cantankerous old woman."

"Did Ms. Ortega appear to know about your mother's relationship with Miss Petty?"

"How did you find out about that?" I said, shock evident in my voice.

"About what?" I was getting used to Garcia's hot-air-balloon sighs. He said, "What else aren't you telling me?"

"It's nothing relevant to the case," I said.

"Does it have to do with Miss Petty?"

"Tangentially."

"It's relevant."

"Oh, all right. According to Jerome Whitaker, Mom and Miss Petty had an affair with him back in the sixties."

A robin landed on the hood of my car, pecked at a leaf, and flew away.

"The three of them? An affair?" Garcia made a noise; it could have been a snicker. "Have you confirmed this with your mother?"

"Not yet."

"Let's get back to Ms. Ortega."

"I've pretty much told you what Mom said."

"What I'm interested in is if Ms. Ortega gave any indication that she knew your mother or about her friendship with Miss Petty."

"None that I could see. But it still gives me the creeps," I said. "I'm thinking of moving Mom to another facility."

"I need you to visualize the scene. Think carefully. Was there something specific in Ms. Ortega's behavior that made you nervous?"

"Not exactly. It's more like there's that potential there, you know? Even though Mom can be pretty crazy, this feels real to me. She went into detail about Phillipa's weight loss after the housekeeper started cooking for her—that kind of thing." I started picking at a small piece of foam coming out of my dashboard. "And St. Kate's has messed up recently as well." I told him about Mom's two joyrides and how the administration took no responsibility for them at all. "What would you do, Detective Garcia? Do you think she's in danger?"

"I don't have enough information to answer your question. But if she were my mother, I'd err on the side of caution."

"Can't you do something about Ortega?"

"I'll check into your mother's accusations. Hold on," he said. I heard a rubbing sound and figured he'd put his hand over his receiver. "Sorry. I've got to get going in a minute. About your mother, if there's any truth to her accusations, believe me, we'll do something."

"But what am I supposed to do in the meantime?"

"What you've been doing all along—what you think is best." He harrumphed. "Actually, what you think is best isn't that good. What I'd do if I were you . . . I'd be careful."

"Great."

"Ms. Solomon, I appreciate your call and hope, for your sake, that you're not keeping anything else from me. I'll be in touch."

I sat in the car a few minutes more, wishing life were black and white, that there was only one answer to any question. Moving Mom would be a royal pain. Paul and I had done extensive research on local facilities before we showed St. Kate's to her in the first place. Mom was used to the therapists—physical, occupational, speech—who helped her feel like she had some semblance of a normal life, of hope, of forward momentum.

To rip her away from this familiar environment would be devastating. Phillipa's death had seemed to bring her closer to her own. I didn't want to precipitate a further decline. I rolled up the window again and went back into the rehab facility.

An after-dinner hush descended on the place. Rustle replaced bustle as people settled in for their long nights. Mom dozed with the television on, *breaking news* flashing pictures of another DWI-related car wreck. Paul sat by her bed, a magazine in his lap.

"What are you reading?" I moved close to him in order not to wake her.

"An article about Elie Wiesel." Paul had survived Auschwitz. Though he rarely spoke about his experiences there, I knew he'd lost most of his family during those horrid years.

"Can I talk with you for a minute?" I laid my hand on his.

"Of course," he said.

"Outside?"

He answered by getting up. We went into the hallway.

"What is it, Sashala?"

"I think we're going to have to move Mom."

"I've been thinking the same thing." He shook his head. "I don't know. A move now is going to be hard, so very hard on her."

"What should we do?"

"For now?" Raised eyebrows accompanied his resigned smile. "We'll call her friends. Bring her meals."

"Don't you think someone will catch on?"

"Not if we do it right. I'll eat the food Miss Ortega serves, if it comes to that."

"Mom might be wrong," I said.

"I don't want to take that chance. Do you?"

"Shouldn't we notify Ortega's boss?"

"I don't think that's wise. It's possible Miss Ortega doesn't realize your mama knew Miss Petty. And, we both know it's possible Hannah is remembering incorrectly."

"Oh, God, I don't know what to do, Paul." I stretched my arms over my head, then touched my toes—almost. "We can't stay with her around the clock. How do we know she'll be safe after visiting hours?"

"We don't."

"Then we'll have to move her right away," I said.

"We can't."

"So, what are we going to do?"

"We might be able to find out Miss Ortega's work schedule. That would help. Maybe Rita could ask."

"I haven't seen Rita today," I said.

"Nor have I. But she gave me her home number once," he said, sneaking a quiet look into Mom's room. We could hear her moving in her bed. "I could call. I'm sure she'll have good advice."

I nodded.

"Jack?" said Mom, her voice panicky. "Jack, what are you doing here?"

Heads both bent with worry, we went to her. She clawed the air in restless sleep. We held silent vigil over her. A nurse kicked us out twenty minutes after visiting hours ended.

forty-one

THE SWEET, MULCHY, AND earthy smell of autumn's decay accompanied me home. On the freeway, I drove with the window down to keep my attention focused on the road rather than on the swirling details of a potential move for Mom.

In my less generous moments, I'd often wished my mother would just go away—a hideous, selfish thought born of frustration and fatigue. Now, faced with the real possibility of her death, I felt an excruciating emptiness, a seizing of stomach and heart. What a lousy conundrum: move her, she dies. Keep her at St. Kate's, she dies.

I could call my sister, ask her to help. To what end? She had a family, a full-time job, and lived two thousand miles away in West Virginia. While she could offer suggestions or an ear to bounce ideas off of, calling her about this would only cause her worry, a feeling of impotence, and too much guilt. She couldn't drop her day-to-day life to fly to Albuquerque anyway.

Paul and I would have to decide.

I turned into my driveway, thoughts whirlwinding. A flash of fur streaked in front of the car. I slammed on the brakes. "Damn it, Leo!"

He stopped at the front door, eyes reflecting the brash headlights, and waited for me to open it. I nudged him out of the way with my foot.

Lethargy enveloped me when I walked through the darkened living room. I wondered if this could be the beginning of depression. I tried a dramatic sigh but it wasn't satisfying. Where had all the fun gone in my life? Another sigh, deeper now.

The answering machine's light strobed red with several messages. I sat down on the couch and stared at its neurotic blinking in the unlit room. Unimpressed, I got up and went to my liquor cabinet for the bottle of Glenlivet. In the kitchen, I fumbled around in the dark until I found an empty jelly jar. Poured a hefty shot. At least I think it was a shot . . . maybe two.

My actions felt slow-mo, like I'd never be able to walk with a spring in my step again—doomed to trudge. Too much had happened in too little time this week. I couldn't go on with this intensity. I'd go mad and no little pills, of any origin, would help.

I drank for a few minutes and then decided to confront those who'd dared to leave messages on my poor, overworked machine. First up, Bob's voice. I fast-forwarded. Then a possible client in Placitas. I went to the bedroom, turned on the light, found a pen, and wrote down the name. Back to the machine. Bob again. Four hang-ups. There were a few more messages but I didn't have the heart to listen to the dial tone—if there were more hang-ups. Instead, I went back to the couch and drank. Leo climbed on my lap, kneaded my thighs, and purred. When I'd finished the scotch, I lay down and let him stretch onto my belly.

Sleep must have come because I jolted awake to a thwack in the kitchen. The wind blew, salt-cedar branches scratched against my windows. I rubbed my eyes and went to see what had caused the louder sound. The back door stood open. I locked it and went to the answering machine again—picking up that interrupted action as if my hourslong sleep had been mere minutes. I pressed the button and walked back toward the kitchen.

"Butt out, bitch," said a gruff male voice.

What on earth? I returned to the machine and rewound the message. "Butt out, bitch."

I replayed it two more times and then shivered. "Leo?" I said. "Leo, where are you? Here, kitty, kitty, kitty." In the bedroom, I looked under the bed, in the closet. "I've got some tuna, Leo. Come here, kitty."

A thump in the front room, then another. Leo must have been on top of the credenza. He ambled into the room toward me, head high. "Yowlrr?"

I picked him up and he went limp, purring and being adorable in a mercenary way.

"Was someone here?" I said. Josie had changed the locks. As far as I knew only the two of us had the proper keys. My suddenly cute cat purred some more, nestled his head near my breast. "Come on, Leo. Did you see anyone?"

He started the kneading routine on my arm, drooled a bit. I dropped him without ceremony.

"I won't give you any tuna if you don't answer my question."

He twined around my legs, purring even louder.

"What am I doing?" I said, heading to the kitchen to get him the fish. At one time, I would have expected answers from him. In English. With a Bronx accent. Lately, I'd begun to relish the silence. The open door reminded me of Peter O'Neill's ruby. It was only nine-thirty. I decided to call, to tell him about his rock and find out if he was the one coming in and out of my place. *I'm being an idiot. How do I even know he got in the first time? Is he a stalker? If he's a stalker . . . no way am I going to call him about a dumb ruby!*

Phone in hand, I faced the wall and banged my head against it—not too hard—and repeated the action until it hurt. This was ridiculous. I was looking for demons where there were none. But who'd left that message? I returned the receiver to its cradle. Why had the outside door been open yet again? Back and forth, kitchen to front room to kitchen. The impromptu stroll did nothing to reduce the tension. In the front room again, I poured a spot more of the scotch and headed toward bed.

I passed the blinking answering machine on my way. With a fatalistic sigh—this one could have won an Oscar—I pressed the button. A couple more dial tones and then, "Sasha, this is Jack Whitaker. Give me a call."

Jack Whitaker. Dad? Daddy Whitaker? I tried all of them on for size and, a breath later, froze. Mom had spoken of a man coming back to rape Phillipa after her first nightmare this evening. And she'd had a second one and had cried, "Jack."

Oh . . . my . . . God.

Whitaker exuded sexuality. A wild, scary hormonal overdrive. For a moment I'd even been afraid he'd try to rape *me*. I stood up, began pacing the front room, and pulled the clothes off the Nordic Track. I hopped onto it and slowly worked my legs back and forth, releasing a small cloud of dust. I sneezed and got off.

Whitaker had admitted to having been Phillipa's lover.

Holy shit!

He'd written a book, called *Teutonic Honey*, in which a man sought vengeance on a former lover. The rape scene had been both brilliant and brutal. Why hadn't I thought of it before?

Whitaker killed Phillipa.

But why?

forty-two

I SPENT THE REST of the night building a case against my potential dear old dad.

Maybe he'd killed Phillipa in an act of passion. No, that didn't make sense. She'd been gassed. It couldn't have been spontaneous. Not unless there was something Detective Garcia wasn't telling me, like she'd been hit with a blunt instrument before she'd been poisoned. No, that sounded too made-for-TV.

And anyway, I wasn't in Detective Garcia's confidence—especially now. He probably had reams of information he'd never share with me.

Oh, oh, oh! Maybe Whitaker and Ortega were in it together. Maybe Celia was Phillipa and Jack's love child—put up for adoption soon after birth and raised in a devout Catholic family. Okay. That idea verged on ludicrous.

Round about four in the morning, I decided I'd call Detective Garcia at dawn and lay all my theories on the table. He could do what he wanted with them and I could concentrate on work.

I didn't bother to go to bed.

Over a strong cup of coffee, I reread the two Harvey House proposals and began planning my final steps in making a recommendation. I'd been haphazard in my approach, interviewing willy-nilly. At this rate, I wouldn't be satisfied unless I interviewed the whole town.

Ernie Merkin had offered to teach me about trains, but I wrote that off as a frivolous use of time. Plus, I didn't really want to see him again. Something about him didn't sit well.

After I got Detective Garcia out of the way, I'd go back to Belen and do a final look-through, really assessing various parts of town for tourist potential. I wanted to check out the P & M Farm Museum, and spend some time doing "man-on-the-street" interviews, maybe at the White Way and then again at the Dayspring Deli. Just quick questions for the locals about which proposal they liked the best.

I knew the answer already: The B & B and train museum. No one loved Phillipa. They liked her work even less. In a deeply religious town, she'd stood out in all the wrong ways. It didn't matter that she made her home in Las Jefas. That community was the size of a mouse's nose. No, Belen was her birthplace, and most of Belen hated her guts. Any art museum with her work at the fore would have negligible community support. On top of that, I doubted the kind of people who appreciated her subject matter would be popular with the likes of Wally and Sugar Crawson and Belen's other moneybags.

In the shower, I argued with myself about the job. I knew I wasn't trying as hard as I could to be fair to the art museum proposal. How much of that was my own bias against Phillipa's work and charmers like Lydia Herndon? The reasonable thing to do would be to interview a few more artists. But what I really *wanted* to do was to see if I could spend a night in the Harvey House and meet Eulalia. I could rationalize the request in terms of a test run for the B & B concept. Get a real feel for how many trains came through town when people were supposed to be sleeping. I'd talk to Crawson or Gracey about it.

With the sun's first flirtation, I dressed and then called Detective Garcia.

"It's an interesting theory," he said.

"You've got to admit Jack Whitaker should be a prime suspect. He knew Phillipa, he's a sex fiend—"

The detective laughed.

"No, really. He's been married at least four times. And Mom said he'd been violent with Phillipa before."

"Your mother said that?"

"Not exactly. Yesterday afternoon, Mom had a nightmare. She said something about a man who had raped and abused Phillipa every time they had sex. And then later the same day, Mom had a second nightmare and called out, 'Jack! Jack!' It has to be the same person."

Garcia didn't respond.

"Don't you agree? Jack has to be the one who did that to Phillipa. He's a good suspect," I said. "Right?"

"Like I said, it's an interesting theory."

"Why do you always do that?"

"What?"

"Negate what I'm saying by belittling it. It must be something they teach in police 101."

"Yep. Right along with letting people waste our time."

I slammed down the phone. *Wonderful. I've just hung up on a policeman.* I dialed again.

"Garcia," he said.

"I'm sorry," I said.

"You ought to watch that temper."

"I just don't understand why you're not considering Jack Whitaker."

"Who said we weren't?"

"You've got to admit, he looks good for it," I said.

"What's missing here is a motive, Ms. Solomon. Jack Whitaker and Phillipa Petty were friends. Maybe once, long ago, they were lovers. During the last few years, they were frequently seen together, and always, they appeared to enjoy each other's company. There's nothing that points to Mr. Whitaker as an abuser or a killer."

"What about Mom's dreams?"

"From what you told me, it's not clear who your mother was dreaming about."

"Jack. I told you." I got up to check out food in the fridge. Opened a jar of kalamata olives and ate one.

"There are a lot of Jacks in the world."

"I know that."

"Ms. Solomon, I've got a meeting to go to. But don't hesitate to call me with your ideas, or with more information from your mother," he said, dismissing me.

"Why bother? I give you something and you think it's totally irrelevant."

"Nothing you say is irrelevant, Ms. Solomon. Goodbye."

Another cup of coffee, two more olives. I dressed in all-purpose professional clothes. One good thing about the last few days: they'd been so hectic, I wasn't eating as much as usual. My slacks fit a fraction less snugly. But the olives wouldn't hold me until lunch. I hauled my sorry self out to breakfast at the Flying Star on Rio Grande.

The green-chile muffin lay half-consumed on my plate while I thought about Jack Whitaker. The man still bothered me, the way he'd acted at our interview, the thick sexuality. He was capable of rape; I was sure of it.

Rape.

Another meal stopped tasting good.

forty-three

VISITING HOURS FOR FAMILY could be stretched at St. Kate's, especially in the early mornings when staff members were either too tired to notice or just settling into their shifts. I walked past the unmanned receptionist's desk and headed for Mom's room. With any luck, she'd be up and coherent.

Paul had beaten me there.

We exchanged hellos and pecks on the cheek, and before Mom got whisked away to one of her many therapy sessions, I jumped in.

"Mom, what can you tell me about Jack Whitaker?"

She looked at me as if I were mad.

"Mom? Are you all right?"

The smile on her face almost embarrassed me, it was so full. "Jerome Whitaker?"

"Yes."

"I haven't thought of him in years. How did you . . . what made you . . . ?" The grin remained goofy. She emitted a girlish giggle.

"Mom?"

"Oh, honey, forgive me. I just haven't thought of him in such a long time." She straightened the blanket over her lap, patted it down. "Why do you want to know about him?"

"I met him."

"Really? Where?"

"In Belen."

"Oh, my," she said. "How does he look? Is he still as handsome as ever?"

Paul signaled me, a question in his eyes.

"Mom knew Mr. Whitaker when she had the gallery in Old Town," I explained.

He nodded.

"He's handsome, Mom. But his hair's white and he's got wrinkles."

"Oh my," she said again, tugging at the sleeve of her robe. "Did he mention me? Does he know I'm in here?"

No problemo with coherence when it comes to a former lover.

"I told him you'd had a few strokes."

"Oh. I wish you hadn't."

I sat on the edge of her bed. "Mom, yesterday you had a couple of nightmares. You were talking about Phillipa being beaten and raped by someone. Later, in your sleep, you called out the name 'Jack.'"

"And you thought it was my Jack? Jerome?"

"Yeah," I said.

"Oh, absolutely not. Jerome Whitaker was the gentlest man I've ever known." She remembered Paul and held out a hand for him. "Except for you, sweetheart."

"Jerome Whitaker, the writer?" he said.

"He lives outside of Belen, near where Phillipa lived," I said.

"Why are you talking about Philly like she's dead?" said Mom.

"She *is* dead," I said.

"No, she's not. I spoke with her this morning."

"Mom, did Jerome Whitaker ever hurt Phillipa?"

"Jerome? Of course not. They're lovers."

"Mom, that's impossible. She's dead."

"No, she's not. She called this morning."

I held back the urge to tear something into molecules. Okay, okay. Detective Garcia said to go on these mental journeys with her—to see where they led. "What did Phillipa say?"

"She'd just found out she'd been admitted to the Art Institute," Mom said. "In Chicago. This is such an honor. A kid from New Mexico . . . there."

"Did she tell Jerome?"

"He was with her when they found out. You should know that. They practically live together."

"Aren't you lovers, too?"

"Sasha," said Paul.

"I'm married," she said. "Even though you wouldn't know it. Armand travels *all* the time."

"Jerome told me that didn't stop you from a little fling," I said.

Indignation brought new color to her face. That, combined with the coquettishness, gave me a glimpse of what she must have been like as a young woman—full of piss and vinegar, the kind of woman who'd pour garbage on people.

"Sasha, you're upsetting your mother."

"No. I need to do this," I said. "Mom, is Jerome Whitaker my father?"

The change was horror-flick fast. Fury mottled her face, bugged out her eyes. Ugliness emanated from her in tidal waves. "Get out!" she yelled. "Get out this instant!"

"Hannah, calm down," said Paul.

"I want that conniving bitch out of here!" If I'd been in range, she might have tried to scratch me. I got the feeling she aimed her anger at someone else, an old memory confused with the present. "Get out!"

"I'm sorry, Mom. I didn't mean to—"

"Get out! Get out! Get out!"

"What's going on in here?" A large nurse rushed into the room, a male aide following her. "Mrs. Solomon, are you all right?"

Mom's speech therapist—a lanky blonde with green eyes—walked in, saw the crowd, and retreated to the doorway.

"Mrs. Solomon?" said the nurse.

"Get her out of here!" Mom pointed at me.

"Mom. I'm sorry—"

"I never want to see you again," she yelled.

Paul and I exchanged glances, his face creased with blame.

"Mom."

"I'm going to have to ask you to leave," said the nurse.

I went to the doorway and stood next to the therapist.

"What's going on?" she said, her voice a whisper.

"I touched a nerve."

"No kidding," she said. "Are *you* all right?"

"I don't know."

I watched them circle around Mom, seeking to calm her down, murmuring platitudes. She lay in the center of their concern, her breathing rapid, her hands clenching the blanket. Tears in her eyes.

The therapist patted my shoulder and said, "With any luck, she won't remember any of this tomorrow."

"Yeah," I said, giving her a numb smile.

Mom's extraordinary reaction could only mean one thing.

Sasha Whitaker. Catchy name.

forty-four

A BIG FAT ONION. That's what this puzzle had become. A big, fat, fetid onion. At first, I had wanted to find the prick who had poisoned me. That was the outer skin of the bulb. Then, Mom got involved and I agreed to try to find Phillipa's murderer; it had to be the same guy anyway. Remove another layer. Mom's and Phillipa's lives intertwined in ways I was only now discovering—ways that affected the very core of my self-image, my self-knowledge. Ah, here's layer number three.

Phillipa's murder unkegged secrets with a distinctive stench. Jack Whitaker could be my dad. Celia Ortega could be my half-sister. Was I related to that nice Lucy Whitaker, too? I wanted to know more, and yet my eyes watered and my psyche rebelled against the potential rankness of a dredged-up past.

Mom, wacko Mom, lay at the center of it all. She needed protection. How was I going to do it without her knowing? Damn, I wish Paul had a cell phone.

I stopped the car in the Winrock Mall parking lot. A little after nine in the morning—few employees had shown up for work yet. I dialed Mom's room. If they'd calmed her down enough, she'd be having her speech therapy session now and wouldn't be there to answer.

"Hello?" said Paul.

"Hi. Is Mom all right?" I whispered.

"Yes," he said. "Speak up. I can barely hear you."

"Is she in the room?"

"Yes," he said.

"Okay. Look, I didn't mean to upset her."

"Who is it?" Mom said.

"That contractor I told you about," Paul said. I knew it pained him to lie—Mom must still have been unhinged.

"Have you seen Celia Ortega today?" I swatted a confused fly that had flown in the window.

"No. He won't be here today," Paul said.

194

"Who?" said Mom.

"David won't be home to let him in, Hannah," he said.

"You found out her schedule?" The fly landed on my thigh. I concentrated on keeping relaxed—not giving away my death wish—and struck. Missed.

"Yes." Paul's voice was tight.

"Well, that's good news," I said. "Can we talk later?"

"I'll be glad to do it, Mr. Gonif," he said. "Why don't you call back this afternoon? Maybe we can arrange a time then."

"Is Mom still upset?"

"Yes. That's right."

"Okay."

"Goodbye," he said.

The fly got bored and zipped out of the car. I squinted to watch its journey. Pretty soon, all the brittle yellow and brown leaves would fall and the flawless sky would be sculpted through bare branches. The fly would be dead, too. A morbid mood slithered round my heart. No. Depression wouldn't help anything.

Mom had called me many things in my life, but never a conniving bitch. She had to be thinking of someone else. Someone who knew her when she'd flirted—or more—with Whitaker. It could have been Phillipa, but I didn't think so. I'd met one woman who fit the description. Realizing I could accomplish at least one item on my agenda and find out the answer to another question, I dialed again.

"Hutchins residence," Cherry said.

"Hi, this is Sasha Solomon. I'm not sure you remember me but—"

"Of course I do. How're you coming on the proposals?"

"Well, that's what I wanted to talk to you about. You said you'd be willing to help me interview Lydia Herndon again. Are you up for it?"

"Are *you*?"

Cherry told me she'd take care of the details and to meet her at her house in an hour. "Look for a blue mailbox and turn right. Go six miles. Turn left at the boulder," and so on. A half hour later, I hung a left at Reinken Avenue, crossed the tracks, and headed south on a curvy and badly paved road.

If Phillipa's place was isolated, Cherry's house sat a couple of miles past nowhere. I made it to the homestead, a weird conglomeration of buildings that resembled barnacles clinging to a doublewide trailer. Several cars—including a shiny Ford circa 1950—littered the front yard. All older than me and in better shape.

The patchwork roof—shingled in some places, corrugated aluminum in others—covered the buildings like an oversized umbrella. Fall flowers, zinnias and determined marigolds, flecked the dirt yard. Dogs barked and kids hollered in play. Color and chaos. I wondered what Cherry's art would be like.

My hostess came out the door, wiping her hands on a dishtowel.

"Did you have any trouble finding us?" Her face dimpled in a smile.

"Not a bit."

"Come on in. I hope you're hungry," she said.

"Always," I said.

We walked through a tube of a hallway plastered on both sides with ill-lit photos and emerged into a great room. Several skylights and windows gave it an unexpected airiness. I blinked several times and with each opening of my eyes, I saw more. Paintings, photographs, mosaics, yarn on the floor and on a long wooden table, a clay bust in one corner.

Cherry didn't pause in the room, but continued on, talking all the time. Another tunnel masquerading as a hallway led into a dinosaur-sized kitchen with three tables, ranging from six- to twelve-seaters, complete with a guest I recognized.

"Miss Solomon," said Lydia Herndon.

"Good to see you again." I hoped the response sounded polite, even a tad submissive.

"Want coffee?" Cherry stepped into a mammoth walk-in fridge, one you'd find at your local restaurant. Without waiting, she handed me a gallon of milk. "Here's your cream."

"Well, what do you want to know?" said Mrs. Herndon before I could sit down.

"I have a few more questions about the art proposal." I put a homemade blueberry muffin the size of a dinner plate on my napkin. *Did you do something terrible to my mom, say, forty years ago?*

"You've read it, haven't you?" she said, then turned to Cherry. "I bet she hasn't read it."

"Lyddie, remember what we talked about?" said Cherry.

Mrs. Herndon emitted a fast, protesting breath.

"Read what?" I said.

"What would you like to know, Sasha?" Cherry served me a mug of cinnamon-laced coffee. I felt like a Lilliputian at Gulliver's table.

"I know Phillipa's art would be the initial draw, but what would sustain it? Have you thought about how you'd market it over time?" I slathered the muffin with soft butter and thought about how I'd rope Herndon into telling me the truth about mom.

"We're thinking that we could showcase southern New Mexican and Mexican talent. Do a kind of Borders Art Exchange with well-known artists," Cherry said. "We've already been in touch with a couple big names down there."

"What about the trains?" I said.

"What about them?" said Mrs. Herndon.

"Won't they shake everything off the walls?"

"Oh, they're not that bad," said Cherry. "And plus, Phillipa gave us the name of a guy who can make sure the art is secured correctly. She said she'd put the money for it in her will."

"Have you seen her will?" I said.

"Not yet."

"I did," said Mrs. Herndon.

Cherry and I put down our drinks and in unison said, "You did?"

"You haven't?" she said to me, her smile smug. "Bet you'd like to know what's in it."

"Lydia, what did it say?" Cherry's voice had descended a couple of octaves—from jovial to dead serious.

"I'm not talking in front of her," Herndon said, looking at me.

I pushed back my chair. "I can go into another room until you're done."

"Don't be rude, Lydia," said Cherry. "Why can't you just say whatever you've got to say in front of Sasha? She's not the enemy, you know."

"Her mother might be," said Mrs. Herndon.

forty-five

"**EXECUTRIX? WHAT ON EARTH** was she thinking?" I said, swiping at the coffee I'd spilled. "There's no way Mom's competent to do that." It could, however, explain several things.

"Don't worry about it, Sasha," said Cherry, following my ineffective cleaning with an oversized sponge.

"Was she absolutely insane? How could she have done something so stupid?" I said.

"Maybe she didn't know about your mom."

"She did," said Mrs. Herndon. "She knew and she didn't care. Or worse, she thought it'd be funny."

I let Cherry take over the swabbing. "I don't get it. Why would she want to play so loose with her fortune?"

"She was an evil woman. Her and that hoity-toity mother of yours. Fornicating, slutty—"

"Lydia!" said Cherry.

"No, really. It doesn't make any sense," I said. "Phillipa had been in contact with Mom. She had to have known about her strokes."

"She must have thought it was a good idea at the time." Cherry shrugged.

"And she had no way of knowing she'd be killed," I said.

"Lydia, why did Philly show you that will?" Cherry squeezed out the sponge and continued with round two.

Mrs. Herndon's tight mouth shrunk to miserly.

We waited.

"Lydia," Cherry said again. "Why?"

Mrs. Herndon got up and put her cup in the sink, keeping her back to us.

"Lyddie."

Mumble, mumble.

"We didn't hear you," said Cherry, rolling her eyes at me.

"She didn't. I looked at it," said Mrs. Herndon. "You satisfied?"

"Tell us." Cherry guided her friend back to her chair.

"I'd gone to Philly's to talk about the darn proposal, and she was acting up again."

"How long ago was this?" I said.

"About one, two weeks ago." She didn't look us in the eyes; instead she found a spot of dried egg on the table and chipped away at it with a fingernail.

"Go on," said Cherry.

"Philly got a phone call and, after a few minutes, she went in the other room to talk in private. And there was her will, plain as day, just sitting there on her desk. I read what I could before she came back." Mrs. Herndon started working on another glob of dried food.

"If you're going to clean, at least use this," said Cherry, handing the older woman a smaller sponge. "I can't believe you'd snoop like that. Now you tell us everything before I whip you myself."

Herndon used the sponge. "She'd been acting all high and mighty about how she was going to save this 'hell-hole'—that's what she called it, a 'hell-hole.' And I wanted to see if she really was. That's all." She opened her hands, palm down and inspected them.

I mouthed my question to Cherry, using one hand to mimic the act of writing on the other. Lydia Herndon wouldn't consider answering me right now, her anger too apparent.

"What did it say?" said Cherry.

I nodded.

"She's leaving money to the whole wide world."

"Lyddie, can you be a bit more specific?"

"The chamber of commerce, the art museum project, Nila Markowitz—of all people. You, the Artists Guild, that bitchy little housekeeper she had. Mike Gracey. Jack Whitaker—can you imagine? Mayor Flores, the train museum project—if the art project falls through. Philly was a regular Santa Claus and all I get is coal. Can you believe it? Not a penny to me. And that Hannah Solomon gets whatever she wants and is in charge of it all. And you can bet she won't give me the time of day." She regarded us with defiance. "I would've read more but Philly came back."

"Did Philly catch you?" Cherry again.

"No. She wasn't paying any attention to me at all. She was crying about something. Serves her right, whatever it was."

"I still can't believe it," I said. "She had to know Mom's memory was shot."

"Maybe she had faith that your mother would do the right thing no matter what." My hostess brought me another cup of coffee.

"Mrs. Herndon?" I addressed her finally. "Did you tell the police about what you saw?"

"Why should I? They've got her will."

"I know, but . . . don't you think they'd be interested in that phone call she got?" I said.

"I don't see how it could help," she said. "Just some crackpot. That's all."

Comprehension slapped Cherry and me across the face and then came back for another hit.

"The phone," she said.

"What did you hear?" I said.

"I'm sure I don't know what you're talking about," said Mrs. Herndon, sitting even straighter in her chair and avoiding our faces with determination.

"Lyddie, did you listen in on that conversation?" Cherry's soft voice struck home.

"How dare you!"

"Lydia Herndon, did you?" Her voice still gentle, Cherry let the obstinate woman know she'd shuck the answer out of her.

"Maybe a little."

"My God! What did she say?" I said.

"Young lady, that's no way to talk to me."

"Lydia, get off your high horse and tell us what she said." Cherry's tone no longer held compassion or kindness; it seethed.

Mrs. Herndon opened her mouth. Closed it. Opened it again and bit her tongue, then shook her head. "It's nobody's business."

"No, it wasn't anybody's business but Philly's. Then you eavesdropped and now it's everybody's business. You know darn well that Moises needs to know about this," said Cherry.

"I didn't recognize the voice," said the older artist.

"That has nothing to do with it," said Cherry. "What did you hear? Tell me this instant!"

"I just listened for a minute."

"Tell me," Cherry said.

"He said he'd been too patient—"

"About what?" I said.

"And that he'd waited too long."

"To do what? What are you hiding, Lyddie?"

I couldn't tell if Mrs. Herndon's rage was because of Cherry's insistent questioning or the tears now forming in her eyes.

Then in a burst of pure fury the old woman said, "He said it was his. All his. And he'd kill her before he'd let her give it away."

forty-six

IF LYDIA HERNDON HAD betrayed Mom—or Phillipa—years ago, I wasn't going to find out about it today. Not long after Cherry's call to the police, Detective Garcia showed up, his exasperation creating a tick-tack-toe of wrinkles on his face.

"What are *you* doing here?" he said to me.

"Interviewing about the Harvey House."

"Well, find somewhere else to do it."

Thus discharged, I left. Whoever had made the phone call to Phillipa might have been the killer. He might have been my poisoner and the person who was now precipitating a decline in Mom's fragile health. I'd find out who he was. I still suspected Pop Whitaker—and intended to find out more about him.

For now, I'd check out a Belen tourist destination on my list of must-sees: the P & M Farm Museum. The literature said it was open by appointment, so I called.

An elderly woman answered the phone, her English rich with a native New Mexican accent—Spanish had to be her first language.

"Can you come now? We don't have any doctor's appointments until this afternoon," she said.

"With whom am I speaking?"

"Monica Cortez."

I drove the short distance to Jarales, a small townlet like Las Jefas, and went bumpity bump over the second train track. Per the woman's instructions, I looked for two miniature windmills and turned onto a graveled drive. When I did, a shrunken, sun-bronzed man with thick glasses greeted me. He wore a blue workman's outfit and matching cap. His chin had gray and white hairs that wanted to become a beard.

"Are you the one who just called?" he said.

"Yes."

"I'm Pedro." He reached in the window to shake my hand.

"Where should I park?"

"Anywhere."

The main building was shaped like an L. Another larger building didn't quite join the first, creating a U out of the complex. While I contemplated alphabetical things, a slightly stooped woman walked to the car. Her hair was neon red.

"Are you the lady who called?" She wore an apron and wiped her hands on it.

"Yes. Are you Mrs. Cortez?"

"Monica. And that's my husband, Pedro. See?"

"Pedro and Monica? P and M," I said.

"That's right." She nodded. "How much time do you have?"

"Just about an hour." I wanted to eat lunch at Pete's before it got too crowded. Plus, the restaurant might be a good place to do my man-on-the-street interviews.

"Oh," she said, her voice quieting in disappointment. "In that case, I'll show you the first three rooms and then, maybe, you could come back some other time."

Mrs. Cortez opened a door and we stood in a room dominated by a dark, hand-carved dining-room set from Mexico. Down one hallway, a washing machine hummed. Display cases, jammed with everything from flowered porcelain teacups to plastic dolls dressed in crocheted finery, surrounded us. Small china saints prayed over miniature ceramic deer and donkeys. Framed reproductions of famous religious art from the Prado hung willy-nilly on discolored walls.

"I started collecting when Pedro went into the service in 1943. Ramon, my oldest, was just a few months old." Mrs. Cortez unlocked a wooden door to our left. Tacked to its front was a commemorative poster of the firefighters and policemen who died in the September 11th attack on the Twin Towers.

When the lighting stuttered on, Mrs. Cortez's patter served as a melodic accompaniment to a strange scene for which I was totally unprepared. Before me stood a presidential diorama comprised of two life-size cardboard cut-outs—one of Bill Clinton, the other of John F. Kennedy—in the center of several mannequins dressed to resemble various presidents' wives. Hats askew, wigs so fake they resembled helmets, the figures were arranged in a social setting, as if they were at a party, perhaps, or having tea. Completing the weird conglomeration was the kind of furniture you might find in a Western honky-tonk from, maybe, 1910. Two antique wooden radios rounded out the display.

"They both work," said Mrs. Cortez, watching me.

"Amazing," I said, thinking the Hub Motel's decor looked barren compared to this place. "Do you have many visitors?"

"Oh, well, it depends," she said.

We walked into another room and, again, the onslaught of its contents bombarded my senses. Rocks—both bought and found—small plastic farm animal toys that had been the Cortez children's playthings, an autographed photo of Jackie O and JFK. No white or empty space anywhere. A collection of Barbie dolls, a hand-operated washing machine, a mannequin wearing a wedding dress. A priest's robe mounted on a face-less dummy in front of an old, smoke-damaged organ.

"How do you manage to keep all of this up?" I asked, catching my balance as best I could.

"My kids help when they can. And we receive some private dona-tions." Her pride rippled through the air, imbuing each area she showed me with a tender sanctity.

"From whom?"

"Oh, this person and that. We've got some famous people here in Belen. Artists and writers and the such." She picked up a polished amber egg.

"Did Phillipa Petty ever come here?"

Mrs. Cortez fussed with a tacky doll dressed in a Flamenco dancer's costume. "Maybe."

"I think she would have loved this museum," I said by way of encouragement. "And I bet Jerome Whitaker likes it, too."

"Yes, well." She extinguished the lights before I was ready to leave.

"Excuse me, Mrs. Cortez, did I say something wrong?"

Instead of answering, she headed out of the building and toward my car. She couldn't have been more obvious if she'd pulled out a gun and shot it at my feet. She wanted me off her property.

"Mrs. Cortez?"

"Phillipa Petty was such a good girl. I don't know what happened to her," she said.

"You knew her?"

"Everyone around here knew her. But I suppose we didn't know her well enough. Why else would she have done the things she did?" Mrs. Cortez had her hand on my door handle, as if she was going to open it for me.

"Are you talking about her art?"

"That, and her loose ways. I don't understand it. She was such a good girl." She shook her head. "We all thought once she got married she'd settle down, but she didn't. Never did."

Mrs. Cortez yanked my car door open—and I think she would have pushed me in it if she could have.

"Thank you so much for the tour," I said, not knowing how to save the moment. I tried to press my $5 donation into her hand. She pulled back her arm.

"There's no need for that," she said.

"But I'd like to contribute something to help with your work."

"Oh, we're fine. We've got all the help we need."

Before I'd started the car, she'd turned her back on me. I felt as if I'd been shunned. She hadn't been rude, but the subject of Phillipa Petty had cut short what could have been an hours-long tour. Why?

On the drive back to town, I thought about the Cortez's place. For people who loved the wigwam hotels on Route 66, who'd love the Hub Motel for its eccentricity, the out-of-the-way museum would be close to nirvana. Years of collecting, of caring for and reworking the displays, had created something unique. Although, with Monica's and Pedro's age, I feared it might not last long enough to reach the audience who would appreciate it most.

As I passed the White Way Restaurant on the right, I thought about the white wedding dress Mrs. Cortez had shown me. Weddings. Marriage.

Miss Petty had been married. Where was her husband now?

forty-seven

PETE'S RESTAURANT LOOKED LIKE a dive from the outside. That's because the owners spent all their money making the inside so perfect. From the tiled floors to the *nichos* with Mexican art, from the intimate dining areas to the skylights, this Belen mainstay lengthened the plus side on my tourist-attractions list. Located right across from the Harvey House, the restaurant was poised to benefit big-time from either proposal.

The waitress led me past a room where I saw Mayor Flores, Sue Evans, and two others in conversation so intense they almost glowed.

Seated in a corner, I ordered my chicken enchiladas and side of guacamole. While I waited, I watched the crowd. People here were having business lunches, as serious as any in a big city. To disturb them would be rude. So much for the man-on-the-street concept.

Lunch came quickly. The guacamole zinged with garlic, the red chile–smothered enchiladas had generous strips of chicken, and the sauce radiated homemade flavor. Everything was so good, in fact, that I ordered the flan for dessert. A minute burst of orange in the creaminess made me moan. If I could have rolled in the stuff, I would have.

Pushing back from the table, I wondered if I really needed more information to make my decision about the two proposals. Only two things tempted me to come back to this little town. I wanted to find the creep who'd put such a dent in Mom's and my life . . . not to mention Phillipa's. And, I wanted to spend the night in the Harvey House to see if people would actually be able to sleep there. Well, that wasn't quite true. I wanted to spend the night in the hope of meeting Eulalia. For once, I wanted my stupid hallucinations to bring me pleasure.

A cell phone chirped and, as usual, several people—me included—opened purses or briefcases and felt in pockets to make sure theirs wasn't the culprit.

"Miss Solomon," said a man's voice.

"Yes?"

"I don't know if you remember me. We spoke the other morning."

"Of course I do. How are you, Mr. Merkin?"

"I'm fine." He coughed—a wet, phlegmy noise. "You talked about going to the train yard. You still interested?" His voice sounded wrong, as if he was reading unfamiliar lines from a cruddy play.

"I don't think I'll have time during this project. But thank you," I said, thinking that the nasty message on my machine could have been left by him, too.

"Oh."

"Could I take you up on the offer some other time?" I didn't want to talk to him.

"I guess."

"Great."

He held the line open but didn't say anything.

"Did you want something else, Mr. Merkin?"

"I don't think I was very helpful when we spoke before. I was feeling under the weather, if you know what I mean."

"Yes . . ."

"And I'd like to make it up to you." He'd gone off script and his delivery was even more stilted. If this was Merkin sober, I liked him better drunk.

"That's not necessary. I thought you were just fine."

"So, I was thinking, if you didn't have anything better to do, maybe you could swing by for another chat."

"I'm in Albuquerque," I said. Something about this conversation, about his voice, gave me the heebie-jeebies.

"No, you're not."

I looked around the restaurant.

"You're at Pete's," he said.

"No, I'm not."

"Yes, you are. I can see you."

I hit the disconnect button.

A waitress who'd been in our section came to me. "Are you all right, ma'am?"

I shook my head to release the fear and said, "I think so."

"Would you like anything else?"

"Just the check."

Outside, I walked from the parking lot through a bright alley to where I'd left my car in front of the municipal library. The alley smelled sour, of old garbage. I kept cranking my head this way and that, feeling exposed, I guess, like Ernie Merkin was tracking me—a stupid quarry.

My discomfort increased as I unlocked the door. Rather than get in, I locked it again and entered the library to be in a very public place.

Merkin came in a few minutes later and walked right up to me. I thought about running, about yelling or making some kind of a scene to protect myself. But what had this man done to me? Nothing until this moment.

"Miss Solomon, there's no need to be scared of me," said Merkin. "I'm harmless."

Oh, great. That makes me feel just wonderful. "I'm not scared. But I'd like to know why you're following me."

"I'm not. I saw you in Pete's when I went to pay the bill, but I was with the guys and you looked busy, so I left with them. But then I got to thinking that maybe I could arrange for you to see the trains," he said. "How come you lied?"

"I don't know, Mr. Merkin," I said not quite trusting his story, though it sounded plausible enough.

He pulled out a chair at the table where I sat. With a grunt, he bent forward. "That train museum idea is the one you should choose." Beer breath escaped his mouth, strong and sweet.

I recoiled from him. "Why?"

"It'd be best for everyone concerned," he said.

"Why? I want to know."

"It just would," he said.

"Is there something you're not telling me, something in particular I should know about?"

Merkin's grin held a crystal disdain. His eyes became clearer, sharper in his washed-out face. He got up, pushed in his chair to its original place, and regarded me with a scornful smile. "There're a lot of somethings you'll never know, Miss Solomon. Just trust me. You'd be better off to choose the train idea. That's all."

forty-eight

"**THIS WILL HELP WITH** your decision?" Wallace Crawson sounded put out.

"Absolutely," I said, biting a fingernail and watching a crow fly overhead.

"I'll see what I can do."

I hopped in the car, immensely pleased with myself. Since I'd lumped the retired railroad manager and the conductor in the same mental file, I'd thought of Crawson seconds after Merkin left. Unlike Merkin, Crawson had influence and money. He'd be the person who could arrange for me to spend the night in the Harvey House.

I sat in my Tercel and avoided the call I really needed to make. At this point, I didn't want a cup of coffee or to interview anyone else. I didn't want to work. Merkin's little story was as real as imitation margarine. The guy gave me the creeps. I shook my head and frowned. This whole Belen job had been full of lousy surprises.

New rule of thumb: If I ever find a dead body on my first day on the job again, I'll quit.

And then there was the question of my patrimony. Who cared if I was a bastard? Well, that technically wasn't correct. Mom had been married when I was born. Just possibly to the wrong guy.

Phillipa, Jack Whitaker, Mom. Was Mom still safe at St. Kate's? Questions tornadoed together with Mom at the eye of the funnel.

"Oh my God!" I said aloud. Open-palmed, I hit myself hard on the forehead. "What an idiot!" Starting the car, I headed back to Albuquerque. On the way, I thought about where to begin my search and blurted again, "How could I have been so stupid? I'm a screaming idiot."

Less than twenty-five minutes later, I pulled onto the brick driveway in front of Mom's house. Her ivied and groomed yard yielded no sign of her incarceration at the rehab center. Thank goodness for dependable gardeners. I unlocked the wrought-iron gate and the brass doors festooned with bunny butts. Mom had had them custom made.

Bunny butts to the world, Asian bunny faces on the inside for her own silly pleasure.

That pretty much summed up Mom's attitude toward most things.

The house, a semi-museum filled with modern and Asian art, had been my childhood home. I'd learned to walk carefully, never running for fear of breaking this invaluable Chinese porcelain or that one-of-a-kind sculpture. When I'd finally taken over paying her bills, I'd had them transferred to my address. I hated this house and all it represented: Mother's love for her antiquities so much stronger than her love for us, her children.

Enough self-pity, idiot. Where to start?

Mom, the ultimate collector, never could throw out a letter or card. Somewhere in her 3,400-square-foot house or in the seven outdoor closets that adjoined her garage, there was an answer.

In her bedroom, I rifled through dresser drawers, on the top shelves of her closets, feeling dirty, like a thief. If she'd been more coherent, would I have asked for permission?

Don't be stupid.

I did find letters, but none that mattered.

The phone rang. I ignored it at first, sure the machine would pick it up. The multiple beeps told me her tape was full, too. I climbed down the stepladder into her television room to listen to the messages. There were several hang-ups, probably telemarketers. A call from two charities that Mom regularly gave to, "just checking in." Read that to mean, "Where's our money?" A couple of long-winded come-ons that started, "Yes, this is Bill so-and-so, and I just got back to the office. I wanted to tell you about a great investment opportunity. . . ."

I fast-forwarded.

". . . live."

I rewound the tape and listened to the full message.

"Bitch, I know where you live."

Oh, *wonderful*. Mom wasn't safe at St. Kate's and now, someone was threatening her at home. But why?

The man's voice slurred as if he had a speech impediment or was very, very drunk. Mom didn't have the kind of machine that recorded times or dates, so I had no way of telling when the message had been left. I played it again. It sounded enough like the one that had been left on my machine that I decided to call Detective Garcia.

Later, on the same tape, "Hannah, Jack here. I just met Sasha. She's almost as beautiful as you were at that age. Call me. We need to talk about Philly." He left his number.

On the plush silk rug covering Mom's floor, I dug my fingers into the designs of bats and plum blossoms. How I wished she could answer my questions head-on. Not that she would, even if she could. As I let the tape run out, I stretched my legs, then lay down to stare at the ceiling. Rolling over onto my stomach, I noticed a box underneath the old Fisher phonograph she'd had since before I was born.

I pulled it out. It was metal with a substantial lock. I jiggled it but nothing happened. I got up and carried it into the utility room and found a tool kit. Using a screwdriver as leverage, I pounded away until the lock broke and I could open it.

Letters, brittle with age and bound together with gummy rubber bands that disintegrated at my first tug, lay under fawn-colored velvet. I glanced halfway down the first one.

I know a good doctor in Los Angeles. He helped Lydia. He has a clean office, wrote J. W. on May 9, 1959. *You don't have to do this alone.*

forty-nine

I READ THE LETTERS until the feeling of voyeurism overpowered me with revulsion.

Mother and Whitaker had been lovers a lot longer and a lot earlier than he'd let on. His missives to her spanned eight years. No wonder she was willing to put up with Dad's peccadilloes—'cuz, Armand Solomon wasn't my dad. My veins ran bluer than that.

In the master bathroom, with cupped hands, I drank cold water and then splashed my face. All those times of feeling like I'd been adopted, all those moments of questioning if Mom and Dad were my real parents. I'd been half right.

Back in Mom's TV room, I replayed Whitaker's—Dad's—message. Then farther back to the nasty one. If I stretched it, the voice could be Ernie Merkin's, just as I suspected he'd made the call to my machine. Could I trust myself on this? Or was I too biased because of our encounter in the library? I played it yet again. Could be Merkin. Could be someone else. I was trying too hard. I fished out Detective Garcia's phone number and left him a message, asking that he call back me at his earliest convenience.

Why would Merkin want to go after Mom? Or Phillipa? He didn't strike me as particularly religious. Since Mom had spent a lot of time in Belen, it's possible she and Merkin had met. The idea of him traveling in the same circles as the chichi arts crowd bordered the outlandish. Uneducated and—if his house was any indication—possessing as much culture as a dust mite, Merkin would've been workin' on the railroad rather than going to gallery openings.

My cell phone rang.

"Miss Solomon?"

"Yes." Why did all of the men in Belen insist on calling me "Miss?" Hadn't they heard of "Ms."? Of Gloria Steinem and Women's Lib?

"Wally Crawson here. It's arranged. I've got someone who'll spend the night with you at the Harvey House. She'll meet you there at six tonight. Her name is Mrs. Alley and she'll make sure you have everything you need."

I don't need a chaperone. "Thank you. But I don't want to put anyone out."

"Don't worry. Mrs. Alley is in line to be our general manager when we establish the new project. She's delighted to have the opportunity to show off the Harvey House and it'll satisfy our insurance carrier in case anything happens to you."

"Thank you. I'll be there at six." Chaperone or no, at least I had the chance to see Eulalia. That'd be worth the trip back to Belen no matter what rules they thrust my way.

Time to go home and pack an overnight bag. I'd take the laptop and begin zeroing in on the written recommendation I wanted to provide Mayor Flores. After all, he'd need a carefully worded rationale to guide the project through to a final vote.

Above the big-screen television in Mom's room, a Chinese-numeraled timepiece showed three o'clock. On the TV's blank screen, my reflection presaged an intangible danger—whether to me or to Mom, I wasn't sure. Before I left, I'd have to make one more call.

"Hello?" said Paul.

"How is she?" I sat cross-legged on the rug.

"Sleeping."

"Is she all right?"

"As good as can be expected."

"Paul," I said.

"What, Sashala?"

"She had an affair. I have proof."

"None of us are perfect," he said. "We all make mistakes. Why upset her with this now?"

"My dad wasn't her husband."

"So? I ask you again . . . is this important now?"

"To me, it is."

"Then it's good you found out." I heard him swallow, as if he'd taken a sip. "Don't bring more trouble to your mama. Her mind is troubled enough just living."

"You're right." I sighed. "That's not why I called anyway. Can you talk?"

"Yes."

"Do we need to move Mom? What do you think?"

"I think it would kill her," he whispered.

"Do you think you can keep track of Celia Ortega's schedule?"

"I know I can."

"How?" I said.

"I've made a friend in the kitchen."

"You rascal."

He laughed quietly. "I think we can control it here, Sasha. I spend most of my time with Hannah anyway. But don't forget tomorrow."

"What's tomorrow?"

"It's shabbat. I'll be at temple."

"Oh, yeah. Sorry," I said, reminded of what a lax Jew I was. "I'll come."

"I know you will." There was a sudden intake of air. "She's waking up. Why don't you come by this evening and kiss her goodnight. I'm sure she'll be happy to see you."

"She's not mad anymore?"

"I think she's forgotten."

"Paul?" Mom said in the background.

"I'll come before dinner."

A futile sadness kept me on the rug though I wanted to leave my mother's house. Why hadn't Mom divorced Dad and married Whitaker? The letters he'd written her were full of love, tenderness, far more than Dad had ever shown. I'd have to get over thinking of Armand Solomon as Dad. Or should I? Was Paul right that I should let it all stay buried?

No. I didn't want to. If Jack Whitaker was my dad, that meant I'd been given a new parent. Someone to help me in this world. Someone who'd care about my successes and failures. Someone whose short-term memory still worked. This was a second opportunity to get everything right.

Who the hell was I fooling? Jack Whitaker had about as much interest in me as a sea slug. Well, when I was done with the Belen job, I'd change that. I'd force my way into his life. I'd make myself so intriguing and valuable to him that he'd have to pay attention. I'd—

My damn cell phone chirped.

"What?" I said.

"Sasha?"

"Peter!" My delight at hearing his voice plummeted as I remembered my suspicions about him breaking into my house. "Hi, Peter."

"How are you?"

"Okay, I guess."

"Have I called at a bad time?"

I didn't know what to say. Could be I was wrong. I had no proof he was a maniacal stalker. Could be he was a wonderful cutie—born to be my next boyfriend.

"Sasha?"

"So, uh, Peter. Did you ever get your ruby back?" Not subtle, but not accusatory either.

"No. Why?"

"You didn't take it back?"

"From where?"

"Oh, never mind."

"Did you lose my ruby?" *I* wasn't being accusatory, but he was.

"Sort of."

"Did you or didn't you?" I heard music in the background, salsa— and people laughing.

"What's so special about it anyway? I mean, besides the fact that it's a ruby?"

"It's a long story. Ruby is my birthstone . . . July. It was a gift from my mom, Sasha. She gave it to me a few weeks before she died." It sounded like he'd put the phone down to turn off the music. "Damn."

"I'm sorry."

"When did you last see it?"

"The other night. I called the police and made a report. I sort of thought maybe you'd come in and taken it back."

"What?"

"Well—"

"You thought I just waltzed into your house—that I broke into your house to get back my ruby? Are you crazy?"

I could hear the anger in his voice, but that wasn't what upset me. I'd spent a couple of milliseconds running through scenarios. If Peter hadn't taken back his ruby, then who'd broken into the house? Twice?

"I don't like this," I said.

"Neither do I."

"I don't know what to think."

"I do. I think we need to talk."

"When?"

"Right now, face-to-face."

"Okay." I wanted to see him again—even under these circumstances.

"I mean it. Right now."

"Fine."

"I'll meet you at the Flying Star on Menaul," he said.

"I'll be there in a few minutes," I said before hanging up. Then, nodding at nothing, I grabbed the lockbox and fled Mom's house. God willing, I wouldn't need to go there again for a very long time.

fifty

CAR BUSINESSES—FROM DEALERS to mechanics, from body shops to chop shops—love Albuquerque. Why? The constant influx of customers. Yep. Albuquerqueans are lousy drivers. I'll admit, I speed on occasion. I might even press the accelerator when I see a yellow light. But today, when my cell phone rang for what seemed like the hundredth time, I swerved across a lane trying to answer it. The guy I cut off flipped a finger and screamed something as he passed me.

"Sasha?"

"Hold on, Paul, I need to pull over." Heart thumping from the near miss, I drove into a convenience store parking lot. "I'm back. Sorry about that."

"You need to come here right now." A panicked insistence tinged his voice.

"Why? What's happened? Is Mom all right?"

"Just come."

Flying Star was on the way to St. Kate's. I stopped there to tell Peter our talk would have to wait. He stood outside the restaurant.

"I can't stay." I rolled down the window, not even bothering to get out of the car. "I've got to go to the hospital."

"What's wrong?"

"Something to do with my mom. I don't know yet, but I've got to go."

"You want me to come?"

I shook my head. "Thank you, but you don't even know my mom."

"How about for you?"

My breath caught. Bob had never offered to come to St. Kate's, not once. "That's really sweet. But I don't think it'd help. Call me later and we can reschedule." I pulled out of the lot and didn't look back when he yelled my name.

Minutes later, I rushed into Mom's room. Paul was there; Mom wasn't.

"Ohmigod. Not again. Where is she?" I'd run in from the parking lot—the receptionist's voice admonishing me to slow down barely registered a blip in my consciousness until I sat down.

"At physical therapy."

"Oh." The chair coughed as I plopped into it. "What's going on? Why the emergency?"

"Look at this." Paul reached into his pants pocket and pulled out an innocent-looking white pill.

"What is it?" I said.

"I don't know."

"Where did you find it?"

"Six," he said. "She always has six pills in the afternoon. This one makes seven. And I've never seen this kind before."

Someone tapped on the door, though it wasn't closed. Unaccustomed to civility in this facility—most people entered the rooms like Visigoths— I turned at the noise. "Peter?"

"Hi," he said, not meeting my eyes. "You were so upset. I thought you might need help."

"Peter works at Poison Control. He's a doctor. And a pharmacist," I said to Paul, who'd stood up to shake hands. I handed my private doc the pill. "Do you know what this is?"

Peter examined it between forefinger and thumb for no more than two seconds. "Amoxicillin. Why?"

"Amoxicillin?" Paul and I said together.

"Two hundred and fifty milligrams. It's a common dosage."

Paul's face lost its last bits of color. He sat down again. I know I blanched, too.

"What's wrong?" said Peter.

"My mom's deathly allergic to anything remotely related to penicillin."

"Where did you get this?" Peter looked at me, then at Paul.

"It was in her medicine cup. They just delivered it. I didn't recognize it, so I took it out," said Mom's boyfriend.

"Where's her chart?" Peter said, going back out the door to see if someone had left it in the wall holder. "Who's her doctor? That's a fatal mistake. This should be reported. " He came back into the room and picked up the little pill cup. "These are diabetes and heart medications. Here's something for cholesterol. No wonder you noticed this." He put the container down. "Where's the pharmacy department here?"

I shrugged my shoulders. "I don't know."

"Will you excuse me for a minute?" I'd never seen someone frown with his whole body, but Peter was doing it now.

"Just bring it back. Okay?" I said.

"Oh, I'll bring it back." Strands of his luscious hair stuck to his sweating forehead. "Just as soon as I find out who's responsible for this." Without warning, he kissed my cheek. "I'll be back in a second."

When he'd left, I asked Paul, "How?"

"I had a feeling, Sashala. That's all."

"You saved her life."

"*Modeh Ani.*" I knew enough Hebrew to know Paul had just thanked God. He looked at his age-spotted hands, then up at me. "You've got a new boyfriend?"

"Bob and I broke up." I went into Mom's bathroom to wash my hands. "Peter's just a friend."

Paul's straight face gave away his disbelief more than any words could have. "A doctor?"

"And a pharmacist." I walked back to the chair next to him. "I mean it. He's a friend."

"You don't have to explain your life to me. He's smart. Much more of a looker than Bob. Definitely more hair." His eyes lit with amusement. "Is he Jewish?"

"Paul, stop deflecting." I took his cold hand in mine. "Tell me about the pill."

"What's to tell? They know me here, so they left her medicine. I noticed that new one right away. I had a bad feeling, so I called you."

"Maybe her doctor ordered something different and the pharmacist made a mistake." I didn't believe it for a minute.

"I would have known," he said. "The doctors all know me, too. They would have told me. They always do." Paul, more than anyone else, had been Mom's advocate since she'd had her very first stroke. He'd made it his mission to take care of her. His devotion enabled my laziness. I didn't have a clue which meds she took or when. Or what this particular groan meant as opposed to that one.

"Plus, you're spooked about Celia Ortega," I said.

"I just know that pill doesn't belong to your mother." He put his other hand upon mine. "Sasha, you asked if we should move your mama. I didn't want to say yes, but I find myself not trusting anyone here anymore." He reached to straighten a picture of my sister and me on Mom's beside table. "Since Rita's been gone, your mama isn't getting good care."

"Rita's gone? Since when?"

"I'm not exactly sure. One of the nurses said she quit," he said. "I think it has to do with your mama's disappearances. Rita was so mad about how the hospital treated us."

"That could be good news, Paul. Maybe we can hire her to help Mom at home." I stood up and went to the window. Mom's view extended to a roof with an exhaust fan serving as the only aesthetic element. "What do you think? I know it'd be expensive, but it'd sure be better than paying this place when both of us are so worried about her safety. Mom would be happier, too."

"She would," he said.

"You've been waiting for me to suggest this, haven't you?"

"Sasha, you always do what's best for your mama."

We both knew that wasn't true. Having Mom in a facility was best for me—at least until today. I hadn't had to rearrange my life at all with her care assured, the therapy sessions predictable. If we moved her home, I'd have to take on a bigger chunk, accept more responsibility for transportation, doctors' appointments, meetings with ancillary health professionals. Just thinking about it soured my stomach.

I sighed because there was nothing else to do. "Would you mind calling Rita to see if she'd be willing to work for us? You know her a lot better than I do." I realized I really didn't know anything about the woman. Was she married? Did she have kids? What part of town did she live in? Well, we could deal with that later. "If she doesn't want to do it, I bet she'll know some good people who might. Don't you think?"

"I think we need to do something."

"Soon."

"Today."

"Paul, I've still got work to do in Belen. I can't move that fast." And I didn't want to, either. The more I thought about this change for Mother, the more I realized it was about to change my life too. Oh, I should be a good daughter and just suck it up, but this was happening too quickly.

"You sign her out," said Paul. "I'll take your mama home and you come when you can. But you need to sign the papers. You're the only one who can do it, legally. I don't count."

"You want to do this right now?"

"Yes."

"You want to just take her?"

"Yes."

"Paul, you can't lift her!" *Neither can I.* "We don't have any of the equipment she'll need. Plus, you said you're going to shabbat services tomorrow night." I started clearing off the tissues on her bed stand. "Let's shoot for Saturday. I'll start calling around tomorrow to try to line things up."

"I don't think we should wait that long." He went to her closet and opened it. "There's not much here. We could move her tomorrow. You could help me pack tonight."

"Tonight? I can't. I've got plans."

"With that Peter?"

"No. I have to be out of town for work."

"You can't put it off until tomorrow?"

"I can't." I probably could have, but I didn't want to. This was the last piece of research for the Belen project. Finish this, write the recommendation, and then I'd be done. Tomorrow, after Darnda's afternoon interview with Karen Kilgore, I could devote my full time to taking care of mother—at least until we got her settled at home.

The rubbery noise and metallic clunk of a walker sounded down the hall. Mom entered the room with her therapist.

"Sasha, sweetheart, what a wonderful surprise," she said. Thank goodness for short-term memory loss.

"Mom, I've got to go," I said.

"Why, sweetie? I just got here."

"Sasha, we need to make a decision," Paul said.

"About what?" Mom said. "Why do you have to go?"

I'd already withdrawn to the door, one foot over the threshold. "I need to find Peter. Then I have to get back to Belen."

"Phillipa Petty lives near there. You remember Philly, don't you?" Mom smiled. "Let me call her. I'm sure she'd be glad to help you with whatever you're doing." With a wink of collusion, Mom said, "She owes me big."

Time to go with the flow. "Why, Mom?"

"I launched her career. There's nothing she wouldn't do for me now. Do you want me to call her?"

I didn't have the fortitude to break her heart again. "You already did. Yesterday. She's waiting for me, Mom. Okay? Do you want me to tell her anything?"

"Just that I can't wait to see her again," she said.

fifty-one

"**HOW DO I KNOW** you're who you say you are?" said the pharmacy tech. Chubby, his face acne-pitted and mop-topped with cinnamon hair—it had to have come from a bottle—he reminded me more of an unhealthy cherub than a trustworthy medicine dispenser.

I pulled out my driver's license and placed it on the counter. "Will this do?"

"I suppose," he said. "It's not my rules, anyway."

"*They're* not," I said, correcting his grammar.

"Huh?" He nudged the license so that it fell onto the floor. "Oops," he said without a trace of contrition. "Look, like I told Peter—I didn't put Amoxicillin in your mother's cup. There are allergy warnings all over her chart. The woman's allergic to her own shadow." His voice had a prissiness to it. I wanted to strangle him.

"You told *him*, but you asked *me* for identification?" I took out a crumpled receipt from my purse and wrote down his name on the back of it.

He eyed this activity with a frown. "I know Peter. He's a doctor. Plus, I've called him at Poison Control before."

"Where is he, anyway?"

"How should I know?" said the tech.

"Who put the pill in my mom's cup?"

"Sorry I can't help you. All I know for sure is it weren't me."

"Wasn't," I said. "Aren't you supposed to have a pharmacist supervisor?"

"You a teacher or something?"

"No." Wasting time here. "Do you have access to the intercom? Can you page Peter?"

"The intercom is for official business only," he said. "Finding your boyfriend wouldn't count."

What a piece of work. I wanted to take the brightest lipstick I could find and smear it all over his smug face.

"He's not my boy . . . oh, never mind," I said, ready to stop sharing air with him.

Where *was* Peter? I sneaked back to Mom's room and peeked in, but didn't see him there. Next, I did a circuit of the rest of the brain injury unit, then went to the cafeteria. No luck. I dialed his number and got the same boring message I'd gotten before. The man was impossible to reach. We'd have to talk about that, too, when we rescheduled our chat.

The sun sparred with a thick cloud outside. I stopped at the hospital's entrance to look at the Sandia Mountains, now a mass of blue in the distance. I didn't really have to go to Belen today. I knew it. Worse, Paul knew it, too. Key in hand, I headed to the car feeling low—like the world's worst child. I'd put my curiosity before Mom's needs.

Sure, I could have turned around and gone back into the hospital, but there wouldn't be much use for it now. Though he said nothing, Paul's disappointment—the slow shake of his head coupled with the unconcealed frown—more than showed when I'd left.

Eulalia, you'd better be worth it.

With my self-image already in the toilet, I opted to reinforce the feeling. On the way home, I stopped by Flying Star to pick up a pastry of some sort. It didn't matter what kind, just so it was gooey, and had lots of chocolate and nothing healthy. I ate the mocha-whipped pie with chocolate sauce without a fork while driving. My steering wheel was a mess by the time I reached home.

Leo stood at the door, waiting for me. One of his ears had a new chunk missing.

"You've got to stop fighting, Leo. No one likes a pugilist," I said.

"Rowllll?"

"How's it hanging?"

"Mmmmmrowllll." Leo pushed past me, ran into the kitchen, and wove in and out of the chair legs under the table. I should mention something: Leo had food and water bowls inside and outside. The current starving-cat melodrama played a bit false. At the sink, I poured myself a glass of tepid water. Leo rubbed against my legs now, purring loudly.

"I'm spending the night in Belen, so I'll give you some wet food," I said. "But don't expect this treatment every day."

He stopped to look at me. I was certain he understood. Darnda said he was unusually smart. Did I see him nod his head in acknowledgment? Then he went back to the rubbing and purring act, a drop of drool hitting his bowl as he ran to eat from the can I laid on the floor next to it.

When Leo first came into my life, he'd served as a kind of madness meter. That was during the bad days, the days of active hallucinating brought on by stress. If he quipped back at my comments or initiated a conversation, it was a pretty sure bet that I'd be out of commission for a while. My strategy worked for months. When Leo told a joke or displayed verbal sympathy, I knew to avoid important meetings—if possible—and stay close to home.

If I'd had the inclination, I might have been able to put out a shingle and pass myself off as psychic. For a brief time, I'd considered it seriously. However, to use Karen Kilgore's words, I wasn't "the real deal." I couldn't make sense of the things I saw and I couldn't control the altered states. They worked on me, not the other way around.

So, after more than a year of unbalanced reality, I started going to the D.O.M. and the hallucinations had mainly gone away. Would I even be able to see Eulalia, or would she be closed off from me, too?

In the bedroom I stared into the open closet, pondering what to wear to a haunted house. I didn't think I'd have to impress Mrs. Alley. And I didn't plan to stay in Belen after tomorrow morning. This would be a quick in-and-out trip. Talk to the ghost, try to sleep, prowl the rooms on the second floor of the Harvey House to assess its real suitability for the B & B concept.

Into the overnight bag went another sweat suit, a change of underwear. I debated taking my make-up bag. Informality won. I tucked in the latest *New Yorker* and an *Economist* that Paul had given me, gave fish-breath Leo a kiss, and locked the door.

When my cell phone rang, I wanted to throw it across the driveway. That's how it always was—scads of calls one day and then none for a week. I leaned against the front of my car and watched a late-season hummingbird flit at one of the many feeders I maintained; when you live in drought country, you have a special compassion for wild animals without food or water. His iridescent chest shimmered with blues and greens. He sampled the sugar water. Buzzed near me and then returned to his meal.

The way I knew that the phone had stopped ringing is that it started up again.

"Solomon," I said, annoyed that the new noise had frightened the little fellow away.

"Sasha, it's Peter. I'm just confirming . . . you said your mom's boyfriend found this with her other medications?"

"Yes." I could just spy the hummingbird on a branch in the cottonwood in Josie's backyard. "Where are you?"

"That's not important. What is, is that I've been talking with a friend of mine about Hatch Healthcare. Seems these kind of mistakes aren't uncommon."

"What kind of friend?"

"Someone I trust. In law enforcement," he said. "I've gotta go. Bye."

His abrupt conclusion to our conversation reminded me of someone else. I climbed onto the hood of the car and dialed Detective Garcia's number, expecting to leave another message on his machine.

"Garcia."

"Hi, this is Sasha Solomon."

"Ah, Ms. Solomon. I just got your message."

"Celia Ortega is trying to poison Mom now."

"And you base this on what?"

"We found Amoxicillin in her medicine cup. Mom is deathly allergic to anything in the penicillin family."

His silence indicated I'd gotten his attention. "Tell me what happened."

"Paul, Mom's boyfriend, found a pill he didn't recognize. He knows all her medications backwards and forwards. And this pill was different."

"Someone unfamiliar with her medical history could have made a mistake."

"The pharmacy technician I spoke with at St. Kate's says he didn't put the pill in her cup. He also said her allergies are flagged all over her chart." I looked at my fingernails. Who'd chewed them so far down?

"Did you ask the nurse on duty about it?" said Garcia, his calm maddening me.

"No." A whiff of roasting green chile hit my nose, making my mouth water.

"It's possible your mother got someone else's medicine."

"I doubt it." Amazingly, a roadrunner strutted across my driveway, his tail feathers up. "The other pills were her normal ones."

"Okay, let's say you're right. Someone put a life-threatening pill in your mother's medications. Why do you believe this was intentional?"

"Oh, come on. You know Celia Ortega poisoned Phillipa Petty," I said, feeling like he was being deliberately obtuse.

"We don't know that."

"I do." I stifled a sneeze to remain undetected by the roadrunner. "First you tell me I need to believe what Mom says, and now you tell me it's fantasy."

"I understand your frustration, Ms. Solomon."

"Stop handling me like I'm a kid," I said. "What are we supposed to do? Wait until Mom's murdered like her friend? I'm not going to do that. We're moving her as soon as we can."

"I don't think that's necessary."

"Can you tell me why not?"

"Calm down," he said. "Miss Petty hadn't been systematically poisoned. We've spoken with her doctor, her masseur, her nutritionist, and her personal trainer. There's no evidence of anything out of the ordinary before she was murdered."

"She had a personal trainer?" I don't know why I fixated on that.

"She wanted to stay in shape."

"Huh," I said.

"Miss Petty was in fine shape until someone killed her."

The roadrunner noticed me finally, but didn't seem bothered. He ate the dried corn I'd scattered near bushes at the side of the house. "So, Mom just made that up."

"Your mother was mistaken," Garcia said.

"It's too much of a coincidence that Ortega is working where my mom is. Something's up with that," I said.

"You may be right." Garcia coughed. "But I doubt it has anything to do with poisoning."

fifty-two

A SHINY, SILVER CADILLAC and an old, beige Volvo coupe sat in the dusky light of the Harvey House parking lot. Wallace Crawson bent like a stalk of pampas grass over a petite woman dressed in khaki-colored sweats. I parked next to them.

"Miss Solomon, this is Mrs. Scott Alley," said Crawson in one breath—as if he were missing another, more important, meeting by being here.

"Hi, Mrs. Alley. Mr. Crawson," I said with a nod of my head.

"Call me 'Scott.'" She shook my hand in a no-nonsense grip.

"Sasha." I liked her eyes—unadorned and unafraid to make contact. "I'm sorry to inconvenience you."

"No trouble. It's my pleasure." Her salt-and-pepper hair was cut in a pageboy that accentuated her oval face. Not a choice I'd make in hairstyle, but it suited her. I guessed her age to be between sixty and seventy. She wore sensible shoes, the kind old-time nurses or maids wore—kind of like Lucy Whitaker's, come to think of it—padded and white with rubber soles. "I love to spend time here . . . and Ernestine is always glad for company."

I looked at Crawson for a clue about Scott's sanity and received only a bland stare. "Well, if you girls are ready, I'll go home now. Sug's got dinner in the oven." He'd already pressed the auto-unlock on his car.

I doubted Sug knew how to warm a muffin in a microwave.

"That's fine, Wally. I'm sure we can manage," said Scott.

We watched him drive out of the lot.

"*Girls.* The only person who dares call me a *girl* is that good old boy," said Scott, walking to the front of the Harvey House. "Some men are so dense."

"Yeah, he seems pretty old-school."

"Like last century," she said. "But that's the way it is with a lot of these railroad guys—the managers especially—they assume everyone else is of a lesser order. You know . . . they're the wheat and we're all the chaff. "

"I thought it was just me," I said.

Scott snorted in response and pulled the door toward her, struggling with the lock. "Damn thing sticks. I'd better tell Ned to get some WD-40 on it."

"Do you need help?"

"Nah. I just like to be dramatic." With a crunch, the door opened and we stepped into the dark building. It smelled lemony, of wood polish and people's deodorant. Scott went to the little office off the main exhibit area and turned on a light. "There isn't any lighting on the stairway. I'll go ahead and turn on a couple of lamps. It'll only take a minute."

"Do you want me to follow? I could turn off the light down here."

"Oh, I'll do it," she said.

"I can."

"Actually, Wally was very particular about that. He doesn't want anything to happen to you, no broken legs or arms."

"Is he worried about a lawsuit? That's silly."

"I think he's more concerned about you getting a bad impression of the place. He wants to win you over for the B and B idea." Scott yelled the last sentence to me from upstairs. Sound carried well here. I wondered how that would work for the overnighters.

I wandered into the sunroom, thinking about how it could be transformed into a cozy eating area. They'd have to have an up-to-code kitchen to make the restaurant fly—but it could be charming on a small scale. Was there some kind of licensing process to use the Fred Harvey name? These weren't my problems, but I considered them anyway. With my recommendation, I'd make a whole new set of friends and enemies. I wanted to be clear in my decision, to look rationally at the pros and cons of each proposal.

"Sasha?" Scott stood before me.

"Did you say something? I'm sorry."

"Want to see your room? We got you a nice air mattress and everything." She started up the stairs again. "Come on, let me show you your digs."

"I can't wait," I said, and meant it.

"You'll wait for sleep, that's for sure."

"Why?"

"The trains. They're relentless . . . but that's part of the experience, the charm and excitement of staying here." She stopped at the corner room with four large, naked windows. "I assumed you wanted to be in Ernestine's room."

"Thank you." We stood there a moment before I said, "Scott, have you seen her?"

"Absolutely."

Outside, the sky had turned a smooth, dark blue. I felt exposed to the workers in the train yard below. The putter-putter of vehicles that looked like souped-up golf carts carried on the quiet night air. I'd seen them travel to and fro during the day but hadn't expected them to be operational now.

"I'll be next door," Scott said, turning to go. "If you need anything, just holler."

"I haven't had dinner yet," I said. "Would you like to catch a bite at Pete's? My treat?" Two times in one day would be just fine with me.

"I've already eaten. You go on over." She fished around in her purse and handed me a card. It identified her as President of the Valencia County Historical Society and listed three phone numbers. "The last one's my cell. Just call when you're ready for me to open up downstairs."

A few minutes later, I stared at the Harvey House through the window at the restaurant. Light could be seen on the second floor but from this angle Scott's temporary lair wasn't visible. Neither was mine. I felt a hand on my shoulder and jumped.

"Hello, Sasha. How's your mom?" said Jack Whitaker.

"Mr. Whitaker, Ms. Ortega." I flipped into formal mode to mask my shock at the sight of the two of them together.

"Mind if we join you?" said Whitaker.

"I'm only going to be here for a few minutes."

"We're just here for a quick bite ourselves." He pulled out a chair for Ortega and then seated himself. "Well, isn't this nice?"

I didn't think so. Ortega's pinched lips and steely eyes showed she didn't either.

"So, how's your mother?" said Whitaker again.

"She's all right." *Given she was almost poisoned by your dinner companion.*

"Celia tells me she met Hannah at the rehab hospital." Whitaker sounded too damn jovial.

"That's right," I said.

"You're not a journalist," Ortega said to me.

"Nope."

"Why'd you lie?"

"I didn't know who you were," I said, picking up a chicken taco.

"That a policy or something? You always lie to strangers?"

"It's too long of a story." I took a bite so that I wouldn't have to speak.

"I've got all the time in the world," she said, moving her butt forward and feigning a relaxed attitude.

"You two know each other?" said Whitaker.

Yeah, Dad.

"We met at Miss Petty's," said Ortega.

"Really? That's nice." Could he really be that oblivious?

"How do *you two* know each other?" I said.

"I'm Celia's godfather."

"Why, you're just everyone's dad, aren't you?" I said.

"Excuse me?" Whitaker reached into his ear with his pinkie and fiddled with something. I hadn't noticed he wore a hearing aid.

230

"I found the letters you wrote Mom," I said. "Not quite the story you told me."

"What's she talking about?" said Ortega.

Whitaker shot me the kind of glance that could wither one of those giant redwoods in California. "She must be confusing me with someone else."

"I don't think so, Pop."

"You're her father?"

"It's possible."

"No, it's definite. I won't tell Ms. Ortega here what you suggested to Mom when she found out she was pregnant."

"That's quite enough," said Whitaker.

"You dare to tell me what to do? Dad?" I hadn't meant for it to sound so venomous.

A thought took form as we sat there in our triumvirate of uneasiness. Dear old Dad was Ortega's daddy as well. Ewwww. Okay. That would make her my illegitimate half-sister. Yech. And Phillipa's daughter. That was it! They had motive.

It'd give them both a good reason to kill the artist. Celia Ortega would be Phillipa's only living heir and if she were *my* mommy dearest, I'd contest the hell out of her will—or get rid of anyone who stood in the way of my inheriting millions of dollars. Bingo! Mom, as executrix—and a mentally incompetent one at that—would definitely be in the way.

No, wait, Ortega's dark skin and hair didn't match either Phillipa's or Whitaker's. That'd have to be one hell of a recessive gene. Maybe Phillipa had had dark hair once upon a time. She was a native New Mexican after all; maybe her family was third- or fourth-generation Spanish. Why not? I didn't really know anything about her childhood or parentage. Nothing of that sort, anyway.

Or maybe Dad and my half-sister were lovers. Yuck! I shivered and looked at the two of them, trying to imagine that scenario. It wasn't pretty. They returned my stare. A vacuum of silence surrounded us.

A moment later, Whitaker and Ortega decided it wasn't such a good idea to join me for dinner after all.

fifty-three

TENSION. STRESS. NORMALLY, I'd shy away from both, but tonight I felt glad for my encounter with Daddy-O and his other illegitimate progeny. I shed the urge to cast Ortega as Madame X in favor of the daughter theory. No matter which proved to be true, seeing the two of them together might counteract my grip on reality enough to see Eulalia.

Still dressed in her sweats, Scott let me into the Harvey House and yawned. "I'm not used to staying up this late."

"Late?" It was eight o'clock.

"I'm usually on the four-to-noon shift at the hospital, so I go to bed early to get my sleep," she said.

"You're a nurse?"

"Lab tech."

"There's a hospital in Belen?" I should've known that. "I thought everyone came up to Albuquerque."

"No." She headed for the stairs. "I go the other direction, to Socorro."

"I'm sorry I woke you." I let my fingers glide on the wooden banister as I followed. "I can't thank you enough for tonight."

"I'm off tomorrow, so it's no problem. That's why there was the rush, though. If you couldn't have come tonight, we would have had to wait until next week," she said, stopping in front of my room. "Wally thought you wanted to be done by then."

"He's right," I said. "Do you mind telling me what *you* think of the proposals?"

"Well, I'm head of the Historical Society, so I have an automatic bias. But my wanting the train museum goes beyond that. I always liked Phillipa as a person—I don't want to speak ill of the dead—but her deliberate mockery of other people's beliefs was downright mean."

"Do you think that's why she was killed?"

"Lydia told me she'd had death threats through the years." Scott shook her head.

"Lydia Herndon?"

"Yes. She's my sister-in-law."

"Is everyone related to everyone here?" *Oops.*

"I bet it seems that way to an outsider." Scott's laugh made everything seem all right. "It's a small town, Sasha." She took off her glasses and wiped them on her shirt. "You know that expression about six degrees of separation? Well, in Belen it's more like a half-degree."

"You were talking about death threats," I said.

"Yes, well, I know you've talked to Lydia. It'd be better if you just asked her directly."

"I don't think so."

Scott laughed again. "Perhaps not."

"Do you think vandalism would be a problem if Belen goes with the art museum?" It was a long way down to the air mattress, but I made it. I turned to face Scott.

"Absolutely. And I'd hate to see this old building suffer because of it." She stroked the wide, polished doorframe. "This Harvey House is the best preserved in the state. You can really imagine what it must have been like in its glory days." She leaned to one side, let the frame hold her up. "At night sometimes, when I'm here working, I can almost hear the laughter of the railroad men and the Midwestern twangs of the Harvey Girls as they served them." A kind of longing passed across her face. "I'd hate for someone to burn down this place or break the windows because of Phillipa Petty's work."

"So would I."

"Well, enough of that. No good comes of looking for trouble." Scott slapped her hands on her thighs. "I'm going to bed. I hope you and Ernestine have a fine time tonight."

I thought about what Scott had said. There was no doubt the train museum and B & B proposal would cost more to bring to fruition. It would also require more volume, more tourists to make it viable. But it belonged in this community a lot more than a modern-art museum. The artists just hadn't convinced me their idea could fly. I kicked off my shoes and lay down, my forearm under my head, to read.

Outside, the low-level humming of the train yard yielded to a distant rumble that grew in intensity until a locomotive pulverized my concentration. It was a full-body experience. The floor shook. The mattress shook. My teeth shook. Train lovers would go crazy with delight.

I was in for a long night.

After finishing *The New Yorker* and getting depressed by *The Economist*, I turned off the lamp and waited. The room was clothed in a velvety orange indirect light due to the work in the yard below. Nothing happened. Well, nothing but two more trains.

"Come on, Eulalia," I said. "Let me see you."

"Did you say something?" said Scott from the other room.

"You're not asleep?"

She appeared at the doorway, her hair ruffled, no glasses. "Every time I manage to do it, a darn train comes through. I can't imagine paying for the experience."

"I know. But train buffs are a completely different breed."

Scott chuckled. "Have you gotten chummy with Ernestine yet?"

"She's not here."

"Yes, she is. She's right there," said Scott.

I sat up, looked left to right. "Where?"

"In the corner there. She's doing something with her hands." Scott's voice gained warmth. "Hi, Ernestine. Would you like to meet our guest?"

Very still, I squinted, trying to see the apparition.

"You're looking in the wrong corner," said Scott. "She's coming toward you."

I held out my hand as if to shake hers.

"No, not there. She's on your left. You really can't see her?"

"Not yet."

"She's practically on you." Scott sounded concerned, then smiled and said, "Why thank you, Ernestine. How lovely." She held out her hand to accept a ghostly something that I couldn't see.

"Eulalia?" I said.

"Eulalia? Who's Eulalia?" said Scott. "She looks really upset. Oh, darn! She's gone."

"What?" I stood up and walked to Scott, whose hand was still held out. "She's gone? What do you mean she's gone?"

"I've never seen her upset before. Who's Eulalia?"

"It's not important."

"You really didn't see any of that?"

"No, damn it, I didn't. What did she give you?"

"Oh, you poor thing. I'm sorry," said Scott, putting a hand on my shoulder. "Maybe you wanted to see her too much. Maybe she'll come back."

I held up my hand, shook my head. "Damn it."

"Well, I'd better get back to pretending to sleep," she said.

"Scott, wait," I said. "What did she give you?"

Maybe it was the lighting, maybe not. The older woman's expression was almost goofy with pleasure. "Would you believe . . . I think it was a cup of coffee."

fifty-four

ELEVEN. I COUNTED 'EM. Eleven trains. That's more than one an hour. Granted, I wasn't your average train devotee. But people who wanted to spend the night in the Harvey House would have to be more than average to enjoy the experience. They would have to be rabid. And deaf.

Scott probably looked better than I did. Brown smudges shadowed the bottoms of her eyes, the rest of her face ashen, multiplied by two.

"How did you sleep?" she said. "No, don't tell me. If you slept at all, I'll be envious."

"Do you think people will really pay for a night like that?"

"Once."

"So much for sustainability."

We both giggled. What else could we do with our time-fugued sleepiness? I stuffed my pajamas and magazines in the duffel bag and stripped the mattress of its linens.

"Sorry you didn't see Ernestine," she said.

I yawned. "I was going to say, 'maybe next time,' but there won't be a next time if I can help it."

My balance felt askew, as if someone had walked next to me and shoved my side so I'd trip. I leaned against a wall, acting as natural as I could. This tired, I knew I'd need to tank up on coffee—no, not coffee, just straight caffeine, intravenously—to safely make the short drive back to Albuquerque.

"This probably isn't the proper time to ask, but have you made a decision about what you're going to recommend?" Scott avoided my eyes, as if the question wasn't really her own.

"I'm too tired to think."

"It's okay. I don't really care what you do as long as this building is still standing at the end of it."

"Have there ever been plans to destroy it?"

"Not really." She opened the front door for me. "It's just that that's always an option. Stick a hamburger joint in here and the railroad would be happy."

"Do you think they'd kick in for the kind of restaurant you're proposing here? I mean invest in it?"

"Probably not. But the workers would eat here. That would help with that sustainability you were talking about."

"Before I do any more thinking, I need a good night's sleep."

"Me too."

We shook hands in the parking lot and I thanked Scott for giving up her night to stay with me. After she left, I sat in my car. The milky dawn sky looked as clear as my fuzzy brain felt. Whitaker and Ortega, Eulalia and Phillipa buzzed through my semi-formed thoughts like static electricity.

And then there was Mom.

I was supposed to get Mom moved today—or at least arrange it all. I hit my forehead with an open palm, then rubbed my eyes and picked the sleepers out. Inertia, that most tempting of coping mechanisms, nudged my resolve to head back to Albuquerque. What I really wanted was an artery-clogging plate of comfort food: biscuits and gravy, hash browns, french toast with real maple syrup, Canadian bacon, and maybe a slice of melon. Well, maybe not the melon. One final meal in Belen.

When I got home, I'd write up my recommendation, my decision obvious. As to Phillipa's murder, I debated telling Detective Garcia my theories. When I'd been in a similar position in Clovis last spring, I'd shared my ideas with the homicide detective there. He'd scoffed. And though we'd had a nice little flirtation, he'd never apologized for his rudeness. Not really.

But what if I was right? What if I'd solved Phillipa's murder? I looked at my watch. 7:00 A.M. If I stopped at the White Way for break-fast, I could be done quickly. The restaurant was on the way to Petty's house. A little look-see, one last attempt to figure it all out, probably would yield little more than splinters if I got into her house. But then I could go back to Albuquerque with a clear conscience. I could tell Mom that I'd really tried. I could tell her there was nothing else I could do. I could feel a little better about a really crummy situation.

I started the car and headed toward breakfast.

The air in the White Way smelled of sausage and pancakes. I sat at the only free stool at the counter and closed my eyes after ordering coffee.

"Here you go," said my waitress a few minutes later. The huevos rancheros—yeah, I changed my mind—swam in a sea of green chile atop a homemade oversized tortilla.

"Thanks."

"Need more coffee?" The teenager had round, dark doe eyes and two black braids that glistened bluish in the restaurant's florescent lights.

"Sure."

"You want anything else?"

Why was she hanging around? The place was hopping; she had other customers signaling for her attention.

"I'm fine," I said.

"You sure?"

"Yeah. Why?"

"I don't know, you just look upset." She shrugged her shoulders and walked away. I felt like I'd missed an opportunity. I closed my eyes again and let the smell of the food carry my thoughts. Why was I feeling guilty about Phillipa? I'd done everything I could. Anyway, who was Mom to ask me to do this kind of thing?

"Miss Solomon?"

"Cherry." I didn't want company. Didn't really want to be alone, either. "Would you like to join me?"

"Just for a minute. I'm grabbing some take-out before heading to work." She perched on a stool that had emptied next to me. "I'm kind of surprised to see you here so early."

"I spent the night at the Harvey House."

"Really?" She raised a finger to get the waitress's attention. The young girl brought her a glass of water. "Did you get any sleep?"

"Not a wink. But I wasn't really expecting to."

Trying too hard to be casual, Cherry said, "Have you made any decisions about the proposals yet?"

"Not quite."

"Does the art proposal stand a chance?"

"Why do you ask?"

Cherry scratched her cheek, leaving a small dry line. She put a hand over her eyebrows as if she were protecting her eyes from my scrutiny. "I've been thinking about Philly's murder," she whispered. Even so, the restaurant grew quiet. "I know we've said we'll get insurance and we'll work on making the building secure, but . . ."

"Is something the matter?"

She dropped her hand. Her lips trembled and her eyes reddened. "I think I know who killed Phillipa."

fifty-five

"WHO?" I MOVED CLOSER to her.

"I don't know his name," said Cherry.

"What did he look like?" The murderer. The man who'd poisoned me, threatened my mom, and killed a bitchy but brilliant artist. I wanted some alone-time with him.

Tears burst past her self-control and wet her cheeks. The place where she'd just scratched welted red. "I don't know. He called me on my cell phone. Can you believe it? He threatened me and my family on the damn phone."

"Did you call Detective Garcia?"

She shook her head.

"Why not?"

"The man said he could kill all of us at once"—she snapped her fingers—"like that."

"Do you have any kind of I.D. on your phone? Do you have his number?"

"I didn't recognize it."

"Why are you telling me this? What can *I* do?"

"*You* can call Moises for me." Cherry looked up suddenly and glanced around the restaurant. Her eyes widened. "We can't talk here. Every man I look at could be him. I don't know what to do." She said it so softly I had to lip-read most of it.

"We can eat in my car."

Without exchanging another sentence, I got a to-go container for the remainder of my food and she picked up hers. With ballet precision we rose together and went into the lot.

"Tell me what he said." I balanced my food on the hood of the car. The plastic eating utensils cut through the styrofoam, leaking chile onto my pants.

"He said we'd better forget about the art museum idea."

"That's it? No greeting? Straight to the threat?" I dropped a piece of egg on the ground.

"Yes." She picked up a sausage link. "I said, 'Who is this?' and he said it wasn't any of my business. I said, 'You made it my business when you dialed my number.'" Her defiant voice seemed a lot more natural than the timid one a few minutes earlier.

"I bet he didn't like that. Bullies don't like to be challenged," I said. There was a slight breeze. It picked up my napkin and carried it off the car.

Cherry nodded. "That's when he said he had a surefire way to kill a whole group of people all at once."

"Did it sound like bragging or a threat?"

"I'm not done." She ate another sausage link. "He told me my address and said he had a poison he could get into our house real easy . . . that we'd be dead before we knew what hit us."

"Was there anything about his voice that you recognized?"

She stared at her breakfast.

"Cherry?" I said.

"He sounded old."

"As old as your husband?"

"He had that same coarseness to him that Nick did when I first met him. Like he'd spent most of his life being angry and without any love." Her compassionate tone upset me.

"Cherry, you can't feel sorry for the creep."

"Wouldn't you? I mean, a man who has to go around threatening people? Who's so angry at the world he wants to kill?" she said. "I wouldn't be able to live with myself if I were him. It must be horrible."

It was my turn to stare. I tried to think of someone like that, old and full of hate. Whitaker seemed like a stretch. Merkin? He fit the description but seemed like a real long shot for this kind of action. I doubted he had the initiative.

Cherry bit into her breakfast burrito. "I don't think he was bluffing, Sasha."

"You want me to call Detective Garcia?" I used my spoon to ladle chile into a tortilla. Folding it as best I could, I made a burrito. "You know he'll just come straight to you."

Mouth full, she nodded slowly, then closed the top of her container. Her hug surprised me. "It's been good meeting you, Sasha. No matter what you decide about the proposals, please don't be a stranger."

"I won't." I hugged her back and watched her get into her truck. Her smile held fear along with the kindness. She waved when she pulled onto the street.

I waited a count of ten, opened my purse, and freed the cell phone. I'd called him so many times I had his number memorized.

"Garcia," he said.

fifty-six

FORMAL AS EVER, THE state policeman repeated the details of my report. The only time I could tell he lost his cool was when I mentioned how scared Cherry had looked.

"You said she's on her way to work?" he said.

"Yes."

"I'll kill that sorry bastard myself if he hurts her." With that, he disconnected.

Okay, so he wasn't quite so formal.

The drive back to Albuquerque had a surreal quality, like that Salvador Dali painting of the clock melting off the side of a table. As I pulled onto I-25, my cell phone chirped. I was beginning to believe that it was alive. Malicious and needy. I wanted to ignore it, but knew the number on the display.

"Hey, Darnda. What's up?" I said, making the curve at Isleta Pueblo. On the radio, KANW played "New Mexico music." I bounced in my seat, keeping beat with the percussion by banging my hand on the steering column.

"I can't do it," said my friend.

"Do what?"

"Any of it. Talk to Karen Kilgore, go on a national tour, sell my damn book. None of it."

"Hold on," I said, pulling off the freeway and driving into the parking lot at the Isleta Casino. "I'm getting off the road. Stay with me." I turned down the radio. "Okay. Now tell me what this is about."

"I watched the tape you made," she said, her voice low. "I look like shit and act like an over-the-hill slut. Why didn't you tell me I was so awful?"

"Because you're not." I yanked the emergency brake and cut the engine. "All that tape is supposed to do is give you some idea of how you appear to others. You didn't have make-up on. You were caught totally off guard. It's not a final product, it's a starting place."

"Well, I don't like where I'm starting and I don't think we have time to make it better in a couple of hours." The whirring noise in the background came from either her blender or a mixer, I was sure of it. When Darnda got upset, she made milkshakes or smoothies or baked brownies. Today it sounded like she was working on all three.

"Listen to me." I half-watched a couple emerge from a mountainous motor home with a satellite dish on its roof. Beyond them, the casino's sign flashed names of upcoming entertainers. "Dress like you do when you work for one of your wealthier clients and meet me—"

"You don't understand, Sasha. I don't have to dress nice for anyone. My clients usually stick me out of the way in a quiet, private place. I can wear whatever I like."

"Darnda, this isn't about clothes. It's about your unique abilities and the fact that you can teach some of your techniques successfully to other people. Don't forget the good you do."

"But I look like an idiot and sound like a moron on that tape, Sasha. I go on and on and on. It's disgusting."

"Well, then, stop it," I said with less sympathy than I could usually muster. Hearing Darnda in self-pity mode was a new and disturbing experience. "You're not a teenager with no impulse control. You're a grandmother, Darnda. You've given birth to five kids, healed yourself of cancer, survived the murder of one of your children. Don't you think you can talk to some fluffy reporter about what you do best?"

"This is how you support your clients? By yelling at them?" I couldn't tell if she was teasing me or still upset.

"That's the problem with having a friend for a client, I guess," I said. "I know you too well. You're the most incredible survivor I've ever met. I can't believe what I'm hearing from you right now." I took a breath. Darnda was right. I would have handled another client differently. "If you really want me to, I can call Kilgore and try to arrange for another meeting. But my sense is that she just wants to have a brief talk with you—nothing major—just to see if you're presentable on camera, that kind of thing. But if you want me to cancel, I can."

Darnda didn't say anything for a couple of minutes. However, I *could* hear her breathing. The casino sign flashed: Neil Young tomorrow! Chicago! Big acts in little ol' Isleta. Amazing. I leaned over to the passenger's side to roll down the other window.

"What would you advise your client?" she said.

"I'd advise you to relax and treat this initial meeting as a fact-finding exercise. You need to see if you're comfortable with *her*."

"What would you advise your friend?"

I wished she could see my pleased smile. She'd already gotten past her own jitters and was thinking clearly again. "To meet with Kilgore and vibe her out. See if she's worth the effort to become more media savvy. And, I want you to meet with her now because you need to prove to yourself that you can do it." The fountain outside the casino had turquoise-colored water. I watched the liquid flow down the slabs and into its pool again.

"But what should I wear?" Now, she definitely was teasing.

"Something a little looser than usual."

I started the car. Traffic was light back on the freeway—even after I'd hit the city limit—and my cell phone lay on the seat next to me. Though I think people who talk and drive are obnoxious, I transcended my aversion and dialed Mom's number. With the phone nestled between ear and shoulder, I turned onto Fourth Street.

"I've got wonderful news, Sashala! Rita can start tomorrow," Paul said after we'd exchanged greetings. "She's going to move in with your

mama. It's all arranged. We're meeting at the house this morning to see
what needs to be done for when Hannah comes home."

"What a relief." Along with gas exhaust from the busy street came
a yeasty, rich smell from the French bakery in a strip mall three blocks
from the turnoff to my street. I needed a croissant, a chocolate croissant or, maybe, an almond one. Two, perhaps? I parked the car to finish
our conversation. "Okay. What are we doing today to make sure
Mom's safe at St. Kate's?"

"You're spending the day with her," he said.

"I can cover tonight." Even that was going to be difficult—my
nerves were already frazzled from so little sleep. "I have an appointment this afternoon," I said, not wanting to blow up at Mom because
I was tired. As a matter of fact, what I really needed to do was get in
bed now and sleep until an hour before Darnda's interview.

"Oy! You can't make time for your mother? Not for one day?"

"Paul—"

"I can't be in two places at once! Her house isn't ready! We need
to line up the therapists, put in ramps over the stairs, tack down the
carpets. We need to tell all her friends and organize shifts to help Rita
. . . and to shop. I can do this, Sasha, but I need time." Paul had never,
ever, told me what to do before. Not like this. "Get to that hospital as
soon as you can, and stay with her as long as you can, so that I can do
what needs to be done."

"I'll do it," I said.

"Thank you."

"Paul. . . ." I didn't want to hang up. "Paul, are we bringing Mom
home to die?"

"No, we're doing it to keep her alive," he said in a whisper.

fifty-seven

THE CROISSANTS DIDN'T MAKE it into the house, though some chocolate got smeared on the doorknob. Fortified with sugar, caffeine, and fat, I struggled to save my imploding day. Since I wasn't going to get a nap, I needed to organize myself, to grab control of what I could. If everything went okay, I'd work at the hospital while Mom slept. If everything didn't, I'd have to sneak five-minute sessions at the laptop while she was in the bathroom.

My exhaustion had an up side. In spite of my sleepless night, I knew my recommendation now. No matter how much I tried, I couldn't create a scenario where the modern-art idea could really sustain an audience over time. In today's repressive climate, I wasn't sure that blatantly hostile representations of religious icons would be the major draw they had been in the rebellious sixties. As a matter of fact, the country seemed to be regressing. People I knew who'd never been particularly spiritual were pretending they were—just to keep below the radar. I felt bad for Cherry, Nila, and Lydia, all hoping to have their showcase. But in good conscience, I couldn't champion their plan.

Most of the train folks I'd met weren't a nice bunch—not pseudo-suave Wallace Crawson nor drunken Ernie Merkin—but their idea had a better chance for success. It was light-years less controversial. Though the train museum and B & B would be noisy, the locomotive rumblings would contribute to the excitement and atmosphere of the place. The trains had it.

I felt sold-out, queasy, and conservative. Choosing the safer of the two options upset my sense of self. There would have been a time in my life when I would have nixed anything smelling of ease or banality. The events of September 11th had had many effects. People, in the U.S. at least, seemed to crave unruffled feathers, sure things, and simple joys. The Good Old Days were rarely as good as anyone thought, but they sure looked a lot better than tumultuous riots and protest marches. Baby boomers, alas, were turning into white bread. They also had money and would grow into the main audience for the Harvey House project.

In the kitchen, Leo slinked around my ankles, purring with selfish goodwill. I bent to pet him and noticed a millipede undulating across the kitchen floor. I stepped on it.

"We're all murderers," I said.

The cat sat down at my feet and looked up at me. He blinked in that feline way that hints of deep wisdom passed cat–to–cat from the time of ancient Egypt. Then he stretched, stuck out a paw, and scratched my leg.

"Damn it, Leo, that hurt."

He resumed his campaign for food.

"No way are you getting a treat now."

In the bedroom, I threw my overnight bag on the bed. *A shower.* I needed a shower. I stank. Mom would surely comment on it. For the both of us, I decided to clean up before doing my filial duty. I twisted the head to low-flow as soon as the water was hot enough and let the heat do its work.

What continued to aggravate me?

Taking care of Mom held all kinds of foreseeable problems, the most obvious being our difficult relationship. The lavender and rosemary shampoo splurted out in a glob into my hand. I saved as much as I could and slapped it on my head before it slid down the drain.

Truth be told, a lot of things were bothering me. Mom. Jack Whitaker, Celia Ortega. I hadn't even processed the whole break-up with Bob and was already planning to jump in bed with Peter. What a mess. Who'd taken that ruby?

My life paralleled a soap opera. None of the problems had any hope of resolution. *Stay tuned for next week when Sasha fights with her mom, confronts her newly discovered illegitimate dad, meets her evil half-sister, finds the dastardly murderer. . . .*

Even that seemed hopeless now. My indignation at being poisoned, at Mom's pain, and at Phillipa's death had ended up with more questions and a whole lot of answers I would have been happier not knowing. Worse than that, I still couldn't explain squat about her murder.

I slathered oatmeal soap over my body, inspected the hair on my legs. I could go another couple of days without shaving. The problem was—well, one of the problems was—that even if I could hand Mom the name of the murderer in calligraphy and gold leaf, chances were she'd forget it within minutes, or hours, or days.

She wouldn't remember that Phillipa had been killed. In a way, that let me off the hook. *Who am I fooling?* Mom had asked me to find her friend's murderer and I'd failed. Even if she didn't know it, I did.

What else could I possibly do? Camp on Garcia's doorstep and demand he tell me when he found the man who'd threatened Cherry? I'd interviewed a slew of people who might have a motive. Just because I'd talked to them didn't mean they were the only suspects. I sounded like a heroine in one of those murder mysteries—the kind that features someone who has no business sticking her nose into the investigation in the first place. But if I'd been one of those heroines, I could call all my suspects together in a room. I'd have a plan. I'd watch them interact, squirm, and give it all away.

Lacking that convenient plot device, I got out of the shower and toweled off. Though the old red sweatshirt with a black cat on the front called to me, I had to don clothes fit for a national celebrity. I wouldn't have time to come home again before Darnda's appointment. I put on a short-sleeved black dress, black stockings so that my cruddy black shoes wouldn't attract attention, and a subtly flowered, long silk blouse that didn't call for a jacket to cover my excess weight. Think billowy, comfy but classy.

"What are you looking at?" I said to Leo, who lay on my bed in an imperial pose, one front paw crossed over the other. His languid blink preceded purring so loud I could hear it across the room.

On the plus side of this dreary assessment of my life was the tying-up of the Belen project. Then, in the too-near future, I'd help Darnda develop a more cohesive PR and marketing plan. I needed to help train the kid in Clovis. And I had a lead for a new job in Placitas.

If I couldn't help Mom by solving her friend's murder, at least I could keep from being a mooch.

fifty-eight

TIME DIDN'T PASS. IT coalesced. I felt like a cricket trapped in zinc oxide. Mom alternated between dozing and wanting my full attention. She didn't like the clicking sound of my fingers on the keyboard. She didn't like that I bit my nails. She didn't like me turning down the volume on yet another inane talk show. I closed my eyes tight against the image of months or years of this nitpicking.

We didn't even get the relief her therapies could have provided; they'd been cancelled. "Staff training," the management called it. I called it, well . . . it's better left unsaid. At least we'd survived lunch and noon pills without incident.

"Mom, I'm going to get some coffee." I stood up and stretched, tried to touch my toes and got as far as my knees. "Do you want anything?"

"No—thank—you," she said, each word a crisp indictment.

In the hallway, I sought a friendly face. After on-and-off months of visiting St. Kate's, I expected to see people I knew. Not today. It was as if the very air was on hold. Waiting for *Godot*, no doubt. The midday sky mimicked the blue of imagined seas, turquoise and royal, made bluer by the contrast with the white stucco walls of the little garden area in which I sat for a moment's respite.

Today's sunlight warmed with the gusto of a last hurrah. Soon we'd have the New Mexico version of winter, bearable cold with leafless trees. Perhaps snow in the higher elevations would dust the mountains with strands of white, ski trails seen from miles away.

The crappy coffee steamed. I'd feigned an allergy to nondairy creamer to doctor up the flavor with real milk. It made it worse. I looked at my watch. Only twenty minutes had passed since I'd left Mom. Twenty more minutes and I'd need to go downtown to meet Darnda and the infamous Karen Kilgore. I looked at my fingernails: nothing left to bite.

Inside once again, whispers hung in the stale air, their sources unseen. I passed rooms where family members held silent vigil, as if their presence could convince Death to abandon his efforts.

Mom slept, her hands remarkably relaxed, her breathing regular. I couldn't have planned a better time to escape.

My car retained the sun's heat far better than I would have liked. Solar power can have its disadvantages when you're trying to look polished. Sweating now, with my hastily applied make-up feeling greasy, I zipped onto I-40 and through the latest construction zone with minimal hassle.

Downtown buzzed. Why did I always avoid it? Local businesses had created a coalition to revitalize the area and they'd done a good job. No boards covered windows on Central Avenue—once known as the old Route 66. Japanese, Thai, and Brazilian restaurants gave the area a cosmopolitan feel—as did the upscale stores and art galleries.

Women in heels I'd trip in—and men in suits equally sharp—crossed streets with cell phones open and Blackberries at the ready. A particularly chiseled twenty-something crossed in front of my car, sparking one of those fleeting nostalgic memories of when I felt totally invincible and super smart.

The underground lot at the Hyatt had free spaces aplenty. I parked close to the elevator. The cool of the subterranean structure assuaged my worries about looking like a melted candle.

Darnda waited in the hotel's lobby. Subdued. She'd dressed like she was going to a funeral. Okay, it was probably a funeral for a rock star. From the elevator door I counted four sparkling rings on her chubby fingers in addition to the chunky crystal necklace, but the combination worked—right down to the fishnets.

"Oh, Sasha, I'm glad you're here," she said, rising from a couch upholstered with fabric in a fake Native American design. Cowboys, coyotes, and flute players for people who don't know anything about the Southwest, but think they do. Something was different about Darnda's lips. Lipstick. In the years we'd known each other, I'd never seen her wear it.

"You look fabulous, my dear," I said, bowing. "Divine."

"It's not too much?"

"*C'est magnifique.*" I hugged her. "Are you doing better now?"

"I am," she said with a diamond finality.

"What did you do?" I said.

"The most therapeutic thing I've done in a long time. I busted up your videotape with a hammer." Her smile dared me to object.

I shook my head and raised my hands in the universal motion for *oh well*. "Whatever works, Darnda. That's what it's all about."

We took the elevator up to the twelfth floor of the hotel—Darnda had already gotten Kilgore's room number—and knocked at the door. A dog yipped, something fell, and we heard giggles.

"Who is it?" called a woman's voice. There were some mumbles, a loud laugh, and more moving around.

Darnda and I looked at each other, both trying hard not to crack up. I had to put my hand in front of my mouth to keep control. Darnda yelled through the door, "It's Darnda Jones and my agent, Sasha Solomon."

"Agent?" I mouthed.

She shrugged. "It sounds better than *publicist*."

"Oh, great," said the voice. "Is it two-thirty already?" A sliding door—or window—opened or closed. "I'll be right there."

"What are they doing in there?" Darnda whispered.

"Can't you tell?"

"It wouldn't be right." She grinned.

"But it'd be fun," I said.

Before Darnda could answer, we heard footsteps approach the door. When it opened, there stood Karen Kilgore in tight jeans, a see-through purple blouse—her lacy bra matched—and bare feet. Her chin-length blonde hair framed her face in two symmetrical sheaths. She held a dinky Chihuahua—I think they're called "teacup" or "shot glass" dogs—roughly the size of a jumbo shrimp.

The reporter extended her free hand and said, "Great to meet both of you. I'll call room service and order another . . . a bottle of champagne."

Remember the nice-looking hairdo? It didn't work so well from the back. There was a big matted knot sticking out. Darnda turned to see if I'd noticed. I had my hand in front of my mouth again. How the hell were we going to play this with straight faces?

Kilgore sat on the bed and let her dog go. She jumped up, surprise apparent on her face. "Oopsie," she said, removing something that looked too much like a sex toy.

"Have we come at a bad time?" I asked.

"Why would you say that?" she said, standing. She walked over to the dresser and picked up a yellow legal pad and transformed into Ms. Serious. "Well, Darnda, I've heard wonderful things about you. Carol raves about the work you did for her daughter's wedding last year. Not a single bug in sight."

"I do what I can," said my friend, struggling mightily for composure.

"Do you think you could do a little demonstration for me right now?"

Darnda smacked her lips. "What did you have in mind?"

"Oh, anything," Kilgore said. "Just give me a teensy sample of what you can do."

Darnda looked around the room for something to work with. Her gaze landed on an orchid. "I'll see if I can get one of the buds to bloom on that Cataleya," she said. "Would that be good?"

Kilgore's expression grew greedy—as if she could already see herself accepting the Emmy. "That would be just fine."

For the next few minutes, Darnda sat very still. I'd seen her work before, her concentration so complete she'd probably sit in the very same position through a major earthquake. Kilgore's stare volleyed between Darnda, the orchid, and me. Every time the correspondent began to open her mouth, I held my finger to my lips and shook my head.

"Ah," sighed Darnda. One of the buds popped open, its tendrils unrolling like a miniature lavender carpet.

"Holy shit," said Kilgore. "How did you do that?"

"It wanted to bloom. It was ready. I just asked it to do it a bit early, that's all," said Darnda, acting as if she'd done nothing exceptional. I could see through the humility, though. She was playing with the correspondent, messing with her mind.

"I don't fucking believe it," said Kilgore.

Lovely vocabulary.

A knock at the door. The doggie yipped. A yell of "room service," and Kilgore was up. The champagne had arrived. Of course, she hadn't called for it while we were there. Kilgore signed for the bottle, her back to us. Darnda touched my knee, her eyebrows raised, her head tilted in question. I shook my head.

"Well, that was certainly impressive, Darnda," said Kilgore. "Astounding, in fact."

Something crashed in the bathroom. Someone said, "Damn it!" Kilgore didn't even try to smile.

"Help yourselves," she said, proffering the bottle and glasses. "I'll be right back."

Darnda leaned over to whisper, "Sasha, we've got to get out of here. She's got a hot *boychick* in that bathroom and he's suffering with a hard-on you wouldn't believe." She shook her head. "Poor dear."

"How do you know that?"

"Trust me, I just do."

I nodded and poured the champagne—Gruet Blanc de Blancs—a tasty, dry New Mexican brand. (I'm not kidding, it's great.) We clinked our glasses, drank, and got little bubbles in our noses. Beyond us, in the bathroom, the noises progressed from conversation to chuckles to a thud. Another giggle. Her dog pawed to get in.

"This is getting old," I murmured, remembering the last time I'd heard those mating sounds through a door and how rotten the outcome had been for me.

Darnda nodded.

"Okay, I think I know what to do," I said, walking to the bathroom door and knocking on it. The room became resoundingly quiet. "Ms. Kilgore?"

"Yes?" Her operatic answer scaled at least one octave. It was accompanied by a snicker I'd swear wasn't hers.

"Darnda is feeling quite tired now. Would it be all right if I overnighted a press kit to you early next week?" Never mind that

I hadn't even developed one yet; Kilgore owed us. I bet she knew it, too. "We can talk about the interview on Friday." I winked at Darnda and put my lips close to the door. "Would that work for you?"

Kilgore cleared her throat. There was a repeated bumping sound. In a breathy voice—with unnatural pauses, she said, "That . . . would be . . . just . . . great."

"All right then," I said. "We'll be in touch."

"I'd say she's being in touch enough for all of us," said Darnda when we'd let ourselves out. In a flurry of adolescent laughter, we chortled all the way down to the parking structure.

fifty-nine

FROM AN X-RATED MOVIE back to the geriatric hour, I entered St. Kate's in a lighter mood than when I'd left. The humor of our big interview with the celebrity lingered as I walked to Mom's room, still grinning at selected vignettes.

Paul sat next to Mother's bed, the fatigue stained on his face. I stopped smiling.

"Sashala, tell your mama how wonderful it will be to go home."

"It'll be great, Mom," I said, wondering why I needed to say anything.

"You just want me to die. Both of you," she said.

"Oh, Mom! We want you to get better," I said. "Staying in a rehab hospital won't bring you health. Seeing your antiques, your beautiful art, your lovely home, those'll heal you."

"I'm not going to get better. You know that."

"Not with that attitude, you won't," I muttered.

"Ladies," said Paul. "Enough."

Paul's tone made us pay attention. Both of us inhaled, angry words a breath away. How could my emotions have traveled from such fun to fury so quickly?

"Sasha, I'd like to speak with you for a minute," he said.

"Telling secrets about me again? Just like you planned to move me without my permission?" Mom said.

"You, I'll talk to in a minute," he said to her. In the hall, he pointed a thin finger at me. "I can't trust you to take care of your mama for a few hours? Where were you?"

"I had to help a client with an interview. I told you I might have to leave for little while. Why are you so upset?" I hadn't had enough sleep to gracefully accept being berated.

"Look at this." His hand trembled and I suddenly feared he might be getting Parkinson's Disease. He dug into his pocket and showed me another pill. A white one.

"Again?" The inane comment came from disbelief—and exhaustion.

"In the cup right by your mama's bed."

"But she had her lunchtime meds before I left."

"Eight . . . eleven-thirty . . . three . . . six and nine—probably more—those are the times she gets her medicines," he said, scanning the hallway. "Have you seen that Ortega woman around today?"

"No, I haven't," I said. "Who's doing this?"

Paul shook his head. "I don't know."

"Who knows Mom's allergic to penicillin?" I exhaled loudly. "Stupid question. Anyone who can read her chart knows that." Why was someone targeting Mom? She was dying well enough on her own. I didn't get it. It had to be Celia. She had to be Phillipa's daughter. Money. The only answer that fit both crimes.

"Paul? Sasha?" Mom's weak voice entreated us to come back.

"Thank the Lord, we'll be done with this place tomorrow," Paul said, going into her bathroom without closing the door. I heard a flush. He must have gotten rid of the pill.

My phone chirruped while I stood in the hallway.

"Hello?"

"Sasha, do you have a minute?"

"I can't, Peter. I'm at the hospital with Mom."

"Is she all right?"

"She's okay, but I'm a little busy right now." I remembered the conversation with St. Kate's pharmacist. "Where did you disappear to yesterday?"

"I had to go to work."

"Oh."

"Why are you so busy?" he said.

"We're moving Mom home tomorrow."

"She's not very moveable—not with that complicated med schedule and what she's taking."

"We're moving her anyway," I said.

"Because of the Amoxicillin? That was a one-time deal, Sasha. Don't overreact."

"Two times, Peter." I let that settle. "Today, too."

"That's it," he said. "I'm going to report St. Kate's. It's unforgivable."

"Do that. But right now, I'm sorry but I've gotta go." I disconnected the phone, turned off the power button, and went back into her room.

"Sasha, explain to your mama why we need to take her home," said Paul.

"I thought I did." The pique in my voice silenced her protests. Her glare told me no rationale would cut through her objections. I went to her bed and tried to think of what I could do to help her see why we needed to get her out of St. Kate's. The truth. I decided to tell her the truth.

"Mom, we think someone is trying to poison you."

"Don't," said Paul.

I took her bird-claw hand in mine. "Someone is slipping Amoxicillin into your medicine cup. Hoping you won't notice."

Mom pulled her hand away, crossed her arms under her sunken chest. "That's ridiculous. Why would anyone want to kill me?"

"It's got to have something to do with Phillipa's death." The look of shock on her face made me want to cry.

"Philly's dead? That can't be," she said. "We talked today. This morning."

"Oh, Mom. Not again." I wanted to crawl into a very dark place.

"No. You're lying. I can't believe it."

Tears now flowing, I said, "Neither can I."

sixty

I ATE A PSEUDO—BEEF stroganoff dish with thick egg noodles for an early dinner in the cafeteria, away from Mom and Paul. For comfort, I bought a serving of chocolate pudding. And then a banana pudding with wafers. None of it helped. Tonight was my last night of freedom before becoming Mom's primary caretaker—no matter what Paul said, or Rita did—ultimately, I'd be responsible for her well-being. God save us both.

Things had happened too quickly, I hadn't even called my sister. With a shrug of shoulder and a sigh, I dialed her number and left a message for her to call me. I'd taken a generous hour for dinner. Paul and Rita still had work to do at Mom's place. He also had temple services tonight for the Sabbath. I'd take the night duty—something I definitely wasn't looking forward to—sleeping in a chair, listening to her breathe, smelling hospital smell all night.

Wah, wah, wah. Rita would scold me for my bad attitude. No matter how much conflict I had with Mom, she'd taken care of my sister and me when we'd needed it most. When it had been most difficult for her to do. This was payback time. I ambled back to her room a few minutes later.

Paul kissed Mom goodbye, then patted my shoulder and whispered, "Watch your mama's medicines. I'll be here first thing in the morning."

Mom stared at the television with a kind of desperation—as if she could zap the upcoming change in her life with the remote. The news was on, the volume loud. In the hall, dinner trays clanked and banged as they were removed from their carts. A heavy, dead odor grew stronger as footsteps approached the room.

"Good evening, Hannah," said a gray-blond woman, mid-fifties, whose crusty voice betrayed a lifetime of smoking. "Are we ready for dinner?"

Mom ignored her.

"Let's sit you up," said the worker. "Your physical therapist wants you to start eating in the dining room again as soon as you can. What do you say? Want to try for tomorrow?"

"Mom, she's talking to you," I said.

My mother turned to the woman, whose negligent smile insulted intelligence. "First of all, I don't know you, so my name is 'Mrs. Solomon.' Second, *we* are not doing anything. You're doing things to *me*. And third, I doubt I'll be here tomorrow."

"Of course you'll be here," said the woman, her lips stretched into whiteness with the strain of being pleasant.

"No, I'm leaving," said Mom.

"Of course you are, dear." She turned her back on Mom and rolled her eyes, assuming my complicity in her insolence.

"What's for dinner?" I said, trying to distract the two of them.

"Well, we've got Salisbury steak and mashed potatoes. A nice salad. And sugarless Jell-O for dessert. Would you like some coffee, Hannah?"

"Mrs. Solomon," I said.

"Mrs. Solomon," Mom said.

The supercilious woman wiggled the coffeepot. "Want it or not?"

"We'll both have decaf," I said.

"I'm sorry, but you'll have to go to the nurse's station," she said. "I'm not allowed to serve family members. Policy, you know."

I hated this place. "Forget it."

She poured Mom's coffee and left in a wake of discontent.

"Are they always like that?" I said.

"Most of the time." Mom sipped her drink and turned down the television. "Or worse. Sometimes they don't even ask questions. They just talk at you—blah, blah, blah. In love with their voices, I guess."

"I'm sorry. I should have spent more time with you here."

"No, sweetie—it's gotten worse in the last little while," she said.

"So, you're glad we're taking you home?"

"Couldn't be happier."

I kissed her on the forehead, then settled in the chair next to her bed. Outside, the sunset burnished the pale blue-pink sky with brilliant gold. Mom turned up the volume again. I watched with her for hours, neglecting—maybe avoiding—work. I didn't mention Phillipa again and felt dishonest in the silence. I'd let Mom down, even without her knowing, and the feeling sawed at my heart.

Evening segued into night. By the time the ten-o'clock news came on, Mom's fitful snores—high and unpredictable—accompanied the anchors' monologues about police chases and "breaking news." Unwilling to think about more crime, I turned it off.

The overhead lighting had gone off a little after nine. I worked under the glow of a bedside lamp. My laptop humming, I tried to type quietly and kept making mistakes. In order to cut down on noise, I had to move at a deliberate and consistent pace—not at all copacetic with my fast thoughts and even faster fingers. I gave up and began to read. Soon, even that became too much.

With my full awareness on the long night ahead, the chair became uncomfortable. My butt hurt, my elbows were too big, my back cramped. I decided to walk to the nurse's station and get a cup of hot water to help me sleep. I turned off Mom's lamp. I'd never been here this late. It was eerie. A woman somewhere wailed—no words, just pure sorrow carrying down the otherwise quiet hallway.

I wondered how many of the people here would be dead in the morning, their active lives brought to a crappy end by bodies that turned on themselves, brains that no longer worked the way they should. I didn't understand why living things had to get old and die. Maybe Phillipa had a point with her cruel mocking of religious icons. In the dark hours, it was difficult to believe in a compassionate God.

What little I knew of my own religion neither comforted nor repelled me. Reform Judaism had more to do with living a good life because it was the *right thing to do*—no promise of afterlife, no God damning you to Hell if you blew it.

With my cup of water—still too hot to drink—I walked the entire two-minute circuit of the brain injury unit and then returned to Mom's room. Someone had closed the door. It was a courtesy since that woman's wailing had grown louder.

I slinked into the room, feeling my way with my free right hand. The darkness was pitch. I felt past her bed to the chair. My hand brushed the drapes and I stopped, not remembering having drawn them. I sat down, took off my shoes and heard it.

Someone else was in the room.

sixty-one

THE BREATHING WASN'T QUITE in synch with Mom's. My stomach reacted first, tight with fear. My gut rumbled and turned on itself. The room's blackness transformed into white shapes as I tried to penetrate it, the vessels in my eyes contracting with the effort. I stood and heard a movement in response to mine. Still holding the hot water, I waited. If I could get a fix on Celia, I'd burn her with the water and slam her to the ground.

Mom's breaths changed. They sounded distant, as if muffled. I heard a brushing, pressing kind of sound, a soft, steady bouncing. The woman was suffocating Mom!

"Fire! Help! Fire!" I screamed, lunging beyond Mom's bed—not wanting to burn her—to the other side. I stumbled on a pliable lumpy thing—a foot—spilling the water, but not all of it. "Fire! Fire! Help!"

I tossed the water in the direction of the foot, hoping to inflict major pain.

"Sasha . . . what's . . . happening?" Mom said, her voice feeble.

"You bitch!" It wasn't Celia's voice, but a man's. Familiar, noxious.

I thrust toward it with all my strength, my fisted hands in front of me pumping through the air, striving to make contact. Anything to stop him from hurting Mom.

He locked me in his arms. I felt the pudge of his torso, smelled old alcohol emerging with his sweat as he pinned me to him. A dry, scratchy hand clamped over my mouth and nose.

I wriggled my head back and forth, freeing my jaw, and bit him with every ounce of fury and frustration I'd felt during the last week.

"God damn it!" he yelled. With his other hand, he punched inward and got me hard in the breasts.

My turn to scream. "Ow!"

"Sasha?" Mom's voice was stronger now.

"Hush," I said.

"I had the strangest dream." She turned on her bedside light. The sudden brightness froze all action for a split second. Mom blinked at the two of us. "Ernie? What are you doing here? Sasha? What's Ernie doing here?"

Head cocked, he looked at Mom, then backed his steps toward the door.

A nurse opened it. "What on earth?"

Merkin turned and shoved the nurse out of the way. But not fast enough.

"Get help," I said, lunging after him and stretching out—feet off the ground with the effort—for his belt. I yanked him back from the door. It closed. He swung around and connected full force on my face. I felt something crack. Eyesight blurred, I held on anyway.

Footsteps pounded in the hall, and the door swung open again, hitting Merkin with a thump as he struggled to free himself from my grip. A big man, one I'd never seen before at St. Kate's, punched Mom's attacker until he fell, pulling me down with him.

Merkin landed first on the unforgiving floor and sputtered, "Goddamn bitches. Bitches. Fucking bitches."

Pressure built around my nose and eyes. The big man who'd come in with the nurse pushed me roughly aside and plopped down on Merkin, bouncing to assert dominance. Through a squint, I saw that he wore one of those cheesy rent-a-cop security uniforms. I swore to never scoff at anyone wearing one again.

"Ron, that's enough. Stop it," said the nurse. "Just hold him." She went to Mom. "Hannah, are you all right?"

"I think so," said Mom.

I lay on the floor, face down now, trying to control my breath. Ernie Merkin. What possible reason could he have for hurting Mom? She'd never mentioned him. But I was sure now—he'd left those nasty messages on our answering machines.

"Miss?" said the nurse. "Can you turn over?"

I obliged, and the look on her face told me more than I wanted to know. "We need to get you to a hospital," she said.

"This is a hospital." I didn't want anyone to touch me, to move me. Not an inch.

"We can't handle this," she said.

"In my purse," I said. "In my wallet there's a business card for Detective Garcia. State police. Please call him." I tried to sit up but fell back, my skull hitting the floor without slowing.

More footsteps running down the hall toward Mom's room. Uniformed policemen. One surveyed the scene and spoke into a shoulder microphone. "Get an ambulance here as soon as you can." The other cuffed Merkin before helping him up.

The nurse attended to Mom while Ron, the security guard, came to sit next to me.

"Thank you," I said.

He shook his head. "You're not going to thank me when you see what he did to you."

sixty-two

HERE'S SOMETHING YOU DON'T get to say everyday: "I shared a paramedic with my mommy." Let me tell you, I could have done without the experience. At the hospital, Mom's frailty radiated under the attention. She attracted the night's healthcare professionals with a potent pheromone and was sent back to St. Kate's quickly. Since I was youngish and healthy-ish, I got to stay—my nose puffing and purpling.

A policeman questioned me and then another showed up and did the same. The after-midnight shift came on duty—minus one doctor. Have I mentioned that Albuquerque is suffering an emergency-room physician shortage?

Detective Garcia meandered in at about three-thirty in the morning. His face had acquired additional crags in the short time I'd known him. I had that effect on men.

He exchanged a couple of quips with the policeman.

"So," he said when just the two of us remained in the curtain-enshrouded area. "What happened?"

I tried to shake my head, but that hurt too much. "I've already told everyone a hundred times."

"Ah, but you haven't told me," he said. "And I want to know every tiny thing."

I spoke, slowly. My mouth ached. Sharp pains shot through parts of my face I'd never known about. Did I have extra nostrils, cheeks? Bone must've shattered and scattered behind my eyes. I guess since I could talk, the triage nurse assumed I'd live. I, of course, imagined microscopic slivers working their way into my brain.

When I finished my monotone narrative, Garcia nodded once and then got up, pulling out his badge as he left the curtained area. "Just when do you plan to see Ms. Solomon?" he said to someone beyond my view.

I couldn't hear the response.

"I happen to know she's been waiting here for more than five hours. She's in pain. Can't you at least give her something for the pain?" he said.

With more effort than I would have liked to admit, I got up and peeked out of the cloth womb. Garcia had a nurse and two other people in scrubs looking plenty upset.

They mumbled. I heard "short-staffed."

"That's not acceptable," Garcia said.

Mumble, mumble, came multiple responses.

"I don't care. This woman needs attention *now*," he said.

The nurse spotted me spying and said something.

"I don't care if she can get up," said Garcia. "She's in pain. She's a witness to a crime and I want someone to take care of her *now*."

My hero.

A man in aqua scrubs followed him back to where I lay once more. A cell phone rang somewhere. Garcia answered it. "They're checking her out." He nodded. "Good."

The detective could have said other things; I wasn't paying much attention to him. Instead my focus centered on not screaming. The doctor's beside manner was as tender as a feral hyena's. Each push and squeeze felt like a personal vendetta.

"I'm ordering an X-ray," the doc said finally. He could have at least pretended to care.

"How long will that take?" said Garcia.

"It depends on how busy they are."

"Give me a time frame."

"I can't, Detective." The doctor readied himself to leave.

"What happens after the X-ray?" I said pitifully.

The doctor turned, perhaps seeing me as a suffering person for the first time. "Well, if there's more than one break around the orbital bone, it could make the whole area unstable. In that case, you'll need to see an ENT."

"For what?"

"He may need to wire the bones together."

"Oh, God," I moaned.

"We can't tell anything with all your swelling." He'd acquired a milligram of compassion in the last two minutes. "Let's see what the film says and we'll go from there." But he didn't stick around.

Garcia returned to his place by my bed—or whatever it's called in a hospital. "It'll be okay."

"No, it won't," I said. "I still don't have health insurance."

He shook his head.

"I know it's dumb. But after getting poisoned, who'd have thought I'd need to see a doctor again so soon?" I started crying and feeling very sorry for myself. "What happened to the law of averages?"

"Don't worry about that," he said. "I'm sure your mom can cover it."

Forty years old. Mom shouldn't have to clean up after me—or pay my bills. I hated it. I hated that I hurt so much. The white of the room, the dingy curtain and fluorescent lights glared into a headache. My eyes throbbed. Exhaustion flowed through my bloodstream. To keep myself awake and to feel some justification for all this pain, I said, "Why do you think Ernie Merkin attacked Mom?"

Garcia shook his head. "I don't know yet." He looked at his watch, grunted. "I'm sorry but I've got to go."

"That's okay. I've got a feeling I'll be here for a decade or two."

"Is there anyone you'd like me to call?"

Darnda would be at home with her grandkids; I didn't want to bother her this late. Peter came to mind. I couldn't ask him for help—not yet. I closed my eyes. "How's Mom?"

"She's all right. Mr. Katz is at the rehab hospital with her."

"Good."

"Do you want me to call anyone to come stay with you?"

"No, that's okay," I said, wanting very much to be alone so that I could keep crying without feeling embarrassed.

"I'll check in on you in a couple of hours. Maybe I can swing by and take you home."

"Thank you."

He patted my shoulder with ill-ease and said, "Everything is going to be all right."

I closed my eyes again. I didn't hear him leave.

"Ms. Solomon?"

Movement woke me. I hadn't known I was asleep. "Huh?"

"Hi, I'm Bernice. I'll take you up to Radiology now," said a girl in a green uniform. She helped me get into the wheelchair.

"Can you hand me my purse?" I opened it and checked the cell phone for messages. Nothing. I turned up the volume in case Garcia wanted to reach me.

We rolled along through the hallway, lights pulsing with rainbows of color. People we passed were glowing. The punch to my face—or the swelling—had affected my eyesight. Or, it was hallucination time at the OK Corral. Bernice hit a large, round metal button and double doors opened. She signed me in, hobnobbed with another woman behind the reception-ist's desk, and left me in the waiting area without a backward glance.

Not long after, a middle-aged Hispanic man fetched me. "Wow. You been playing hockey or something?" he said.

"Don't I wish." I welcomed the humor even through my discomfort. Tears came unbidden in another monumental bout of self-pity.

"Hey, I'm sorry," he said.

"It's not you; it's me." I wiped at my face and cried harder. "Damn it, this hurts."

"Didn't they give you anything for the pain?"

"Not yet."

"Poor thing," he said, helping me to sit straight for the X-ray. "Let's get this done quickly. Okay?"

I blubbered a yes.

He positioned my head in a variety of ways, reminded me to hold my breath, offered encouragement.

"God, I hope nothing's broken," I said. "There's no way I can afford surgery right now."

He frowned. "I tell you what. Wait right here and I'll be back in a second."

The pressure from the swelling made holding my head up difficult. I let the weight of it fall backward so that my neck was stretched. Someone could have come by and sliced through it and I would have been grateful. Though breathing through my mouth became strained, my nose felt better in the new position. I think I fell asleep again because I awoke to his voice in mid-sentence.

". . . show you something," he was saying, wheeling me into an area smelling of photo-developing chemicals. He had two X-rays on a light window. "See that crack? That's where your nose is broken. And here, on your cheek, there's this one crack on the flat part. Now, I'm no radiologist, but I've worked as a tech for thirty years. I'd bet you don't have any other breaks. And if I'm right, you won't need surgery."

"I could kiss you."

"I'd like to see you try." He grinned and held out a hand.

"That is such good news."

"Before you get too happy, I've got to say that break on your nose looks pretty bad. They'll probably have to set it once the swelling goes down."

"As long as I don't need surgery, I'm happy."

"Well, good."

Bernice stood in the waiting area once again. "Ready?"

"Can't I just go home?" I said.

"Not yet," she said. "The doctor needs to read your films."

Through the haze of pain, I heard my cell phone. Expecting the caller to be Garcia, I answered and said, "It shouldn't be too much longer. Can you come pick me up?"

"Sasha? You sound funny."

"Oh, hi, Peter."

"Why do you sound funny?" His confusion reassured me.

"Well—"

"Pick you up from where?"

"I'm in the hospital. Someone broke my nose and I'm waiting to go home."

"Where are you?"

"Kaseman."

"I'll be right there."

"Don't bother," I said. But he'd already hung up the phone.

sixty-three

"SASHA?" PETER WOKE ME up with a kiss as soft as milkweed down.

"Hi."

"How're you feeling?"

"Horrid," I said.

"You want to get out of here?"

"Please."

"You really shouldn't be alone." He glanced at a clock on the wall above the nurse's station and said, "I can't stay with you; I've got a twelve-hour shift coming up."

"You can drop me off at my mom's." I sat up and gingerly touched the top of my head. It only ached. "We've hired someone to take care of her and she'll make sure I'm okay, too."

After the discharge instructions—take it easy, follow up with an ENT, call my primary care doc—the rest was predictable. Not much could be done for a broken nose or single cheek fracture. Not until the swelling went down. That took time, warned the nurse who'd rolled me to the curb while we waited for Peter. An old white Carmanghia purred to the designated area. I wasn't sure even Peter was worth bending that low for.

The sun was up now. A chill graced the air, fresh coldness against my overwrought body. It felt so good. I don't really remember much about the drive to Mom's. I gave directions; Peter followed them. He tucked me into bed in my old room, now converted into a weaving studio, then kissed me once more on the forehead and promised to call.

Since it was after 9:00 A.M., I phoned Paul and told him where I was. The receiver hurt against my cheek. He said not to worry, that he and Rita were packing Mom up as we spoke. They'd be at the house in a matter of hours.

After the call, I lay debating whether I really needed to get up and go to the bathroom. Personal hygiene squeaked past the alternative. Even the smallest gesture hurt. Thank goodness I'd signed all the papers for Mom's release yesterday and had already given them to Paul.

At some point, I remember a door opening and Rita tsk-tsking at me. Later, she woke me with a mug of chicken soup with thick noodles and a sprig of fresh parsley on top.

"Paul told me what happened. Why one earth did that man want to kill your mother?" She held a spoon to my mouth. "Come on, now. Drink it. Just because you've got a broken nose doesn't mean your mouth doesn't work."

"I'm not hungry."

"Don't fight me, Sasha. I'm bigger and meaner than you are."

I took the mug and began to drink. I don't think soup has ever, in the record of the world, tasted better. "Thank you."

"Apology accepted."

"How's Mom?"

"I think she's happy to be home. She'll probably be less disoriented than in the hospital, what with all of her things around her." Rita took the empty cup. "You did the right thing."

"I'm so tired," I said.

"Don't worry about your mama. Paul's with her. She'll be fine. You just concentrate on taking care of yourself."

I closed my eyes and fell asleep once more.

Hours later, I awoke with a start, then realized where I was. My car was still in the parking lot at St. Kate's. Maybe Darnda—or her latest boyfriend—could pick it up for me. I'd have to call my landlady to put more food in Leo's bowl.

Rita had laid out a pill—probably for pain—and a glass of water by my bed. I heard voices and applause in the other room. Antsy, I decided to see how Mom was doing.

The heavy drapes had been drawn closed. Alone, Mom lay asleep in her empress-sized bed, her skin albino pale in the television's flickering light. On her bedside table, a plate with pills and a glass of water.

I thanked God for Rita, for her willingness to help us with Mom.

And then I stopped. Something caught my attention. Quietly, so as not to awaken my mother, I went to her nightstand and looked at the plate. The white pill shone against the multicolored ones.

I forgot to breathe.

"Sasha," said Rita, coming into the room, her eyes lively and tone cheerful. "I'm glad to see you're up and around. Do you want a little dinner while your mama sleeps?"

"Sure," I said, hoping my voice didn't betray the loop-de-loops in my gut. "Where's Paul?"

"I told him to go on home. I'm used to taking care of fifteen patients at a time. I think I can handle the two of you." Her smile seemed brighter than usual, her teeth whiter.

I followed her back to the kitchen. From a distance I could hear my cell phone ringing. "I think I'd better get that," I said.

"You shouldn't be walking around too much right now. Not with the trauma you've had," she said, leaving the kitchen. She returned a minute later with the phone to her ear. "Yes, I've got her right here."

"Sasha? How are you?" said Peter.

"Hi, sweetheart," I said. "I've missed you."

Rita looked up.

"Why, thank you," said Peter. "That punch must have affected your brain more than we thought."

"Rita, I think I'd like some privacy," I said. "Mind if I take this in the other room?"

"Of course not. I'll get dinner ready," she said.

I went to Mom's bathroom and closed the door. Sitting on the counter near her medicine cabinet, I whispered, "Peter, I need you to come over here right away."

"Why? What's wrong?"

"I've got another pill. Here. I think it's Amoxicillin."

"I'll come as soon as I can. What's the number on the pill?"

"I don't know. I don't dare go get it."

"Sasha?" Rita knocked on the bathroom door. "You okay in there?"

"I'll be out in a minute." I listened for her footsteps to recede down the hallway. "Look," I said to Peter. "You remember that detective you spoke with on the phone . . . the day I was poisoned? Can you call him? He's state police . . . based in Los Lunas."

"Garcia. Right?"

"Yeah."

"I'll do it."

"Sasha?" Rita again.

I flushed Mom's toilet, pocketed the phone, and opened the door. Her hefty arm under my elbow, Rita escorted me back to the kitchen. After she had me seated at the table, she began chopping an onion with one of Mom's big cleavers. I watched her, disbelieving. Could she really be the one who'd been trying to kill Mom all along? I couldn't put her together with Ernie Merkin—they didn't fit. All of this had to be tied to Phillipa's murder, somehow.

"You're awfully quiet," said Rita.

"I guess I'm sort of in shock."

She nodded. "All you need to do is heal." She turned to face me. "I noticed you didn't take your painkiller, Sasha. Don't be brave about this. There are studies that prove people heal faster when they're not in pain."

"Really?"

"Yes. I'm a firm believer in appropriate medication."

I'm sure you are. "Rita, you've been so good to us. I realized— just today—that I hardly know anything about you," I said with utter sincerity.

Did she tense or was it my imagination? She wiped her hands on the dishtowel she'd been using. "What do you want to know?"

"Gosh, anything." I shrugged. "Where are you from? Do you like red or green chile better? Do you have family here in New Mexico?"

The second I asked it, her expression clouded. "Why do you want to know that?"

"Which one?" Could she see through the feigned innocence?

She peered at me, as if searching for something in my eyes. I worked at the most guileless expression I could.

"My past is pretty boring," she said, resuming her chopping. "Ask me something else."

"Okay. Well, how'd you get into nursing?"

"Actually, I wanted to be a doctor, but my family didn't have enough money to send me to medical school. So, I went for this instead."

"Where'd you train?"

"TVI," she said. The Technical Vocational Institute had a good reputation.

"Here in Albuquerque?"

"Yes."

"So, you're from here?"

She stopped her chopping and looked at the knife she'd been using. "Now, why do you want to go back to my past again, Sasha? What do you really want to know?"

"Nothing in particular," I said, picking at a cuticle. "You don't meet many native New Mexicans. Most people leave as soon as they can."

"Blacks, you mean. You don't meet many New Mexican Blacks." She washed a tomato and resumed her chopping—harder this time.

"No, that's not what I meant," I said. "I don't think about skin color."

"I do." She washed a bunch of scallions. "Everyday." Chop. Chop. My phone rang, torquing the tension tighter.

"Ms. Solomon?"

"How ya doin', Darnda?" I said, praying Garcia wouldn't hang up. Rita watched me.

"Do I have the right phone number? Is this Sasha Solomon?"

"Sure is," I said with false brio—pretending my best friend was on the line. "But I'll be a whole lot better when you come over."

"What's going on?" he said.

"That'd be great," I said. "I'd love to see you right this minute if you can come."

There was silence on the other end. I couldn't hold my breath without Rita suspecting something, so I held a smile instead and nodded as if he were still talking to me.

"Yes," I said to his silence.

"You're in trouble?"

"You bet."

"You're lucky, I'm still in town," he said. "Don't do anything stupid."

"It's my middle name." I hit the off button.

"Who was that?" Rita asked, the knife still in her hand.

"My boyfriend called a bunch of my friends. One of them is coming over right now."

"I don't think that's wise, Sasha." Her back was to me, but I didn't like the sound of her voice. A threat hung over her every word. "You need to rest."

"She'll make me laugh," I said. "I could use a good laugh right now."

Rita busied herself washing more vegetables, sautéing a portabella mushroom. She served me a vinaigrette salad with mandarin oranges and onion. "I'll make you an omelet, but I'm not cooking for anyone else."

"I'm not asking you to," I said. "You've done so much for us already."

sixty-four

DINNER POKED AT MY stomach like glass thorns. While Rita cleaned up, I went to sit with Mom. Before anything, though, I put that white pill in my pocket. Mom awoke and held out her hand. I took it in mine. Her fingers felt dry, but not too much so. With my other hand, I traced the veins on her forearm, which now bulged with her lack of body fat.

"How are you, Mama?"

"I'm glad to be home."

"Me, too," I said, the double meaning lost on her.

"Open the drapes, sweetheart. I can't see your face."

"It's late." I tried to deflect her request.

"I want to see you."

"That's not a great idea," I said. "I look kind of scary right now."

"Please, open the drapes. I feel stifled."

Perhaps she remembered Ernie Merkin trying to suffocate her. If that was it, I couldn't deny her request. I went to the glass sliding door that led into her private patio. When I pulled the string, the heavy curtains swished, bringing back a good childhood memory—of playing hide-and-seek. Outside, the mostly bare trees had a pinkish hue, a reflection of the setting sun. I took the beauty in for a moment, then refocused on Mom. From where I stood, I saw only shock in the sunken reservoirs of her eyes.

"Oh, my baby. What happened to you?"

"You don't remember?" I said.

She shook her head.

"A man named Ernie Merkin attacked you at St. Kate's. My nose and cheekbone got in his way."

"Ernie." She tented her hands over her face. I went to her and gently pulled them away. She stopped her twitching lips by rolling them inward until their mostly colorless forms had disappeared.

"You know him?" I felt like I had to tiptoe on the corner of a great truth.

"Ernie Merkin after all these years," she said with wonder in her voice.

"Mom? What about Ernie?"

"Philly said he'd started calling her again."

"But why, Mom? How did he know her?"

"Honey, they were married," she said, as if I were an imbecile for not knowing.

"What?" I wanted to hit something. "Why did everybody act like she was single? Why the *Miss* Petty?"

"They only lived together a few months. Back then, getting a divorce wasn't easy and Ernie refused to give her one. Since she'd promised his parents she'd always take care of him, they weren't disposed to give permission either." She closed her eyes. "He was a minor, you know."

Merkin had said something about having been married in our first interview.

"Was he violent with her, Mom?"

She didn't answer.

"Mom? Did he beat her?"

In the silence, I heard the squeak of Rita's rubber-soled shoes on the polished brick floor.

"Never mind," I said, regretting my timing. "Don't answer."

"Don't you two just make a picture?" Rita said when she entered the room. Then over to the nightstand. "Hannah, you haven't taken your pills. Come on, now." She held up the plate and dumped the medicine into her hand. Mom picked up her glass of water and sipped from the straw.

Rita shook the pills in her hand. Slowly, her eyes met mine. We held the stare.

"Why'd you do it?" I said.

"I don't know what you're talking about," Rita said.

"What?" said Mom.

"Nothing, Hannah," said Rita, patting Mom's upper arm. "Sasha's had a concussion. She's imagining things." To me, "You really should lie down, dear. You're not doing anybody any good here."

"Oh, I think I'm doing a whole lot of good, being right here, right now."

Rita reached into her pocket and pulled out an orange medicine bottle. "You seem to have dropped one of your pills," she said to Mom, putting the other meds back on the plate.

"She's trying to poison you," I said. "Don't put anything in your mouth."

"Rita?" Mom's incredulity thickened the oppressive air. "She'd never do that."

"That's right, Hannah," Rita said, pressing down on the childproof container. "Don't listen to her."

The doorbell rang. I didn't dare leave Mother alone.

"Aren't you going to get it?" said Rita, a look of horrid victory on her face.

"Why don't you?" I said.

"Your mother needs her medicine."

The bell continued to ring—ding dong, ding dong, ding dong—as if someone was leaning on it. Garcia would never be able to get in the house. Mom had fortress-grade wrought iron on almost every window. The alarm was on, too.

"Sasha, please, answer the door," said Mom. "That ringing is giving me a headache."

"Not unless Rita comes with me."

The bell stopped.

"Well, I guess my friend went away," I said, praying with every molecule of my being that Garcia hadn't given up that easily.

"Well, good. We don't need company right now," said Rita. "Hannah, take your medicine."

"No!" I shoved Rita, knocking her off balance and sending several of the pills spilling onto Mom's bed.

"Sasha!" screamed Mom.

"Don't take it, Mom! She's trying to kill you!"

Mother began picking up the pills—no problem with her fine motor skills.

"Mom! Do you hear me? She's trying to kill you!" I held onto Rita, who struggled to grab any part of my face she could.

"Did you kill Phillipa, too?" I said.

She fought harder, pushing me down backward. Thank goodness for plush carpeting and the abundant foam pad underneath it.

"Hannah, take the fucking medicine," Rita shouted, jumping up.

"Rita?" Mom looked at the pills. "Oh, Rita," she said with unbearable sadness.

And then three things happened: Rita put a pillow over my mother's face, the house security alarm went off, and there was a loud crash. Someone in black stepped on my hand and pushed past me. Another person—a man—grabbed Rita from behind and forced her away from Mom.

"You've ruined everything! Everything!" Rita yelled. As the man pulled her back, she stomped on my other hand—I could tell she'd been aiming for my face—and spat at me.

"That's enough, Mrs. Woodson," said Detective Garcia, kneeling to wipe my cheek with a tissue. "Bill, would you mind controlling Mrs. Woodson for a minute? I need to talk to this young woman." To me, he said, "Twice in twenty-four hours. You ever thought of going into law enforcement?"

"Hardee har har." Even a microscopic smile hurt.

The noise from the alarm overpowered my awareness. Rita struggled against the second policeman, but it didn't make much difference. He was the biggest human being I'd ever seen—even bigger than the St. Kate's rent-a-cop.

"Do you know the code?" said Garcia.

I nodded.

"Tell me."

I did.

He left and the sound soon stopped, replaced by Mom's weeping. "Rita, why?"

"You wouldn't understand, Hannah." With a shimmer of remorse, she said, "It was nothing personal."

"Nothing personal? Murder's not personal?" I said.

"Ms. Solomon, calm down." Garcia reentered the room.

"No! I want to know what the hell she thought she was doing," I said, discovering that indignation is a powerful analgesic.

"We'll find out. I promise." He helped me up and steadied my wobbly steps. "Let's go somewhere quiet."

I led Garcia to my room. When I lay in bed, he made several phone calls. Within minutes, sirens blared down Mom's normally sedate street.

"Where do you keep the key?" he asked on his way to open the door. I followed, not wanting to be alone—and got my wish. Paramedics, policemen, and a reporter and cameraman.

Great, I'm going to be "breaking news."

Paul showed up. I told him briefly what had happened. After making sure Mom was okay, he left again to pack a suitcase, promising to stay with the two of us as long as we needed.

I stumbled back into my room on liquid legs and fell into blessed sleep.

sixty-five

SOMETHING NIBBLED AT MY ear. Leo? I opened drowsy eyes and saw Peter. I closed them again.

"You ought to eat something," he said.

"What time is it?"

"Eleven."

"Damn! I've got to get home. Leo must be starving." I sat up, put a reflexive hand to my face, and winced.

"Your landlady helps out, right? I can call her."

"No, she goes to bed really early. I don't want you to wake her." One leg out of bed, I tried to rise, but Peter pushed my shoulder down.

"Sasha, it's eleven in the morning."

"Oh."

He pulled back the drapes and the brightness came in with a cleansing wash over the room.

"How long have you been here?" I said.

"Since last night."

"Thanks for calling the police." I touched my tender nose and cheek. Shook my too-heavy head. "Why would Rita do such a thing?"

Peter's lips dove downward, revealing those dimples. "Detective Garcia said he'd stop by with some lunch."

"Peter, thank you."

"Sure."

"I mean for all your help."

"They found my ruby," he said after a short pause.

"Where?"

"I guess that guy Merkin took it. He was some kind of rock hound. Anyway, Detective Garcia mentioned something about it last night and I identified it. He thinks they can give it back to me in the next couple of days."

"Merkin broke into my house?"

The doorbell sounded and Paul passed through the hall saying, "I'll get it."

Men's voices hummed in the foyer. I heard the door close and a laugh. A rich, full laugh.

Darnda and Detective Garcia came in. She wore her trademark floozy-tight T-shirt and capri pants. He dressed in jeans and a T-shirt.

"Oh, thank God," said Darnda. "I didn't know where you were." She sat on my bed, her face white with worry and relief.

"How are you feeling?" said Garcia.

"Crappy. But alive." I looked at my hands.

"Could we have a few minutes?" he said to Peter, Paul, and Darnda. Almost, but not quite, a folk-singing group.

I'm going bonkers.

When we were alone, I said, "So, is this where everything ties up in a neat bow?"

"Not a bow yet . . . more like a knot. But I can fill you in on what I know."

"Let's start with Rita. Why was she trying to kill Mom?" She was the biggest betrayal.

"Her full name is Marguerite Merkin Woodson," Garcia said.

"She's related to Ernie?"

"Stepsister. Younger by several years." He drew the drapes against the direct sunlight coming in my window and came back to a chair near the bed. "Apparently, they're quite close."

"What does that have to do with anything?"

"Ernie Merkin was married to Phillipa Petty."

"I know that."

Garcia frowned. "Think about it."

"Mom told me . . . yesterday . . . after everything happened . . ."

"Yes?"

"They were still married."

He nodded. "All this time, ever since Miss Petty got famous, Mr. Merkin has been waiting for her to die. Did you know they married when she was twenty-three and he was seventeen?"

"Mom said his parents wouldn't *grant* a divorce. That's screwy. Wasn't she his guardian?"

"We're still trying to figure that one out. What we know is that his parents were devout Catholics."

"I bet they loved her art," I said.

Garcia continued as if he hadn't heard me. "Miss Petty promised them she'd take care of her young husband, that she loved him more than life itself, or some such nonsense."

"So what happened?"

"She got bored with him about the time her career began to take off."

"And he just waited?"

"Long enough for most people to forget they'd ever been married or to assume they'd been divorced." Garcia cleared his throat. "You know that circle of reflected light you caught in that photo? Mr. Merkin has some nice telescopes. We think he was watching Miss Petty die when you found her."

"Oh, that's too . . . it's too creepy."

We didn't speak for a while. I heard a train's whistle in the distance and remembered all the times I'd dreamed of going to exciting places, of having real adventures. Now, all I wanted was peace and to understand what had happened to me, Mom, and poor Phillipa.

"Why didn't he just wait a few more years? Why kill her now?" I said.

"Miss Petty rewrote her will. She was giving away her millions—to everyone but him. And to make things worse, she'd left control of her estate in the hands of your mom."

"Oh."

"She didn't name a successor to your mom, either." Garcia's phone rang. He looked at the number and turned it off. "With your mom out of the picture, the will would go to probate and Mr. Merkin would get control as the closest living relative."

"So Merkin killed Phillipa and Rita was supposed to kill Mom."

"More or less."

"How long had she been planning to kill my mother?"

"Not long. No one knew the contents of the will right away. Remember?"

I nodded.

"Mrs. Woodson got a sinus infection and Amoxicillin was prescribed. With Mr. Merkin calling daily with reports of the money being given away, Mrs. Woodson figured she could help her stepbrother and get a healthy portion of the inheritance, too. I think they both planned to blackmail each other."

I felt sick. This wasn't how things were supposed to be—hideous and filthy. I wanted to take a shower, to cleanse the taint of their corruption from my thoughts.

"Nice, hunh?" said Garcia.

"What about Celia Ortega? Where does she fit into all of this?"

"We're still trying to figure that out. Ms. Ortega is Mrs. Woodson's husband's niece . . . I think I've got that right. Anyway, they're related. And Mrs. Woodson got her the job at St. Kate's." Garcia stood and went to the window, moved the drape slightly, and looked out. "Remember your theory about Ms. Ortega poisoning Miss Petty?"

I watched him but didn't speak.

"While we don't think you were right about that, we *do* think you may have been right about her role in trying to poison your mother. Especially given that Mrs. Woodson wasn't near your mother's room for a few days." That sounded like the closest thing to an apology I'd get out of him for not taking my ideas more seriously. "Of course, there may have been someone else helping Mrs. Woodson at the hospital . . . but right now it doesn't look that way."

"What about Jack Whitaker?"

The detective turned back to me. "What about him?"

"Celia is his goddaughter."

"So?" he said. "Even if Ms. Ortega had a part in this, there's nothing anywhere to implicate Mr. Whitaker. Being related to a criminal—by blood or by friendship—doesn't make you one."

"Tell that to Rita."

sixty-six

EACH DAY MY FACE shifted through the flag patterns of various African nations—the major colors being purple, green, red, and yellow. Darnda and Peter shared Sasha duty and made sure I had platefuls of comfort food within easy reach. Chocolate had the strongest recuperative powers.

I felt so good in fact that I sat at the computer now. My cat hopped onto the desk and stepped onto the keyboard. He released a line of hhh-hhhhhhhhhhhhhhhhhhhhhhhhhhhhhhhhhhhhhhhhhhhhhhhhhhh.

"Damn it, Leo. I was almost done with this."

He stopped to look at the screen, then began his new ritual—one that had started with my return. Purring loudly, he began to lick me, his stinky tongue continuing its upward motion on my good cheek.

I pushed him off the desk. "I've got to get this finished."

During the first few days at home, I'd finished the press kit for Darnda and she'd already shipped it off to Karen Kilgore. The project I worked on this morning was the final report to Mayor Flores. In it, I urged him to pursue the train museum and B & B. My work provided several rationales for the recommendation. In so doing, I felt like a traitor to Phillipa's memory. However, Mom would do the right thing with the famous artist's paintings—and I'd help contact art museums that would give her works the displays they deserved.

My faith in the world and the future improved. In less than a week in her own surroundings, Mom had gained weight and seemed much more coherent. It made me wonder if someone had been giving her other kinds of drugs—sedatives, maybe—to subdue her. Detective Garcia said I was crazy—but he wrote my comments down this time and looked like he might follow up on them. Peter and I talked about asking other patients' families if they had noticed a similar change once they brought their loved ones home.

Paul, Mom's friends, and two competent, thoroughly bonded home-healthcare nurses provided food and stimulation for her. We'd begun to look for private speech, physical, and occupational therapists. Why not? Mom could afford to stay at the Ritz with forty of her buddies for the rest of her life and not put a dent in Philly's fortune.

I leaned back in my chair. Tonight, Peter and I were going to go to dinner. Our first "date" and my first time in public since all the excitement.

The denouement of Phillipa's murder continued—along with the resolution to Mom's formerly threatened life. Ernie Merkin and Rita Woodson were scheduled to appear before a grand jury. Merkin's indictments included murder, attempted murder, and tampering with evidence. The details of how he murdered Phillipa iced my optimism for days. And I'm sure Detective Garcia wasn't telling me everything.

What I did know is this: Merkin had knocked his wife unconscious and, with a plastic tube shoved directly up her nose, had administered hydrogen sulfide, a caustic gaseous acid. Apparently he had canisters of the stuff at his house—something to do with his rockhounding, I guess. The memory of that toxic smell made me cough again. My healing face screamed. Worse than the pain, though, was imagining the sheer hate, the fury, Merkin must have felt toward Phillipa.

In contrast, Rita's role in all of this looked positively benevolent. Opportunity and greed, rather than extraordinary hatred, drove her actions. On some level, I could understand her motivations—in spite of her targeting my own mother. Rita was being charged with accessory to murder and attempted murder.

Garcia assured me they'd both be in jail for a long time.

The investigation into Ortega's activities was less clear cut. Neither Ernie nor Rita had said she was involved in the poisoning at St. Kate's. And no one at the hospital had noticed anything unusual. Garcia didn't buy it. He told me he was keeping an eye on her.

"Ortega'll trip up sooner or later," he said. "And when she does, we'll be there."

Mom decided to change her will. She put the responsibility for disposing of Philly's art—after her death—on me and my sister, along with hefty stipends for the work. And she divided the rest of her funds among the three of us—Paul getting an equal share.

If it sounded like Mom was totally better, it wasn't true. She was better than before, though, and that was something.

For now, I'd keep on working. Darnda's project was heating up and the lead for Placitas looked good. I owed Mom for the hospital bill and for signing me up for health insurance.

I owed a lot of people.

The best thing about the changes in Mom and what had happened was, well, we'd started talking a little bit more—about life, about what it was like when Dad, I mean Armand, had left her. I'd begun to see more of the spunk, of the cocky refusal to give up, that had carried her through those many years alone when she had to raise us on a secretary's salary. She even identified the person who'd snapped the photo I'd lifted from Phillipa's house. Lydia Herndon. Mom called her "Lyddie." The man leaning against the car, well, Mom claimed every woman in Belen adored Jack Whitaker.

But whenever I mentioned her former lover, Mom refused to talk.

Tomorrow, with luck, I'd drive down to Belen one last time to hand-deliver my report. The mayor had promised me a lunch at Pete's. *Almost through.*

A timid knock, then a harder one, broke my concentration. I peeked out the window.

Jack Whitaker stood at my front door with a bouquet of flowers—lilies, gladiolas, and roses—garish, outlandish.

"Hello," I said, after an awkward moment.

"Hi."

"This is a surprise."

He looked down. "To me, too."

"What? You didn't know?"

"Of course I knew."

"Then where's the surprise for you?" How dare he show up? My whole life, I'd never felt a father's love. I wondered if Armand knew the truth, if that was why he'd been so mean.

"Sasha, may I come in?"

"I'm not sure, Mr. Whitaker."

"Please," he said, lifting the flowers almost to my face. "Please, Sasha. I've got a lot to explain."

I closed the door all but a crack. Did I really want this man in my life? Another person to disappoint me?

"Please," he said.

I stepped back to let him in.

Acknowledgments

On my exploratory trip to Belen, I met Beverly McFarland, the director of the local library. From that moment, I knew I'd have fun with this book. My gratitude goes to the many people in this wonderful little town who answered my sometimes odd questions without a blink. In particular, thanks to the Chavez family, the docents at the Harvey House, and the nice policeman who told me what he'd do to a person who'd parked too long in a thirty-minute zone. Thanks also to Bob Anderson, a true train enthusiast, who suggested books and sent me information so that I might understand his addiction.

Three brave women bid—for charity—on the dubious honor of having me use their names in a book. Thanks to Sue Evans, Karen Kilgore, and Scott Alley for their sense of humor and philanthropic spirit.

The mystery literary community is one of the warmest and most welcoming anywhere. Thanks to the bookstore owners and staffs, readers, reviewers, authors, and cohorts at conventions who make my life such a joy.

Without the help of family and friends, this book would be just a stack of typing paper and spent dreams. Thanks to Bob, Zane, Dara, and Greg for their titanium support. Mike, Susan, Tracy, Gayle, Donna, Lindsay, Elaine, Deborah, and many others buoyed me during some of my most discouraging moments. And, I've got the best awful agent around. Thank you, Joshua. Peter, Hope, Lily, and Finn—my love for you grows with each breath.

The University of New Mexico Press undertakes with vigor, and professionalism, its goal to promote local authors. Everyone there has shown me the utmost kindness. I'd like to extend a particular nod to Amanda Sutton, Valerie Larkin, Kay Marcotte, Melissa Tandysh, Ernest Earick, Maya Allen-Gallegos, Glenda Madden, David Holtby, and Luther Wilson.

Finally, I wrote this book—and took my car trips—to the accompaniment of one of the best radio stations in the country. Thank you to KANW-FM for playing the heartfelt music of my native state. Whether the songs are filled with wailing violins or giddy trumpets, they speak to my soul.